Praise for
FREAKY IN FRESNO

"*Freaky in Fresno* is a fabulously fun read about the importance of family and forgiveness, the butterflies of first crushes, the pitfalls of fame, and not really knowing someone until you swap places. I freakin' loved it."

ELIZABETH EULBERG, author of *Better Off Friends* and *Past Perfect Life*

"A little bit of magic and a whole lot of makeup. Against a backdrop of classic horror films and contemporary influencer gigs, Ricki and Lana discover important truths about themselves while seeing the world through each other's eyes. *Freaky in Fresno* is full of heart and full-on fun!"

JEANNE RYAN, author of *Nerve*

"*Freaky in Fresno* is a fun and funny take on *Freaky Friday* . . . so appropriate given that main character Ricki adores scream queen Jamie Lee Curtis. But this amazing story takes that old trope to new depths, with moments as dramatic and emotional as they are comedic, so by the time you finish the story, you'll be careful what you wish for . . . and appreciate the life you have."

PATTY BLOUNT, author of *Some Boys*

FREAKY *in* FRESNO

LAURIE BOYLE CROMPTON

BLINK

BLINK

Freaky in Fresno
Copyright © 2020 by Laurie Boyle Crompton

Requests for information should be addressed to:
Blink, *3900 Sparks Dr. SE, Grand Rapids, Michigan 49546*

Library of Congress Cataloging-in-Publication Data

Names: Crompton, Laurie Boyle, author.
Title: Freaky in Fresno / Laurie Boyle Crompton.
Description: Grand Rapids, Michigan : Blink, [2020] | Audience: Ages 13+. |
    Summary: Two estranged cousins—horror movie fanatic Ricki and online
    makeup guru Lana—accidentally switch bodies and share a fateful day
    filled with a mini-road trip and keeping up appearances for Lana's fans
    and Ricki's crush.
Identifiers: LCCN 2019038441 (print) | LCCN 2019038442 (ebook) |
    ISBN 9780310767473 (hardcover) | ISBN 9780310767312 (ebook)
Subjects: CYAC: Body swapping—Fiction. | Cousins—Fiction. | Internet
    personalities—Fiction. | Motion pictures—Fiction. | Friendship—Fiction.
Classification: LCC PZ7.C8803 Fr 2020 (print) | LCC PZ7.C8803 (ebook) |
    DDC [Fic]—dc23
LC record available at https://lccn.loc.gov/2019038441
LC ebook record available at https://lccn.loc.gov/2019038442

All internet addresses (websites, blogs, etc.) and telephone numbers in this book are offered as a resource. They are not intended in any way to be or imply an endorsement by the publisher, nor does the publisher vouch for the content of these sites and numbers for the life of this book.

Cover design: Brand Navigation
Interior design: Denise Froehlich

Printed in the United States of America

---

19 20 21 22 23 24 / LSC / 10 9 8 7 6 5 4 3 2 1

• • •

*To Jamie Lee Curtis,
the ultimate scream queen
and ambassador of self-esteem.*

• • •

chapter 1

nearly have an out-of-body experience as I watch Jake lean in to kiss me.

It's the moment I've been dreaming of, and my adrenaline is pumping so hard I'm afraid I'll pass out. It feels like everything has shifted into slow motion as a voice in my head screams, *This is it, Ricki! Your first kiss from a nonrelative!*

Jake is so close I can sense the warmth of his breath on my lips as I draw in the fresh afternoon air. I close my eyes and . . . execute a full-body spasm to duck out of the way.

I basically react as if the two of us are in a slasher flick and Jake is coming at me with a butcher knife instead of those perfect lips of his.

My evasive action is *not subtle*.

The fact that Jake's romantic timing is completely wrong really shouldn't matter. After all, I've been hoping for a kiss from him for the past three months as we've worked side by side, trying to save the Starlight Drive-in movie theater from closing forever.

And it makes perfect sense that Jake would be caught up in our victory—getting ready to light up the enormous outdoor movie screen we're currently painting. A kiss right now would make our impending triumph even sweeter.

But when I envisioned our first kiss, never once did I picture myself covered in spatters of bright white paint and buried under eight layers of perspiration.

All afternoon Jake and I have been painting over the stained and rusted places on the Starlight's giant outdoor movie screen in preparation for Friday's grand reopening. We've been goofing off and "accidentally" getting paint on each other while working our way down the scaffolding to where we're now standing on the ground, and my stomach muscles ache from laughing so much.

Despite my two-dollar sunglasses, I'm fairly blind from the sun's constant glare off the giant wall of white, and on top of everything else, my lips are so dry, I'm afraid a soft, tender kiss from Jake could draw blood. Not to mention I'm hours beyond the power of my last breath mint.

It's not like I'm the type of girl who needs things to be overly romantic; I'd just prefer my first kiss to be minty fresh.

And okay, since I'm listing things, I'd really love for it to happen Friday night underneath the stars at the drive-in's grand reopening. The magical movie night Jake and I have been working toward for months. I know that makes it sound like I *am* overly romantic, but trust me—my favorite romance is the 1935 horror classic, *The Bride of Frankenstein*.

Jake and I actually met at a Classic Horror Movie Tuesday right here at the Starlight last spring. The theater could never afford to switch to digital projectors, so it hasn't been able to screen new movies for a few years now. Wes, the owner, who is so bonded to the Starlight he probably sprang to life from the drive-in's dust, was doing his best to stay afloat showing only older films.

Wes was working really hard, making up theme nights for every day of the week based on classic films. He had things like Monday Movie Musicals featuring *Grease* and *The Sound of Music,* as well as Eighties Movie Saturdays with a John Hughes tribute each weekend.

Jake and I share an obsession with classic horror flicks, but not everyone appreciates the iconic sensation of sitting in a folding chair beside your car, watching a double feature of *The Birds* and *Creature from the Black Lagoon.* Ticket sales at the drive-in were already dangerously low before the big flood forced Wes to close last fall.

The fancy, high-tech digital projectors for showing newly released movies are astronomically expensive. I'm talking, like, eighty-thousand-dollars expensive. So, six months ago, when waist-high floodwaters ruined the outdated equipment that had allowed the theater to keep barely scraping by, Wes was sure he'd need to close the Starlight's front gate forever.

The passion Jake and I have for the drive-in inspired me to write a stirring letter to our local paper about how important the Starlight is to our community. The paper printed my email address along with the piece, and Jake and I were thrilled over how many volunteers wrote to ask how they could help. That one letter kindled a fund-raising drive that is actually on the verge of saving the Starlight.

Besides contacting local businesses to donate supplies (including the white paint I'm presently speckled with), Jake had the brilliant idea to organize a weekend Park 'n' Swap right here on the lot. Professional vendors paid to participate, and the flea market folks gave Wes a portion of their profits. The way people in the community rallied was truly inspiring, and we raised enough money for all the necessary repairs as well as extra funds to rent a digital projection system for our big reopening in two days. Someone even donated a new speaker sound system that's being installed tomorrow.

All Wes needs now is a successful night on Friday to prove to the bank they should give him a loan. If he can just borrow enough for a down payment on the digital projector system, he can start showing new releases, and the future of the theater will be secure. Of course, he's already promised Jake and me he'll keep running Classic Horror Movie Tuesday once a month as a thank you for all our hard work.

Out of everything Jake and I accomplished, I think Wes is most excited about the T-shirts we designed, because he wears one constantly. The front of the shirt has a cartoon silhouette of two people about to kiss inside a car with the words "Experience the magic of the Starlight" written among the stars over their heads. For the design, we wanted to play up the local legend that claims a first kiss exchanged at the Starlight guarantees a long and love-filled relationship.

After all the stories Jake and I heard from so many couples of all ages, still together after sharing their first kiss here, I don't even think it's false advertising to call kissing under the stars at the Starlight "magic."

Which is why I *can't believe* Jake decided to try and shift our relationship from buddy comedy to blockbuster romance right *now* instead of waiting two days for opening night on Friday. Magic never happens on a Wednesday afternoon.

"Whoops!" I say as I flinch away from his near-kiss.

We're almost done painting the bottom section of the screen, standing in the grass with our paint rollers on long extension poles. Jake must've interpreted the quick wink I gave him before detaching the pole from the handle of my paint roller as a *"this is it"* moment.

Except that I've turned it into a *"what was that?"* moment by acting like Jake just tried to murder me. I'm practically shaking as I try to act casual, bending down to dip my roller into the tray. I pretend my maneuver was just to reload with paint, despite how awkward the angle of my arm is now.

Jake blinks a few times in confusion and quickly shoves his long bangs out of his eyes. I look down at the now-dripping paint roller in my hand and try to come up with a diversion. Inspired, I wave the long, detached pole back and forth, wishing it were a wand that could turn back time and give me a do-over.

Jake just blinks rapidly as he watches me.

In desperation, I give the pole a playful spin, knocking myself lightly in the forehead. "Ow!" I drop the paint-filled roller onto the grass at our feet.

I laugh and Jake doesn't, and my heart clenches as I bend back down to pick up my roller. Green blades of grass now stick out from the white paint. *Great.*

By the time I've finished picking the grass from the roller, Jake has turned his focus intently to the section of screen just above him. His face is bright pink as he rolls on yet another coat, ignoring the fact it has plenty of paint already covering it. I clear my throat, but he refuses to look my way, and so I turn my attention to my own *already-very-much-finished* section.

I've been crushing on Jake ever since we first made eye contact, each setting out our lawn chairs beside our cars at dusk early last summer as cartoon hot dogs and sodas paraded by onscreen. We lined ourselves up close enough to start a casual conversation and quickly discovered our mutual obsession with old horror films.

It was a happy accident that the battery in his Bronco died from having the radio on throughout the whole movie and I had to give him a jump from my parents' minivan after the film ended. Which of course turned into the perfect excuse to keep our connection sparking.

And now, after having so much fun together for almost a year, summer is starting again and we're finally getting to the part where we share a magical kiss, and I've just ruined everything. My mind feels as blank as the screen we're both over-painting.

Finally, an idea moves into the white space of my brain. I simply need to get us back on track by casually mentioning I'm super psyched about going to opening night together. Surely he'll get the point I want to save our first kiss for underneath the stars during the movie.

Except that now the dryness has moved from my lips to my throat and I can't seem to say anything.

Finally, Jake says, "Hey, Ricki, I'm sorry about that, um—" He gestures to my general mouth area. "I hope I didn't make you uncomfortable. I just thought . . ."

"Oh no, don't be *sorry*!" I'm shocked he's choosing to actually talk about what just happened. I was fully prepared to never ever, *ever* acknowledge it. "That was, um, cool."

"That was *horrible*," he says. "I just tried to kiss you and you dodged me like I was the Wolf Man or something." He gives me a small smile, and I'm so grateful he's still clearly into me that I could kiss him. On Friday night, that is.

I joke, "I'd call it more of a dodging-Dracula move." I pretend to cover my neck.

Jake doesn't laugh, and I wonder if I can use the leftover white paint to cover up how much I am blushing right now.

I must shift our conversation to how great our first kiss will be at the grand reopening. But instead, all my idiot blank brain comes up with is, "So, who're you coming as on Friday?"

It's actually a valid question since we've given the reopening a fun costume theme. People who come dressed as their favorite movie character get a free bag of popcorn. But asking Jake about his costume now just sounds like I'm refusing to acknowledge our near-kiss and changing the subject. *How am I so bad at this?*

After a few beats, Jake says, "I was actually considering classic Dracula. Or maybe the Wolf Man."

"Such a *coincidence*," I say, trying to pretend away the lingering awkwardness. "But either one of those guys will take a *lot* of work to get right. And I can't imagine you shaming Lon Chaney or Bela Lugosi with some nonauthentic version."

"True," Jake says. "I'd need to go all in. Wouldn't want to embarrass myself with a lame, generic attempt."

I smile, but it feels like this whole conversation is a lame, generic attempt to hide our embarrassment. The silence washes over us as I continue my futile paint rolling, while also trying to think of something else to say about dressing up on Friday.

"I'm just happy for a chance to use my horror makeup skills," I say. "I was thinking about being the Bride of Frankenstein, but I haven't figured out a way to get my hair to stand up so high."

"Cool." Jake's voice sounds like he's forcing it to sound casual. "I'd love to come as something over-the-top, like a giant tomato from *Attack of the Killer Tomatoes*, but I have a feeling Wes would like us to wear costumes we'll actually be able to work in."

"Yeah, he already warned me, nothing super gory." I laugh, and it feels almost natural. "He still hasn't forgiven me for the time my cousin Lana and I did our faces all 'bloody victim' for a Halloween Horror Night here at the drive-in."

"I didn't know they did a Halloween theme night."

"It was a year and a half ago," I say. "Before you started coming. Wes only remembers because I gave him a bad jump scare as my dad was buying our tickets. He still sometimes calls me 'Gore Girl' as a joke."

I frown at the memory of goofing off with Lana. We had a total blast that night, but it was probably one of the last times the two of us hung out together, totally engaged and doing something fun.

Jake must feel the shift in my mood because he says, "Looks like this screen is as painted as it's going to get. Here, I'll rinse off the rollers and you can go wash up."

"Thanks," I say. "I'm sweating so much I'm starting to stink." Jake looks vaguely grossed out, which just further proves I've killed any romantic tension that may've still been lingering between us.

I blame my stupid cousin Lana, which I know is a stretch, but it's *her* fault we don't hang out anymore. She utterly rejected me, and now just thinking of her makes me automatically frown unattractively.

All I can hope is that I'll be able to redeem things with Jake by Friday night. And maybe *then* I'll get that perfect first kiss and truly experience the "Magic of the Starlight."

chapter 2

I t's still light out when I get home, so I lower my blackout shades and block the horror of my exchange with Jake by watching Hitchcock's *The Birds* in my darkened bedroom. During a break in the movie's soundtrack of screeching and fluttering and screaming, I hear a knock at our front door. This movie always creeps me out, and I'm unusually nervous as I hit *pause* and head to see who's here.

The sun is low in the sky, and I squint at the beams of light streaming in through the bay window in our living room.

Jake made a fast departure when he dropped me off, and yet I'm hopeful he's come back.

When I fling open the front door, I picture my tall, lanky crush standing there. But instead, I find my petite and loathsome cousin, Lana, giving me a smug grin. I frown.

I can tell right away she's just finished filming one of her makeup tutorials. Every last one of her freckles is buried under thick foundation and her eyelashes look ready to crawl down her face like two spiders.

"Hello, Ricki." Lana's vivid lips are tightly pressed together. "I'm here to smack you with an epic proposition."

"As long as you don't *literally* smack me." I close the front door behind her. "Or attack me with a makeover blitz."

"It's not about that," she says. "Although your eyes would look *epic* with a little purple liner to accentuate your brown eyes. And those cheekbones—"

"I have no desire to put on one of your phony masks, Lana," I say.

"Hold on." She yells up the stairs, "Aunt June! Can we talk?" I marvel at the volume achieved by such a tiny creature.

"I'll be right there," my mother calls down. "Let me grab the new top I found for you."

Lana gives quick little claps and squeals, "Yay, new clothes!"

It figures my cousin is actually here for my mom. I curse the glamour gene that bonds the two of them together. That gene totally skipped me. Along with my father's dark hair and tan skin, I inherited a brain that blocks my ability to care about what clothes I wear. Lana says it's a crime I don't wear high heels because she loves tall girls who can rock a pair of stilettos, but I'm pretty sure a blurry photo of me would end up on some website with the headline, "Sasquatch Discovered in Fresno, California."

"I'll wait for your mom to come down so I can tell you two together." Lana flings herself into my favorite spot on our leather couch. I can't help but think her bony bottom is going to ruin my perfectly formed butt groove. "You're both going to freak."

"I'm *freaking* already," I say in a dull voice.

"You still wear that shirt?" She points to my Wolf Man movie poster T-shirt. I put it on when I got home as a tribute to the least-cringy part of my embarrassing exchange with Jake.

I gesture to the faded front of it. "Um, *obviously.*" I wonder if Lana remembers she was with me the day I bought it at the mall. Of course, that was before she evolved into the beauty guru who's too cool to be seen with me. Particularly at the mall, aka her tribe's mecca.

"Huh," she says while staring at my shirt. She definitely remembers being with me.

"Do you still have that *Beauty and the Beast* shirt you bought?"

"*God* no. I mean, I didn't throw it away, but I have no idea where it is."

"Yeah, you never were all that sentimental."

"Oh, but Ricki, I am *totally* sentimental! And just *wait* until I tell you. This news that I'm about to share is seriously *epic.*"

"I think you may be abusing the word *epic.*" Lana blinks her spider-rimmed eyes at me and I shrug. "I'm just saying . . ."

"You'll understand when you hear," she says. "Epic-ness is guaranteed."

My mother walks down the stairs with her Chihuahua, Zelda, prancing neatly at her heels. The tiny white dog is perpetually attached to my mom like a pointy-eared parasite.

Mom gives a baby-voiced, "*Wookie who's here to see us, Z!*" to the Chihuahua, and holds up a gauzy-looking scrap of white fabric to my cousin. "This will look so cute with those lime jeans we found for you on Saturday."

"Thank you so much, Aunt June!" Lana says. "You're the best!"

As my mom passes, I reach down to pet Zelda's little apple head and as usual the Chihuahua growls at my hand. Anytime Z snaps at someone, my dad likes to put on a country drawl and say, "That there's a *lookin'* dog." Mom and Lana are the only two who can touch her without risking a nasty bite.

It's obvious Zelda is pure evil in the form of a teacup Chihuahua, but I can't seem to stop trying to win her over. Clearly, my rejection issues run deep.

Mom smiles at the new top as Lana holds it up to her chest and Zelda paws at Lana's lower legs, begging to be held. I'm getting antsy to exit the Lana Lovefest happening here in my living room.

The Birds is still on pause in my bedroom and someone is about to lose an eye in extremely gruesome fashion. Nobody makes me swoon quite like Alfred Hitchcock. I mean, aside from Jake, of course, but I'm trying not to think about the cringy way I ducked today when I should've let myself be swept away.

I move to escape back into my movie.

"No, wait, Ricki. You need to hear this too." Lana slaps the seat beside her and looks at my mom. Mom plops down on the couch and Zelda leaps onto her lap in one synchronized motion. I take a half step back, propping myself against the wall and crossing my arms.

Lana hooks her hair behind both her ears, which is something she would never do on camera since she has Nona's sticky-outie ears. We all do, but Lana's the only one who refers to them as the "family curse."

Looking back and forth between Mom and me in order to build dramatic tension, Lana finally says, "Aunt May has decided how she'd like to spend the money."

Our aunt lives in a yurt about an hour and a half north of us, where she raises wolf dogs and makes jewelry from the rocks and crystals she finds on her daily hikes. Apparently wolf dogs need a *lot* of exercise, so she covers a huge stretch of ground each day. She recently discovered a modest vein of gold and it turns out that gold is worth, well, more than gold nowadays. Aunt May has always lived free and simple and acts like having so much money is an unnecessary headache and a waste. My mother has been predicting her free-spirited sister will find a way to blow it eventually.

My mom's not a huge fan of the whole yurt-and-wolf-dog lifestyle. Under her breath, she refers to Aunt May as "selfish," although I don't see how my aunt's choice to live unencumbered by stress is hurting anyone.

Lana looks up at me. "Aunt May is buying something *epic* for us to share."

"Us? As in you and me?" I try to envision Lana and me sharing anything. A Venn diagram of our tastes would show very little overlap.

Lana nods. "She's decided she's going to get us . . . a *car*! How cool is that?"

I picture how nice it would be to not have to borrow my parents' minivan anymore, but I refuse to leap right back on the Lana train to Rejectionville.

"She thinks you and I are going to share a car," I say. "Like *both* of us together."

"Me and you. Fifty-fifty. Fair and square." Lana grins so big I can practically see the lies oozing between her teeth. Lana does not share.

Mom folds her arms across her thin chest. "Typical May move. I'm sure this sounds like a *fantastic* idea to you two, like she's the coolest aunt ever. It's easy to act like a cool aunt when you're not responsible for anybody but yourself and a few wolf dogs."

"You're a cool aunt too," Lana says, hugging the shirt on her lap.

I don't say anything since Lana's mom, my aunt April, is super stressed lately and consumed with being Lana's fulltime "momager." If I claimed April was a "cool aunt," we'd all have to crack up laughing.

"What kind of car is May buying?" Mom asks. "And *who* is going to pay for the insurance?"

"Aunt May says she'll cover all costs." Lana looks back and forth between us. "And the car? That's the best part! Are you ready for this? She found us a 1966 . . ." She stands up and raises both hands in the air as she announces, "Buick. Skylark. Convertible."

Mom and I uncross our arms at the same time and I lean forward off the wall.

"Yup." Lana nods. "It's even cotton-candy pink. Just like Nona's old car."

It's the only thing all the females in our gene pool absolutely agree on. That was one fantastic car. Nona used to bond with her three daughters by taking them on individual road trips to northern California. That's why Aunt May ended up living there.

"I need to talk to May." Mom stands up, tucks Evil Z under her arm, and strides down the hallway.

A pink Skylark convertible. I picture a shining cloud of pink cotton candy on whitewall tires.

Once, when Lana and I were in sixth grade, we all took a

cross-country trip to New York in Nona's Skylark. The three sisters sat across the front bench seat in order: April, May, and June. Or sometimes the reverse: June, May, and April, with Aunt May always in the middle and never driving. They whooped down the highway like wild teenagers while Lana and I laughed in the wind-tunnel back seat.

We blew bubbles from long wands and wore fake dog noses that people would point to and smile as we drove past. When Lana's mom got pulled over for speeding somewhere in Iowa, Aunt April told the officer he needed to blame her fast driving on the rocking tunes on the radio. She turned up the volume and we all danced in our seats to Elvis until the officer started laughing—which I think as a law meant he had to let us off scot-free.

It was the best road trip of all time, and I still remember that feeling of connection Lana and I had to each other and to our mothers and even to Nona, who had just that year gone up to heaven.

Generations of women riding free.

Of course, this was back when my cousin cared more about having goofy fun with me than she did about scrutinizing lipstick shades and huffing face powder. Back when wearing an actual rubber dog nose was way better than using some selfie filter.

Now Lana has her own BubeTube channel called *Lookie Lana!* On it she airs these three-to-five-minute makeup lessons that have become unreasonably popular. She's closing in on one million eager subscribers, who seem to miss the fact that her heart-shaped face and naturally clear skin are not things they can learn to have. Her *Lookie Lana!* channel was recently mentioned on some big fashion website, which is when Aunt April quit her law firm job. Managing her daughter is apparently way more appealing and potentially lucrative.

Lana is studying me now. "We are going to have the best summer ever with that car," she says. "Aunt May's one condition is that we need to spend most of our time in it together. And she wants photographic evidence to back up our tales of adventure."

I scoff. "So Aunt May wants us to, what, hold up a newspaper with the date on top in our pictures? Like we're kidnap victims?"

"Don't be silly. A timestamp on our photos will be fine." Lana gives me another big, phony smile.

"I'm honestly thrilled about the car and I'm happy to work out a schedule with you but . . ."

"Aunt May is adamant," Lana says. "We need to pick the car up together. Drive away together. And send her updated stories and pictures of the two of us enjoying ourselves—together."

"Why on earth does she care so much about us spending time with each other?" I ask.

"She says she wants us to get back to being best friends."

"Ha," I say. "There's no way we'll be able to fool her into believing we're back to besties. You may be a pro, with all of your fake relationship experience—"

"Hey! Erik and I are *not* in a fake relationship."

I put my hands on my hips and stare her down until she looks away.

Under her breath she mumbles, "We're not." But here's the thing. We both know that they are. Erik has his own popular

BubeTube channel and the two of them benefit from the crossover boost from each of their fan bases.

Of course, Erik has tons of girls crushing on him and so Lana *also* got a crossover boost of teenagers obsessed with hating her. According to my mom, she's received an endless stream of mean comments and messages because of their "dating," which makes it seem completely not worth it to me. But like I said, I have rejection issues. I'm not even going to *pretend* to understand Lana's choices.

"Did you know I'm about to hit a million followers?" She flips her hair now. "I've been recognized out on the street. Girls have actually *squealed* over seeing me."

"Is that a good thing?" I say.

Lana rolls her eyes and starts scrolling on her phone.

"Yeah, I'm pretty busy these days too," I say defensively. "Working over at the Starlight Drive-in and planning to be there full-time this summer. Our reopening is this Friday night and it's going to be truly *epic*." Lana looks up at me so I add, "And I do *not* abuse that term."

"Cute," she says smugly. "Friday's Digifest is going to put me and my channel over the top. In fact, my mom has already been talking to Norealique Cosmetics about possibly starting my very own 'Lookie Lana!' lipstick line."

"As if people can purchase that pout."

Lana shoots me one of her signature pouts. "But will it persuade you to share an epic Skylark convertible with me?"

I scowl at where she's still sitting, wrecking my butt groove. "Let me ask you, Lana. You have all of these people following your channel, and *squealing* at you in public, but do you have a single friend who truly knows you?"

Her face falls for a microsecond and recovers so quickly I wonder if I imagined it. Putting down her phone and rising gracefully, Lana straightens her tight skirt and walks over to where I'm standing. She completely ignores my personal space, moving in so close I can smell her hair spray.

"What are you doing?" I ask as I feel the wall against my back.

"You're the one who needs to take a look at your life, Ricki." Lana purrs like a smoky-eyed cat that's about to pounce. "Stop wasting all your time watching movies. We are going to have an epic adventure in that Skylark this summer, even if I have to chain you to the hood."

I glance down at her perfectly sculpted arms and wonder how ten thousand hours of Zumba translates in a fistfight. The last physical tussle Lana and I had was ten years ago over a pink popsicle, but I'm practically double her size now so I'm pretty sure I can take her this time.

Still, my heart is beating fast as she leans in close.

When our noses are nearly touching, she tosses her head back and laughs. "You looked so scared just now." Her voice gets serious. "But I really do need that car for my appearance Friday night. It will be perfect for my grand entrance."

We look at each other for a full minute. "That car would actually be a *sa-weet* attraction at the drive-in for our grand reopening on Friday," I say. "And that's why there's no way this can work. You and I will never be able to work out a fair schedule."

"I guess maybe you're right," Lana says. "It's sad, really. Aunt May is so desperate for me to hang out with you. She's tried bribing me with other things, you know. Gift cards, facials . . . she even offered to buy me the pet hedgehog I've always wanted."

"Always wanted? When did you decide a prickly rodent would make a good pet? And wait . . . you're saying Aunt May has been giving you incentives to hang out with me and you *still* haven't done it?"

Lana says, "Sorry, I didn't want you to find out."

"You literally just *told* me."

"You deserved to know." Lana pretends to check her perfect nails a moment before giving me a look of pity.

"Well, I haven't really had time to hang out with you anyway," I say. "Jake and I have been busy day and night getting the Starlight ready."

"Who's Jake?" she asks, suspiciously.

"Just my friend Jake," I say, but this time I hear what she must've heard the first time I said his name. A certain richness to the A sound that only someone who really knows me would notice.

"Right. *Friend.*" Lana moves back out of my personal space, thankfully sitting on the couch opposite my favorite groove.

"What do you know about friends?" I say. "Jake and I have been working together to save the drive-in, and a *lot* is hinging on a successful reopening."

"Well, Digifest will basically determine my whole career and future," Lana says. "I'll be doing a VIP meet and greet, performing an original song, and hopefully attracting a slew of new followers. It's the kind of thing that can cement my Norealique affiliation and possibly even get me a book deal."

"Well, good luck then," I say. "I guess sharing a pink Skylark just wasn't meant to be."

"Come *on,* Ricki." Lana sounds enraged. "You are so super stubborn."

I shake my head. "I don't really care if Aunt May wants to give you the car. I'm not going to lie to her."

Lana pauses. "Do you know how at the end of my videos I always say, 'Be beautiful . . . to each other'?"

"Yes," I say. "The perfect phony tagline for your perfectly phony show."

She gives me a Lana Pout™. "Why did you and I stop being beautiful to each other?"

Which is an infuriating question, coming from her. "You know why!" I say. "You left me flat! Out of the blue, you wouldn't even return my text messages—who *does* that to their own cousin?" Inwardly, I lash out, *You were my best friend, Lana!* but I tighten my fists and pull back my rage.

She growls and stands up again. "Ricki, I need that convertible to be mine."

"I thought it was going to be *our* convertible," I mock.

Lana lunges and pushes me hard enough that my back slams against the wall.

She's strong, but I'm angry. I shove her back and my height/weight advantage sends her reeling backward with pinwheeling arms.

"Oh, it's *on!*" Lana flies at me again, this time with even more momentum.

I close my eyes and brace for impact, but she suddenly pulls back mid body strike. She twists so her shoulder bumps into my left boob, barely hard enough to make me grunt. *Does Lana finally realize she should feel bad for ditching me?*

Then I hear the real reason Lana held back: the approach of tiny claws clicking on the floor.

My mom comes into the room, shaking her head. "I can't believe May is serious about this whole thing." Zelda walks neatly beside her and perks up at the sight of Lana and me glaring at each other. As if Evil Z can sense the threat of violence and she likes it.

A huge grin bounces back on Lana's face and ricochets to my mom.

"It will be just like old times." Lana dramatically pulls her phone back out and hits the button to show her current home screen. It's a photo of Lana and me, side by side in the little motorized pink Jeep we shared when we were five. We're laughing in the photo, and our dark and light hair swirls together as we hold up pool noodles like swords.

Of course, Lana's driving.

She flings both her arms around me now, and I almost have to use my fingers to stop my eyeballs from rolling at this whole display.

But Mom looks misty.

"Where did you even find that picture?" I pull away.

Lana grins. "You used to say we were just like sisters, but without all the drama of sharing the same parents."

"No, *you* used to say that." I say. "I always said we were more like sisters who got into way more trouble together than we ever did on our own."

She laughs and nods like she's thinking of one of our funny antics.

I add, "Except that sisters are *always* there for each other and we both know that didn't happen with us." I close my eyes to stop myself from tearing up.

When I open them again Lana's face has fallen and Mom is giving me a stern glare. Of course, she can't see how phony Lana is acting—or realize just how terrible her sweet Glam Girl niece can be.

"Ricki," Mom says. "What has gotten into you?"

Of course, *I'm* the bad guy here. I'm always seen as the bad one. "It's just . . . Come on, Mom. Lana and I haven't been like sisters in a really long time."

Lana says, "But now Aunt May would like to *fix* our sisterhood with an amazing cotton-candy pink, vintage Skylark convertible."

"Aunt May has always been pretty delusional," I tell her.

Mom nods in agreement even as her face turns red and she says, "Ricki Marie Pumadero! You apologize to your cousin *right now.*"

Lana stands up from the couch and punches her fists onto both hips in a stance of victory. My eye is drawn to the gauzy white top she's left on the couch and something in me snaps.

"Really, Mom? You think *I'm* the one who should apologize?" I say. "I'm so sick of everyone acting as if Lana is perfect when she's the one who dumped our relationship in the garbage."

Mom scowls. "That's enough, Ricki."

Zelda snarls at me threateningly, like she needs to prove she's on Mom and Lana's side.

Lana puts a hand on my mom's arm. "It's okay, Aunt June. I guess my big success has just been too much for Ricki. We all know she struggles with jealousy."

"*Jealousy?*" I shout before I can grab the emergency valve on my rage. "Gee, Lana, you're right. I guess I'm just *really jealous* of your fake life and your *fake* relationships and your *fake face.* Everything about you has turned fake, fake, *fake!*"

"Stop this," Mom says firmly. "Ricki, I can't believe you can't get along with Lana well enough to share an incredibly generous gift from your aunt May."

Lana sits again, and Zelda chooses her lap over my mother's. Of course. The evil dog is naturally drawn to any source of aggression.

Lana looks back and forth between me and my mother while Zelda imitates her movements. I can't tell what either one of them is thinking, but I know them both well enough to know it's not good.

Lana gives an obviously phony sigh and says, "I guess Aunt May's terms are just too harsh. It's a shame, but she should probably keep the car herself."

A part of me is super disappointed about the Skylark. I picture the convertible with a bench front seat and whitewall tires and a perfect pale-pink paint job, and I give a genuine sigh. But not even something that wonderful will convince me to allow Lana to reject me all over again.

I don't need to relive being discarded by my cousin.

"I'm going back to my movie," I say as I head down the hall toward my bedroom. I can hear Mom apologizing to Lana in a low voice and feel a pang of guilt.

Blowing up at Lana in front of my mom was stupid of me. I'm still really upset about wrecking things with Jake, and I shouldn't have taken out my dark mood on her.

My mind flashes to the image of me and Lana laughing together in the back of Nona's Skylark and I nearly turn around.

But I'm *always* the one who feels bad and apologizes, and I'm sick of it.

I play memory after memory of Lana starting to focus on her phone when we'd hang out, and then canceling the plans we'd make over and over, and then finally not even bothering to respond to me.

In the end, I slam the door to my bedroom so loud I hear Zelda bark back at me from the living room.

At least I'm the one who did the rejecting this time.

chapter 3

The next morning, I'm still worried things will be weird between Jake and me when he pulls up in his red Bronco to give me a ride to the Starlight. We're supposed to help Wes test the sound system for tomorrow's opening day by walking down each row of the drive-in lot, making sure everyone will be able to hear the movies loud and clear.

Over the years, the Starlight's audio evolved from giant metal speakers on individual poles that moviegoers would hang on their car windows to a dedicated radio station that would often result in drained car batteries, like Jake's, at the end of the night.

But now, thanks to the used equipment donated by our local Speaker Shack, we'll have a sweet sound system for people who like to sit on chairs and blankets to watch the movie out in the fresh air, underneath the stars. Plus we'll still have the radio option for those people who prefer viewing the movie from inside their vehicles.

Of course, an open convertible offers the best of both worlds and the ultimate drive-in experience. But I close the top on that thought.

"Tomorrow's the big day!" Jake says as I slide into the passenger seat of his Bronco. "You ready to rock this sound check?"

"*What*?" I yell, pretending to be deaf, and Jake laughs and blasts the eighties song "Super Freak" playing on the radio.

And just like that, the cringy kiss-miss from yesterday is forgotten and everything is back to being great between Jake and me.

When we make the turn into the Starlight we see a flatbed truck parked by the projection booth. We turn toward each other with giant grins on our faces because we know this can only mean one thing.

"The projector's here!" I practically squeal.

"*Rented* projector," Jake corrects but then whoops, "This is really happening!"

Our shared happiness completely erases any residual traces of weirdness from yesterday.

Of course, Wes has to go and make everything all awkward again as soon as he walks out of the concession shack.

"You two *lovebirds* ready to sound check this place?"

We both blush and Jake kicks at the asphalt.

I ask Wes, "What movie are we using for the test?"

Jake's head snaps up. "May I suggest Hitchcock's *The Birds*?" He cups a hand around his mouth and gives an impressive squawk. "The sound effects set that masterpiece apart."

"Yes!" I say. "I *just* re-watched that last night." I cup a hand around my mouth as well and give Jake an ominous screech.

He answers me with more creepy bird noises and it feels like everything is going to be okay. *Better than okay.* Our bird shrieks dissolve into funny little cheeps and tweets.

Wes frowns. "I guess you two haven't noticed Brad and Gwen, the two hanging out in the projection shed. They're still setting up the system and it looks like it's going to *be a while yet!*" Wes loudly directs the last part toward the big shed that serves as the projection booth. The door is open and inside we can see a man and woman in overalls, moving back and forth around a giant metal box that must be the rented projector.

Gwen has a wrench in each hand and Brad looks over and calls, "It will just be a few more hours to get everything online."

"They've been saying that since five a.m.," Wes tells us, then raises his voice. "As long as you hook it up *perfectly* for tomorrow night." Wes may take movies even more seriously than Jake and me.

"So, should Ricki and I maybe head out to grab a bite?" Jake asks. "Fat Jacks? My treat."

I nod at Jake and picture the two of us surrounded by life-sized cutouts of Marilyn Monroe and Elvis as we listen to fifties music and share a vanilla milkshake with two straws.

We look at Wes, but he says, "Sorry. We need to get each one of these speakers checked in case there are any problems. We'll just use music to test the acoustics."

"Sure. Rain check on Fat Jacks." Jake winks, and the way the sunshine reflects off his face makes my stomach *do the twist.*

"But Jake, this is May. In *Fresno.* It's not going to rain here for a very long time."

"Right," Jake says. "Sun check then."

"I like that." I close my eyes and tilt my face upward. "*Sun check.*"

When I open my eyes, Jake is watching me, and the two of us hold the moment for a beat. I take a mental picture of every sharp detail. *I want to cling to this feeling.* Thankfully, our romantic tension has been fully restored.

Wes invades our taut force field, giving Jake a rough pat on the back. "I'll go put on some rock 'n' roll!" he says, and then notices Gwen and Brad are watching us instead of working. He claps his hands a few times. "Let's go, people! We have a theater that deserves a second chance!"

Just like Jake and me.

• • •

It turns out, when Wes said "rock 'n' roll," he actually meant something closer to classic eighties death metal.

Jake makes a face of agony at the aggressive music and the two of us burst out laughing as we split up to walk the rows. We map out which speakers need to be made louder and which ones have a slight rattle or hum. Each time the two of us cross paths close enough, we pantomime dramatic rocking out. After a few passes I pretend to shout along with the lyrics and make air guitar moves that are both passionate and hilarious.

I love making Jake crack up and can hardly wait until tomorrow night for our magical first kiss.

Finally, the two of us meet in the wide center aisle in the middle of the drive-in. We greet each other with a wild improvised dance that's a cross between the twist and something that I think may qualify as head banging.

Jake takes my hand and swings me around, and the two of us shift into a kicking, thrashing, over-the-top mash-up that ultimately leads to us galloping arm in arm around the lot as we whip our heads up and down.

All the nodding and swooning makes me so dizzy I

almost fall, but Jake scoops an arm around my lower back and catches me.

I burst into laughter, but when I look up at Jake's serious expression I stop.

And, okay, so I'll admit this is a *much better* moment for Jake to kiss me than the perspiration-and-paint-speckled scenario from yesterday. And I will say I'm feeling a certain gravitational pull toward his lips. I even have minty-fresh breath this time. But it *still* isn't Friday night, and there are zero glittering stars overhead, and so therefore this moment could never count as our Magical Starlight First Kiss Under the Stars™ that will last forever.

Which is why, when Jake starts moving his face toward my face in that perfectly angled way that means he's about to kiss me . . . I duck. Again. For the second time in less than twenty-four hours, I flinch away from the lips of the boy of my dreams, and this time it's even more obvious and awkward. There are no paint rollers or poles to hide behind.

It's just me. In his arms. Outright *recoiling* from his kiss in horror.

I stammer, "I-I-I . . . I'm so sorry."

"No." Jake's face is instantly bright red. "I'm the one who's sorry . . . I just thought . . . I should've asked . . ."

Before I can explain about waiting for our magical under-the-stars-at-the-Starlight kiss, there's a loud roar of an engine and a giant cloud of drive-in dust rolls toward us.

"Listen," I say quickly, "I've been saving my first kiss for—"

But Jake is looking to see who's speeding into the closed drive-in in the middle of the afternoon. "What's happening?"

Two sharp barks ring though the air as if in response, and that's when I recognize the vehicle racing toward us. It's my Aunt May's black vintage pickup truck with her three wolf dogs riding in the open back.

The drama of my second near-kiss with Jake is forgotten as the truck circles us and the wolf dogs bark joyfully.

Heroically, Jake places his body in front of mine, facing off the dogs as if they might jump out of the truck and attack us.

"Whoa," he calls to my aunt, "we're dog-friendly, but we're closed until tomorrow night."

"It's okay," I say, putting a hand on his arm. "This is my Aunt May, who I told you about. She lives about an hour and a half north and these are her wolf children."

"Oh!" Jake relaxes instantly. "Nice to meet you. Beautiful pups."

Aunt May jumps out of her pickup and runs a hand through her long, wavy red hair. She's almost as tall as I am and her jewelry chimes with laughter as she envelops me in an earthy-scented hug.

When she releases me, she starts nodding her head to the death metal music. "Righteous tune."

"This is Wes's mixtape," Jake says. "And yes, I'm talking about something that gets played in an actual cassette player, which he insisted the new system keep as an option."

"Brilliant." Aunt May laughs. "And who is *this* fine young man?" She waggles her eyebrows at me and tips her head toward Jake.

"This is Jake. My, er . . ." *Crush*. "Friend."

Jake reaches to shake her hand and instead finds himself dragged into a jingling hug as well. "Hello, Jake," Aunt May says, "Ricki's *er* friend." She gives me a quick wink that makes me wonder if she's psychic, or if my feelings for Jake are really that obvious.

"What brings you to the drive-in, Aunt May?" I say. "I was hoping you'd make our grand opening tomorrow night, but we're still getting things prepped right now."

"Don't worry one bit, my dear," she says. "I'll be here tomorrow with bells on." For emphasis she shakes her bracelet, making it ring. "I'm just here to see you and Lana together in the car."

"Wait . . . what are you . . . *what?*"

But before I can properly articulate my confusion, a second cloud of drive-in dust rises up accompanied by the roar of an approaching engine.

"And here she is now," Aunt May says ecstatically. "In the pink convertible, *exactly* like your Nona's."

The cloud of dust grows larger and thicker until I see a long pink hood emerging from the giant puff of smoke.

I silently mouth the words *pink Skylark convertible* as it drives toward us. It really does look just like Nona's car.

Jake, Aunt May, and I all stand stock-still, and the wolf dogs bark gleefully as Lana drives around us once before stopping right in front of me. When the dust clears, I can see that my cousin's smile is phony and her eyes are imploring. Like she's begging me to *please, please, please* just keep quiet and swallow whatever hot mess she has cooked up.

Lana calls, "Aunt May insisted she witness our first ride together in the car and your mom said you were here." Her words all smoosh together in the way they always have when she's lying about something. "I can't wait, so come on, Ricki! Get right in and let's go, go, *go!*"

I narrow my gaze at her. "You didn't tell her?"

"What?" Lana says. "About the agreement we made to allow the car to work its magic and bond us back together again?" She is smiling so hard I have to laugh.

"Not that . . ."

Aunt May is suddenly behind me, shoving me toward the passenger side of the car. "Don't worry, honey, you'll get your turn to drive, but it's only fitting that Lana take the first spin. After all, she is the older cousin."

"By a month and a half," I say reflexively. Being considered younger has always seemed unfair when the two of us are so close in age, and Lana is clearly the selfish child here.

I look into Aunt May's hopeful and happy face and can't bear to bust her bubble right now. She is obviously thrilled by her inspiration to "fix" our cousin relationship, and this vintage Skylark is in mint condition. It must've been expensive.

With a sigh, I climb into the passenger seat and shift so I'm facing Lana. I introduce her to Jake and she jokingly holds out her hand as if he should give it a kiss. He gingerly shakes it instead.

"So, you are Jake," she says, and gives me an obvious wink that makes my face burn.

Aunt May says, "Now this is what I envisioned when I found the car for sale. My two beautiful nieces. Together like a double-scoop cone all over again."

I push out a smile for Aunt May's sake before I sit back in my seat and give Jake a weak wave. My hair whips backward as Lana peels out and heads straight for the Starlight exit.

Between my clenched teeth I say, "What do you think you're doing? We agreed we weren't going to share the car."

"Listen," Lana says. "We can work this out, Ricki. I need this convertible and I won't allow your stubbornness and hurt feelings to rob me of this epic car."

"So, you're saying you'll let me use the Skylark for the drive-in's grand reopening tomorrow night?"

Lana grips the steering wheel and speeds up even more. "*Grrrr!* I can't believe Aunt May didn't trust me enough to drive away with the car on my own."

"So that was your plan?" I say. "To ride off into the sunset alone and lie to the rest of the family for as long as you could?"

"Well, it didn't take much time to get found out, did it? And now we need to follow through with sharing the car."

"Fine. Starting tomorrow night when *I* get to use it," I say.

Lana is silent for a few beats, and I actually have time to hope that she'll be reasonable and let me have the car for my magical first kiss with Jake.

"It's perfect for the drive-in," I say. "Like a good luck charm for opening night. After all, it's not as if you could drive it up on stage with you at Digifest anyway."

Lana slaps the center of the steering wheel and the Skylark coughs a sharp honk. "That's it! The extra *zhoosh* my appearance needs. Thank you, Ricki. I am *absolutely* driving this car directly onto the stage and will present my song from the driver's seat. I can't wait to tell my mom."

"You can't just drive up onto a stage," I say. "And besides, I'm telling Aunt May that this whole thing is a charade and that you are too selfish to share anything, just like you have been our entire lives. You could never even share a stupid popsicle!"

"Popsicles are not sharable treats," she shouts. "They are designed to be enjoyed *individually*."

"Agree to disagree," I say, which I know drives her nuts. "My point is, you are completely incapable of sharing this amazing car."

"You are so frustrating," Lana says. After a beat she gives a Cheshire cat grin and guns the engine. "But this car *is* truly amazing, isn't it?"

As the wind swirls through my hair, I can't stop it from pulling the tiniest smile from my lips too.

"The car's *all right*," I mumble under my breath, but it isn't easy to keep that smile small.

Especially when Lana circles back and we drive underneath the Starlight's archway marquee with nothing but the open air between me and Jake and our dream of saving the drive-in coming true.

chapter 4

By the time we get back to where we left Jake and Aunt May, the music has stopped and the wolf dogs have jumped out of the truck to wrestle each other wildly in the dust. Aunt May's wrists jingle as she claps her hands for them to behave, but the pups completely ignore her.

Jake is laughing at their gleeful insubordination. "Sweet ride," he says to me when we pull back up. "Your aunt explained you two are sharing the convertible. You must be stoked for this summer!"

Lana is typing on her phone. "I'm texting my mom about taking the car up on stage tomorrow night."

Aunt May says, "My one rule is that the two of you always look out for one another no matter what. Can you promise me you'll have each other's backs?"

My cousin's only plan for my back is to stab me in it. I swallow. "I'm sorry, Aunt May. I didn't get a chance . . ."

"Oh, yes!" Lana cuts in as she places both hands back on the steering wheel. "We abso-toot-o-lutely promise to have each other's backs."

Wes appears beside us and steps up to Aunt May with his

hands hidden behind his back. "Hello." He smiles. "I don't believe we've met."

Aunt May is distracted trying to corral her wolf dogs, so from the passenger seat of the convertible I say, "Sorry, Wes. This is my cousin Lana . . ." Lana smiles at him. "And this is our aunt May."

"May," he says like it's poetry. "What a lovely name."

Aunt May is still trying to convince the dogs to stop wrestling each other. "My sisters are April and June," she says without looking up at Wes. "Middle child here. Always trying to force everyone to get along." She emphasizes her words with tugs on her dogs' collars.

"Do you think your dogs might like a little snack?" Wes pulls his hands from behind his back, revealing a small, wilted-looking bouquet of hot dogs. "They got a touch of freezer burn, but I've warmed them up and I doubt the pups will mind."

Aunt May stops struggling with the dogs and gives Wes a genuine smile. He grins back, and for the first time I notice Wes looks different. Less covered in drive-in dust than usual. Like maybe he took a moment to comb his hair and put on a brand-new Magic Under the Stars T-shirt before leaving his office inside the snack building.

He holds up the hot dogs like he expects Aunt May's wolves to sit neatly and wait for him to hand out the wieners one at a time. Instead, Wes is surprised by a three-way furry tackle-hug.

Aunt May lunges to help Wes and giggles as they both struggle to stay standing.

"They're not exactly what you'd call *trained*," she says as they feed hot dogs to the wagging pups. Between accepting wolf kisses, Wes introduces himself.

"I've been working here at the Starlight for over thirty-five years," he says. "Started helping out at thirteen, and I've been the owner for going on twelve years now."

"That's amazing," Aunt May says as she wrestles one of her wolves to the ground. "Most people don't stick to one thing that long."

"What can I say? I love movies." Wes stiff-arms a pup who's trying to steal the last hot dog.

"Now, Wulf," Aunt May scolds the pup mildly, "say *please* to the nice man."

Wulf leaps up and places a paw on each of Wes's shoulders, nuzzling his face until Wes is laughing so hard he hands over the final hot dog.

"I don't think I've ever seen him so affectionate with a stranger." Aunt May's bracelets jingle as she runs a hand through her hair.

Wes grins at her. "And all it took was a pack of old hot dogs."

Aunt May moves her hand to rest on his arm and I squint at Wes, trying to see him through a forty-five-year-old woman's eyes. But I can't do it. He's still just *Drive-in Wes*.

Lana looks at me from behind the wheel and widens her eyes as if to ask, *Are you seeing this?*

I nod and cover my mouth with my hand.

Just then, Jake gives a loud, "*Oh!*"

Aunt May grabs at empty air as Wes is knocked facedown and instantly buried alive under all three dogs.

"I'm okay!" he insists while blocking the thank yous from the pups grateful for their hot dog party.

"Dang, I missed recording that," Lana says, pulling out her phone.

"Not everything needs video documentation, Lana." I wave Aunt May over and say, "Can I have a quick word with you about the car?"

Aunt May calls out, "Come on, Lana, it's Ricki's turn in the driver's seat now."

Which makes me realize it's actually pretty silly for me to pass up the chance to at least *drive* the pink Skylark with the top down. I mean, it's only fair.

"That's right, *Lana*." I climb out and walk around the front of the car. "It's time for me to take my proper place behind the wheel."

Grudgingly, Lana slides across the bench seat to the passenger side and starts scrolling on her phone.

The second I slip my body behind the wheel of the Skylark I feel something shift inside me. *This seems familiar.* I allow my hands to trace both sides of the steering wheel. A thick stripe of chrome runs the full length of the dashboard, and the round gauges are spread wide like expectant eyes watching us.

The emblem in the center of the steering wheel inexplicably blurs.

For a surreal moment, I am a child again, playing pretend driver in Nona's old car while Nona gives a full-bellied laugh beside me at the way my feet don't reach the pedals. I blink, and now my knees are back to being crammed against the dashboard and Nona is gone. Lana and I have to work together to move the bench seat backward to make room for my long legs. Once it locks into a perfect fit, I give the engine a rev.

My heart races as I slide the beautiful chrome gear shift into the *drive* position.

Almost before I know what's happening, the pink convertible is peeling out of the drive-in so fast Wes hollers for me to slow down. I wave to him in the rearview mirror and laugh as we roar down the wide center aisle, making a sharp turn at the playground in front.

I drive the convertible through the exit and underneath the Starlight marquee. The wind immediately grabs my hair and whips it above my head. Like it's telling me, "*Wake up!*"

I look over at Lana with her swirling blonde hair, and for a moment I am transported back to a sunny grass field in our shared Barbie Jeep as we crown over the peak of a too-steep hill and gleefully lose all control.

But I can't allow myself to get sucked into all of this. After all the rejection, I can't let myself be overcome by nostalgia and give Lana a free pass to drive away in this amazing car she does *not* deserve.

Because if I give in now, it will definitely become *Lana's* car.

"Unless I get to keep the Skylark for opening night," I say, "I'm telling Aunt May that this can't work and she should just return the car."

Lana looks at me though her dancing hair. "I can't believe you'd be that spiteful."

"Try me," I say, and start working up the strength to resist the liberty coursing through my limbs right now. *Am I nuts to not just play along?* I mean, semi-part-time use of a cotton-candy pink convertible is much better than *no* cotton-candy pink convertible, right?

As I slow the car to make the turn back into the Starlight, Lana pulls down the sun visor and leans forward to check her face. Her makeup is perfect, of course, but she cringes at her reflection. In one smooth motion, she opens the archaic ashtray in the middle of the dashboard, pulls a pink lipstick out from underneath the built-in cigarette lighter, and holds back her hair so she can trace her pout.

And that's what does it.

Lana has already started moving herself into the car. Like a dog marking its territory, that pink lipstick in the ashtray is her way of claiming full ownership.

She's still looking in the mirror, watching herself glide the lipstick around her mouth for a second time, when I slam on the brake. Lana's head nods forward from the force, and her lipstick leaves a wide pink streak across her cheek.

"Ricki!" she wails like I've just stabbed her.

"I'm not kidding, Lana," I snap. "I get the car tomorrow night or neither one of us does."

She turns and grins at me, her eyes crazy-wide. "Yeah, but see the thing is . . ." She runs her fingers down her cheek, smearing the lipstick into streaks. "I'm betting you don't really have the willpower to give back this car."

Before I can move, she grabs my face and wipes matching pink streaks on my cheek like war paint.

I don't flinch. "Just watch me." I hit the gas and the Skylark peels out, kicking up gravel as we fly across the wide-open lot toward Aunt May's pickup. I can't wait to give Aunt May a speech about what a selfish liar Lana has become.

Except that as soon as we get close to Aunt May's pickup, I see that the dogs are already loaded into the back and she's sitting in the driver's seat with a big grin on her face. Wes is sitting next to her with a double-big grin.

"Wes is showing me his old-fashioned candy supplier," our aunt says out the window as she pulls her truck forward. "I can't believe they carry Bottle Caps and wax lips!"

"I can't believe your aunt never tasted a Zagnut bar," Wes says from the passenger seat and she shoves him playfully.

"Bye, girls. Love you," Aunt May says. "Ricki, I'll see you here tomorrow night for the grand reopening. I'm trusting the Skylark will draw you two together, closer than ever. Drive it mindfully."

"Keep an eye on Gwen and Brad," Wes calls out to Jake, who's walking toward us now. "I'll be back before they're done. Probably *long* before they're done . . ."

"Aunt May! Wait!" I call, but she and Wes are already pulling away. "*This isn't going to work!*"

May slows her truck. "What's that, Ricki?"

Lana covers my mouth with both hands and calls after our aunt, "She says she's *so happy she could twerk*!"

"You girls and your crazy dance moves," Aunt May says with a chuckle. "Oh, hey, looks like you both got something on your faces." She points to her cheek and gestures to ours. "Pink taffy or something."

She turns to Wes and we hear her squeal, "Oooh, do you think they'll have Laffy Taffy?"

Wes nods as she pulls forward, and with three sharp barks and one long, low cloud of dust, they're gone. Leaving Lana and me on our own to war over the pink convertible.

chapter 5

crank the gearshift into park as the dust settles, and Lana and I simultaneously turn in our seats to face each other. Our eyes lock and the two of us embark on the most intense stare down of our lives.

"Terrific car," Jake says, reminding me he's here. I just nod slowly in response without breaking eye contact with Lana. We stay focused on our no-blinking stare for so long that I can feel the lipstick on my cheek begin to melt and run liquid down my face.

Eventually Jake mumbles some excuse about checking on Gwen and Brad and says, "A dark screen tomorrow night will mean everything we've worked for has been in vain."

I nod again, feeling like I'm already throwing everything away. But my deep anger toward Lana keeps me glued in place. Locked into our stare.

Once Jake's gone I swear I hear a low growl emitting from my cousin's throat.

But I'm still the one in the driver's seat.

Cherishing the control I wield, I narrow my eyes at Lana and dance my fingers mockingly across the top of the steering wheel. I'm surprised to find it's covered with a fine layer of powder.

Rubbing my fingers together, I feel the abrasion of grit and break eye contact to look around the inside of the car.

Not only is the entire interior of the car covered with drive-in dust, I realize Lana and I are both blanketed in a thin layer of the shining powder. Tiny silver particles gleam in the sunshine. It's as if the Starlight is laying claim to the vintage car. I'm emboldened by the thought.

"I'm not moving," I say. "I'll just hold the car hostage here until tomorrow night."

Lana says, "My mom already texted me back and this convertible is now a crucial part of my epic appearance at Digifest tomorrow night. There's no way you will deny me this."

"Your fans are not going to remember you a year from now. Or even six months!" I say. "They're like goldfish with tiny little attention spans. What are you going to do to keep them clicking, Lana? How do you plan to keep gaining more and more followers?"

Apparently, I've made a direct hit on a nerve because Lana's left eye twitches as she springs across the seat, lunging at me with both hands. Before I can react, she's grabbed both my wrists and is trying to wrestle my grip off the steering wheel.

I'm impressed by her strength, but I refuse to let go.

Lana shoves her small body against me so hard, the two of us are both in the driver's seat. All four of our fists clutch the thin steering wheel as we sit tightly together as one. Lana digs the spike of her high heel into the top of my foot, making the engine rev loudly.

If I popped the gear from park to drive right now the Skylark would speed straight for the playground, launch off the slide, and send Lana and me flying right through the towering white movie screen.

In frustration, I start honking the horn with my elbow. Jake comes running out of the projector room, followed by Gwen and Brad in their overalls. They all watch us, trying to figure out what on earth is going on between the two of us in the front seat of this convertible.

"I am keeping this car for our Friday night reopening!" I screech at Lana. "This drive-in means *everything* to me and it is so much more important than some stupid Digiwidgifestivalcon."

"You know it's *Digifest*," Lana screams back. "And my whole future is hinging on attracting more followers tomorrow! This car is perfectly on-brand for me!"

"You think your fleeting fame is all that matters," I say. "This amazing drive-in could close down *forever*."

At the exact same time, we both yell at each other, "**You are so selfish!**"

Ahead of us, the giant movie screen spontaneously flashes to life.

A bright light projects onto the screen and begins to strobe, while Brad releases a Wilhelm scream to our left.

Jake puts a protective arm around both him and Gwen while Lana and I continue wrestling for the Skylark's steering wheel, using our elbow bones as weapons.

Suddenly, it's as if the steering wheel gives us both a huge electric shock. With a loud crackle, the convertible fires off tiny sparks in every direction.

Lana and I both shriek in pain and surprise, but neither one of us lets go of the wheel. In fact, I squeeze my fists around it even tighter.

The movie screen in front of us continues flashing and snippets of short movie clips begin to play. Despite the sunlight making it difficult to recognize the picture, I swear I see the image of a grown woman wearing bell-bottoms and riding a skateboard as she blows a giant bubblegum bubble.

Lana and I finally stop elbowing each other and stare straight ahead as the screen flashes with a spiky-haired Jamie Lee Curtis confidently walking toward us in heels and an amazing black dress. I can't help but feel soothed by her image.

"JLC," I say out loud.

"What?" Lana says.

"The ultimate scream queen." I gesture to the screen, but it's now showing Lindsay Lohan yelling at a little kid. "Not her," I say. "Jamie Lee."

The heavy metal music that was playing earlier begins to speed up and get louder. It almost sounds like we're on a carnival ride, and I instinctively let go of the steering wheel and grab for the door handle. But when I pull on it nothing happens.

My stomach gives a lurch and I feel an inexplicable panic rising in my throat. "My door's locked."

Lana leans over and pulls on the passenger-side handle. "Mine too!"

"What's going on?" I say. "It's like the car is going all 'Stephen King *Christine*' out of nowhere."

"It looks like the movie projector is possessed too." Lana points to the kaleidoscope of twisting colors now dancing onscreen. "It's making me dizzy!"

I shake my head but can't look away. "I guess the new equipment must be malfunctioning."

As we watch, Jamie Lee Curtis reappears to rock out on an electric guitar for just a blip before the screen switches back to strobing colors. Next, we see a clip of a teenaged Jodie Foster riding on the top of a waterskiing pyramid. Or rather, a very obvious green screen shot of Jodie Foster *pretending* to water-ski. That image switches to Lindsay Lohan angry-kissing a guy and shoving him behind a tree before the skateboard mom reappears, now dealing with a washing machine overflowing with a giant heap of bubbles.

The images begin to flip by faster and faster until a flash of pink light and a blast of music explodes so bright and so loud that Lana covers her face and I squeeze my eyes shut.

screech

    whoock

        zzzap

My scream is loud enough that I can barely hear Lana's scream beside me. But when I stop she continues her unrestrained shriek for a full thirty seconds. Finally, she gives a few stammering, "What the—what the—what the—?" and I hear her dissolve into a long, high-pitched whine.

I keep my eyes squeezed shut as I try to catch my breath. Everything goes quiet.

When I dare to look again I see that the screen in front of us has stopped flashing and both Gwen and Brad are clinging to Jake. Brad's blond head is tucked tightly into Jake's armpit and Gwen announces at the top of her lungs, "This drive-in has a poltergeist!"

"Are you girls okay?" Jake calls. "It looked like the convertible was covered in static electricity just now."

Brad yells out from his position in Jake's armpit. "How did movie clips play without the projector hooked up?"

Gwen wails, "It's not even plugged in!"

I lean back and rest my hands on the steering wheel, and Lana slides along the bench seat away from me. When I look over, I can feel the shock on my face mirroring hers. For a moment, I'm just happy to be okay and I'm glad that Lana seems to be fine too.

I ask loudly, "Are you all right?"

"My ears are ringing," Lana yells, covering her ears with her manicured hands.

"Mine too," I call. "Guess you wish you'd captured that on your phone, huh?"

Lana drops her hands from her ears and I can see by the set of her mouth that the shock is already wearing off. Her eyes dart around, as if she's scheming how she can get me out of the driver's seat and claim the convertible as her own.

As if to confirm my thoughts, she reaches over, turns off the ignition, and takes the key.

Cupping her small hands together to hide the car's pom-pom key chain inside, she says, "I don't know how you did that, Ricki, but nice try. This car is mine."

"I didn't do anything," I say loudly. "I don't even know what just happened."

Lana says, "Okay, cuz, but answer me this: What are you going to do with no key?"

I sigh. "Well, cuz, I *could* just unhook the battery and leave the car parked exactly where it is until tomorrow night."

Lana looks perplexed, like she hadn't thought of this possibility.

"But I don't really feel like camping in a convertible overnight just because you are the most stubborn and selfish person on the planet." *I give up.*

"I am not the most . . . But wait, does this mean I win? I get the car for tomorrow night?"

To answer her, I reach around to pull up the lock. I swipe at the lipstick on my face as I open the door and climb out of the pink Skylark.

"We've wasted enough time," I say and then call out to Jake, "Let's get to work on that old popcorn machine."

I don't even look back when I hear Lana restart the car.

She lets the engine idle a few moments before putting the Skylark in gear, but I just keep walking and don't turn around to watch her pull out. By the time she zooms past I've reached Jake and the others.

"You guys okay?" I ask.

"Girls should not fight like that," Gwen says. She pulls a hankie from the bib of her overalls and wipes the side of my face. "Not to be sexist or anything, but that was *incredibly* unladylike."

From the corner of my eye, I watch the convertible disappear down the road. "My cousin and I have never been accused of acting *ladylike* when we're together. Even when we used to get along."

"Hard to believe you two ever got along," Jake says.

"Yes, it is, Jake." I feel wrung out. "Yes, it is."

With that, the four of us follow each other through the arched front doorway of the concession shack, while my ears continue ringing from the . . . well . . . whatever the heck just happened.

chapter 6

'm trapped in a clear plastic bubble of shock, and everything feels too loud and bright as Jake and I set about cleaning the snack counter. We sanitize the hot dog maker and shine every inch of glass and chrome in the whole concession area. The two of us spend almost an hour exclusively scrubbing the soda machine without speaking.

Underneath my stupor, I'm still seething with anger toward Lana. *I cannot believe she got exactly what she wanted*: driving off with the Skylark all to herself.

When Wes walks back in with an armload of bags filled with candy, he has an amused look on his face and seems distracted. Jake and I try to explain the strange anomaly with the movie screen, but he just shakes his head.

"I knew Gwen and Brad were going to be a nightmare." He opens the glass door and calls out toward the projector shed, "You two are a *nightmare*!"

Gwen's voice streams back. "Just a few more hours to get everything online." Which is exactly what they've been saying all day.

"See," Wes says as he begins unloading the candy into the

glass case. "No poltergeist. Just ordinary incompetence com-
bined with a poor work ethic."

"You don't understand," I say. "Jamie Lee Curtis was there,
but not as she appeared in any of her slasher movies. I mean,
Freaky Friday is *not* the first thing that comes to mind when you
think of Jamie Lee Curtis."

"The ultimate scream queen," Jake says.

"That's exactly what I said." I flash him a grin, but the way
Jake looks at the ground reminds me of our near-kiss 2.0. *Why
must I mangle everything?*

Wes says, "Let's just hope the projector is rolling properly by
showtime." He clears his throat. "Speaking of which, Ricki. I'm
wondering if you happen to know your aunt's favorite film. I'd
love to have it cued up as an after-party bonus movie following
tomorrow night's double feature."

"I don't really feel all that well," I say, because if we're going
to have a post-show flick it definitely should not be *The Wizard
of Oz*. But also, I genuinely don't feel well.

As we go back to cleaning, Jake keeps asking if I'm okay and
giving me worried looks. And to be honest I'm worried about me
too. Something is definitely wrong.

I am absolutely to-the-bone tired and I keep getting vaguely
confused. Like, I'll have my hand on a tall stack of cups and
suddenly forget if I'm in the middle of lining them out in rows
or if I'm supposed to be gathering them up in a tower. Or I'll
start cleaning out the inside of the popcorn maker, and the light
gleaming off the metal makes me feel so claustrophobic and
panicky that I need to run outside for some air. Then I forget
what I came outside for.

I ask so many odd questions and end up undoing and redoing things so many times, Jake and Wes eventually begin taking over every task I start before I get a chance to mess it up.

Finally, after I've dropped a tall stack of oversized popcorn buckets for a third time, the final traces of calm euphoria leave Wes. He growls with frustration as he tries to catch the cardboard pails rolling along the tiled countertop and asks Jake to please just drive me home already.

"I'm sorry," I tell Jake as he helps me into his Bronco and buckles my safety belt. "I know there's still so much work to do. I'm just all fogged in right now."

"We need you healthy and at your best for tomorrow." Jake walks around the front of his vehicle, and I marvel at how cute he looks through the windshield. Opening the door, he shoves his bangs out of his eyes and I struggle to remember what's so important about tomorrow.

As he climbs in the driver's side I say, "Wait, tomorrow's Friday? I can't miss the grand reopening!"

"No, you can't." Jake starts the engine and pulls out of the Starlight. "Who else am I going to impress with my old-school Wolf Man costume?"

"Wolf Man?" My brain goes blank for a moment as we drive.

I picture the two of us standing in front of a big, white screen, talking about horror movie costumes. And then I remember the moment had something to do with an embarrassing attempt at a kiss. "That's right," I say. "The Wolf Man and I almost *kissed*." I pinch my fingers together and hold them up. "We were *this* close!"

Jake's face goes red and I scramble to remember if I was the one trying to kiss him or vice versa. *He is so cute!* It must've been me trying to kiss him.

But then I remember it was him trying to kiss me and proudly announce, "But I *ducked!*"

"Heh, yeah," Jake says. "*Twice.*"

I realize I've just reiterated our most awkward experience and cover my face with both my hands. I really need to stop talking now. I drop my head against the side window of his Bronco and can hear my loud snores just before releasing consciousness.

When I wake up we're already at my house. I'm so unsteady, Jake has to help me climb down from the passenger seat. He keeps an arm around me as we make our way up the walkway to my front door, and it feels as if my wooziness is now from being so close to him. *I really, really want. To. Kiss. Him.*

"You smell *good*," I say.

My mom flings open the door just as I'm puckering up and closing one eye to take aim. In my mind I'm getting ready to plant a kiss directly onto Jake's lips. Except I'm moving in slow motion, and as I watch helplessly, his face moves farther out of reach. He's trying to hand me over to my mother, but I won't let go of him.

"Are you okay, honey?" Mom asks in a concerned tone as she wrestles me off of Jake's arm. "Wes called from the drive-in and said you weren't feeling well."

"I'm fine," I say, trying to wave her off. "Jake-Jake-Jake-Jake . . . Jake, you are a *thank-you* boy!"

I reach out to pet his face and he laughs. Squeezing my hand, he says, "Ricki, you are a *you're welcome* girl," which makes no sense, but he's already turning away and walking back to his red Bronco.

"No, but . . . Friday is coming!" I call after him, trying to convey a lot of very important information about our first kiss and magic and the drive-in. "Jake!" I repeat, "Friday is coming!"

He gives me a thumbs-up as he climbs into his truck. But I don't think he understands.

I start making loud kissing noises in his direction and Mom says, "Okay, Ricki, that's enough of that," as she practically carries me inside.

I'm discouraged but *at least things can't get any weirder between Jake and me.*

Mom shifts into Nurse Mom mode and says, "Let's get you all fixed up."

My mother always rates between "adequate" and "quite decent" on the mothering scale, but when I'm even the slightest bit sick, she pops solidly into "world's best" mom zone.

She tells my dad to fend for himself, and locks Zelda away in the bathroom while explaining in a high-pitched baby voice, "Sowwy, but my *other* baby girwl is sick."

Me feeling queasy right now is Mom's time to shine.

I'm barely inside my bedroom when I find myself tucked into bed in my comfiest flannel jammies with a spoonful of mystery medicine sliding down my throat. The ringing in my ears gradually stops, and my perfectly darkened room gently hums with a humidifier blowing a soft cloud of mint mist into the air.

My head finally stops spinning and my thoughts turn to how unfair it is that Lana gets to keep the Skylark. I desperately want to tear off her fake makeup mask and show the whole world what a big, selfish phony my cousin truly is.

I can't believe we were ever besties, or that Aunt May

thought things between us were fixable. *I wish Lana and I weren't even related.* From now on, I plan on seeing as little of my cousin as humanly possible. In fact: I'll have no problem completely avoiding her all summer.

Into my darkened room, I actually growl a sarcastic, "See you at Thanksgiving, cuz," just before rolling over and going to sleep.

chapter 7

The first thing I notice when I wake up the next morning, before I even open my eyes, is that the soothing smell of mint has been replaced with a thick, fragrant odor. The sickly sweet scent is so dense it actually makes me start coughing.

Why would Nurse Mom dump perfume into my humidifier?

My eyes try to fly open, except . . . they *don't*. They're stuck closed as if they were glued shut while I slept. I manage to get my right eye unglued, but my left eyelid is stuck shut as I look around my room.

Through the haze of sleep, I realize that the smell and gluey eyelids aren't the only things that've changed. The morning light that usually shines from the window to the right of my bed has shifted so now the sunbeams are coming from the window near the foot of my bed. Except that I don't normally *have* a window near the foot of my bed.

I squeeze my eye closed again. That must've been some very strong medicine Nurse Mom slid down my throat last night.

Maybe that explains the odd sensation of having something heavy resting on my chest right now. I picture Zelda sitting on my front and baring her teeth at my face as she watches me sleep. That Chihuahua is so terrifying, just imagining her on top of me makes me panic and blindly flail at my chest.

Except that my body seems to have shrunk in the night and I'm actually grabbing at air. *Where has my chest gone?*

My right eye flies back open and I use my fingers to pry at my left. My eyelashes are so stiff they feel like they could draw blood. Panicking, I tug hard on my upper left eyelid, trying to force my eye to open, and my upper eyelashes *peel off my eye* in one long stream.

I hold up the long strip of lashes and scream like I've just pulled an insect out of my eyeball. Which is basically what I've done. I drop the multi-legged parasite and slap at it until I'm sure it's not alive.

Hyperventilating while I look around, I discover that another *major* thing has changed while I was sleeping. That is: *my whole room!*

Gone are my posters of Alfred Hitchcock and *The Thing*, replaced with a series of silver-framed mirrors in all different shapes and sizes. My long shelves, which are normally occupied by realistic-looking monster masks, have morphed into neat displays of makeup on each and every available surface area.

Across from my bed sits an oversized desk with an assortment of large, white lightboxes aimed at a clear acrylic chair on wheels. Stacks of wide compacts are piled high, and white canisters holding bouquets of brushes surround a perfect army of lipsticks standing in creepily even rows.

Instead of blood and gore everywhere, my room is suddenly pink and white and delicate-looking.

I scream in horror.

"MOM!" I call as I begin to hyperventilate.

I hear angry mumbling coming from the next room. I sit straight up in bed and call faster and louder, "*MOM-MOM-MOM-MOM-MOM—*!"

Finally, thick footsteps come stomping toward my door.

But instead of my mother, Aunt April bursts into the room. Her hair is a snarled mess and her eyeliner is smeared all the way down to her cheekbones.

"What the heck, Lana?" Aunt April is so angry I'm stunned into silence. "It's *insanely* early! Unless you are injured, go back to sleep!"

I hug the pink blanket up to my neck and stare at her.

"*Are* you injured?" she demands.

I shake my head, and she takes a step closer, looking at my face intently.

I wince as she scowls in anger. "You fell sleep without washing off your makeup?"

"What?" I'm so confused.

"What on earth were you thinking, Lana?"

Aunt April's look of disgust makes my insides wither. I hold the blanket tighter around my neck. *Why is she acting like I'm Lana?* She must be drunk.

"I can't believe you'd risk a breakout the night before Digifest! Seriously, Lana. Your complexion is our livelihood." She spins on her heel to leave. "Go wash your face!" Aunt April slams the door and I hear her footsteps marching all the way back down the hallway.

I have *so* many questions right now.

Looking around at the photos and pictures on the walls,

I know I'm in Lana's bedroom, although I barely recognize it without the *Ghost World* movie poster and underground comic décor I remember from the last time I was here.

Now, in addition to the elaborate vanity table, Lana's room is littered with strategically placed mood candles and bland, semi-inspirational wall art. Her shelves are packed with glass perfume bottle sculptures, and a giant, glam, old-Hollywood-style light-up mirror is centered like a holy icon.

I get the willies so bad I have to jiggle my arms to fend them off and give a shuddering *"Aaaaaaaaghblahblah"* as I shake my head to clear it.

I have zero clue what I'm doing in Lana's bedroom. And why did Aunt April freak out over face washing instead of me being in her daughter's bed? *And if this is all some elaborate prank, then where have my boobs gone?*

I clutch my new A cups and have a terrible thought.

I'm possessed.

Or worse, I've taken possession. Which means *I'm* the evil one.

My mind whirls with horror movies like *Invasion of the Body Snatchers* and *The Thing*, but in those situations I'd just be some monster or alien right now and my body wouldn't have changed at all. This is more like the opposite, where *only* my body has changed.

The horror movie *Thinner* comes to mind, where a guy makes a wish to lose weight and then can't stop, but I've always been extremely body positive and would never wish away my C-plus cups. Besides, even that poor *Thinner* guy's curse had a more gradual weight loss effect. I seem to have dropped at least

fifty pounds overnight and even my rib cage feels like it just . . .
shrank.

I think of the voodoo that put a dying murderer into a three-
foot-tall Chucky doll in the cult classic *Child's Play.* But as crazy
as things seem right now, even I know that's too far-fetched. I'm
not into voodoo, also not a murderer. And I may be small now,
but I'm hardly doll-sized.

I eye the desk covered with perfectly arranged bottles and
brushes and recognize it as the spot where Lana films her makeup
videos. I creep out of bed and make my way toward the vintage
glam mirror dramatically framed with round light bulbs.

The heaviness in my chest gets even worse when I stand up
and hug one arm tightly around my mini-middle. I reach up to
rub the eye that didn't peel apart in my hand but feel a sharp
eyelash and immediately drop my hand back down.

As I approach the waist-high desk, I push the rolling acrylic
chair out of the way and brace myself. *This is it.*

Without looking, I reach over and click on the light bulbs,
take a deep breath, and wait a beat before moving so I'm facing
the brightly lit mirror.

I'm disoriented for a moment because instead of my own
reflection, I see a very realistic and lifelike image of Lana.

She's a complete mess, but she looks *hyper*-realistic. Like,
when I blink, she blinks her lopsided, crazy-looking lashes, and
when my mouth falls open in shock, Lana's lipstick-smeared
mouth does the same exact thing in the mirror.

We both close our mouths and give a gulp. Numbly, I raise a
hand to wave, and the wild-looking Lana reflection waves back
at me.

I think of the powerful jolt the two of us got in the Skylark back at the drive-in while *Freaky Friday* clips flashed onscreen. I fully believe that the Starlight is magic, and that Aunt May's pink Skylark is an ultra-special vehicle, but none of *this* can be real.

I lean forward and the Lana in the mirror leans closer too. The heaviness in my chest shifts to a sense of hopelessness. Out loud I say, "This isn't happening," and Lana's lips move with mine.

I reach up to touch my face, which is when I notice my nice, strong, functional hands have grown long, manicured nails overnight. I give my left hand a few shakes, as if that will release the foreign pink nails from my fingers, but they're a part of my new, graceful-looking Lana hands.

The hopeless feeling in my chest expands like a balloon until it reaches my head.

This is real.

And that is when my legs give out a little.

In desperation, I grab for something to hang on to. But the clear acrylic chair I lunge for rolls away and I'm left grabbing at a waist-high display of small bottles.

The room starts to go dim as my flailing arms send lotions and creams sailing in every direction.

clatter

> *smash*

>> *crash*

Bottles explode as they hit the floor, and the cloying scent is released into the air in fragrant waves that grow more and more overpowering.

I can't breathe.

My mind swirls as I fall to the floor, gripping a bottle in each hand.

I struggle to hang on to consciousness:

> *How did I wake up in*
> *Lana's bedroom as LANA?*

> *And what is the deal with this*
> *heavy feeling in my chest?*

> *Why do I feel so hopeless and*
> *depressed right now?*

> *Actually, scrap all of that:*

*Can I please, please, **please** just be dreaming right now?*

Maybe if I close my eyes and rest a minute, I'll wake up among the comforting gory masks and horror-show movie posters of my own bedroom.

And with that thought, the screen of my mind flickers and goes completely dark.

• • •

When I open my eyes again, Aunt April is leaning over me with a look of concern on her face.

I'm not sure how much time has gone by, but I don't think I passed out for very long. The aggressive scent of perfume hasn't changed and my aunt is breathing heavily, as if she just ran back into the room.

The way she's studying my face right now is starting to make me nervous. I wonder if she can tell I'm not actually Lana and if so, *How long before the people in white lab coats take me away to be experimented on and eventually dissected?*

Aunt April says, "Lana, sweetheart, are you okay?"

"I'll be . . . fine." I look around at the broken bottles scattered across the floor beside the desk. "What a mess. Sorry."

"Oh, honey, please don't apologize," she says. "I'm the one who's sorry. When you called for me I had no idea you were about to faint. I should've known something was really wrong for you to have gone to bed without washing your face. Not to mention waking up this early."

I weakly nod and glance at the white clock on the night-stand. It's nearly eight thirty. Hardly the crack of dawn.

Aunt April helps me back to the bed, drags the garbage can from the corner, and starts to clean up the mess. But she only uses two manicured fingers to pick up each piece of broken glass one at a time, so her progress is painfully slow.

I picture the way my mom would clean up a mess like this, grabbing a dustpan and getting the job down-and-dirty-and-done. I'm glad I'm more like her.

Aunt April says, "You really should go back to sleep and rest up so you're fresh for Digifest tonight."

"I don't think more sleep will . . . Wait," I say. "Digifest is *tonight*?"

Aunt April comes over and sits on the edge of the bed beside me. "Do *not* joke around about this appearance, Lana. The concert organizers were so excited when I pitched them your pink Skylark idea!"

"I'm really not feeling well." *And I'm not lying.*

"Oh, honey." Aunt April brushes back my hair with her hand and I feebly smile. "You need to kill it at this event," she soothes. "Your fans are expecting you. Erik will be there by your side, and there's already a reinforced ramp all set up so you can drive the convertible directly onto the stage."

"Maybe we can send the Skylark up there in my place."

My aunt's expression turns harsh. "I said do *not* joke around, Lana."

It hits me that Aunt April doesn't seem to be all that worried about the fact I just passed out. Or even consider canceling tonight's Digifest performance because of it.

After a moment I say, "I guess quitting your office job put a lot more stress on *Lookie Lana!*'s success, huh?"

Aunt April looks at me strangely and says, "You know I got laid off."

I look at my hands in my lap and begin picking at Lana's perfect manicure. "Sorry, I—"

"It's fine. I guess the truth seems a little blurry. Better this than letting it slip to Aunt June that my law office got shut down. I hate her being right about that place."

Wow. "Yes, it's easier for me to pretend you quit," I say. "This way I have less remembering to keep my lies straight." No wonder Aunt April is so anxious about Lana's appearance at Digifest. Not to mention her *appearance*. Their livelihood now depends on her daughter's clear complexion. I could manifest a stress zit just thinking about it.

Aunt April smooths her wild hair and says, "I think you should lie down now. Relax for tonight. All day if you need to."

I shake my head. "I think I need some fresh air." There's no way suffocating in this chamber of stank will improve anything about my current situation.

"If you're sure you feel up to it," Aunt April says. "I mean, extra beauty rest might be just what you need."

"It'll do me good to rally," I say, ignoring the pull in my chest that begs me to climb back underneath those covers. I wonder how much time Lana has spent in bed "extra-beauty-resting" away her days. I'm fully tempted to just give up and lie back down.

"Oooh, I know. You can take the convertible for a little drive." My aunt gives me a big grin. "Get used to how she handles and maybe gas up for tonight's show."

I give her a few sticky blinks. "The Skylark?"

"She's right outside in the driveway."

"Oh, right. Because *I* drove it home last night."

Aunt April gives me a look of concern. "On second thought, are you sure you're okay to get behind the wheel?"

"I'll be fine," I say. "I'm almost positive."

"Well, you'd better be," Aunt April says. "Because there is a ton of pressure on you to totally slay at Digifest tonight."

"Okay." I give her two thumbs-up as I head for the door. "I'm *totally* stressed."

"Great, sweetie. Use all that stress to keep you sharp."

Which is the opposite of what my mom always says about stress being the root of mental illness and robbing people of their peace of mind. Mom even has a cute little plaque in our kitchen that says, "Stressed spelled backward is desserts."

As my aunt turns her attention back to her two-fingered cleanup, I wonder how it is that all three sisters can be so wildly different. My heart breaks just a little for my aunt April, trying to keep up appearances with the family after losing her job. I guess I can see where Lana learned to cover things up.

I look around for sneakers, but all the shoes I see have six-inch heels or higher. I spot a pair of flip-flops that are bedazzled for some reason and hold one up to allow the light to reflect off of it. I wonder, *Why?* With a shrug, I slide them onto my feet and grab the pom-pom key chain perched on Lana's end table. I'm focused on the fresh air that awaits as I head for the door.

"Love you, Lana," Aunt April calls over her shoulder as I leave the room, and I stop cold. *Would Lana normally answer her or not?*

I respond with a half-hearted, "You too," as I make my escape.

But I can't move fast enough to outrun the pang of sadness hitting my heart.

chapter 8

As soon as I'm in the Skylark I drive straight to my own house. That is, after I put the convertible top down, of course. Because, hey, I may be stuffed inside my nemesis cousin's tiny body, but come on . . . it's a pink Skylark convertible and I haven't completely lost my mind. *Yet.*

The wind soothes me as I make the drive, and I take a deep breath of fresh morning air. The heaviness in my chest releases just a bit and with a spark of hopefulness, I check my reflection in the rearview mirror.

Nope. Still Lana's blue eyes looking back at me.

I think back to the electric shock she and I got at the drive-in yesterday as we were wrestling over the convertible's steering wheel.

Wait. "Hello, Lana?" I say out loud, and feel around in the back of my mind. *Nope.* I'm definitely alone in here, so not in one of those mutual-possession situations like in the movie *All of Me.*

I decide a straightforward body switch between me and Lana is the simplest explanation that doesn't involve one or both of us already being dead. Just your basic everyday body swap between two cousins who hate each other. Hardly worth getting upset over.

I push down the impulse to openly sob.

When I reach my front door, I take a deep breath and stare at it a moment before bending down for the fake rock that holds our hide-a-key. As I slide the key into the lock I realize it would be odd if Lana just let herself into our house. Better to simply pretend I'm her until I see what we're dealing with.

I stop and replace the key.

I'm sure Mom's up by now, and I wonder if she's already figured out what's happened. She'll definitely freak out and probably try to dose me with enough drugs to sleep until next Tuesday. Plus I imagine she'll be much quicker to realize something is wrong than Aunt April was.

My mom's pretty tuned in.

"Good morning, Lana," she greets me sweetly when she answers my knock at the door. "How're you feeling today?"

"All right, I guess." I watch her carefully to see what she knows.

"Wait," she says, and I brace myself. "Did you sleep in that outfit?"

I realize I didn't bother checking what I was wearing before fleeing Lana's bedroom. But when I look down, instead of sloppy PJs, I have on a wrinkled-yet-adorable shorts romper. It's the most fashionable outfit I've ever worn.

I say, "Yes, but my glitzy flip-flops dress it up, right?" I try to iron the romper using my favorite trick of sliding the palms of my hands down along the fabric, but it has little effect.

"Are you doing okay, Lana?" Mom asks, examining my face. "Your makeup seems . . . off."

"I'm fine, really. Just left my house in a hurry."

Mom laughs. "Here, let me help you." She drags the remaining parasitic lashes off my right eyelid and gently rubs her fingers underneath my eyes. "If this is a product test, I'd call it a *fail*." She smiles. "There you go, all set."

She's so nice to Lana that I wonder for a second if maybe *she* made us switch places so she could finally get that Glam Girl daughter she's always wanted. My mom's Christian, so not exactly into casting spells and curses, but she does believe in the power of prayer.

Still, this is a really weird thing for her to pray for.

"Thanks, Aunt June," I say.

My mom looks back to where Zelda sits waiting for her to return to her reading chair. "That's odd," she says. "Zelda's usually happy to see you." She raises her voice to a high-pitched, "Sweetums? Come see Wana?"

But Zelda only eyes me suspiciously from the comfort of the living room. Which is the way she normally greets *me*.

I tell my mom, "I'm actually here to see Ricki—is she awake yet?"

Mom's eyes narrow and I remember that Lana and I had a big fight in front of her a day and a half ago.

I quickly add, "She and I need to work a few things out." I'm not lying.

"Ricki's usually awake by now, but she wasn't feeling well last night so I'm letting her sleep in." Mom gives a small smile. "Sounds like you really want to work on getting that Skylark, don't you?"

"Oh, I forgot to tell you. I mean *Ricki* probably forgot." I take a step back and point to the convertible parked in the street. "Aunt May gave us the car yesterday."

Mom flails her hands with excitement for a full sixty seconds. "Oh, Lana! I'm so happy! I was hoping you two would rise above your differences and reconnect. It's *beautiful*." She practically has stars in her eyes as she looks at the car.

"Here." I hold out the pom-pom key chain to her. "Why don't you take her for a little ride?"

"Oh, no, I couldn't. It's for you and Ricki to share." She pauses a moment, licking her lips. Finally, she says, "Well, maybe I'll just sit in the driver's seat really quick."

"Enjoy," I say. "I'll go check on Ricki."

"She still may not be feeling well," Mom says in such a caring, protective way it erases any chance she wished for this to happen. Then she adds, "You know how *cranky* Ricki gets when she's sick, so watch she doesn't bite your head off."

"*Hey*," I say defensively.

"Oh, Lana." Mom smiles warmly. "I want you to know that I've been lifting you up in prayer. Every single day."

I wonder what is going on with Lana that Mom feels the need to let her know she's praying for her. "Uh, thanks?" is all I can think to answer, since it would be odd to ask her for specific details.

Mom heads out the front door and Zelda runs to catch up, clearly more curious about the pink convertible than she is about me.

I turn and make my way down the hallway toward the bedroom I *should've* woken up in this morning. My heart pounds at what I might find, and the sound of birds singing outside turns ominous. The hallway seems more shadowed and creepier than ever before.

Hitchcock would love every second of this. But I decidedly do not.

• • •

When I open my bedroom door, I'm instantly comforted by the dim light shining on the gruesome monster masks lined along my shelf. I run my hand down the long row, touching each of their familiar, disgusting faces, as if they're dear friends who I haven't appreciated enough lately.

"Hey there, Frank. How's it hanging, Swampy?" I whisper to Frankenstein and the Swamp Thing. I actually give a quick kiss to the Wolf Man and pat a zombie on the top of his head, avoiding the exposed brain portion of his rubber skull, of course.

When I turn to look at my bed, goose bumps tickle my forearms.

There, underneath my dark-green comforter, is a body-sized lump.

And I'm not talking about some little delicate, petite bump either. I'm talking about a *me*-sized lump in my bed. That's definitely *me* sleeping underneath the covers.

Unless I'm dead! The thought comes with a flash of panic.

I lunge across the room to my bed, draw back the covers and . . . *Wow, do I always sleep with my mouth wide open like that?*

As if to answer, a loud, unflattering snore resonates from my sleeping face. I cringe at the rumbling volume, but at least I'm breathing.

My heart beats fast as I reach out one manicured finger, and in a squeamish rush I give my—well, my *body's*—soft cheek a quick poke. When that doesn't wake me up, I take sleeping Ricki's face by the chin and shake her head back and forth.

I'm usually a pretty light sleeper, but the only response I get is another loud snore from that wide-open mouth.

Are you kidding me right now?

"Hey," I say, shaking the shoulders of the body in my bed. "Wake up."

With a grunt and a face scrunch, the Ricki figure rolls over and continues snoring heartily.

"Come on!" I shake her shoulders harder. "Lana? Are you in there?"

I lean in and marvel at the size of my own ear up close. *Maybe my cousin is right and they are a family curse after all.*

"Wakey, wakey," I say sweetly while slapping her cheek hard.

I get a grunt in response. "*Mmmppph!* I need—*mmmph*—beauty *rest now!*"

"Hey!" I call sharply, "time to get up!"

With a startle, Ricki version 2.0 rubs her face and opens her eyes. She immediately sits up in the bed and looks around the room. A confused expression closes over her face and her head rotates back and forth and then slowly up and down as she takes in her surroundings.

I follow her eyes to the bloody horror paraphernalia and gory masks around my room and worry that if this *is* Lana, she may start screaming any second. No need to conjure Nurse Mom to the scene.

She takes a deep breath that hitches in her throat and I get ready to cover her mouth. Her eyes land on the coffin-shaped Dracula lamp sitting on my nightstand. "What the—?" She looks more confused than scared.

Her fingers tentatively reach toward the coffin lamp, but she freezes when she sees her hand.

I'm actually impressed by how cool and collected she is about my grisly-looking room. I fully expected her to lose it over the horror masks. But now, as she touches her short, plain nails with her other hand, she begins breathing harder and faster. She softly whines.

"My hands," she wails and adds an even more tragic-sounding, "My *nails*!!" so loud I'm afraid my mom will hear from all the way outside. She continues whimpering as she examines her fingernails.

I whisper, "Lana, is that you? You need to keep it down so we can figure this out."

And that is when my Ricki-looking cousin in the bed turns to look directly into my Lana-looking face.

Her eyes widen so big the whites show all around, and I get to see what I might look like if I were in a Stanley Kubrick film.

"It's me," I say. "Ricki."

With that, Lana opens her mouth and lets loose with a terrified scream that would rival the best B-movie horror victim.

She slides her hands into either side of her hair and continues screaming like she's reacting to a gruesome fifty-foot monster. Her lung capacity is truly impressive, and I wonder if her singing talent has transferred into that body as well, or if maybe now that I look like Lana, *I'm* the one who's able to carry a tune for the first time in my life.

As if to prove she's still the singer here, her screaming rises to a higher note and her whole body trembles. Or rather, my body. I try to put an arm around her shoulder to calm her down, but she flinches away, points at my face, and screams even louder. Then she looks at the stubby nails on her hand again and her scream hits a glass-shattering pitch.

I want to explain what's going on and assure her that everything is going to be okay. Except that I realize I have absolutely no idea what is going on. And I have zero assurance that *anything* is going to be okay.

Before I know it, my mouth is opened wide and I am screaming in harmony right along with my awful, loathsome cousin.

At least the two of us finally found something we can agree on.

This right here, waking up inside each other's bodies, is something to scream about.

chapter 9

Our harmonized screams continue until they're cut off by sharp shouts coming from the doorway.

"Ricki!" I turn to see my mother standing with her hands on her hips and Zelda at her heels. Evil Z is offering her usual morning greeting; baring her teeth at my cousin in the bed. Mom snaps, "What is going on here?"

"I have no idea!" I wail.

"I could hear your screams the whole way outside. What's wrong?" I realize Mom's addressing Lana, but Lana hasn't even seen her own reflection yet.

"Oh, Aunt June, it's horrible!" Lana says. "Just look at these!" She holds up her short nails for my mother to see.

Mom's eyes narrow and she looks back and forth between us. "What am I looking at here? Are you girls really going to start your funny business antics already? I *will* ground you from that car, Ricki."

I cut in, "*Ricki* is just messing around, Aunt June. We wigged out for a second over it getting late already when we have *so much* to do today."

"It's only a little past nine," Mom says. "I was letting you sleep in, hoping you'd feel better for the drive-in tonight."

"Right!" I say. "The reopening tonight is *super* important!"

"You're going to that, Lana?" Mom asks me. "Don't you have some appearance to do in LA?"

"Digifest!" Lana wails. "Digifest is less than twelve hours away! And it takes over three hours to get to the venue so that means I need to leave in, like, less than nine hours! And now on top of everything else I need to fit in an *emergency manicure*."

My mom tilts her head at Lana with confusion. "Ricki, I didn't know you were following your cousin's career so closely. Or that you cared about your nails. *At all*."

"Why are you calling me Ricki?" Lana asks.

Mom holds up the pom-pom key chain. "I'm serious, girls. I will *take that car*. Now tell me why I can't call you Ricki all of a sudden." Mom hates "funny-business," but I think she mostly wants the pink Skylark for herself.

Thinking quickly, I say to Lana, "Oh yeah, we forgot to tell *your mom* you're going by your full name again."

Mom and Lana say in unison, "Lyric?"

They both burst out laughing at the same time. Lyric is my actual name, given to me because when a person is a baby nobody can tell that they won't be able to carry a single note when they get older. My mom and my aunts all sing, and of course Lana has a gorgeous voice, but once I got old enough to try belting out actual "lyrics," my part-time nickname, Ricki, became my name, and *Lyric* became a family joke.

"No, really," I say. "She's gotten better at singing, watch!"

Mom looks expectantly at Lana and Lana looks at me in confusion. "Come on, Lyric," I say. "One and two and . . ."

She obediently opens her mouth and starts to sing, "You are my sunshine, my only sunshine . . ." with such melodic beauty, my mom is utterly speechless.

"Ricki, er, I mean, *Lyric*," Mom says. "You've found your voice."

My mother has actual tears in her eyes, which makes me realize just how important my being able to sing has been to her. I feel bad for giving her this false hope, especially since on top of still being tone-deaf, I'm also out of my mind now. Literally.

I notice Zelda has jumped onto the bed and is wagging her tail now as she sniffs Lana. Which of course looks like she's greeting Ricki without growling and snapping for the very first time ever. With a snuffle, Zelda actually tucks into to my cousin's neck and starts licking her face.

I instinctively reach over to pick her up before she tastes the Ricki-flavored skin and attacks.

Zelda growls at me, and I pull my beautiful Lana fingers away just as her teeny teeth loudly snap at the air.

Lana reaches over to comfort the evil Chihuahua and Zelda kisses her cheek. Apparently, it's not the face she hates. It's just me.

"That's odd," Mom says to Lana. "Since when does Z prefer you to Lana?"

Lana looks at my mom in confusion and I know I need to get my mother out of here before we all end up spending the day stuck in some psychiatrist's office. Today is too important to waste, because no matter what else happens, I'm still determined to get my magical kiss from Jake at the Starlight tonight.

I grab the gray throw blanket from the bottom of my bed and use it to pick up Zelda. The dog immediately goes wild, growling and trying to bite me, but I hold her out away from my body as I hand her to my mom.

"You should maybe get her to the vet, Aunt June," I say. "She's acting *very* strange."

My mother takes the small white vessel of evil from the blanket and Zelda immediately calms down. Mom looks back and forth between Lana and me for another long moment while petting her Chihuahua. Finally, she says accusingly, "I don't know what you two are up to, but I know it's *something*. And I don't like it."

She turns to go, and I give a sigh of relief before she spins back around.

"No more screaming." Mom holds the pink pom-pom key chain up in the air. "I'm going on a little test ride to check how the car drives, but any more funny business and that Skylark is *mine* for the rest of the day." Her eyes sparkle as she adds, "Imagine everyone's reaction if I pull up to book club driving *that*."

As soon as my mom and Zelda leave, Lana turns to me. "What is going on here?" she says. "Why do you look exactly like me?"

I stand and pull the small mirror off my wall, careful to aim it at the floor as I walk back over to the bed. I look Lana in the eyes. "Remember. No screaming."

I raise the mirror up to Lana's face. She takes a deep breath and I quickly clap one hand over her mouth.

She screams into it hard.

As Lana runs out of scream and begins hyperventilating, I

loosen my grip on her mouth. A small whimper escapes as she looks with sorrow at my face reflected back at her in the mirror. When I drop my hand she says, "This is the worst thing that's ever happened to me."

"All right, already," I say. "No need to be insulting."

Lana's expression turns to anger and she shoves the mirror away. "Right, because *of course* you'll make this insane situation all about *your* hurt feelings."

"*You're* the one acting like it's only happening to you. I'm just saying you don't have to act like you're completely deformed."

"I'm not allowed to have a reaction?" She points to her/my face. "This sucks!"

"Well, I'm pretty sure this is all your fault. If you hadn't tried to trick Aunt May into giving us the Skylark, we'd probably be in our regular bodies right now."

"Our fight over the Skylark!" she says. "Back at the drive-in."

"Yeah, that's what I was thinking. Something must've shifted when the screen started flashing and we got shocked."

Lana springs out of bed. "Wow," she says. "Other than the mental break from reality, I feel really good right now. Do you feel *good*? Like maybe getting switched gave us a jolt of, I don't know . . . expectation?"

I look at her a moment and think about the weight I noticed sitting on my chest when I first woke up. It's shifted to more of a dull ache, but it's still there. Like my heart is made of stone. "I actually feel kind of tired."

"Yeah, maybe you didn't sleep well or something? That body is used to sleeping in pretty hard during the summer."

"Or maybe the hopeless feeling in my chest is a sign that something's wrong."

"Something's *obviously* wrong, cuz," Lana says. "And we have less than nine hours to get ourselves back into our proper bodies, or my career is over. Do you know how many beauty gurus would kill to be in my position?"

"Lana . . ." I say calmly, but the panic in her voice only increases.

"There's this top icon who calls herself Her Highness, who has been in an online *war* with me and would love to watch me tank tonight . . .

"Lana!" I say louder, and she finally looks at me. I sigh. "Your mom told me your channel has to support you financially. And that she didn't quit her job, she got laid off."

Lana bites her bottom lip so hard it turns white.

I ask, "Why would you two keep that a secret?"

She closes her eyes and her head lolls back. "My mom didn't want the family to know," she says. "Everyone tried to tell her she was wasting her talent at that firm, and it turns out they were right. She didn't want her sisters judging her."

Lana tucks one of her newly dark curls behind her ear and I'm hit with a pang of sadness for her. "She should've at least told my mom."

"Right, sure," Lana says. "Because your perfect mother needs a yet another way to rub her perfectness in my mom's face."

"You *know* my mom doesn't do that," I say. "And she's *not* perfect. Just *mostly* perfect."

"Yeah, well, maybe if my mom didn't feel like she was always seen as a screw-up for her past mistakes, she could be more open and honest." Lana frowns. "Maybe even ask for help."

"The two of you are lying to everyone because your mom is worried about her sisters' opinion of her?"

"Yeah, but it backfired anyway," Lana says. "Your mom thinks she's super selfish for purposely putting all this financial pressure on me, so I guess there's no escaping being judged in this family."

She fidgets with her hands and I have an urge to cover them with one of mine. She must feel so alone in this. "I'm sorry our moms have a screwed-up relationship," I say.

I look at her, waiting for her to apologize for rejecting me. She could easily blame our breakup on our moms, and I can feel myself softening toward my cousin.

"Ugh, the *worst*." Lana flattens one hand and examines her nails. "How do you live with these nailbeds?"

Or not. "Okay, so let's maybe deal with our mom's sisterhood issues *after* we've figured out how to switch our bodies back. Any ideas?"

Just then, the back pocket of my romper starts vibrating and I jump straight into the air as if I've been goosed. "What the . . . ?" I didn't even realize the shorts had a back pocket. "Why is my heinie vibrating?"

"Oh, my phone!" Lana says. "I can't believe I haven't even thought about it all morning."

"You *just* woke up five minutes ago." I pull the phone from my pocket. "Also, you sleep with your phone?"

"You don't?" Lana says. "Give it here. I have the do not disturb set until after nine thirty."

"How is it nine thirty already?"

But Lana ignores me as she scrolls through her phone.

"Maybe this is just a 'wait until it ends' sort of switch," I say. "The ones in movies are usually over in one day."

Lana continues looking at her phone but says, "There's that old Disney one with Katherine Heigl where she and her sister switch for a whole week."

"Can you please put that thing down?" I snap. "We need to figure this out because even if it's just a twenty-four-hour shared psychotic break, we're both doomed for tonight."

"Fine, I'll focus." Lana puts her phone into the pocket of my comfy flannel jammies. "Any ideas?"

"No," I say quietly. "And I don't know that Katherine Heigl movie—what's it called?"

"*Wish Upon a Star.*"

"Is it good?" I ask.

"No, it is not," Lana says matter-of-factly. "But it's also not bad. It wasn't particularly original or creative, but it was loads of fun. Fluffy popcorn movie through and through. I'd give it three and a half stars rounded up to four for being mildly funny."

"Nice review," I say. I know the value of a clear movie opinion. I don't care much for social media, but I do have an IMDb presence where I'm known to write occasional passion-fueled and maybe even ranty movie reviews.

We're both quiet for a long moment. "Hey," Lana says. "How about that hand slap game we played all the time as kids? I remember we'd get going so fast it felt as if we were sharing a brain." She gives a sharp snap. "Maybe it could *spark* a connection and switch us back."

"Down-down baby?" When we were younger we'd recite verses and make up our own complicated hand motions for hours on end. I say, "It's worth a shot."

The two of us stand on my carpet facing each other and awkwardly start, failing to connect palms at first and slapping at the air. It takes us a few tries to remember the moves, but we gradually get it together, and the next thing we know we're slapping and clapping faster and faster.

"Shimmy, shimmy cocoa pops, shimmy, shimmy pow," we recite together as we stomp and clap and snap and slap.

As we pick up speed we begin moving together more intuitively, like our muscles are remembering the repeated sequence we made up as kids. I feel the slightest flutter in my chest, like the heavy weight that's been pulling down on me ever since I woke up is finally releasing a hint of pressure. I look over at my cousin, who's smiling with the triumph of mastering each move, and wonder if the fluttering could be the start of us changing back.

We go faster and faster until it's impossible to keep up and we just start trying to slap each other, which is actually the way the game has always ended.

We chase each other around my room, swinging and ducking until I catch Lana and slap her so hard across the heinie it makes my hand sting.

"Ow! That actually hurt," she says, rubbing her butt.

"Sorry." I grin. "Guess I don't know your own strength."

"Well, that was a bust." Lana gestures to our still-swapped bodies.

"I don't know," I say. "It felt good to release a bit of pent-up frustration."

"Yeah, on my heinie." Lana rubs it again and lunges to smack mine hard.

"*Ouch!* This isn't helping anything," I say, and give her another sharp smack. "Ha!"

"Wait a second." She holds up both hands in truce. "I think I might know what could switch us back." Her eyes widen with excitement. "And you're going to hate it."

chapter 10

The next thing I know, I'm looking into the mirror over Lana's shoulder as she puts the finishing touches on making her/my face look absolutely glamourous.

"And how exactly is a makeover supposed to switch us back?" I ask as she dabs a small brush along my blood-red lips. They are *literally* blood-red since Lana only had my monster special effects makeup to work with, so they're covered in fake blood. She's used bruise makeup to create a dramatic smoky eye and somehow managed to manipulate skeleton contour to change the shape of my whole face.

"I thought that maybe making you gorgeous was my quest," she says, dramatically gesturing to her handiwork.

"Your *quest* was to make me look like I'm sucking in my cheeks and giving kissy lips," I grouse. "Yeah, right."

"So maybe I have been dying to accent these cheekbones." She points to one. "Just look." I have to admit she's not wrong about the enormous-seeming cheekbones.

"Wait a minute, maybe the curse is just waiting for *me* to make up *your* face," I say.

"Great idea! Do you want some help?" she asks.

"Oh, no. I've got this." I get to work while Lana opens my closet, releasing the pile of laundry I recently shoved inside.

"I have to get out of these frumpy pajamas," she says and starts rifling through the clothes on hangers. "Why on earth do you own so many hunting outfits?"

"They're not for hunting—I just like layers." I get to work on my elaborate face makeup. "Don't wreck my closet."

"Your closet was a wreck before I got here," she says. "A *fashion train* wreck." She laughs at her own joke.

I ignore her as I work quickly. I know my cousin's face so well it looks odd to see it reversed in the mirror.

"Oooh, wait! LBD! LBD!" Lana shrieks excitedly as she pulls out a short black dress. "And are these actual . . . Prada *heels* in your closet?"

"A little fancy, don't you think?" I say. "That's my junior prom dress from last year. And my mom bought me the heels as wishful thinking. I wore sparkly Doc Martens with the dress instead."

Lana slides the heels onto her feet and she is instantly six foot three. "I'm so tall!" she says with amazement. "And these shoes are gorgeous. I can't believe you never wore them." She holds up the dress and poses in the mirror that hangs on the inside of my closet door.

"I can't walk two steps in those things," I say.

Lana gives a few expert stomps toward me and stops short when she gets a look at my face. "Really, Ricki?" She's furious.

"What?" I say innocently. "You gave me a makeover and so I gave you a makeover." I snarl at my reflection and a sick-looking zombie girl snarls back. I adjust a strategic bit of rot on my left cheek and spin around to grab at my cousin. "Braaiins!"

Lana flinches. "That's so creepy and disgusting!"

"Thanks." I smile, showing off blackened zombie teeth.

Lana slips into the black dress and tries to convince me to change the sleep romper I'm wearing. But this romper is super comfortable. I point out that nothing in my closet will fit Lana's tiny body anyway.

We're still arguing over belting options when there's a quick knock on the door and my mother opens it without waiting for our response. Zelda struts in behind her.

"Aunt May was so right about that car being magic." Mom's hair is windblown, and she has a wild look in her eyes as she swings the key chain around her finger.

Lana and I look at each other. "The convertible must hold the key," Lana says.

Mom quickly shoves the key into her own pocket and looks at Lana. "You look amazing, Ricki!" she says and then turns and startles at my zombified face. "Oh! And, wow, look at you, Lana. Just . . . look at you."

I ignore her. "That Skylark is definitely magic," I say. "We need to get in touch with Aunt May right away."

"That's sweet you want to thank May," Mom says, "but you know your aunt. She's can be tough to track down—probably off hiking through the California wilderness without a care in the world."

Aunt May uses a primeval flip phone, and insists her yurt and truck remain zero-tech, Wi-Fi–free zones. Plus, most of her time is spent hiking with her wolf dogs in out-of-range places.

Sure enough, when Lana dials her, it only takes a moment before she growls, "Straight to voice mail."

"And she never responds to texts on that fossil she calls a phone," my mom says.

"Let's just go see if we can catch her at home," I say. "It's only an hour and a half away, and this could be really important."

Lana is still distracted, scrolling on her smartphone, and Zelda sniffs my ankle like she's looking for something to nosh on. I hook my foot to slide the Chihuahua neatly underneath the bed.

"Let's go!" Grabbing Lana by the hand, I head for the door and give my mom a quick peck on the cheek as I move past her.

"Wait," Mom calls as she steps into the hallway after us. She holds up my phone. "You left this charging, Ricki."

I slink back to grab the phone from her and my mother furrows her brow. "Oh," I say, "I'm letting Ricki use mine to map the way to Aunt May's." I hold out my hand and accusingly add, "Keys please?"

Grudgingly, Mom pulls the pom-pom key chain from her pocket and I take it.

The Chihuahua sees an opportunity to go for blood and I quickly shut the bedroom door just as Evil Z charges for my toes. I hear a small thump and tiny yelp.

Handing my phone to Lana, I say loudly, "Here you go, cuz. I can't believe you almost left without it."

"Sorry." Lana takes my phone and stacks it underneath hers. "I'm not feeling myself today." She laughs at her own joke.

"*So* not funny." I wave the pom-pom key chain in the air and sprint outside. "I call driver!"

I expect Lana to move slow in the high heels, but when I turn back at the walkway she's right behind me. We both dash for the car and reach for the driver's door together. I give the keys a shake. "I called driver."

Lana towers over me. "Really, Ricki? You're going to turn this into a thing? I've had my driver's license longer and have more experience, so—"

I cut her off. "Don't you remember the big spark? When the random movies started playing?"

"Hmm . . . let me think a second . . . *OF COURSE* I remember," Lana scoffs. "That had to be the moment our switch began."

"Exactly." I smile at her. "So maybe we should, you know, sit on the sides where we were? Try grabbing the wheel again?"

"Good idea," Lana says as she gestures for me to walk around to the passenger side.

"Actually," I say, "I was in the driver's seat at the time, so . . . ?"

I wait.

Lana doesn't move so I gesture with a nod to the passenger seat. I have to point my head so hard I can feel the fake pus on my cheek trickle slightly toward my jaw.

Finally, she rolls her eyes, hands me my phone, and stomps around to the passenger door like a surly toddler forced to go to her room.

I climb in the driver's side and Lana slides all the way in close. When we're both in position I count down slowly, "Three. Two. One," and the two of us reach for the steering wheel at the same time. And . . .

Nothing happens.

I try to imagine the weight in my chest being released out into the open air as I turn the key, but there's no breakthrough of relief as the engine rumbles to life. In fact, I've never felt so trapped.

I put the Skylark into gear. "Hopefully Aunt May can help us."

Lana slides to the passenger side as we roar away from the curb and says, "Well, at least we're road tripping in style."

"Right," I say. "*Tripping in style.*"

The Skylark picks up speed, and the fresh air kneads at us.

Finally, Lana flings her arms wide and stands so she's hugging the wind that wildly whips her now-dark curls. She calls out, "I may be crazy, but I feel so free!"

"Well, I feel like I've had something sitting on my chest ever since I woke up this morning."

Lana sits back down and looks at me. "Is it like an invisible crushing that makes it so hard to breathe that you feel like you might suffocate on just plain air?"

"Why?" I ask. "Have you felt it before?"

"No. No reason." Lana reaches for the radio dial and turns up the music. "Maybe a little car dancing will help you feel less anxious."

She makes twisting arm motions to the beat of the song she's put on. Turning to me, she unsticks a clump of her hair from the thick glamour makeup layered on her face. "Car dance!!"

Lana gleefully moves to the music, and I think about the heavy weight I've inherited. She definitely knew what I was talking about. I can't imagine what it could mean, but I do think my mom's theory may be right about our bodies manifesting tension as we hold on to stress.

And I suspect Aunt April's firing isn't the only secret Lana is holding back.

As Lana's front seat rave continues, a Volkswagen SUV filled with cute guys approaches us on the passenger side. Lana flirtatiously shimmies her shoulders in their direction and the young men woot and cheer in a way that surprises me, since I've never in my life been "wooted" at by a carload of boys.

Lana eats up the attention until we stop at a light and I put the car in park so I can lunge all the way across the car to her side. I stretch past her, grasping at the air and reaching for the guys with zombie hands.

I call out, "Brains!! Braaaaiiiins!" and the boys immediately stop flirting and speed off ahead of us.

Rubbing at the pressure in my chest as I slide back to my seat, I shift back into drive and turn the music to an indie rock song that better matches my mood. "While you're me, you might want to try staying in character," I say. "I would never flirt with strangers that way."

Lana crosses her arms and makes a pouty face. "Fine. Now I'm you."

"Yeah. That's the problem," I say, and gun the motor, speeding faster toward Aunt May's yurt.

chapter 11

In case you don't know what the heck a yurt is, it's basically a round tent serving as a living space, that's big enough to fit a bed, a couch, and an entire kitchen, but is in no way designed to house three wolf dogs.

We can hear the dogs barking before we even pull up to Aunt May's, but her pickup is nowhere in sight. I park the Skylark on the front section of lawn that serves as a driveway and cut the engine.

"I guess she's not here," Lana says. "But doesn't she usually bring her dogs everywhere with her? She's like your mom that way."

"Yes, because carrying Zelda, the evil purse dog, is exactly the same as running errands with three wild wolf dogs."

Lana laughs. "I guess Aunt May's wolves aren't welcomed everywhere."

"Hardly fair since they're so much friendlier than that cranky Chihuahua will ever be." I step out of the car and make my way toward the yurt.

Lana dials her phone as she follows me. "Aunt May could be at the supermarket, or the doctor's, or basically anyplace you're not allowed to have wolf dogs."

"It's safe to assume she didn't leave them to go hiking in the woods by herself."

I see the indents of fist-sized paws punching the tent walls as we approach. As if the three of them want to claw through the canvas to give us giant big-dog hugs.

Lana hangs up her phone. "Still going straight to Aunt May's voice mail."

We both call out "Hello!" and knock on the wood door frame, which only makes the dogs go completely nuts and bash the tent harder.

I pat the soft outer wall. "It's okay, puppies! It's just us."

Lana reaches for the door handle.

"No, no, no . . ." I say, but it's too late. She is immediately knocked down by a massive collection of hair and paws and wet noses that sniff and huff and lick her face all over.

"Ugh, dog slobber," Lana wails while using both hands to push away the overwhelming degree of affection. One of the pups calmly walks over to me, places his head underneath my hand, and sits at my feet.

While struggling to dodge canine kisses, Lana blurts out, "I was just testing the handle! *Ugh*—I thought it—*mph*—would be locked."

"Ha! I guess Aunt May trusts her place is secure."

"She is not wrong." Lana laughs.

I help lift my cousin up off the ground and the dogs run to the convertible to inspect it as if they're the pit crew.

"Maybe they can feel it's magic," Lana says.

One of them lifts his leg and pees on the back tire.

"Yup. Magical," I say. "Come on, let's look around. Maybe we can figure out who Aunt May bought the car from."

Lana reaches up and touches her face. "I hope dog slobber doesn't make your skin break out."

Aunt May's yurt is warm inside and smells of spices and dirt. The sun shines through the window and onto a large dream-catcher hanging from the center ceiling beam. The only thing it seems to be catching successfully is dog hair.

Lana walks over to the desk against one angled canvas wall and starts rifling through the uneven papers piled high on top of it.

I kneel in front of the long, low bookcase that's bursting at the seams with books. Most of the titles are related to either self help, peace of mind, or dog training.

"I guess Aunt May never heard of feng shui," Lana says as she adjusts a huge stack of papers threatening to topple.

"Oh, she's heard of it," I say, pointing. "In fact, she has four books devoted to it right here. They're all covered in dust." I pick up a fat volume titled *Declutter Now!* and blow a cloud in Lana's direction.

Lana giggles, and the dogs come running back inside to see what's so funny. One immediately recommences giving her a slobber makeover while the other two take turns leaping up to gently nibble at my phony wounds.

We both squeal and fight them off, which only makes them more determined to prove their love to us.

"Ack." Lana lunges over one of the dogs and she and I go back-to-back to ward them off more effectively. It's a trick we developed years ago when the wolf dogs first reached maturity, and as Aunt May would say, "The babies give big cuddles!"

Lana reaches down and grabs a large book off the shelf. Holding it in both hands, she uses it to block one of the dogs and says, "Is this how these dog training guides work?"

"Actually, Aunt May taught me a little trick the last time I came by."

Seizing the closest dog, I firmly take one of his ears in my hand and start massaging it. The dog immediately sits, tilts his whole head toward my hand, and gives a groan.

"What are you doing, hypnotizing him?" Lana asks.

"Just forcing him to relax," I explain, and she immediately begins massaging all the dogs' ears one after another. Soon the pups are well-behaved putty in our hands, moaning and writhing on the ground.

Lana laughs. "I didn't realize you still came out here to visit Aunt May."

"Yeah, some of us didn't get too busy for family," I say.

"I didn't get too busy for family," Lana says. "I just . . . Hey, what's that?" She points to the bookshelf, where a faded red leather volume is partially visible behind the space left by the dog training book. "It looks like a diary!"

Pulling out the thick journal, she brushes a layer of dust off the front, revealing it's embossed with a drawing of silver kissy lips.

"*That* is none of our business." I take the diary from her hands.

Lana immediately snatches it back from me. "This might hold some answers for us."

She opens it and starts running her finger down the page, her brown eyes darting quickly until I grab the book back again.

"If Aunt May wanted people to read her diary, she wouldn't have hidden it in the back of her bookshelf."

Lana grabs one end of the journal and pulls with all her might. I won't let go until she drags me toward her and gives me a hip check that knocks me down flat.

The wolf dogs immediately come over to inspect me as if they're now an EMT squad.

"Whoops." Lana snickers. "I didn't realize a set of hips could be weaponized."

"I miss my hips!" I wail. "Fine, just take a quick look."

Opening the diary, Lana scans the page a moment before reading aloud, "We won *Star Search!*"

"What? Let me see that."

Lana holds the thick book between us. The wolves act as if they're reading over our shoulders as we scan pages of notes detailing dance moves and sketches of ripped fishnets and big 80s teased-out hair.

Lana says, "Here's an oath, vowing to practice every day after school, and it's signed April, May, and June."

"It looks like they entered a local talent competition." I turn the page, whispering, "Please have a photo . . ."

Sure enough, taped in the center of the next page is a blurry Polaroid of all three sisters rocking out like big-haired 80s pop stars. The lyrics to "Love Is a Battlefield" are scrawled underneath in black Sharpie.

Lana looks at me. "They lip-synched a Pat Benatar song—in public!"

"And they must've been amazing!" I point to the gold-embossed first place ribbon tucked into the diary's page crease.

We both squint at the photo, but the idea of our aunt and moms punching lace-covered fists into the air in time to music fails to develop.

I turn the page and find a double-page spread of colorful stickers. "Well, this book serves as a nice eighties time capsule, but it's pretty useless. Let's put it back."

"Authentic vintage scratch and sniff!" Lana squeals. "I need to do a video of these stickers for my channel."

"I don't think our moms and Aunt May would appreciate you making their diary public."

"I'm just making a scan of the sticker page for my story," Lana says as she pulls out her phone and starts filming. "I haven't posted anything *all day.*"

She points a finger at one of the "grape" stickers like she's about to scratch it. Then she sees her short, stubby nail and says, "Oh, right. Can you come over here and scratch this sticker for the camera really quick?"

I point to the analog clock on Aunt May's bookcase. "Lana," I snap. "You're supposed to leave for Digifest in seven hours and we still have an hour and a half drive back to Fresno."

She makes a sad face as she slowly raises the open page of stickers so it's right in front of her nose. She sniffs loudly and brightens. "Still grapey!"

Aiming her phone at the page, she draws it across, careful to keep her hands out of the frame as she captures each colorful row of stickers.

"Could you please just put that stupid phone away and help me look for clues," I say. "Maybe the bill of sale for the Skylark, or at least a receipt for the pom-pom key chain."

"I think it came from Claire's," Lana says. "Hang on . . ." She checks her phone.

"You've *got* to be kidding me," I grumble.

"Oh no!" Lana wails. "Erik is trying to FaceTime me. What am I going to do?"

"You're going to ignore that call, help me clean up all these books, and get out of here so we can figure out how to fix this switch. I am *not* missing opening night at the Starlight so I can pretend to be you, singing badly on some stage . . ."

Without warning, Lana swipes her phone to answer it. "Hi, Erik," she says with a giant grin on *my* face.

"Um, hello?" The confused voice comes from the speaker on her phone.

Lana grins. "I'm Lana's cousin, Ricki."

"Hello, Ricki," he says. "You've got something on your face there."

The wolf dogs have succeeded in spreading Lana's bloody lips over most of the lower half of her face. Lana can see this on her phone's screen but pretends to dab at one tiny corner. "Here? Did I get it?"

"Nope." Erik laughs and gestures to his chin as if stroking an imaginary beard. "It's a little more . . . all over." She wipes a tiny bit more and he says, "A *little* to your left . . ." and the two of them go back and forth flirting like that until I clear my throat.

Lana turns her phone to face me and the screen shows a handsome boy with a flop of blond hair.

His pained expression changes to happiness at seeing my face. That is, *Lana's* face.

"Zombie. Nice," Erik says. "I can't believe you let your cousin answer your phone. Quite the kidder she is."

Lana aims the phone back at herself. "Look who's talking," she says. "I know all about your epic pranks." She hands me the phone. "Here, I need to find a sink to wash my face."

"I think that's the kitchen area," I say, gesturing to the pile of dishes that hopefully signify a sink buried underneath.

"Where are you right now?" Erik asks me. "Did you forget we're doing a livestream together today at noon?"

"OhmyGee," Lana says from the kitchen, "I *did* forget."

"Ricki? Is that you?" Erik sounds confused.

I turn the screen toward Lana again. She's leaning over the pile of dishes and wetting a paper towel. She calls out, "I mean, *I* was supposed to *remind* Lana about the livestream."

"Yeah," I say, turning the phone back toward myself. "She forgot to remind me. We've had a *lot* going on this morning."

"Truth!" Lana shouts.

"Well, you'd better head over here," Erik says. "We're scheduled to go live in a half hour." He lowers his voice and asks me, "Did you catch the new post from Her Highness? She's ruthless."

"Who's Her Highness?" I ask.

Erik grins. "That's the right attitude. Don't let her get in your head."

Lana calls from across the yurt, "We can be at your studio in about an hour and a half to film. Let your followers know we'll be an hour late! Sorry."

I think fast. "Wait a second, Erik," I say. "What do you think of us meeting at the Starlight Drive-in over on Route Eight so we can do our streaming from there?"

I wink at Lana, and she narrows her eyes at me.

"I can grab my portable setup, no problem," Erik says. "What are you planning?"

"Yeah, Lana," Lana says. "What're you planning, cuz?"

Cheerfully, I say, "You'll see!" I look at Erik on the phone. "Meet us at the concession stand at the Starlight at one o'clock."

As soon as I hang up Lana snaps, "What the heck are you doing?"

"What? Was I supposed to blow him a kiss goodbye?"

"Not that," she says. "The drive-in. Are you still really that desperate to win the convertible for the reopening tonight?"

"Seriously," I say. "You do *not* let things go, do you?"

"You're the one who just manipulated things to get the Skylark back to the Starlight."

I say, "I'm hoping that taking the car back to the drive-in will shake something loose in the stratosphere or something."

Lana tilts her head. "I guess it's worth a shot. This trip was certainly a waste of time."

I give the closest wolf dog a rough rubdown and he smiles up at me with his tongue lolling out one side. "No. Not a total waste," I say to him in a wolfy voice. "Not a waste at all, was it?"

He rolls on his back and paws the air in response.

Lana and I quickly wash the dog slobber and remaining makeup from our faces at the dish-filled sink, and I straighten up the books, making sure the red diary is well hidden.

We move toward the door together but Lana doubles back and says, "You go ahead. I just want to fill the dogs' water bowl. I noticed it's empty." She smooshes her words together, so I know she's hiding something.

I say, "Based on the amount of slobber on my romper right now, I'm pretty sure those wolf dogs are hydrated."

"I think I know *one* reason Zelda doesn't like you," she says. "You're a dog hater."

"I am not." I look at the dogs, who have been watching us prepare to go. They look utterly betrayed by our leaving, and their tongues hang to the floor. "Just hurry with the water and I'll go start the car," I say. "Don't bother locking up."

chapter 12

We're already speeding down the highway when Lana shifts in the passenger seat so she's facing me.

"Don't be mad," she says.

"Yeah, sure, Lana. Let's test my temper today," I say with sarcasm.

Lana reaches behind her head and wriggles a moment as if she's trying to unhook her own bra. Finally, she smiles and pulls something out from the nape of her black dress.

"Heavy-duty bras do double duty," she says in triumph as she holds up the red leather journal with the kissy lips on front. "I could never do that with the flimsy, lacy things I usually wear. Pretty bras are useless."

"*Hey*, that happens to be one of my fanciest bras," I say, pushing the twirling blonde hair out of my face. "And *how* could you steal something so private from our aunt's yurt?"

"Look!" Lana is flipping through a few pages. "It's just a bunch of random eighties trivia and stuff about boys that our moms and Aunt May all wrote together."

"Do you want to make our body swap even worse?" I say.

"We're clearly supposed to be learning something here to reverse the curse. *Not* turning into thieves."

"I *am* learning." She continues scanning the journal. "About our mothers and about Aunt May. Aren't you curious? They were around *our age* when they stood onstage declaring 'We are young!' to a Pat Benatar song."

"I just want to switch back," I say. "Things for you will work out fine—your beauty guru success has grown unstoppable. But if we can't figure things out by tonight, I am going to lose Jake forever."

"I have a boyfriend too, you know," Lana says. "Not to mention a cosmetics sponsorship hinging on my performance at Digi."

"Boyfriend. Right," I say. "Just please put that diary away and help me come up with a plan. Jake is going to be waiting for us at the Starlight and things are already super weird between us."

I'm about to tell her about Jake's two near-kisses and how much I'm still cringing inside over them, but when I look over, her nose is buried in the diary. Typical Lana. Ignoring me and acting like I have no life.

With a growl, I paw at my churning blonde hair again and finally notice a rubber band hanging from the gearshift. Using my elbows to steer, I pull my hair up into a quick, messy bun.

"Please do not damage my hair," Lana says without looking up. "Look, here's a collection of questions each sister took turns answering." She begins reading. "'What is your greatest fear?' Then under *April* it says, 'Failing to fulfil my life's dream of becoming famous.'"

"Well, it looks like your mom's greatest fear came true and she's taking it out on you."

"What are you talking about?" Lana asks.

I point to the open page on Lana's lap. "Becoming famous. Your mom is forcing you to live out her dream."

"That's not what *Lookie Lana!* is about," she says. "My mom and I are just trying to get by. And hey, let's see what your perfect mother wrote as her greatest fear . . ."

"Really, Lana, let's just stop—"

"Here it is," she interrupts. "Your mother's greatest fear was . . . Okay, so she wrote down *vampires*, so that's not really anything. I guess she *is* the youngest . . ."

"Actually, I think she has a genuine thing with vampires," I say. "She still sleeps with her neck covered." I look over, but once again, Lana isn't listening.

"Oh . . ." She puts a hand over her mouth.

"What is it?" I glance at a small drawing of a bat beside what I recognize as my mother's handwriting. "Was my mom afraid of something else?"

"No, it's not her. It's Aunt May. Her greatest fear . . . was being alone."

I swallow down a bitter pocket of air, and a chunk of blonde works its way loose from my bun. The two of us ride on in silence as a vast and sparsely vegetated field rolls by.

I picture Aunt May and wonder if she's hiding deep loneliness. She's always been so cheerful and generous, it wasn't even all that surprising she spent her money on this car to draw Lana and me together.

Lana says softly, "Keeping family together has always been most important to Aunt May."

I shove the renegade rope of hair behind my ear and say, "You just *had* to steal that stupid diary, didn't you?"

"Once we figure all of this out and switch back," Lana says, "I'm going to spend more time visiting Aunt May."

"Yeah, me too," I say. "Whether we switch back or not."

●　●　●

When we pull into the Starlight Drive-in, Jake is standing outside the concession shack listening to a conversation between Wes and some slick-looking man I've never seen here before. I can tell right away by the way they're standing that Jake and Wes do not like him.

Jake uncrosses his arms and gives Lana a tight smile when he sees us pull in, and she waggles her fingers at him in a flirty way I never would.

"Stop that," I hiss as I turn off the Skylark's engine. "It looks like something serious is happening."

Jake turns back to listen as Wes starts shouting at the slick-looking guy. *I really hope this isn't something bad about tonight.* Everything feels so fragile right now, and the pressure in my chest begins to throb.

A vintage Audi roars into the drive-in lot with Erik at the wheel.

Wes angrily gestures to Erik's car and continues yelling at the intruder, who points to Erik and shakes his head.

"What on earth is happening?" I ask as I climb from the Skylark. *I wish I knew how to read lips.*

Jake pats Wes on the shoulder consolingly and leaves the two men arguing. As he walks toward us, Lana tucks the red kissy-lipped journal deep under the seat.

Climbing out of the car, she happily calls, "Hey!"

Jake stops short, and I realize Lana has just greeted Erik as he waves from his Audi. And it's *obvious* she likes him. Jake tilts his head at her and my heart drops.

I hiss at Lana, "Please do not ruin things with Jake while you're me."

"Oops, sorry." She turns toward Jake and mouths a seductive *hello* in his direction.

"What are you doing?" I say under my breath. "Stop it. We need a game plan."

Lana bats her eyelashes faster as Jake gets closer. "How about I help you *snag this cutie*."

"Stop!" I say so loudly that Jake freezes in his tracks. "Sorry, I don't mean you," I say. "I mean, hi, Jake, good to see you again. I'm Lana."

"I remember," he says. "Nice to see you two worked things out with the car."

"Yeah," I say. "Kind of."

I lean awkwardly on the Skylark's hood and Lana moves in beside me. Erik starts unloading camera equipment from the trunk of his Audi and the slick-looking guy gestures to him as he continues arguing with Wes.

Jake asks Lana, "I take it he's with you guys?"

"Yes, that's Erik," she says.

I call out enthusiastically, "He's with *me*." Just to make it clear he's Lana's crush, not mine.

"Oh, good," Jake says. "Wes thought he might be a buyer."

I jump up to face him, impressed by how tall he now seems. "What kind of buyer?" I ask, alarmed.

"Don't worry about it, Lana," Jake tells me and turns to my cousin. "Are you feeling better, Ricki?"

"Right," I say stiffly. "Ricki, remember how Jake witnessed your sudden-onset dementia from yesterday? You said you were really struggling to function."

"Actually, I *do* remember," Lana says. "It was almost like I started leaving my body."

She gives me a meaningful look and I realize she must've been experiencing the exact same thing. For a beat I feel grateful that I'm not completely alone in this.

I tell Jake, "Thank you for getting my cousin home safely last night."

But Jake's full focus is on Lana. "Listen, Ricki," he tells her. "We need to talk about what's going on with the drive-in."

My stomach dips with a sickening sense of doom. "Is everything okay? Who on earth is that guy arguing with Wes? Is it about the reopening tonight? Did Gwen and Brad ever even get the projector working? Ugh, that *Brad*—"

Lana cuts in, "My *cousin Lana* is pretty excited about our theater reboot." She widens her eyes at me and I bite down my words. Turning back, she tells Jake, "I'm sure everything is going to work out fine."

Jake shakes his head as if he doubts it, but a voice smoother than liquid butter floats in behind us. "Everything will be better than fine." Erik slides between Lana and me, takes her hand, and kisses the back of it. "Hi, Ricki, I'm Erik," he says. "Nice to meet you in person."

She grins at him. "Hi, Erik. I *love* your pranks!"

The chemistry between them is so obvious I'm afraid Jake is

going to think I like Erik now instead of him. He may even think that's the reason I wouldn't kiss him.

"Aren't you going to say hi to *me*, Erik?" I whine. "I mean, *I'm* the one who's your *girlfriend*, right?"

"Lana is kidding," Lana says. "Doing the needy girlfriend prank. I tried to talk her out of it." She turns to me and widens her eyes.

"Lana is a total kidder," Erik confirms, and embraces me a little too closely. "But right now, we're late to our livestream. Do you need to get ready?" he says to me.

I can feel the blank look on my face. I really just want to know what's happening with the Starlight, but I need Jake to see me connecting with Erik so he doesn't think "Ricki" is after her cousin's boyfriend. *This is already exhausting me.*

I turn to Erik. "Don't I look ready to livestream?"

"You look *great*," Erik says. "You know I *love* the freckles."

I smile and run a hand against my smooth skin. "We got wolf dog facials this afternoon," I say, and laugh too hard at the joke only Lana understands. I slap at her with the back of my hand. "You get it."

Lana says, "You better freshen up before going on camera, Lana."

"I'm thinking I'd like to maybe stay *off* camera today," I say.

"Good one, Lana," Erik says. "Everyone's streaming before Digi. I was thinking we should set up over by the entrance underneath the marquee."

"That'll be great exposure for the drive-in!" Jake tells Erik. "I'm Jake, by the way—Ricki's friend and coconspirator to get this place open and running again."

"Glad to help however I can," Erik says. "The Starlight has been an iconic attraction here in Fresno. Shame to hear it's been struggling to reopen since the flood."

"You don't know the half of it. In fact, Ricki?" Jake turns to Lana. "We *need* to talk."

"Cool—Lana and I have a million eager viewers standing by," Erik says to me. "I'll grab my gear and get set. Meet me in front." He blows me an air kiss and strides back toward the bags of equipment he's left beside his Audi.

Lana says, "Come on, Lana. I'll help you get ready."

Jake tells Lana, "I really need to discuss something with you, Ricki." He glances over to where the stranger is still talking to Wes.

Lana moves so she's eye-to-eye with Jake. "We'll sort everything out, I promise. I just need to help my cousin a minute." She pats his cheek. "Come on, Lana. Let's go wash up."

"*I'm* interested in hearing about what's going on." I point to the slick-looking guy. "Who even *is* that guy?"

But before Jake can answer me, Lana starts pulling me toward the concession shack. "First, the little girl's room." Under her breath she hisses, "Where is it?"

I'm furious that she's *once again* put herself first. Grabbing her elbow rougher than necessary, I pull her sharply to the right since the bathrooms are around the rear, behind the concession shack.

Looking back, I see Jake is tilting his head at us. He definitely caught my redirect, and there's no way the real Ricki would ever forget her way to the Starlight's bathrooms.

Great, I think. *Because Jake needed one more reason to* not *give me my magical first kiss under the stars tonight.*

chapter 13

When Lana and I are alone in the bathroom, I turn on her. "Why didn't you let me talk to Jake?" I snap. "I really have to find out what's happening with the Starlight."

"We need to figure out what you're going to livestream with Erik," she says flailing her hands in panic. "He wasn't kidding about over a *million* viewers waiting." She turns to wet a paper towel in the sink, squeezes it out, and hastily starts wiping her face with it. "Also, you are in *serious* need of an exfoliator, cuz."

"Dead skin cells are *not* my biggest problem right now," I snap.

"Of course not." Lana points to my face. "*That* skin is soft as a baby's backside."

"The boys are going to think we're nuts," I say. "Maybe we should at least *try* to explain our crazy body swap to them."

"Erik will definitely think it's a prank, and Jake will just assume you're trying to blow him off."

"Ugh, you're right," I say. "Everything is the *worst.*"

Lana grows more and more flustered as she struggles to turn the faucet off. "Is this faucet some sort of prank?"

"Here, let me get that." I show her the secret trick of turning the knob all the way on and then off to make the water stop. "I planned on printing the instructions on a little sign for tonight." I had *so many* plans for tonight.

We stand, facing each other a moment.

"What the heck do we do now?" I ask. "I can't go on camera with Erik and be you."

Lana takes a deep breath, pulls out her lipstick, and applies it without looking in the mirror. It goes on flawlessly. "I think our only choice is to do our best to help each other."

"Right," I say, pushing aside my anger at Lana's selfishness. "Helping each other is what Jamie Lee Curtis and Lindsay Lohan have to do in *Freaky Friday*. I never saw the older version with Jodi Foster and that other actress."

"Barbara Harris," she says. "And I'm surprised you know the movie at all. No blood, no monsters. Totally outside your wheelhouse."

"Ah, but it *does* star the ultimate scream queen." I smile.

"Perfect." She scoffs. "Actually, I do love Jamie Lee in the movie titled *Perfect*."

"Never heard of it," I say. "Sounds sci-fi maybe?"

"Nope. It was an aerobics movie she made with John Travolta back in the eighties," Lana says. "She's in *sick* shape and the movie is so bad, it's good."

"I *love* movies that are so bad they're good," I say. "There are a ton of B-horror ones, like, have you ever seen *The Return of the Living Dead*?"

"Okay, nope." Lana holds up a hand to stop me. "We're not going down the horror movie trivia trail. Erik will be ready for you soon."

"But those cult classics may be the key," I say. "I'll just make the livestream so bad it's good."

"Do *not* make it your goal to be bad," Lana says.

"Oh, I am *going* to be bad."

"All you need to do is pretend to be relaxed on camera with Erik," she says. "You're just talking up Digifest. A little flirty banter is all people want to see. You do know how to be flirty, right?"

At my blank look, Lana launches into a quickie tutorial on flirting that covers hair flips, pursed lips, and chin dips. Rolling her eyes at my attempts to copy her, she corrects my posture and forces my shoulders open, and finally says, "I guess that will have to do for now."

"Thanks?" I say.

"You're welcome," she says. "Now for the livestream . . ."

"Wait a minute," I say. "You need to help with my stuff too."

Lana crosses her arms and looks at me. Basically, the opposite of the open flirting stance she just taught me.

"This is important," I say. "I need you to try to help Wes and Jake with that jerk in the suit. He's obviously upsetting things for tonight. Also, try to keep Jake interested, because I really do like him."

Lana says. "Foil the jerk. Flirt with Jake. Got it."

"No, wait!" I say. "Don't flirt *too much* with Jake. I don't want our first kiss to be while you're me."

"Wait a minute, you two haven't kissed?" Lana raises one eyebrow. "I was catching some very strong vibes from him. I thought you two were a couple."

"It's . . . *well*, it's complicated," I say.

"No, *this* is complicated." Lana points back and forth between us. "You and Jake clearly like each other, so what's the problem?"

"Okay, fine," I say. "See, there's this legend about the drive-in . . ."

She nods for me to go on and so I explain about Jake's two near-kisses and me ducking awkwardly to avoid his lips—*twice*—just so I can get my Magical Starlight First Kiss Under the Stars™ tonight.

I sigh. "When I say it out loud I hear how nuts I sound."

"Let me get this straight." Lana steps in front of me and starts applying her lipstick to my lips. "You've worked for *months* to save the Starlight for the chance to kiss this boy. And when you got the chance to kiss the boy, you went all Keanu Reeves inside the Matrix to avoid his lips just to hold out for the *magic* kiss from this same boy?"

"Hey! I love the drive-in theater too . . ." I start to protest, but she holds my chin still, continuing to apply the lipstick to my mouth. I focus on the vintage pink bathroom tiles and try to breathe through my nose.

"I think it's great that you're a closet romantic," Lana says. "All these years you made fun of me for loving rom-coms and meanwhile, here you are, plotting out your first kiss for maximum enchantment."

She swipes her finger under my bottom lip, turns to the sink, and twists the knob. "Now the faucet won't go on?" she says. "If this isn't a prank sink, it should be."

"*That's* it!" I snap my manicured fingers. "I know how we can fix our million-viewer dilemma."

"Please stop thinking up ideas," she says.

"No, this one is good," I say. "We can *prank* Erik as our livestream."

Lana thinks a moment. "That could actually work," she says. "That way he won't notice you're acting all weird."

"Right!" I say. "And I will *definitely* be acting *all* weird." I rub my lips together, trying to get used to the tingly feel of them.

"But Erik is *really* tough to catch off guard," she says. "His friends are always trying to get even with him so he's constantly on high alert. He won't even eat snacks from unsealed bags since a buddy replaced his barbeque chips with nuclear-grade Takis once. He was practically crying!" Lana grins. "That video has almost four million views so far."

"How about if we just do something totally unexpected," I say. "Like tell him you're breaking up with him? That would explain me acting nervous."

"A breakup prank could *seriously* backfire." Lana cringes. "I have no idea how he'd react. Like, he could just laugh and shrug and that would be *mortifying*. Especially on the day of Digifest. Remember, this will be *live*. No do-overs."

"I thought you guys genuinely liked each other," I say. "At least, it feels real when he looks at me. I mean, when he looks at *me* and he *thinks* I'm you."

Lana blushes.

"You were actually right before," she says. "Back when you said our relationship was a publicity stunt. At least, that's how things started."

I realize my lips are getting more and more tingly. "Let me guess. Your momager at work?"

"Of course." Lana explains how her mom researched ways

of boosting subscribers and then interviewed several up-and-coming BubeTubers to play the role of Lana's boyfriend.

"Like a casting call?" I cover my mouth.

"Don't touch your lips." Lana yanks my hand down. "Erik and I hit it off right away, so at least my mom let me make the final decision."

"Gee," I say. "How progressive of her."

My lips are tingling so much I can't help but rub at them with my palm.

"Ricki, stop!" Lana points to my reflection in the warped mirror. "Please look at yourself."

My reflection now shows Lana's face with pink lipstick spread wide around my mouth.

"Why'd you give me clown lips?" I ask.

"I *didn't* give you clown lips," she growls. "I applied the lipstick perfectly, and you've completely smeared it."

"It was burning," I say. "Are you sure Erik didn't already beat you to a prank and put something peppery in your lipstick? A hot sauce packet, maybe?"

She laughs. "It's a *plumper*." At my confused look she adds, "It makes lips fuller. Look how nice it looks on me." She smiles and frames her mouth with her hands.

"It causes swelling?" I immediately wipe the lipstick off my mouth with the back of my hand. "This cannot possibly be good for you!" I lunge to swipe the lipstick off of her too, but she ducks.

"Quit that," she says. "It's also a lip stain, so thanks a bunch, it's going to be really hard to get off the rest of your face. And Erik is probably waiting by now."

I whine pitifully. "Why is it still burning?"

Lana gets to work washing the lipstick off my face while grumbling that I'm worse than a toddler. Finally, she dries my mouth with a paper towel and takes a step back.

"I've never seen anyone so scared of a basic beauty product," she says.

I smile at my fresh-scrubbed face reflected in the mirror. "Now *these* are the Lana lips I remember." I blow myself a quick kiss.

My cousin has been watching me in silence. "I think I have a prank idea I can do as Ricki so you won't even need to fool Erik."

"That would be *great*," I say. "That way I can help Jake deal with the jerk in the suit myself. What's your idea?"

"It's still coming together," she says as she moves toward the door, "but I'm afraid of what will happen if I pull it off."

"Don't you mean you're afraid of *not* pulling it off?" I say.

"No," she says seriously. "Because if this prank goes the way I think it might, it will change everything."

•   •   •

By the time I follow Lana out of the bathroom, Jake and Wes have shifted over to the playground, where they're talking intently in front of the big white movie screen. The slick-looking guy in the suit paces back and forth beside his black sedan while angrily shouting into his cellphone.

Meanwhile, Erik is about four hundred feet away, adjusting a camera on a tripod beside the entrance marquee. The giant Starlight sign has a white light-up box at its center that boasts the two new releases we're showing tonight as a double feature.

The movie titles are written in big block letters that Jake and I had to spell out last week using a super-long pole with a suction cup at one end. We tried to maneuver the pole together, but between all our dropping letters and laughing, it took us nearly two hours to spell out both titles.

I wished it had taken us longer.

"See if you can get Erik to frame our marquee in his shot," I tell Lana. "The theater can use all the promotion it can get."

"Got it. Wish me luck." Lana smiles, and I realize that a fitted dress paired with heels and a lip plumper is perhaps not the worst look on me.

I reach up to give her tall back a pat and she struts toward Erik in a way that makes me hiss after her, "Remember that's *not* your boyfriend." She turns to give me a thumbs-up, causing her to stumble a bit in the heels. She flounders awkwardly a second before reclaiming her confident stride.

Giving me a more realistic glimpse of what *I'd* look like in that outfit and those heels.

• • •

I make my way over to where the slick-looking guy is just rejoining Jake and Wes by the playground. The guy looks pissed.

"Look, Westley," he's saying. "I don't know what it is you have against money, but you could be living out the rest of your years as a very rich man. Do you really want to count on this drive-in taking care of you?"

Wes sits down hard on one of the swings and begins swinging, acting as if he isn't listening.

I whisper to Jake, "What's going on?"

He shakes his head and pulls me aside. "This guy is a real estate agent, and he listed the Starlight on MLA as being in pre-foreclosure without Wes's permission. It's a really underhanded way to make a commission," Jake says. "But apparently, it's not illegal."

"It sounds like it should be," I say. "Why doesn't Wes just tell him to leave?"

"He's been trying, but the guy is determined to make Wes change his mind," Jake says. "There's a ton of money to be made on the Starlight's land, and he already has an offer on the table from MegaMart."

My heart sinks. "How much are they offering?"

"They love the property's location and size." Jake runs a hand through his hair. "Lana, they're offering Wes three *million* dollars." He frowns. "And I'm pretty sure that's lowballing."

"Oh no," I say, and I feel tears spring into my eyes. "The drive-in would take decades to earn that much." I hug my small waist and feel so powerless. "What does Wes think?"

"It's a lot of cash, but the drive-in is special to Wes. It isn't just about money," Jake says, "it's about community, and he loves that Ricki and I have worked so hard to keep this screen from going dark for good. Where *is* Ricki anyway?"

"Oh, she's over by my boyfriend helping us out with something."

Jake gives a suspicious glance to where Lana is talking to Erik at the front entrance. Her hand is on his arm, and even from this distance it looks like the two of them have a close connection to each other.

I want to shout at her to *tone it down*, but instead I move so I'm blocking Jake's view of them.

"It's just a small prank for our live video to promote Digifest," I explain.

"And *that's* more important than focusing on the reopening tonight?" Jake says. "She was supposed to make signs and help me get concession set up."

"Ricki made me promise to pitch in with whatever grand reopening prep I can do in her place," I say. "What do you need?" It's so frustrating to not tell him it's me, but I know in my tiny bird bones this is too much to believe.

Jake cranes his neck in an attempt to see past me. His look is so intense my heart races with adrenaline. *He is so dang kissable.* Why did I have to go and "Ricki" things up between us?

When I follow his gaze, I'm relieved to see Lana and Erik are talking earnestly from a respectable distance apart. Lana puts a hand to her mouth in surprise and Erik swoops close and puts an arm around her.

"Hey," I say quickly to Jake, pushing his shoulder and pointing toward the playground to distract him. "Should we go rescue Wes?" The evil real estate guy is now sitting on the swing beside him, trying to talk to him each time Wes swings back and forth past him.

"I don't know. Wes is acting weird," Jake says.

"I refuse to believe he's considering selling," I say. "He's worked just as hard as . . . you and Ricki."

Jake says, "We can just hope that Wes has such a great time tonight he remembers why he loves the drive-in so much."

"And if this is the end, this night needs to be even *more* incredible," I say.

"You speak truth. Let's do this."

Jake grins at me and I can feel sparks shoot between us. He holds up a hand for me to high-five and I realize there's a chance he mistakenly thinks he's developing a crush on Lana.

I wrinkle my nose and give a repellant snort, breaking off our shared connection.

But Jake just lowers his un-high-fived hand and gives a small chuckle. He shakes his head in a way that says Lana's face looks adorable when it's snorting. *Figures.* And worse, he just might be open to giving up on me and falling for her.

I look over to see that Erik and Lana are still close-talking. I'm curious how the prank is going because their serious looks make me think she told him something important. Like maybe Lana cheated on him or something.

Which would be an especially mean trick to play seeing as everyone thinks I'm Lana now.

"I hope she's okay," I say.

"Who, Ricki?" Jake says.

"I'm not sure how much experience she has with playing pranks."

Jake laughs. "Trust me, Ricki can be quite the trickster."

I look at him, trying to decide if he's talking about our near-kiss. Or possibly our *other* near-kiss.

I say, "I know her really well and there are some things Ricki takes *very* seriously. Like, maybe almost too seriously." *Like first kisses.*

"It's odd." Jake tilts his head at me. "When I talk to you I'm reminded so much of Ricki."

"She and I are awfully close," I say.

"Yeah, well, I thought Ricki and I were close, and yet she barely mentioned you to me before."

This has completely backfired. All I've done is made it seem as if I haven't shared stuff with Jake.

"What I mean is, Ricki and I *used* to be close," I say. "But we're not anymore. I mean, not until today."

"Things did seem pretty brutal between you two yesterday."

"You don't even know the half of it." I laugh.

He grins at me and I feel that flicker of connection again. I realize it's just the same electricity he and I have always shared. Ever since I first helped him jump his battery. I put a hand on his arm and feel a spark so strong I'm worried for a moment that the two of us are now changing places. But apparently one body swap per massively important event-filled Friday is the limit.

He's still watching me. *I'm Ricki*, I think, but say, "Ricki made me promise to help you clean the fryer before she agreed to pull the prank for me. She loves . . . the Starlight."

Jake looks over to where Lana and Erik are still talking by the entrance and his lip twitches into a smile. It's obvious that whatever feelings he might have for me as Lana are nothing compared to the feelings he has for "Ricki-me" in any form.

He barely glances my way this time as he says, "Come on then, Lana. The Starlight's illustrious fryer awaits."

I resist the urge to give a flirty response about things heating up. Because flirting with my crush when he thinks I'm my cousin will not exactly simplify my life at this point.

chapter 14

Jake hands me a sponge and a bottle that says *de-greaser* in big blue letters. "Sorry, we're out of work gloves," he says.

"No problem."

Jake eyes my perfect pink manicure. "You sure? What about Digifest tonight?"

"Oh, right." I waggle my fingers in the air. "I'm supposed to care about these things."

"Maybe you can just use a rag to shine the counter tiles?" he suggests.

Jake hands me a rag, stops, and exchanges it for a cleaner rag. Then he turns to the true work of scrubbing the fry tub. I'm frustrated to feel so useless as I delicately shine the already glossy red counter tiles.

I'm not afraid of wrecking Lana's nails so much as making Jake think she's some sort of super-chick he could fall in love with. Better to just act like a high-maintenance burden right now.

As I pretend to uselessly shine the counter, I say to Jake, "I wish the Property Prince of Doom would just give up and go already." I gesture out the window to where he's *still* on the playground, trying to win Wes over. "Wes keeps walking away to make short phone calls, but the guy refuses to take a hint."

Jake puts down the fryer scrubber and moves over to the window for a better view. The two of us stand side by side, watching together as the men continue their playground game of chase. It's strange to be so much shorter than Jake, and I feel like everything is just so big and overwhelming and out of control right now. The heaviness in my chest gives a ping and I wince.

"You okay?" Jake asks.

"The timing just seems so unfair." *And not just with the real estate guy.* I rub at my chest and say, "That's a ridiculous amount of money to turn down, but Wes would hate to see this place turned into a MegaMart."

"Well, as the Property Prince of Doom kept saying, with three million dollars, Wes could move anyplace he wants and never have to see it change," Jake says.

We've come so far and now it feels like there's no way for us to win. I start to reach my fingers consolingly toward Jake's hand, but then remember and shift away. *Being with him when I can't be myself is agony.*

Jake and I continue watching as the greedy agent finally corners Wes and waves his business card in his face for the hundredth time. With slumped shoulders, Wes finally accepts the card.

"No!" I say out loud, and Jake puts his hand on mine.

Looking satisfied, the man strides back to his black sedan. Wes looks at the card and sits down hard on the swing again. I hold my breath.

"Rip it in half," Jake whispers beside me. "Just throw the card away."

But Wes continues staring at the card as the swing sways slowly forward and back, forward and back. Finally, he stands, slides the card into his front pocket, and starts walking toward the concession shack.

When he gets closer, Jake and I scurry behind the counter, acting nonchalant as he enters the wide front door. Jake actually starts whistling while wiping the tiled counter with the greasy scrubber he was just using on the fryer. Completely destroying my nice clean shine.

"How's it going?" Wes asks as he approaches the counter.

"We're looking good for tonight," I say with a bright smile. "Ricki is busy pushing social media out front and we're getting the feed station all geared up."

There's an awkward pause, and Jake and I look at each other. I want to ask Wes if he's thinking about selling the drive in, but realize I'm not ready to hear the answer to that question right now.

Wes turns to me and asks, "Have you spoken to your aunt May this morning, by any chance? I was trying to reach her but can't seem to get through."

"Oh, don't worry. She's not ignoring you," I say.

"I didn't think she was," Wes says. "That is, until just now when you said that. *Is* your aunt May ignoring me?"

Jake laughs too hard, and Wes and I both look at him. He gestures out toward the marquee where Lana and Erik are standing way too close, and says, "Girls, huh, Wes? They'll drive you nuts if you let them."

"Listen, Wes," I say. "May doesn't have Wi-Fi at home and she often turns off her little flip phone, but I think she's planning on coming tonight."

"Well, yeah, she *said* she was coming." Wes looks back and forth between us and I realize Jake and I are both interrogating Wes with our stares. "I'll be in the office," he finally says. "There's some paperwork I need to look at."

As soon as he leaves, Jake says, "Wes was furious about that guy this morning. And now he ends up taking his business card?"

"I can't believe the nerve of that guy, showing up and trying to force a sale today of all days," I say.

"Wes never even agreed to hear offers on the Starlight," Jake says. "That real estate crook had zero right to list this property."

"Well, we won't know anything until tonight either way," I say. "Because unless the crowds show up, none of it matters."

"I feel a little sick to my stomach thinking about it," Jake says.

"I'm still hoping for the best. Maybe Wes is planning to give my aunt May one of those magical Starlight kisses tonight."

"What are you talking about?" Jake looks skeptical, and I see an opening to fix all our kiss misses.

"Starlight kiss magic! Like the T-shirts say! A kiss under the stars guarantees a great romance. Ricki talks about magic Starlight kisses *all the time*."

"Lana, I don't think you know your cousin all that well," Jake says. "Ricki is *not* the romantic type. In fact, you could almost call her the aggressively *non*romantic type."

"I wouldn't go *that* far." And *wow*, have I ever been blowing it if my crush thinks I'm *aggressively* nonromantic.

He says matter-of-factly, "Her favorite romance is *The Bride of Frankenstein*."

I hide my smile at Jake knowing my favorite romance and

say, "Ricki is actually super romantic when it comes to the Starlight Drive-in and getting her first kiss here under the stars."

He squints at me as if he thinks I'm joking.

"It is *really* important to her," I say. His expression is so frustrating that if I was myself at this moment, I'd just go ahead and kiss him here and now, right over the greasy counter.

I'm imagining that kiss when I feel a hand on my shoulder and spin around to find Erik, burning holes into me with his blue eyes. His hand squeezes my shoulder and he asks me, "Lana, is it true?"

• • •

"Uh . . ." I have no idea what Erik just heard. His grip on my thin shoulder is urgent and I don't like how vulnerable my size makes me feel. "What did Ricki tell you?"

I look around for my cousin. I need to know if Erik's mad at me right now for some prank she's playing. *And if so, what that prank is.*

Just then Lana bursts through the door at full speed, reminding me just how tall and intimidating I look when I burst through doors at full speed. It's awesome.

Erik barely looks at her, but he's staring at me, and I wait for him to say this is just some prank he twisted back around on me. In fact, I realize he has a small camera palmed in his left hand, aimed directly at our faces as if to catch my reaction.

I turn to my cousin. "Ricki? What did you say to Erik?"

Erik runs two fingers gently down my cheek. "Is this why you're not wearing makeup?" he asks. "Not even lipstick?" He smiles genuinely. "Lana, you are so naturally beautiful, you stun me."

He moves closer as if he's about to kiss me, which would be wrong on every level. I mean, Jake is standing *right* there, and he has unsuccessfully tried to kiss me *twice* now. And I *want* to kiss Jake.

"*Ricki*??" I whine like I'm Lucille Ball.

Lana rushes between Erik and me. "It was supposed to be a prank," she says. "Sorry, Lana, I got carried away."

Erik looks disappointed a moment and allows his hand to drop from my cheek. With a deep breath, he looks back and forth between me and my cousin. His small, sad smile lands on me and he turns off the camera he's been palming, placing it on the snack counter.

"What about the things you've been telling me?" He leans closer and lowers his voice. "About the trolls getting to you?"

I think of the dark weight I've been wrestling all day and look at Lana, feeling as if a protective inner wolf dog is waking up inside me. I mouth the word *trolls* at her and she hugs herself, rubbing her arms.

A phone starts buzzing and my cousin glances at hers. Her brown eyes widen at the screen. "We need to fix this!" Her voice cracks. "It's my mom! She must've been watching the live feed."

Erik doesn't break eye contact with me. "Why would your cousin's mom freak out about you possibly quitting your show, Lana?" His laser focus on my face is making me start to sweat.

"Wouldn't that be her aunt?" Jake says, but everyone just ignores him.

"*Lana* is not quitting her show," Lana says. "We just needed something to film to generate some buzz before Digifest. I obviously suck at pranks."

Erik says, "Lana, you need to know that if you do decide to

ghost BubeTube, I'm all in." He laughs. "Or maybe that should be, I'm all *out*."

He dips down again as if to kiss me, and I turn my face so far to the side he kisses my earlobe. He pauses, brushes the blonde tendrils back from my ear, and whispers, "It's okay to walk away."

Lana holds up her phone with one hand and flails the other. "It went to voice mail. It went to voice mail. This is really bad, guys."

It seems like the bond between Lana and her mother has turned into a choking hazard and Lana's the one being choked.

I say, "All moms worry when they can't reach us, but she'll probably just text you . . ."

Lana looks at her phone and gives a high-pitched "*Eep.*" We all look at her. "She texted me."

"See," I say, "she's just . . ."

Lana holds up her phone. "It says, 'I saw the show,' with a nuclear explosion emoji."

My cousin and I lock eyes in fear. "She had to scroll for that emoji." Aunt April is not a fan of emojis and loathes my mother's effusive use of them.

Jake asks Lana, "What's going on, Ricki?"

I say, "Oh, her mom is just, um . . ."

My cousin interrupts me. "She's calling *again*." Lana holds up her phone. "No, worse! Now she's *FaceTiming*." She starts hyperventilating. "I have to answer."

I spring toward her but I'm too late. In a panic, she swipes to answer and winces at her phone.

Looking over her shoulder at the screen, I see a furious-looking Aunt April.

"Ricki, is that you?" Aunt April's voice streams from Lana's phone. "And Lana? I see you! Do not try to hide from me. What were you two thinking, pulling a stunt like that?"

"Hi, there, *you*," I say, taking the phone from Lana and holding it so the boys can't see the screen. "I guess you caught Ricki's adorable little prank."

Jake looks at Lana. "Ricki, why does your mom's voice sound off?"

She blinks and says, "Oh, she's practicing a new character for her improv troupe."

I grab my cousin's arm before she can tell any more unnecessary lies, and head outside. "Excuse us," I shout over my shoulder.

Except now Lana is moving like one of the living dead and I practically have to drag her through the glass doors that lead out the front of the concession stand.

It's as if the stress of all this has finally caught up to her and the idea of facing her mother—or in this case *FaceTiming* her mom by proxy—is weighing Lana down so much she can barely move.

● ● ●

"Lana!" Aunt April's voice explodes from the phone when we get outside.

I hold it up and give her an overly cheerful, "Hey, Mama!"

Lana cringes and shakes her head. "Just Mom."

"Heh," I say. "I mean hi, *Mom*. Just trying something new."

"Well, it would seem you've been trying out *lots* of new

things," Aunt April says. "What the heck was Ricki thinking? I warned you about trusting her too quick—"

Lana grabs the phone from my hand and says, "Hi, Aunt April! I'm right here."

"Hey, Ricki. Didn't see you there." My aunt April's voice goes at least four notes higher. Or maybe it's more like twenty notes—like I said, I'm naturally tone deaf. She says in her fake-sweet voice, "Could you put my daughter back on?"

Lana says, "I just wanted to explain to you what happened." She glances at me. "You see, *Lana* forgot she agreed to do a live show today with Erik, and so we were desperate for a fun idea."

"She *forgot*?" Aunt April's voice is shrill. "Erik's channel starts with a million livestream viewers and just goes up from there. The whole point of working together was so we could cross-post with him and gain followers!"

Lana's mom is clearly in her legendary "scorched earth mode." I'm just glad I'm not the one who needs to deal with her.

"Welp, I tried." Lana shrugs and hands me her phone.

Looking at the screen, I'm greeted by a furious-looking Aunt April. "Walk away, right now, Lana. Out of Ricki's earshot. Right. Now!"

Even over the phone, I'm afraid to disobey, so I stride across the drive-in lot, angling the screen so that Lana can follow me without her mom seeing her.

But Lana doesn't follow me. I wave for her to come along, but she just shakes her head and starts walking toward the play-ground in front. Before I can stop the impulse, I stick my tongue out at her. But then follow her.

Trailing behind Lana, I turn the phone back to my face and

say, "I'm sorry, Mom. Ricki just got a little carried away with a prank." I wish I had some idea what even happened on camera with Erik. "I'm sure she meant well."

"What is with you cozying up to Ricki?" she asks. "She ditched you a year ago. Now you're acting like you two are best buds."

"What are you talking about? *I'm* the one who ditched Ricki," I say. "Don't you remember?" Lana has reached the merry-go-round and runs her fingers along one of the metal rails.

"Did you get hit in the head, Lana? You kept asking Ricki to do fun things, like go to the mall or play mini golf, and she just said *no thanks* over and over."

"Mini golf?" I'm instantly furious. I *love* mini golf. "There was never a mini golf invitation. Not one."

I shoot a glare at Lana and angrily mouth, "*Mini golf?*" She shrugs, kicks off her high heels, and climbs onto the merry-go-round's platform. Pushing off with one bare foot, she moves to sit cross-legged in the center, closes her eyes, and slowly spins around.

Aunt April growls, "Lana, look at me!" I turn my attention back to the phone screen. "You need to explain what on earth possessed you to make a joke about skipping Digifest tonight."

So *that's* what Lana used as the prank. Telling Erik she's skipping the huge, important event that's supposedly about to change her life more than puberty did.

I put on a fake smile. "Come on, *Mom*. Nobody will believe I'm really skipping Digi. And everybody loves Erik's prank shows," I reassure her.

"Lana, you weren't even on camera!" Aunt April says. "Just a big blur of your face at the end, and you *aren't even wearing lipstick*! How are we supposed to score a Norealique sponsorship deal with your face looking like that?"

I bite both of my lips, and Aunt April bears her teeth onscreen.

"And what about Erik's reaction?" she goes on. "Did you have any idea he would say those things? This is a catastrophe!"

"I'm sure it's not a *catastrophe*." I sigh. "But I wasn't watching, so I have no idea what he said."

Wrong answer. Aunt April's eyes flash with so much anger I flinch away from the phone. "What was more important than monitoring the live feed?" she demands.

"I was being useful for once, helping around the drive-in," I say. "I'm sure the livestream turned out fine."

"Erik said he'd quit his show with you in support!" I can practically feel her anger vibrating through the phone.

"Oh, that's bad," I say. "All of his fans would hate me."

"He offered to delete his channel right then and there, and Ricki just stood there looking at him all moony-eyed. Why on earth did you send her on camera in your place?" Aunt April says. "Your cousin is not a front-of-camera person."

"Hey! That's not a nice thing to say."

"*You're* the one who's always saying it!"

I fling a look over to where Lana is still sitting with her eyes closed. The merry-go-round has slowed so much it's barely moving, and I can see her considerable chest rising and dropping as she takes deep, slow breaths. But the protective feeling I had earlier is gone.

"Listen, *Mom*," I say. "I need to go talk to Ricki."

"You need to ditch Ricki, delete that video, and post a new

one with Erik right now," Aunt April says. "And for goodness' sake, Lana, put on some lipstick."

"Fine," I say. "I'll go put on lipstick. Bye!"

"Wait!" Aunt April shouts. "You don't have anything with you! I'm looking at your travel makeup kit right here in your room."

"Ugh, I have a *lipstick* with me." I've moved over to the slow-moving merry-go-round and grab one of the rails, causing it to stop suddenly.

Lana's eyes fly open and I hold out the phone to her. "Hey, Ricki. Do you want to say goodbye to your *aunt*?" I ask loudly. "She's pretty pissed at both of us."

Lana calmly shakes her head *no*.

I clutch the metal rail and give it a shove, making the platform spin more and more quickly. When I look back at the phone, Aunt April's face is practically purple.

"Sorry," I say. "I thought *my cousin* could smooth things over. But I guess she's just being *selfish* as usual."

Lana drops the zen routine and yells, "*My* cousin is the one being selfish. She thinks *she's* the only one who gets hurt feelings."

I leap onto the merry-go-round's spinning platform. Stomping my way toward Lana in the center, I'm disappointed that my body is too light to have the full impact I intend.

"Girls! Girls!" Aunt April is raging through the phone. "You need to focus! Lana, you've already started losing followers after that stupid stunt. *Digifest is all that matters now.*"

I can't deal with my aunt, and since Lana isn't willing to step in, I get an idea. Making static noises in the back of my throat, I say, "Oh no. We're . . . *keeet* Mom! *keeet* We're losing you!"

"Lana, don't you dare—" I hang up.

"I can't *believe* you just hung up on my mom!" Lana leaps up and dives onto me, knocking the phone out of my hand and making me sit down hard on the merry-go-round.

"You weren't helping me, and she deserved it." I grab the backs of Lana's knees with both hands and yank so she falls down beside me. "And what is up with you saying I'm not camera worthy?"

"What are you talking about?" Lana reaches over and pulls a fistful of my blonde hair, forcing both of us to stand.

"Ouch!" I yell. "You told your mom I'm not *front-of-camera* material." I shove my cousin forward and pin her against one of the rails of the merry-go-round.

Lana kicks me with her bare foot, twists herself free, and leaps down from the ride. "Mom was always insisting I get some girl guests for the show so I could perform makeovers. Dramatic befores and afters always attract massive clicks." She grabs one of the rails and begins running in a circle, making the ride spin faster again.

"So that's why you used to hound me about doing a makeover?" I say. "So you could turn me into clickbait?"

"I don't exactly have a girlfriend stockpile, if you haven't noticed. Mom was always tormenting me to pester you." Lana runs faster, kicking up dust with her bare feet. "Finally, I just told her I'd filmed a segment with you, but it was unusable because you were a disaster on camera."

I try to stand up, but the centrifugal force makes me stagger across the metal platform. "What about mini golf?" I practically shout. "You *never* invited me to mini golf!"

Lana shouts, "Why on earth would *anybody* want to play mini golf?"

"You know that *I. Love. Mini golf!*" I take a running leap off the ride and tackle Lana to the dusty ground.

So much for our plan to help each other.

• • •

We're rolling back and forth in the dust when I feel myself being lifted by my shoulders. I rise up and away from Lana, easily removed from our spontaneous wrestling match as I bicycle my feet in the air.

Erik is holding me by my upper arms and places me neatly on the ground.

"What the heck is going on, girls?" Jake asks as he helps Lana up.

"Nice stage dive off the spinner, Lana," Erik says to me and then frowns at Lana. "Why did you attack her, Ricki?"

"What are you talking about?" Jake says. "Lana clearly initiated that attack."

"Jake's right," I say, wiping my hands on my rumpled romper. "I'm always acting terrible. My whole thing is that I'm the *worst.*"

"No." Lana brushes off her black fitted dress. "*I'm* the big bully who *always* acts so sensitive. I love making Lana feel guilty. *All the time.*"

"Oh, yeah?" I say, "Well, *I'm* the one who thinks it's okay to just cut loved ones out of my life for no reason."

Her voice rises even louder as she thumps her chest. "And I'm the one who never even asked you *why* you cut me out."

"Well, I never *gave* a reason," I say.

"That doesn't mean you didn't *have* one!" Lana's face

crumples and I realize she's actually trying not to cry right now. My anger settles.

I look at the boys who are watching us, speechless.

Erik sweeps his long blond bangs from his eyes and places one palm on the top of his head. "I want to be supportive," he says, "but I am *not* following this at all."

Jake says, "Is this some sort of *Strangers on a Train* situation?"

"What're you talking about?" Lana asks. "We're not strangers." Jake tilts his head at her.

"*Strangers on a Train*," I prod her. "That movie where two people commit each other's murders so they won't be suspects."

"Come on, Ricki. It's *Hitchcock*," Jake says. "I'm sure you know it."

Lana's eyes widen. "Oh, *those* strangers," she says. "The ones on that *train*."

I say, "You *love* the way that movie unfolds."

"And I'm a *huge* fan of Hitchcock," Lana says. "Because loving black-and-white films proves I'm all *deep and angsty*."

I resist sticking my tongue out at her again, but only because Jake is watching us.

Erik has been scrolling through his phone and he turns to me now. "I had to disable the comments on the video."

I give him a blank look and shake my head as if to ask, "So what?" But Lana springs to action, putting a hand on his arm.

"Let me see," she says.

"Ricki, I don't think you're prepared for this level of vitriol," he says. "Lana and I built up a thick skin before facing this much hate and it's still a *lot*."

"Trust me, I can handle it," she says.

She takes his phone and solemnly begins scrolling and reading. At one point, she puts a hand over her mouth and at another she actually lets out a gasp that sounds suspiciously similar to an involuntary sob.

Instinctively, I reach for the phone and pull it from her hands.

Instead of looking at it, I hand it back to Erik and envelop my cousin in a hug.

"Do you want me to take it down?" Erik asks, and I realize he's talking to me.

I draw back to look at Lana, but she shakes her head *No*. She whispers, "It will only make things worse."

"Just leave it," I say, rubbing my cousin's back and feeling that inner protective wolf again. It wants to chase away all the menacing birds that I can sense are pecking at her. I turn to the boys. "Can I have a minute alone with my cousin?"

They don't move, and Lana adds, "We're done wrestling, we promise."

Jake holds a hand to the side of his mouth and imitates an announcer's voice. "And now, live from the Starlight Drive-in in Fresno, California, we have the 'lovely ladies of wrestling,' Rick-ck-cki and Llllllaaaaana!"

Lana and I can't help but crack smiles.

Erik says, "Any more fighting between you two and I will turn this merry-go-round around. And around . . . and around."

He jumps up onto the spinner platform and gives a few pumps with his foot until he's rotating quickly. Holding on to the railing, he does an expert handstand and continues going around.

Lana grins as she watches him, and Jake leans in close to my ear. There's electricity in his breath as he tells me, "Please watch out for Ricki. I'm worried about her."

I turn to face him. The concern in his eyes makes my heart clench and I say, "She'll be okay, just please don't give up on her."

"She's been acting so odd," he says. "I mean, *Strangers on a Train*? How did she miss that reference?"

"Yeah," I laugh. "*Crisscross.* That was a good one."

He says, "Thanks," and the spark running between us is so strong I lean forward and upward slightly and . . . remember I'm Lana and need to break our connection *right now*.

"I mean, Hitchcock is *okay* and all," I say. "Like, I haven't seen *most* of his movies." Before Jake can take this as an invitation to binge-watch old thrillers together, I take a running start and leap onto the merry-go-round beside Erik.

I try to be graceful and land lightly, but of course I'm still Ricki on the inside and so I end up knocking into the rail Erik is holding. His legs swing so far, he starts kicking wildly for balance.

"*Oh-my-gosh.*" I lunge to catch him, but he does an agile backflip and dismounts the ride easily.

I'm left on the still-turning merry-go-round, staring at his daring feat with my mouth hanging open.

Lana giggles at my surprise. "He started out as a skateboarder," she says.

"Lana knows that." Erik looks back and forth between us.

Thinking fast I call out, "Ding! Come on, Ricki, it's time for round two!"

Lana joins right in. "And standing in this corner, weighing in at a gorgeous and solid . . ." She looks at me questioningly. "One forty—"

I shake my head and point my thumb up to say *higher*. She grabs her butt cheeks as if she's testing her own weight. She scrunches up one side of her face and sticks her tongue out. "Make that . . . one fifty—"

"One fifty-five!" I holler.

Jake laughs and starts walking toward the concession booth. "Do *not* make us come back here and separate you two."

Erik ventures inside my personal space as he moves past. Leaning in he whispers, "Let me know what you need, and remember, what you do tonight is completely your decision. Let it be all about you for once."

I look at Lana as she watches Erik walk away and realize her fake boyfriend has been doing more to try to help her with her struggles than I've done all year.

I still don't know why my cousin pushed me away in the first place, but for the first time, I see that maybe I'm a little bit at fault for our fallout too.

Because Lana may be wrong for rejecting me.

But I'm the one who let her.

chapter 15

'm curious what Erik and Jake are discussing so keenly as they walk away toward the concession shack together. Erik's hands move animatedly as he talks, and Jake is giving his full attention. I push my concern away and turn to Lana once the boys have disappeared inside the building.

She's sitting on the edge of the merry-go-round, gingerly brushing off her feet.

"So," I say, "what happened during that livestream to make everyone bug out?"

Lana puts her heels back on without answering.

"Come on," I say. "First your mom's reaction, and now the comments. I thought you were going to start crying just now as you were reading them. What was so horrible about the prank video you and Erik made?"

"It's easier to just show you." Lana picks up her phone from where it landed during our scuffle and scrolls through it a moment before handing it to me.

I hit *play* on the video that features a thumbnail close-up of Erik's surprised-looking face and the title *"Girlfriend Quitting! Prank or Not?"* Lana and I sit side by side on the kiddie ride. My feet dangle as Lana kicks the ground with the spike of her heel, making the merry-go-round turn gently.

Onscreen, I see Erik doing a series of stunt poses in front of the drive-in marquee. The Starlight sign is featured nicely with the showtime of 8:15 clearly displayed. I glance at the number of views at the bottom of the screen and gasp.

"It has over nine hundred thousand views already," I say. "And it went up less than an hour ago."

"This is just the beginning," Lana says. "If I don't get close to a million views after four days, my mom considers a post a dud. And Erik's channel does much better than mine."

As I watch the recorded feed, Lana walks into the frame in my body and tickles Erik from behind. He turns with a smile, obviously expecting to see Lana, and does a double take when he realizes it's her cousin Ricki acting all familiar and flirty with him.

"Oh, hi there. Um . . . where's Lana?"

I watch her bite down her smile and say, "Hi, Erik. I'm Lana's cousin Ricki." Obviously for the sake of the camera.

Erik's smile bounces back. "How's it going, Ricki? I suppose Lana's still doing her makeup?"

"Don't mock. Lana is a *beauty guru!*" She says the words like an advertisement, but playfully slaps him on the arm. "You know her look needs to be flawless."

"Oh yes, I know." He laughs. "I've spent about nine months of my life waiting while Lana gets her makeup perfect."

"Stop. You've only been dating *five* months." She dips her chin and looks up at him through the top of her head in the flirty way she coached me in the ladies' room.

"You look a little like her," Erik says, which is funny because that's not something anyone ever says about Lana and me.

"Thank you," she says onscreen. "That's *definitely* a compliment."

I laugh and tell her, "Wow, conceited?"

"I was just getting into my part." She points to the screen. "Now *shhsh*, and watch."

Erik leans down close. "Just between you and me . . ." He eyes the camera, making it clear he knows everyone watching can hear him. "I love the way Lana looks with no makeup on at all."

She wrinkles her nose, making it look like I find my cousin hideous without makeup.

Erik laughs. "Those freckles are to *die* for."

Lana says, "Come on, not even *lipstick*?"

Erik leans in closer. "Easier to get smoochy, if you know what I mean."

Lana elbows him and gives a flirty giggle.

"I really do like him," Lana says beside me. She kicks the ground harder so our spinning picks up speed. "And he has been wanting to get together for weeks. I just feel like once it's real, it's only a matter of time before it's over."

"Gee, Lana. You've given up on love already? When did you get so cynical?"

Lana shrugs while onscreen Erik tilts his head in confusion. Probably wondering why he's feeling a spark of attraction to his phony-and-maybe-future-girlfriend's cousin.

After more flirty banter, Lana seems to decide something. She says, "Erik, I came over here to tell you I'm worried about

Lana. She's talking about quitting her channel cold turkey. Maybe even tonight at Digi."

Erik lights up. "Really? That's awesome!"

Lana takes a step backward. "Erik! She's about to hit a million followers. Sponsors are lining up and her brand is about to explode. Quitting right now would be insane."

"Trust me, I'm up to my ears in sponsors," he says. "It just ropes you in harder. Outsiders trying to tell you what to do on your show. What time to post and which hashtags to use." He pauses, turns to camera, pulls out his sunglasses, and gives a big, cheesy smile. "Thankfully, I genuinely love these Oculies sunglasses."

Lana says, "But cosmetics sponsors make perfect sense for a show like Lana's."

Erik squints at her. "Wow, Ricki. I didn't realize you were all that involved in Lana's show."

Lana's surprise registers onscreen. "Oh, I mean . . . *I* think makeup is *disgusting*."

"Right," Erik says. "Nice lipstick, by the way."

Lana touches her lips with her fingertips both onscreen and beside me.

Erik says, "If Lana doesn't like one of her sponsor's products, she'll have to lie to her fans." He looks at the camera again. "Not that *I'd* ever do that!"

"She'll negotiate her contracts to allow for honest reviews," Lana says. "Even if they're negative."

He laughs. "That's not a thing."

"Lana is good at this," Lana says. "And hey"—she looks into the camera lens—"*someone* has to challenge *Her Highness* for top beauty guru position."

"I agree," Erik says, "but if Lana's thinking about walking away, I think she should! Her channel already consumes her, and things will only get worse. Did you know your cousin has a passion for underground comics? She is so much more interesting than being a *beauty guru* allows her to show."

Lana looks at the ground, and Erik puts a finger under her chin and forces her to look him in the eyes. With her wearing my heels, plus my body, she and Erik are the same height.

His voice is soft. "Can't you see that Lana has many other talents?"

Lana looks at him a moment before shaking her head and pushing his hand away. "She's singing at Digifest tonight," she says. "And she has a really pretty voice too. Usually."

"She doesn't want to be a singer," Erik says. "We've talked about the sacrifice and dedication it would take to pursue music and that's just not something she wants to fight for. She doesn't love it enough."

"Listen, Erik." Lana puts her hands on her hips. "I came over here so you can help me convince Lana *not* to quit her show. You're acting like she should just abandon her channel and her fans."

"I just think a break from all the online stress might be the perfect solution for what Lana's been going through," he says. "Her true *fans* will want her to take care of herself."

Onscreen, Lana holds her hand in front of the camera lens, but between her fingers we can see her step closer so she's in Erik's face. "Are you trying to ruin everything for . . . her?" she says under her breath. "Lana's doing just *fine*."

"She's not, Ricki. And getting in deeper will make the

pressure worse," Erik says in a low voice. "You shouldn't be worried about trying to *stop* Lana from quitting. You should be worried about *Lana* if she *doesn't* quit."

"So, it's fine for you go pimp out sunglasses and reap the rewards . . ."

Erik says, "To be honest, I'll walk away from all of this right now if it will help my girlfriend."

Through Lana's fingers still covering the lens I see her look of surprise. "You'd really do that?"

The two of them talk under their breath a few moments and then Lana's hand moves out of the way and she gives an over-the-top, fake laugh.

"Haaaa, good one, Erik!" she says. "You realized we were pranking you and so you pranked us right back! You'll never quit your show."

Erik looks at Lana. "Ricki, I swear I'm not pranking right now. For Lana, I will walk away. I won't even do Digifest tonight."

Lana just stares at him for a beat and then abruptly turns to the camera. "*Lookie Lana!* will be, heh, *most likely* appearing live tonight at nine o'clock on the main stage at Digifest!!"

Erik says, "I need to talk to her."

He walks toward the camera and pulls it off the tripod.

In the background, Lana calls out, "Make sure to like and subscribe to Lana's channel, and turn on your notifications!"

But the camera is moving quickly toward the snack stand, and the next thing I know, the scene of Erik confronting me as Lana is playing out from the camera's point of view.

Our onscreen exchange ends and the feed goes dark. I turn to my cousin. "What are you going through that I don't know about?" I rub at the pressure still resting in my chest. "Why is Erik so worried?"

"He's just being dramatic." But Lana pushes her words together when she adds, "I have a normal amount of anxiety for the star of a channel with nearly a million followers that happens to attract a steady stream of hateful anonymous remarks."

"I guess it's been a while since I looked at the comments section of one of your videos," I say. "Has it really gotten that bad?"

She scrolls on her phone a moment. Taking a deep breath, she holds it up to show me.

I'm shocked by the number of comments that have accumulated already. "These are all for the video that *just* posted?"

"There's a reason fans are referred to as 'rabid,'" Lana says.

"I think the term is *avid*," I say. "Avid fans."

"Keep reading," she says, pointing. "You'll see."

"Well, this one's pretty nice." I read aloud, "Lana, please take care of yourself. And whatever you do, don't take down your channel. I love your videos!!"

"Some people can be really sweet," she says. "But keep going."

I read on:

Oh gee, poor little Lana.
  I'm too beautiful and have a great boyfriend
  And am ALWAYS pouty.
  Please spare me.

"Okay, so maybe some are less sweet . . ." I say, and keep reading:

Dear Erik, Please dump that whiner, Lana,
and get with me.

Lana, you watching your cousin steal your man?
Careful or he'll realize you're a whore.

Ricki be fattie

Now ruining Erik's show too. #whyIhateLL

You are a dog wit no makeup to cover yur dog face.

And the simple:

Lookie Lana: Go kill yourself.

I close my eyes.

What is wrong with people? It's as if they don't even realize Lana is an actual person with real feelings.

"How do you stand it?" I say. "I barely started reading and I feel sick to my stomach."

Lana shrugs and gives the ground another kick with the spike of her heel, making the merry-go-round continue circling.

I lean closer to Lana so our arms are touching. "I get that not everyone is going to love your show, but it's not like there's a shortage of stuff on the internet. Just move on. Why would anyone spend so much energy spreading toxic bile?" I picture Jeff Goldblum puking up acid in *The Fly* and shudder.

"I've tried to develop an elephant's hide," Lana says. "But

that's really hard to do when your skin routine is so thorough." She shifts so she can lift my arm and runs her fingers along it. "Silky smooth," she says.

I don't laugh.

We both lie back with our legs dangling over the edge and look straight up as the merry-go-round gently turns. The sun's still high in the sky, but it must be after two o'clock by now.

"Look," Lana says. "Even my nice, supportive fans will turn on me if I don't make this right at Digifest tonight. Plus, my mom will never forgive me if I try to ditch." She raises her head. "Ugh. You hung up on my mom!"

"She told me to take the video down too," I say. "Which actually sounds like a good idea." I look at her phone. "How do you un-post something like this? Maybe switch it to private?"

"It's way too late," Lana says. "This is *big* drama. I'm sure someone has done a transcript and screenshots by now. Deleting the video will only get it more attention. I need to spin this."

"Or you could, I don't know, maybe just actually walk away from it all. It sounds like Erik genuinely supports you. You don't really think he was pranking you back, do you?"

"It doesn't matter either way," Lana says. "You have no idea how hard I've worked. Why would I quit when I'm this close to breaking through? I'm on track to be a top influencer by the time I'm twenty."

"Top influencer of what?" I say. "Which brand of glop people put on their faces? Who cares?"

"Hey! Maintaining skin's elasticity is serious business."

"You're seventeen!" I pull the skin of my temples back tight. "Your skin is *riddled* with elasticity."

"Speaking of which, we need to get out of this harsh sun." Lana stands up and starts walking unevenly toward the concession shack. "I think that buzz from the body switch is starting to wear off."

Lana hunches over her phone as she crosses the drive-in lot, now looking less graceful and confident in her high heels. I think about the physical manifestation of stress I woke up with this morning. The pressure in my chest.

And I wonder how long before all of that stress follows Lana, like a flock of squalling birds, migrating from this body into mine.

chapter 16

I chase after Lana as she continues scrolling on her phone while striding toward the snack bar. Despite her deflated posture, her ability to walk in heels without looking up from her screen is quite impressive.

All of a sudden, she stops.

She puts a hand to her chest and says, "Oh no."

After a moment, she doubles over, hugging herself, and I run to crouch at her side.

"What is it?" I put an arm around her. "I don't feel anything. Are we switching back?"

"Not switching," she says between gasps for air. "Just *awful*."

"We'll be okay, Lana," I say. "We talked about this, remember? The switch will probably only last for a day no matter what we do. A week at the most."

"No," Lana says, "this is a really, really bad one."

"What's happening?" I ask as I try to hold her tighter. "Do you need me to call your mom?"

"Unghhh," she cries. "My mom makes these things worse."

She groans and sinks out of my arms until she's all the

way down on the ground in a ball. I pull the heels off her feet, instinctively trying to channel Nurse Mom.

"I don't understand what's going on," I say. "Do you have pills you're supposed to take or something?" I can feel my own heartbeat thudding harder. I'm so afraid for her right now. I kneel down so we're facing each other.

Lana looks at me with tears forming in her eyes. "No big deal," she says. "Just having a little panic attack."

She looks so afraid and vulnerable I want to pick her up and carry her inside, but she's much larger than me now. I do my best to cradle her, trying to block everything out so she'll feel safe. She desperately begs the sky, "*Oh please, please, please!*" in a voice that's so childlike it makes my heart crack wide open.

I'm rocking her as firmly as I can, but she stays rigid. "*How do I help you, Lana?*" I whisper into her ear. "*Tell me what I should do.*"

"*I don't know. I don't know. I don't know,*" she repeats softly, shaking her head back and forth.

I'm frightened, but I know I need to stay calm. I need to be strong. "Okay, Lana? Look at me. Right now."

She closes her eyes and tears squeeze from the corners and run down her cheekbones.

"Opposite. Opposite. *Open* your eyes." I firmly take her by both shoulders. "Lana, I mean it. Look at me now."

When I finally coax her to open her eyes, they're my brown ones and they're filled with terror. I sense how scared Lana is and my heart feels like it's leaking with compassion. Her eyes search around, and I say, "*Right here, right here, right here*" until she focuses on my face.

"This hit me totally out of the blue," she whimpers. "I can't breathe."

"Keep looking at me," I say. "We are going to breathe together, okay?"

I draw a long breath in through my nose until my chest rises up, but Lana starts taking small, shallow breaths.

"No, not *panting*," I say. "We are *breathing*."

I draw in another deep breath and push out my cheeks filled with air. I hold it in and wave my hand, inviting Lana to join me.

She just shakes her head and continues panting.

Finally, I get a wave of lightheadedness and exhale. *This isn't working. Nothing is working.*

"Lana," I soothe. "Just listen to the calm and melodic sound of my voice."

She stops panting but continues breathing fast and shallow while looking at me. I feel like I'm on the right track. I just need to distract her.

"Hey, maybe we can try rubbing your ears," I say. "It always calms the wolf dogs." *It's worth a shot.*

I reach over to rub Lana's ear and she blocks my hand. "I'll rub my own ears." She starts massaging her lobes.

"Anything?" I ask.

Lana shrugs her shoulders and continues rubbing. "It feels soothing, but it's not really making the knot in my chest loosen." She gives another wince of pain.

"I had no idea you were getting hit with panic attacks like this," I say. "This is awful. Does my mom know?"

Lana continues panting, but stops rubbing her ears so she can hug her chest. "My mom doesn't even know how bad these

get," she says. "She thinks I just have regular, everyday anxious-
ness like she does."

"The women in our family are awesome and amazing, but
we do tend to be high-strung." I go back to trying to rock her.

"Not you," Lana says as she comically tucks into my small
chest. "You're never anxious or scared."

"Ha!" I exhale through my nose. "Lana, do you know why I
love horror movies so much?"

She looks at me. "Because you have a *sick and twisted* lust for
blood and gore?"

"Nice," I say. "But wrong. I watch them because they relax me."

"Like I said." Lana shakes her head. "Sick and twisted."

"Hear me out," I say. "I started watching horror movies
because they helped me escape all the big emotions I felt as I
got older. I hated feeling out of control, but I discovered horror
movies are like this practice exercise for stress."

Lana squints at me as her breathing grows more normal. *I
just need to keep distracting her.*

"Really, Lana, think about it," I say. "Take any classic horror
and picture the most intense part of the movie. Like, imagine
Michael Myers is just about to kill Jamie Lee Curtis in the final
scene of the original *Halloween*."

"Are you trying to make this *worse*?" Lana says.

"Stay with me here," I say. "Now picture him chasing her
through the big, creepy house and he has that big knife . . ."

"*Oh my god, Ricki*, please stop talking," Lana says.

I go on. "But just when things can't possibly get *any* worse
for poor, frightened Jamie Lee . . . *Bam!* Michael Myers gets shot
and falls off the balcony like a brick."

"Yeah, but he's still alive and just comes back to torture her again in all those sequels." Lana furrows her brow. "In fact, he's probably sitting around right now in his scuffed white face mask, drinking strawberry lemonade and just waiting . . ."

"That's the thing," I say. "None of it is real. It's all masks and special effects makeup and camera angles and sinister music. We know Jamie Lee Curtis is fine and we get to see her in all these other roles, like that aerobics instructor and the *Freaky Friday* mom. Not to mention children's book author and spokesperson for that yogurt that makes you poop. When you think about it, *Halloween* isn't actually all that stressful at all."

Lana takes a deep breath. "I never looked at horror that way," she says. "And here I always thought you just enjoyed being scared out of your mind."

"Oh, I do," I say. "But in a manageable way that makes me feel like I'm in control. Horror movies taught me that when I'm feeling tense and anxious, it's best to not freak out."

"Because the people who freak out in horror movies end up dead," Lana says.

"Well, let's just say they end up *not on camera* for the rest of the film," I say.

"Right." Lana gives me a small smile and shakes her head. "You have a weird way of dealing with stress."

"Look who's talking, cuz," I say, relieved to see her smile.

We sit together, not talking or phone scrolling—just sitting together—until Lana nods that she's ready to stand.

As I help her up I ask, "Why didn't you tell me about these attacks?"

She smooths back her dark hair with one hand and takes a

deep breath. "I thought I had things under control. This was a little setback, is all."

"A little setback?" I say. "You were just immobilized by stress. I'm pretty sure your body is trying to tell you to make some changes."

"Gee, what on earth could I *possibly* be stressed about?"

"This *has* been a pretty intense day," I say. "Maybe if we just relax and breathe, everything will go back on its own."

With that, the concession door swings open and Jake and Erik come running out at top speed.

Erik is screaming at such a high pitch it makes me laugh a second, until I see how terrified he actually looks.

"What's happening?" I call to Jake, and he shakes his head as if to clear it.

"Is everything okay?" Lana asks. "Erik, if this is one of your pranks, I'm honestly not in the mood."

"It's not a prank, Ricki," Jake says, breathing heavily. "But I do think it's some sort of sabotage."

Wes comes barreling out of the concession shack door yelling, "Aaaaaagh!!! Mice!! We have mice!!"

"Seriously?" Lana says. "This definitely sounds like a prank."

She walks over to the glass front door of the snack bar and flings it open. "Really, Erik, nobody has time for this sort of . . . Eeeeekkkkk!!" She slams the door shut and runs back over to me, pointing toward the concession shack. "Right on the counter. I could see it running along the edge."

I move to put a protective arm around her, but Lana does a "grossed-out heebie-jeebie" dance, shimmying as she gives a long, whiny, "*Yuuuuuck.*" Clearly her anxiety has been replaced by a basic run-of-the-mill, inspired-by-rodent feeling known as "the creeps."

I catch Jake smiling at her, because of course even her heebie-jeebie dance while looking like me is adorable.

"Why would we have mice inside?" I say. "There hasn't been food in there for months."

Wes says, "How did you know that?" He looks at me suspiciously and I give a mental face-palm over forgetting I'm Lana. *Again.*

Thankfully, Jake cuts in. "You're right, Lana. It doesn't make sense. This has to be sabotage. And without concessions, we're sunk tonight."

Wes says, "The bank won't give us funding if we can't prove our income, and we make *half* our money on snack sales."

"What are we going to do?" Lana wails dramatically. "My whole entire life is hinging on this drive-in's success. Without this, I'm just a hopeless loser."

"All right, Ricki, it's not all *that* bad," I say, motioning for her to take it down a notch as I head toward the concession shack door. "Let me take a look."

"I thought you were afraid of mice, Lana," Erik says.

I glance back at Lana over my shoulder and say, "Yeah, well, I'm feeling double courage today for some reason."

Opening the door to the concession shack, I see where the cleaning supplies sit on the countertop, abandoned by the boys when they made their hasty escape.

I call out, "Coast looks clear. I guess you guys scared the little fellow off."

"He didn't seem scared of us," Jake calls back. "At *all*."

Just then, a quick movement catches the corner of my eye. Sure enough, I see a small mouse shadow scurrying quickly across the counter. Before I can fully focus, it's disappeared underneath the popcorn maker. I calmly turn and walk back out.

"Yup, still there," I say. "We really need to do something."

Wes says, "Getting an exterminator to come on short notice will blow our profit margin."

"Worse than that," Jake says, "an exterminator truck pulling in will send a pretty shabby message to customers."

I picture the local exterminator's van with its telltale giant plastic rat on top and the back bumper sticker that says "Rat's All Folks."

"Yup," I say. "Just imagine a black van that says 'No More Mister Mice Guy' parked in front, right where I wanted to park the vintage pink convertible."

Lana says, "You mean where *I* wanted it parked."

We exchange glances.

"How do you get rid of mice without an exterminator?" Erik says. "Because I am *not* going back in there."

"Mousetraps, maybe?" Wes says.

"Those take too long," Erik says.

Jake gives a shiver. "I once had a mouse survive the trap and it was *horrible*."

"What did you do?" Lana asks.

"I opened the spring over the toilet as I flushed, and the little guy started swimming like mad." Jake looks down. "He went around, and around . . . I still feel awful."

I say, "He's probably fine and living in the Fresno sewer system now."

Jake laughs. "Better yet, he could be surviving on toxic waste."

"Mutating as we speak," I say.

Lana steps between us. "Okay, so mousetraps are out."

"Well then," Wes says, "anybody have a cat?"

"That's it." I turn to Lana. "Remember that house mouse Zelda killed a few summers ago?"

Lana laughs. "Yes, she was so proud of that thing we could barely get it away from her before she ate it." She looks around at the guys all watching us. "Zelda is a Chihuahua."

"She belongs to Ricki's mom," I say.

Wes shakes his head. "Chihuahuas aren't bred for hunting."

"Well *this* Chihuahua is half demon," I say. "Evil Z has the soul of a murderer."

"Lana and I can go pick her up," Lana says.

"We need to grab some special effects makeup from Ricki's house anyway," I say. "If we hurry, we can get back here and have Evil Z clear out all the mice well before any customers arrive."

Jake looks at his watch. "It's two thirty. I should probably go home and get changed now too. My costume's pretty elaborate, and we have a bunch of volunteers coming in early."

Wes says, "So, wait, you're telling me you all just saw a mouse and now everyone's leaving?"

Erik puts an arm around Wes's shoulder. "I'm here for you, big guy," he says. "I may not have a killer Chihuahua to help with your mouse problem, but I do have a few fresh ideas for tonight."

Lana smiles at Erik. "Nothing involving water balloons, shaving cream, or plastic wrap, please."

He looks back and forth between us and I say, "My cousin and I don't need any of your pranks today, just saying."

"Seriously," Lana says, "no acting as if our little livestream joke needs retribution. That barely qualified as a prank."

Erik holds up his hands, feigning innocence. "Hey, that 'little joke' was no joke! At least it convinced me to pull out of Digifest tonight. If you'll join me?"

He looks at me hopefully, and I look at Lana hopefully, but she shakes her head no. I sigh. "Still gotta Digi it up." I smile weakly. "But *first*, let's help these guys out with their grand reopening. We have plenty of time."

"That's fair," Lana says. "Lana and I will be back with the killer Chihuahua."

"*Killer Chihuahua.*" Jake laughs. "That sounds like a great B-horror movie."

As we head for the convertible parked near the theater entrance, Jake says goodbye to the others and starts walking toward his red Bronco.

"Please wave to Jake," I tell Lana. "Do you see why I like him?"

She gives him a slight wave and he lights up, waves back, and gives her a thumbs-up. She laughs. "All I can see is that he *really* likes you."

"He's excited for the reopening tonight." I pull out the pom-pom keys. "I just need to get back to being *me* before he decides I'm too problematic to bother with."

"Well, I can't *wait* to give you back your body," Lana says. "Just be warned, it's riddled with stress now."

"Gee, thanks," I say as we both climb into the pink convertible. "And with a wicked real estate villain apparently trying to sabotage the drive-in, I doubt things are about to get any less stressful."

"Unless." Lana looks at me nervously.

"What?" I ask as I start the engine.

"It's just that . . . maybe Wes is the one trying to sabotage the place so he can sell the drive-in without having to be the bad guy."

I cringe at the possibility. "I hadn't thought of that," I say. "I guess a failed reopening would make it easier to close down and cash out." I look over to where Wes is talking with Erik. *Wes practically is the Starlight.*

"I'm sorry I brought it up," Lana says. "I'm sure tonight is going to be awesome."

"Yes," I say. "The magic of the Starlight will pull through for us, I just know it will." *Because it has to.*

chapter 17

A s I steer the Skylark underneath the drive-in's marquee, Lana points up to the sign. "Actually, maybe that *magic of the Starlight* thing is the key to our switching back."

"Yes! Admit it, you'd love to skip Digifest and just come hang at the movies tonight," I say. "We'll dress all gory with my special effects kit. It'll be a blast."

"I won't need horror special effects if I skip out on Digi tonight," Lana says. "Because my mother will turn me into a corpse."

"Lana, you're not responsible for fulfilling your *mother's* dream of becoming famous."

She bites her lip and runs her fingers over the Skylark insignia on the glove box. Finally, Lana says, "Remember that amazing cross-country road trip to New York we all took together six years ago?"

"It was after Nona died," I say. "Our moms and Aunt May were all so close and acted so silly."

"I remember feeling like I was getting a peek at what my mom was like when she was younger," Lana says. "Like, before she became a mom."

"I thought the same thing," I say. "For the first time, I could picture what mine was like before she met my dad."

"We never told anyone, but my mom visited a talent agent while we were in New York City," Lana says. "She talked to me beforehand and we were prepared to move to the East Coast so she could pursue her theater dreams."

"Oh, wow. I'm sorry her audition didn't go well."

"That's the thing," Lana says. "Her audition went amazing and it was going to be my mom's big break. They *loved* her singing voice. But then the five of us had so much fun on that road trip that she decided she couldn't bear to be away from her sisters. So we stayed in Fresno, and she never said anything."

"Wow! I bet my mom and Aunt May would've convinced her to go," I say. "But I would've been devastated if you'd left then."

"I know," Lana says. "Me too. It cost my mom her dream though, so I owe her."

"You don't—"

Lana cuts me off. "You should see her, Ricki." She gives a wistful smile. "She gets so excited every time there's some good news about sponsor interest or a major feature I got. It's like it's happening to her and she *loves* it."

I point to Lana's chest. "But is the pressure of this public life something *you* love? Is the stress even worth it to you?"

Instead of answering, Lana reaches over and cranks up the tunes.

I turn the volume back down and grip the steering wheel. "Lana, you don't owe your life to your mom," I say. "You have a right to make your own decisions."

"That's easy for you to say. It's just the two of us, and this is the one thing that makes her happy." She frowns. "And now we're counting on my income to support us."

"Well then, what are we going to do to protect you?" Lana doesn't answer so I prod, "That panic attack you had back there? That was *really* scary. Do you understand how afraid I was for you?" I push down the emotion that's rising in my throat.

"That was not a big deal," she says. "Really, it was good that you were there—thanks. But my attacks have been worse."

"Not a big deal? And worse than not being able to breathe?" I say. "Your *Lookie Lana!* glamorous life is obviously too much for you to handle."

"Hey," she says. "I'm an inspiration to thousands." I picture her down on the ground at the drive-in, struggling to breathe.

"So, you're just going to ignore the panic attacks that are being triggered by stress?" I say. "Like you don't deserve to take care of yourself? Some *inspiration*."

"I don't need a lecture from you right now, Ricki." She slides off her heels and puts her bare feet up on the dashboard. "It's not as if you're even a part of my life anymore."

"Listen." I rub the still-tight space in my own chest. "I'm sorry. Instead of allowing my hurt feelings of rejection to get in the way, I should've dug in deeper and figured out what was really going on with you. I should've recognized how much you were struggling."

"Forget about it," Lana says. Her voice is casual, but a glance shows me she's squinting like she's trying to hold back tears.

"I *won't* forget about it," I say. "Because I *care* about you. I never should've let you push me away in the first place, and I'm really sorry I haven't been here for you. But I'm here now."

"Yeah, you just want your body back is all."

"That too."

We both give a small snicker. And this time when Lana turns the tunes back up I leave the volume alone.

• • •

When we get to my house, my mother greets us at the door.

"Hi, girls," she says, "I could hear the radio coming down the block. How's the car?"

"The car's *amazing*." Lana is so over-the-top fake-enthusiastic, my mother tilts her head at her. I don't usually smile with all my teeth showing.

"I've never seen Ricki this exuberant," I say. "All that fresh air must be really going to her *head*." I elbow Lana and she dials her phony grin down a notch.

Mom moves back to her comfy chair where Zelda is waiting, one delicate paw on the armrest. She sits, and Zelda immediately leaps onto her lap.

Mom says, "I know Nona's old convertible used to get everyone's blood pumping."

"Hey, Aunt June," I say, "remember that great road trip we all took to New York? Why didn't we ever go on another one?"

"You mean just get in the car and drive across the country?" Mom pets Zelda. "We're all busy. We have lives. It made more sense to sell the car and split the money."

I say, "But we had so much fun together."

"Sorry, Lana." Mom picks up her book from the end table and opens it. "Real life can't be all road trips and wild adventures."

"I guess," I say. "It's just that, that was a *really* great trip."

Mom doesn't look up from her book and I head for my bedroom, then move aside and allow Lana to lead the way.

Once there, I reach for the backpack I keep on the top shelf of my closet. And . . . realize I'm way too short to reach it. I climb onto the pile of laundry on the floor and stretch and grunt as I jump for the bag.

Lana sits on the bed watching me. I stop and turn. "Do you mind giving me a hand?" I put my hands on my hips.

"Why would you store something so high?" she teases as she saunters over to me.

"Very funny," I say. "How do you even function in the world being this short?"

"Why do you think I wear high heels all the time?" She easily reaches up and plucks the bag from the shelf. "Also, *my* closet has a little step stool."

"Good strategy," I say and start loading up the bag with horror special effects and supplies. "I'm not sure what I'm dressing up as tonight," I say. "But I guess it depends on which body I'm inhabiting."

Lana moves around the room, poking at masks. "Do you think our switch could have something to do with our moms and Aunt May growing apart too?" she asks. "I mean, your mom just acted like that road trip was a total waste of time."

"I don't know," I say as I leaf through a stack of assorted scars and gashes. "The three of them argue with each other, but I think they're still pretty close."

"Yeah." Lana picks up a Styrofoam head wearing a latex Frankenstein mask. "But they're not really *there* for each other now, are they?"

I think of Aunt April hiding the fact she got fired. "I guess you're right." I'm scooping bottles of fake blood into the front pocket of my backpack. "Grab a few wigs for me, would you?"

"I thought the theme is supposed to be dressing up like your favorite *movie* character," Lana says.

"Right. I just can't decide which *horror movie* character is my favorite," I say.

I turn toward her and startle at the unexpected sight of her wearing the Frankenstein mask.

I laugh and call out, "It's *ALIVE!*"

Lana stretches her arms straight ahead and takes a few stiff-kneed steps toward me. I fake a scream and pretend to be terrified.

The door swings open and surprises me so much I actually do scream. Which makes Lana start screaming inside the mask.

My mom stands at the doorway with a swath of pink material in her hand, looking back and forth between us. I help Lana pull the mask off her head and put an arm around her shoulder.

"Sorry, I didn't mean to startle you girls." Mom holds up a sundress that's the same cotton-candy pink as the Skylark. "I just remembered I got this cute dress for Lana a while ago and forgot it in the back of my closet."

"My *signature* color," Lana says with a happy squeal, which sounds like a joke since I wouldn't be caught dead wearing pink. Unless I was maybe dressing up to look like an undead baby doll or a zombie prom queen. So I guess, technically, I would *only* be caught dead wearing pink.

"Very funny, Ricki," I say. "That's *my* signature color."

"Try it on!" Lana is way too excited. "It'll be *perfect* for Digifest tonight."

"It's really going to *pop* on you, Lana," Mom says.

"Thanks, Aunt June," I say. "I can hardly wait to try it on. Oh, and do you mind if we borrow Zelda for a few hours?"

"Sure, Lana," Mom says. "My book group ladies certainly won't miss her. They *are not* fans." Zelda has bitten every member of Mom's book group. Mom asks, "Do you need her pink purse carrier?"

I raise my Lana voice, punch my wrists into the air, and say, "A pink purse carrier. *Yay.*"

Mom bends down to pick up the dog at her feet. Holding the Chihuahua close to her face, she asks her, "Zelda? Sweetums, want to go for a wittle *ride*?"

Zelda's tail wags violently, and she gives my mother's nose a lick.

"She's going to *love* the convertible," Mom says. "Where are you taking her?"

"Just to the drive-in to hunt for mice," Lana says.

I say, "We saw one inside the concession shack and need to clear the area fast before the reopening tonight."

"Wow." Mom laughs. "A car ride *and* rodent murder? Zelda will be in her *glory*. Let me go get her things."

With that, Mom hands the Chihuahua to me.

I'm startled into taking the dog and Zelda bares her tiny razor-sharp teeth at me. The deep growl that emits from the belly of the three-pound Chihuahua sounds like it could be coming from the Babadook.

I scream in terror and hot potato the little dog to Lana. Evil Z goes back to being calm as she starts licking Lana's face. Which is my face, of course.

"What is going on?" Mom says from the doorway. "Why is Zelda suddenly so in love with you, Ricki?"

I think fast. "I just lent Ricki some of my perfume," I say. "But let's get Z contained before she realizes Ricki isn't me."

Charging at Lana, I use the open backpack filled with horror supplies to scoop the Chihuahua from her arms and zipper it closed as the dog takes snarling snaps at my fingers.

"That's odd," Mom says. "Sweet little Z normally loves you, Lana."

"Sweet. Right. But see, *I'm* wearing *Ricki's* perfume too." I hold the growling bag at arm's length, away from my body.

Mom walks over and takes the bag. She unzips it without breaking eye contact with me and pulls out her Chihuahua. She gives Evil Z a quick nuzzle and glances at Lana. "I'm starting to think you two are up to funny business and I should maybe confiscate the Skylark . . ."

"Everything's good, Aunt June, we promise," I say. "And I'm sure Z Dawg will be fine once she's inside her little purse."

"It will even *match*," Lana says with enthusiasm as she takes the pink sundress and holds it up to my front.

Lana is brilliant because Mom is distracted by the cute pink dress and even whispers a mild, "Nice."

I give a huge, open-mouthed grin and pose with the dress while making jazz hands.

Mom sighs. "I'll bring Zelda with me to get her things." She walks away with the dog tucked under one arm.

As she moves down the hallway we can hear her high-pitched

voice talking to Zelda. "I don't know what's going on with them," she says sweetly. "But I guess it's nice they're getting awong."

Lana grins and holds out the pink dress. "This dress is so me," she says. "I can't wait to see it on."

"There is no way I'm wearing that dress," I say.

"But it's so perfect. And you need to stop walking around in the wrinkled romper we slept in." She gives me a Ricki Pout™, but I am unmoved.

"You may be the fashionista here, but it doesn't give you the right to dress both of us." I point to the semi-elegant dress she's still wearing. "You get to dress that body how you want, I'll dress this one the way I want."

"I'll change," she offers. "I'll put on jeans and a flannel or whatever you're about. That way you won't be stuck wearing this dress if and when we switch back."

She does make a point. I snatch the pink dress from her hands. "Fine, but you're wearing the softest, most comfortable pair of jeans I own."

Lana makes a face as if comfortable jeans are gross, but once we're both dressed she has to admit my soft jeans do feel great. Admiring them in the mirror she says, "These are actually kind of cute. But I'm pegging the cuffs and keeping the Prada heels *on*."

She combs out my hair, complaining about the knots from the convertible, and motions for me to spin around in the dress. I grudgingly do a turn, and Mom comes back just in time to join Lana in applauding my half-hearted modeling.

I curtsey sarcastically.

"It will be perfect for Digifest," Mom says.

"We really need to get going," I say to Lana. "We don't want that mouse problem to get any worse."

Mom hands the pink dog purse with Zelda inside to me and the Chihuahua immediately begins to snarl and bite at the mesh sides of the carrier. Clearly trying to break out so she can gnaw through my carotid artery.

"I really used a *lot* of Ricki's perfume," I explain as the carrier jerks so hard I nearly drop it. "Bye, Aunt June, wish us luck!"

Lana grabs the backpack filled with horror supplies and chases after me.

"Wait." Mom follows us. "Are you sure Zelda is going to be okay with you?" She addresses the carrier with a high-pitched, "She's my itty-bitty, precious girl."

With murder in her heart. "Don't worry," I say. "Zelda is going to have so much fun."

I'm already out on the porch when Lana turns back and says, "Bye, Mom. See you at the grand reopening tonight."

Mom says, "You know I have my book group tonight." She holds up the book she's only halfway through.

I say, "Well, if you don't finish the book in time, bring Uncle Eddie on a date to the Starlight." Running down the porch steps, I call back, "Movie magic starts at eight fifteen!"

"Bye, Mom," Lana blows her a kiss and follows me to the back end of the convertible. I open the trunk with the key and she neatly tosses my backpack inside.

Standing there holding the snarling purse, I debate for a moment as I look down into the open trunk—like I'm posing for a POV shot in a Quentin Tarantino movie.

Lana gasps. "You're not really thinking of making Zelda ride in the trunk."

She grabs the bag from me and the growling dog instantly goes silent. Lana nods her head toward the front door and I realize my mom is still watching us from the porch. *Whoops*. I wasn't *really* going to put Evil Z in the trunk, only picturing what that might feel like.

I give a big, phony smile and wave to my mom as I slam the trunk shut with just my backpack inside. Walking casually to the driver's side, I jump in and quickly start the Skylark's engine. Lana climbs into the passenger seat and unzips the bag enough so Zelda can pop her little apple Chihuahua head out.

Mom crosses her arms as I rev the engine and Evil Z surprises us all with a glad little yap.

"See," Lana calls out, "Zelda loves the Skylark too!"

Mom finally smiles, and as I pull away she even yells after us, "Enjoy the mouse massacre, sweetie."

I look at the Chihuahua, her face turned upward, ears flapping in the wind. She really can be sort of adorable. In a cutesy, high-pitched voice I say, "Who's weady to go on a wittle kwilling spree?"

Zelda raises half her lip to show me her fangs and gives me another deep Babadook growl.

I quickly break eye contact and step on the gas until the wind inside the car nearly blows Evil Z into the back seat.

Lana puts her arm around the pup to block the wind while consoling her.

"Be nice, Ricki," she says. "This little dog is about to save your drive-in's butt."

"*She's* the one growling at me," I insist. "I wish I knew why she hates me so much."

"It's your fear of rejection," Lana says matter-of-factly. "She can sense it and she finds it off-putting."

"You think my mom's Chihuahua is a *Mean Girl*?" I say. "I think you're giving her too much credit."

"I don't think you give yourself enough credit," Lana says. "Not everyone is going to appreciate you, Ricki. Get over it. Zelda will like you more when you stop worrying about her liking you."

"Fine," I say, "but you can't rule out the possibility that she's been privately plotting to terminate me to get my mom all to herself."

"Well, let's just hope she terminates that mouse in the concession shack when we get back," Lana says. "And any buddies he may have with him."

I laugh. "*The Attack of the Killer Chihuahua*." I raise my voice again and say, "Are you ready, wittle kwiller?"

This time Zelda just closes her eyes and lets her teensy tongue hang out as we speed down the highway toward the Starlight.

● ● ●

When we arrive at the drive-in, there's nobody in sight and Erik's vintage Audi is gone.

I neatly pull the pink Skylark beside Wes's Wrangler. "Wes must be inside."

"I wonder where Erik could've gone," Lana says as she

zippers the Chihuahua back inside her carrier and steps out of the car. "He was supposed to stay and help Wes get things together for tonight."

"Hopefully he's not planning some major prank," I say. "We were only gone a half hour."

"That's plenty of time to plan something," Lana says. "And by the way, that dress seriously does look spectacular on me."

"Um, thanks?" I lead the way to the back door of the concession shack, but when I reach for the handle to pull it open, Lana lunges forward to grab my hand.

"Watch out!" she says. "Every doorway could be booby-trapped."

"Great," I say. "Like things weren't already *stressful enough*."

Slowly, I wrap one arm around my head and reach out to pull the door open at arm's length.

Nothing happens.

With a sigh of relief, Lana and I move inside the concession area. I walk across the room to turn on the lights as she sets the pink dog carrier on the snack counter.

"Do you really think Erik could've been working on a prank this whole time?" I say. "Doesn't he have more important things to do? I mean, he's a famous BubeTuber."

"Yeah, he's famous for doing pranks," Lana says. "They're basically his *job*."

I reach for the zipper of the carrier and a low growl emits. Recoiling, I tell Lana, "You should open it."

She moves to the carrier and starts unzipping it. "You ready?" she asks Evil Z in a high pitch. Gingerly, she lifts the Chihuahua out of the pink purse carrier and places her on the red countertop.

Zelda immediately catches the scent of something and her little toenails *click, click, click* on the tiles as her tiny, long-legged body scampers along the edge.

Her run looks almost spiderlike.

"Thatta girl," I say as she darts into the corner behind the old-fashioned cash register.

We can only see Zelda's back end, her tail straight like a tuning rod, as she roots around in the dark crook near the back wall. The scratch of her nails digging at something gets more and more urgent until finally we hear one loud *squeak* and then silence. Her tail starts wagging happily.

She backs up and Lana closes her eyes as the Chihuahua comes out from behind the register with something gray and furry hanging from her mouth. I see a big red drip of blood and Z's whole body wriggles with joy.

I release the breath I'm holding, just as the furry creature in her mouth squeaks again.

"Aaahhh!" Lana screams and flails her arms. "Just kill it already!"

Instead, Zelda releases the bloody mouse and it runs across the countertop.

The next thing I know, there's a small gray creature hurtling over the edge of the counter and through the air toward us.

Lana and I instinctively run for the closest exit.

Which is the main entryway in front.

With a *bang* and a *flash* and a *whoosh*, we crash into the glass door together. And in one adrenaline-fueled shove, the door swings open and we grapple with one another, trying to escape out the opening at the same time.

There's a blaze of light as the two of us scramble through the doorway, climbing over each other to get away from the wild, bloody rodent that I swear just growled and flashed its teeth at us.

chapter 18

'm breathing heavy when I step outside, feeling silly for reacting so strongly to a little mouse. Then again, that seemed like
a *very aggressive* little mouse. And I definitely saw teeth.

"Was that some sort of immortal mouse?" I ask Lana. "I can't
believe Zelda let—" But then I'm distracted by a blinding glint of
light. I lift up my arm and sunlight reflects off of it, making me
squint. *My arm has turned solid silver.*

I look over at Lana and see she's completely silver too.

"Did we just switch back?" she asks as she holds up her
shimmering arms, twisting them back and forth in amazement.

"I'm pretty sure I'd feel taller if we did," I say. "Wait a—" I rub at
my wrist and tiny flakes of silver float into the air. "Arrrrgh!" I yell.

Together, Lana and I both wail, "*GLITTER!*"

So much glitter.

"The front door must've been rigged with a giant bin of it."
Lana scowls and calls out, "Nice one, Erik!"

I look around. "Is Erik even here?"

"He's not, but I'm sure one of his cameras is." She scans the
parking lot a moment and gestures to Wes's black Jeep and then
to a light post. "It could be anywhere."

"I don't see anything." I shake out my pink skirt, making it rain silver around my feet.

"That's the point. Trust me, it's there." Lana tries to wipe the glitter off her arms, but it doesn't budge. "This is awful. Glitter is *forever*!"

The door to the concession shack opens and Wes strides toward us with Zelda tucked under one arm. He's laughing so hard he can barely walk, and the Chihuahua has her head held high. She's gripping the mouse in her mouth by its tail.

Lana screams and points. "There's *blood* around that thing's mouth!"

Zelda looks even prouder.

Wes gives a fresh bout of laughter, then reaches down and takes ahold of the mouse, trying to wrestle it from the Chihuahua's grip.

"Don't *touch* it," I yell.

Zelda bares her teeth at Wes and hangs on to the tail, but he manages to lift the small, dead creature with two fingers. He aims it in our direction and Lana gives another scream.

"Wait, is that real?" I move in for a better look. The mouse has exposed fangs and blood drips from its mouth. Zelda growls as I get close but not before I'm able to see the mouse was never actually alive.

"It's a fake zombie rat!" Wes laughs.

"I saw it run across the snack counter," I say. "Is it motorized or something?"

"Remote control," he says proudly. "One of Erik's gadgets."

"I should've known," Lana says. "He once got his buddy with a ferret that scampered around like it was loose in his car."

"So then it *wasn't* the real estate guy sabotaging our snack sales for tonight?" I say.

Wes makes a face. "I'd never give that guy time alone in the snack bar, Lana. Although I wouldn't put it past him. He stands to gain a huge commission if he closes the sale on this place."

I burst out, "Are you considering selling?" and stop breathing as I wait for Wes's answer.

He absentmindedly pets the Chihuahua he's holding. Finally, I'm forced to exhale and take in a fresh breath to hang on to. Wes says, "This drive-in has been the one constant for most of my adult life. It's home. Always here no matter what each day deals me." He looks at me and then Lana. "To be honest, it feels like the Starlight and me are a part of each other."

"So, you're not selling then?" Lana shakes her head and glitter rains down on her shoulders.

"I'd hate to see it go," Wes says. "I've watched so many couples come here on their first dates and then continue coming, announcing to me they've gotten engaged and then married." Wes puts Zelda down on the ground and she begins contentedly chewing the bloody-looking mouse. "The next thing I know, here those sweethearts come, driving up to the ticket booth with car seats and little ones in PJs in the back. Bouncing around, excited to see a movie."

"I loved coming to the drive-in in my pajamas as a kid!" Lana says. I can still barely breathe, waiting for Wes to finish his story and give his final answer about the fate of the theater.

"I've had dates and even a few relationships over the years," Wes says, "but I never got to experience the true magic of the Starlight: sharing it with that special someone."

"Wow," I say. "I never thought about how lonely it must feel to watch all that love expanding in that way. Love *you* helped facilitate."

"But see, this drive-in *is* my one great love," Wes says. "It's probably why things never quite worked out with anyone else. Why I never started a family of my own. Open every night year-round is a huge commitment. Women always felt like they came second. But ever since the flood nearly took my love away, I've been thinking it may be time for me to risk a real relationship with someone special. Before it's too late."

I move to put an arm around him, and Zelda gives a warning growl at his feet. I don't back away.

"Wes, you truly are the *heart* of the Starlight," I say. "And I support whatever decision you make about this place."

"What was your name again? Lana?" he says. "You're kind of getting glitter all over me."

I laugh and drop my arm as he ineffectually tries to brush himself off.

"Glitter is *forever*," I say helpfully.

"Thanks," Wes says. "That's comforting."

An engine revs loudly and the three of us turn toward the sound coming from the Starlight's entrance.

Wes lights up and announces happily, "Why, look at that perfect timing," he says. "It's your aunt May."

Sure enough, the telltale bark of a wolf dog rings out across the drive-in's empty lot as Aunt May's pickup emerges from a low cloud of drive-in dust.

"*Finally*," we all say in harmony.

Wes runs a hand through his hair and straightens his Starlight T-shirt. He turns to Lana and breathes in her face.

"How's my breath?" he asks.

She coughs and waves her hand as she takes a step away from him. "We don't have that kind of relationship," she says.

Aunt May parks her truck and hops out quickly, her long, red hair swinging and her bracelets jingling. "*Oooh*," she says. "What's been going on here?"

Lana shakes her arms, creating puffs of sparkles. "There was this glitter incident—"

"Lovely." Aunt May waves her off as if us being coated in glitter needs no explanation. "But why did you three fill up my entire voice mail box?"

With a hand that displays a ring on each finger, she holds up her flip phone and a message I left on the way to her yurt this morning streams from the phone's ancient speaker. I sound more composed than I felt in the moment, only explaining that we were on our way to see her.

It's followed by a message from Lana. "Hi, Aunt May, I need you to call me right away please. Everything is great with the car, thanks again. It's just that, well, there's something kind of wrong with Ricki and me."

The next message begins with, "Hi, May. This is Wes and I'm just calling you to say, you know, *Hi*." There's an awkward pause and he adds, "I'm really looking forward to seeing you at the Starlight tonight."

Lana and I look over at him, and he gives the glitter at his feet a kick and smiles at Aunt May.

Hi, he mouths, and Aunt May says *Hi* back before playing the next message.

It's Lana again, and she sounds like she's barely controlling her voice. "Aunt May, we need to know if you can help us. Please call back. Please call back. Please call back."

"We get the point," I try to interrupt, but May holds up one finger and continues hitting play.

The messages cycle through various stages of grief and panic from Lana and me, while Wes calls with increasingly senseless explanations for why he keeps calling her.

Finally, Wes is stammering, ". . . not sure if I remembered to tell you in that last message that you can come early if you want. We could sure use your help around the theater if you don't mind or, actually, please don't feel *obligated* to help. You can just come and enjoy yourself or . . . don't come. But please come."

Lana reaches over and snaps Aunt May's phone shut. "Okay, so we get the idea. And you, Wes, have zero game, by the way."

I laugh. "I think it's sweet."

The look on Aunt May's face shows that she finds his awkwardness sweet too.

She says, "Well, I wasn't getting your calls because I was busy at my studio . . ." She pulls out a small brown box. "Making this." She hands it to Wes. "To wish you good luck for the reopening tonight."

Wes blushes as he takes the box and opens it. Inside is a thick blue stone, formed into a necklace with wrapped, antiqued copper wire. Wes smiles so big he looks like his face might burst.

"The stone is called an Elistial *Starlight* Sapphire Andara," Aunt May says, and Wes holds it up in the sunlight so we can all see the way the minerals inside light up like stars. It genuinely is amazing-looking.

He asks Aunt May to put it on for him and the two of them

share a touching moment that drags on as Lana and I wiggle with impatience. I feel like we're little kids helplessly wishing the grown-ups would *hurry* already.

"I'll never take it off," Wes says, smiling down at our aunt.

They embrace for too long, and finally I can't take it anymore and say, "Okay, so moving on . . ."

Lana says, "Aunt May? Can Lana and I speak with you? Privately?"

"Of course," she says. "Wes, would you be a dear and let the boys out of the truck? They're probably so thirsty. They barely drank their water this morning for some reason."

"Weird," Lana says as Wes quickly heads to the back of the pickup.

I catch my aunt checking him out for just a beat and see the slightest smile cross her face before he lets down the gate and the dogs knock him down flat.

I instinctively cover my head against the oncoming wolf dog stampede.

Instead of running for cover, or cowering in fear, Evil Z continues gnawing on her bloody-looking prize until one of the wolf dogs sniffs her so close he touches Z's nose. The Chihuahua immediately drops the mouse and plants her four spindly legs in a wide stance.

The wolf dogs startle and tumble into each other as they leap backward, away from the tiny creature.

Zelda growls one of her deep, terrifying growls and the biggest wolf dog tilts his giant head at her, as if trying to figure out if she's prey or if maybe he's the prey. The closest pup leans down to give a tentative sniff and Evil Z bares her teeth and lunges so quickly, the next thing we know all three wolf dogs are running away at full tilt while the miniature Chihuahua aggressively gives chase.

We stand in shocked silence as we watch Zelda pursue the pack of wolves to the faraway end of the drive-in lot. Finally, Wes and Aunt May unfreeze and give chase while Lana and I glance at each other before bursting into laughter at the comedic scene.

"I guess it's all about the attitude," I say, feeling a stir of admiration for the little Chihuahua, wicked as she may be.

The humans chase the canines around and around while Lana pulls out her phone to record the whole thing. When they reach one end of the drive-in, the pack changes direction and starts running the other way with Wes and Aunt May bringing up the rear. Lana is laughing so hard she can barely hold her phone straight.

We watch as Wes trips over a metal pole sticking out of the ground that many years ago would've had a small speaker on top for hanging on customers' car windows. Aunt May stops to help him up but instead he pulls her down beside him and the two of them start howling with laughter. They lean against each other and continue watching the galloping dogs.

"They both seem so happy," I say.

I look over at Lana, still covered in glitter with her phone held high, and she turns to look at me with a smile on her face. I feel a lifting in my chest that makes me wonder if we've successfully bonded enough to change back.

Lana says, "This is going to get over two million hits and bring fresh traffic to my channel."

And just like that, it's as if the whole world has invaded our little moment of delight.

My heart sinks. "Are you truly incapable of staying in reality?" I snap. "What's wrong with just being present? All you care about is trading experiences for clicks and likes and traffic."

"Come on, Ricki," Lana says. "This is viral *gold*." She gestures to the pack of large wolves being chased back across the lot by the tiny teacup Chihuahua. "They're acting like she's Freddy Krueger or something."

I have to admit it's hilarious. But I can tell when Lana's just trying to butter me up with horror movie references.

"Let Aunt May know I'm inside when she's ready to talk," I say. "There's an awful lot to get done before tonight."

I don't look back to see Lana's reaction as I stride away. It's like it's impossible for her to unplug and do what's best for herself. I open the glass door to the concession shack, and angrily step over the mound of glitter still scattered across the threshold.

chapter 19

I'm resanitizing the countertop when I hear the loud metallic scrape of a vehicle bottoming out on one of the pavement bumps as it drives across the drive-in lot. Looking out the window, I see Lana standing beside Wes and Aunt May as they all watch an oversized white van drive past them on its way toward the concession shack. It pulls up right outside, and Erik jumps from the driver's side.

He strides around to the back of the van and yanks open both doors. Hauling out a brightly colored mountain of thick canvas from the back, he drags it onto the ground.

He puts one foot on the waist-high mound and places his hands on his hips, posing as if he's just conquered the rainbow heap in battle.

I move toward the glass doors but stop when I see Lana has chased after the van and is striding up to confront him. He laughs at her sparkly condition and she flings both her hands at him in an attempt to hit him with glitter.

I head out to remind her to control the level of flirting with Erik and reach the two of them just as she's rubbing her glittery hair in Erik's face.

At least Jake isn't here to see this shimmering, flirty display.

"Hey, *Ricki*," I say. "I know you're excited to be tall enough to shake glitter on Erik and all, but don't you think you should maybe give my *boyfriend* a little space?"

"Hey there, doll." Erik grins from ear to ear when he sees me. "Cute dress. I watched the glitter drop in real time." He points to the low roof of the snack shed, where I see a small camera.

He takes two wide steps closer and wraps his arms around me. The next thing I know, he's spinning me around, making glitter sprinkle off of me and into the air around us.

I will never get used to being this light and portable. I thought petite girls were lucky, getting to be smaller than all the guys they like, but I hate being lifted so easily and now wonder how small humans deal with feeling physically powerless. I reach forward and punch Erik's shoulders. "Maybe *ask* a girl before picking her up?"

He immediately places me back on my feet. "I'm sorry, Lana, truly. You've never minded before."

He seems rattled by the fact he's upset me, and I realize he and Lana have built their way up to this level of closeness. It feels intrusive to me because I barely know him. But still, "I don't enjoy feeling controlled like that," I say.

"Perfectly valid. I'm just excited to show you." He runs over to the massive wad of colorful canvas.

"Let me guess," I say. "A giant clown chewed up a life-sized rainbow and spit it out."

"It's a surprise!" Erik says. "To make up for the glitter shower. Which went so *amazing*, by the way. I'd figured just one of you would get hit on your way inside, but then I couldn't *believe* it when you entered through the back door, and *both* came *flying* through the front! It was better than . . ."

He looks back and forth at Lana and me, covered in glitter and staring him down.

I say dully, "Why don't you just show us what you brought."

"Righto." He holds both arms out to the rainbow wad. "It's a ginormous bouncy castle to help with the drive-in's opening night."

Lana unfurls her arms and starts bouncing on her toes. She's always had a special love for bounce houses.

"That's actually . . . a really great idea," I say.

"Yeah it is!" Lana says with grin. "Come on, let's get this thing blown up so we can make a fun gif and promote the heck out of it online!"

I picture the kids in PJs having so much fun jumping around tonight, and my chest tightens at the thought of me missing it all as I'm shoved onto some stage in LA as Lana. We're running out of time to switch back.

"Wait, Ricki," I say. "Did you try talking to Aunt May?"

"Briefly." Lana shakes her head. "I don't think she knows anything."

"What do you mean she doesn't know anything?" I say. "Did you ask her?"

Lana and Erik are working together, carrying the deflated bouncy castle away from the van.

"I hinted," Lana says with a grunt. "But I can tell she's as clueless as we are. Give us a hand, would you?"

I move over to help them get the giant rainbow wad up in the air and the three of us shuffle back and forth, dragging what we can't lift.

"We don't want to obstruct the view of the screen from the picnic tables," Erik says in a strained voice, "but we need to be close enough to the electrical outlets to plug in the blower."

As the two of them discuss optimum bouncy castle placement, I look over to see Aunt May and Wes still talking while all the dogs run in wild circles nearby.

It seems the Chihuahua has effectively established her dominance and is now leading the pack of wolves. She guides them in our direction, where they all run a loop around us before stopping to commence sniffing every inch of the canvas mountain we're again dragging back and forth.

Lana drops her end and says, "This looks like a good spot for it."

"Let's *inflate* this thing!" Erik heads back to the van, pulls out a giant and *very heavy-looking* blower, and sets about getting it plugged in and attached to the bouncy castle's base.

While he's distracted, I pull Lana closer to the concession shack. "What exactly did you ask Aunt May?"

"I asked her if the Skylark got a magical upgrade," she says.

"What?" I say. "You asked her outright if our body switch was some sort of add-on feature that came with the car? That's just silly. What'd she say?"

"Heh, yeah. She stared at me like I was nuts and went back to flirting with Wes."

We both look over to where the two of them are deep in conversation. "So that was it?" I say. "You just gave up?"

"Well, then I saw Erik pull in . . ." I groan, and she adds, "But I did ask Wes if the drive-in was built on an ancient graveyard or something," she says.

"Okay, long shot," I say. "What was his answer?"

"He just looked at me like he thinks I'm nuts too." She pauses a moment. "Well, I guess technically they both think *you're* nuts."

"Thanks." I sigh. "But Aunt May must know *something*. At least about the car. I'm going to give it a shot."

"Fine," Lana says, "let them think we're both nuts."

"Hey, you two nuts, a little help over here?" Erik has somehow managed to get one of his arms pinned underneath the still-deflated bouncy castle.

We take our time walking over and stare him down with our hands on our hips.

Lana says, "We should leave you trapped here after that prank you pulled."

"I'm going to be finding glitter in crevices for months," I tell him.

"Hey, don't blame me." Erik looks up at Lana. "It was all Jake's idea. I mean, I came up with the details, of course, but Jake's the one who said we should prank you two."

"Why would he want to do that?" I ask as I lift one end of the thick canvas.

"He thought it might help you two connect," Erik says while Lana helps pull him out. "Like some sort of team-bonding exercise."

Lana and I look at each other. After a beat, we both burst out laughing.

"What's so funny?" Erik asks, starting to laugh along with us.

"Oh, nothing," I say.

Lana adds, "Just that at this moment, the bond between us is fairly solid."

"Yup," I say. "You could almost call it *unbreakable*."

"So, Jake was right." Erik smiles. "He thought a silly prank was exactly what you needed to start getting along." He flips the switch and the air blower roars to life.

The whirring motor is deafening and the wolf dogs all scatter in fear. Only Zelda walks toward the roaring machine, sniffs it, and immediately lifts both back legs in an attempt to pee on it.

I've seen her "handstand pee of defiance" plenty of times, but Erik starts laughing and pulls out his phone to take a photo. "Is she a circus dog?" he asks.

Evil Z doesn't manage to get pee on the actual blower, but when she finishes, she turns and boldly kicks her tiny hind feet, flinging gravel on the mechanical beast.

Taking the Chihuahua's cue of owning the moment, I mime to Lana that I'm heading over to talk to our aunt. She answers with a thumbs-up, but raises one eyebrow to show she isn't very hopeful.

• • •

When I get close to where Aunt May and Wes are talking, I pause a moment. It feels like I'm intruding on a serious discussion. If I wasn't desperate to learn whatever I can about the car and our switch, I'd slowly back away instead of interfering right now. Because it's obvious they're into each other and, honestly, it's pretty adorable.

Wes leans close. "Hands down, the *best*," he says, and Aunt May laughs.

"Really? You don't strike me as a Pixar guy," she says.

"I wouldn't necessarily call myself a Pixar *guy*. All I know is that *Inside Out* is a beautifully layered exploration of the complicated role emotions play in mental health."

I clear my throat, and the two of them startle and turn to me. "Hi, Lana, what's up?" Aunt May asks, her eyes shining.

"Hi, guys," I say. "Hey, Aunt May, can I ask you something really quick?"

Aunt May glances at Wes. She's clearly not ready to abandon their Pixar debate, but says, "Sure, Lana, what can I do for you?"

I put an arm around her and guide her out of Wes's earshot. "Ricki and I have had an interesting twenty-four hours since we got the car."

"I'm so glad you both love it!" she says. "Ricki told me it's really brought the two of you closer together."

"That's one way of putting it," I say. "Another way would be to say we're kind of . . . inside each other's heads?" I look at her meaningfully.

She glances back at Wes, who gives her a wink before bending to pull some ambitious weeds growing through a small fissure in the pavement.

Aunt May blushes and shakes her head as if she's just remembered she's supposed to be having a conversation with me.

"Your mom and Aunt June and I were like that when we were around your age," she tells me. "We called it our ESP for *extra-sisterly perception*. Like we could read each other's minds."

Her eyes swing back to Wes again as if acting on their own.

Taking my aunt's face in my hands, I force her to look me in the eyes. She registers surprise then reaches up, clutches my hands, and nods. "Sorry, Lana. I'm listening. What's going on between you and Ricki?"

"After you left yesterday, the two of us were arguing over who should get the Skylark for tonight," I say. "We both have big events and both *really* want to use it."

"I totally understand," she says. "Ricki told me all about your Digi performance in LA, but now talking to Wes, I can see that this is a big night for the drive-in too."

"Tonight will determine whether or not the Starlight has a future, but that's not—"

"I'm sorry," Aunt May interrupts, "but like I told Ricki, I can't make this decision for you girls. I gave you the convertible to help with your relationship. It's up to you two to work out the details, even if it gets messy."

Just then, the pack of dogs runs past and loops around us. Aunt May laughs and instinctively looks over at Wes. They share a spark that spans the space between the two of them and I grunt in frustration.

"Aunt May!" I say sharply. "I'm not asking you to decide who should have the car. I'm trying to explain to you that while we were arguing over it, there was a flash of electricity and everything switched when we woke up this morning."

She widens her eyes. "Wait a second . . ."

She looks me up and down as if it's just dawned on her what's really happening. I nod at her and gesture for her to tell me what she knows.

"Ricki was acting strange too," Aunt May says. "Are you girls trying to *warn* me that Wes isn't as amazing as he seems? Is this your way of telling me to not date him?"

She looks over at Wes. He's now petting two of her wolf dogs as they try to simultaneously lick him in the face. The other wolf is lying on his back, kicking his feet in the air as Zelda aggressively bites at the thick fur on his throat.

Lana was right. Aunt May has no idea about our switch.

"No, that's not it at all," I say. "Wes is terrific."

The grin that breaks out on Aunt May's face at this news is so bright I can't help but give her a weary smile. Despite my dread over her *not* having the answer to swapping us back, I'm happy for her.

"Ricki and I were just messing around," I say. "But we want you to know how much we truly appreciate the convertible."

"I'm just glad it drew the two of you together," she says. "That was my only wish."

"So, you *did* make a wish on the car then?" I say accusingly.

She nods and smooths a hand down her long hair, allowing her eyes to slide back to Wes. "And it worked," she says softly.

I give her a tight smile, turn on my heel, and head toward the concession shack. "You have no idea, Aunt May. You have no idea."

• • •

"Well, that was a dead end," I say to Lana when I get back to her and Erik.

Unlike my hope, the bouncy castle is fully inflated.

"Told you Aunt May didn't know anything." Lana gives me a smirk as if this news isn't terrible. Kicking off her heels, she dives headfirst into the bouncy castle and starts jumping around like she's five.

"Come on, girlfriend," Erik says to me, "let's give this house a bounce!"

He grabs both my hands and leads me through the door flap and into the giant air castle. Lana is laughing as she executes a series of bumbling forward and backward flips, and it isn't long before the glitter we're both wearing is everywhere.

Lana pulls out her phone and starts recording me and Erik. He's still holding my one hand as we jump up and down. It's sweet, but since he's not Jake, it's kind of annoying.

"You two would be so cute doing a channel together," Lana says.

Erik stops bouncing. "I'd love to start spending more time with you, Lana . . ."

"That would be *epic*!" Lana cuts in.

"Plus, of course, we would *crush* it," Erik says to me. "But at what cost? It would put so much pressure on our relationship. And you think the stress of building a following is bad? That's nothing compared to the stress of *keeping* a following. Just, *no thank you*."

"What about you?" Lana says. "Your channel does great and you don't seem stressed about it."

"That's because I think of my whole *channel* as one giant prank I'm playing." He does a spin jump and gestures to the mesh castle walls. "It can't be taken seriously. None of this is real."

"None of it?" Lana asks.

He stops bouncing, turns to me, and takes both of my hands.

"Listen, Ricki," he says over his shoulder to Lana. "Do you mind if Lana and I grab a minute alone?"

"I'm not listening," she says. "Or filming." She puts her phone in her jeans pocket and continues bouncing. "Really. Forget I'm even here."

Erik looks back and forth between us, and her bounces gradually slow and then stop. She stands, watching us, and the silent, awkward pause grows until finally Lana says, "Fine. Castle's all yours. I wanted to upload the little dog chasing the big dogs anyway."

She gives me a small shrug before exiting ungracefully through the Velcro doorway. Her nose is aimed at her phone as she puts her heels back on and strides away.

When I turn back to Erik he's looking at me in a way that makes me hyperaware of three things. One, he thinks the two of us are semi-dating. Two, we're alone here inside the bouncy castle. And three, for a place with no roof that's filled up with air, this bouncy castle is *extremely* stifling.

"Is it hot in here?" I ask.

Erik laughs and takes a big jump, making me echo bounce. "You're the one who's heating things up, Lana."

In response, I give a big-toothed donkey *hee haw*, completely shutting down the sultriness of his remark.

Unphased, Erik bounces closer and I bounce away. Finally, my expertise at avoiding kissing is coming in handy. I hold my arms in front of me, bunny-style, and *bounce, bounce, bounce,* until Erik gives up and stops chasing me.

"Lana, hold up," he says. "Can we just talk for a second, please?"

"Fine." I cross my hands over my chest and fall over backward like a corpse. Erik laughs and drops down beside me, and

I shift so he's just outside of my personal space. We stay lying on our backs, looking up to the clear, open sky.

Erik says, "I know you've been struggling, Lana. And I just want you to know that I'm here for you. Whatever you need."

I sit up and look at him. The concern displayed on his face makes it obvious he's been truly worried about Lana. And he's invested in helping her. Meanwhile I've been too busy with my own hurt feelings of rejection to even see how much she was struggling. *But I'm determined to help her now.*

"What do you think I should be doing to help myself?" I ask Erik, since he seems to know Lana best these days.

"You actually seem to be doing a little better today with Ricki around," he says. "So that's good."

"Yeah, we're . . . er, working some stuff out between us," I say. "What else do you think might help?"

"Well, you *know* what I think you should do," he says. "Question is . . . do you have the guts to go for it?"

"The guts to . . . ?" I say, leadingly, but before Erik can finish my sentence and tell me what could really help Lana, her head bursts through the opening of the tent.

"Guys!" she hisses loudly. "Come out quick. Your mom is here."

"My birth mom?" Erik says. "How does she know where I am?"

"Not *your* mom, Erik," Lana says. "And you're not adopted, so stop calling her your birth mom. You know she hates that."

"Well, she did give birth to me." He grins.

Lana rolls her eyes. "I'm talking about *Lana's* mom."

I sit up and cross my arms. "No *way* am I dealing with her," I say. "She must be *furious* with me for hanging up."

"You *have* to deal with her," Lana says.

"Not if I just keep bouncing." I stand and start jumping, but Erik reaches and puts a hand on my foot.

Looking up at me, he says, "This is your chance, Lana. Go talk to your mom."

"Nope." I lightly kick him away and take bouncy steps around the perimeter. When I reach the doorway, Lana has climbed in and is standing directly in my path.

I give a firm bounce that barely jostles her. *Stupid light and tiny body.*

"What does Erik think you need to talk to your mom about?" I ask in a low voice.

"*Ugh.* He has no idea what my mom is like. Can we please discuss this later?" she says. "You need to go out there."

I bounce back over beside Erik and tell Lana, "Make me."

"Seriously, Lana," she says. "Get out there before she . . . Oh god, *she's here.*"

And with that Lana is yanked backward out the canvas doorway as if being dragged under water by a great white shark.

Her look of shock is so funny, I cover my mouth to hold in a laugh.

Aunt April pokes her head into the bouncy castle and points at me accusingly. My hand and smile both drop.

"There you are! How *dare* you do a fake disconnect on me. I *invented* that move." Aunt April's eyes shift to Erik. "And you!" She shakes a finger at him and he moves to hide behind me.

"So much for having my back," I tell him.

He smooths his hands across it. "I have it. Just from right here behind you."

I turn around so I can raise an accusing eyebrow at him.

"Dude! Your mom is scary!" he says.

I have to nod in agreement.

Aunt April looks around the inside of the bouncy castle. "What is this? Some sort of glitter dome?"

"Erik did this," I say. "It'll be fun for the kids to play inside before the movie starts tonight."

I bounce up and down to demonstrate and Erik clears his throat.

He moves from partially behind me to partially in front of me. "There's something I think Lana needs to tell you."

Aunt April puts her hands on her hips and her expression shuts down.

"Go ahead, tell her," Erik says into my ear. "Say you need a break from the pressure of making videos."

I clear my throat. "I just think that if I were to consider taking a step back from *Lookie Lana!* tonight might be a good time to—"

"That's just your nerves talking," Aunt April says. "Do you have any idea how many girls would give their left ovary for this kind of opportunity?"

"That doesn't mean it's a good fit for me," I say. "I'm already under so much stress."

"Lana, stop acting insecure. You are great at this!" Aunt April smiles and it sends a creepy shiver down my spine.

"That's not—"

"*That's enough now,*" she snaps. "My turn to talk, because I have a surprise." She looks at her watch. "But we need to leave right now."

"Now?" I say. "We don't have to head to Digi until six."

"It's already after three thirty."

"How?" I feel like time is skipping forward.

Aunt April takes a bouncy step toward me and grabs hold of my arm. "Let's go." She gives a tug. "I've been on the phone all afternoon setting this up. Where are the keys to the Skylark?"

"We can't take the convertible," I say. "Ricki needs it for the drive-in's reopening."

Aunt April says, "Fine. We'll just take my car now and then circle back for the convertible after. Ricki can't complain if she's getting the Skylark for half the day."

"But that's the *wrong half* of the day," I whine.

"Stop stalling, Lana," Aunt April says. "I have your makeup in my car. You can put on your face while I drive."

In desperation, I look at Erik and mouth the word *help*.

"Wait a minute," he says. "Can you please just listen to what Lana is trying to say?"

Aunt April spins around and points an accusing finger in Erik's face. He's so startled he actually falls back, bouncing once and standing right back up.

She moves in for the kill. "You," she says to Erik. "You were supposed to be *helping* Lana with subscribers, not *sabotaging* her with some stupid prank."

"I'd never sabotage her," Erik says. "I care about Lana. In fact, I care much more about *her* than her channel stats."

He puts an arm around me and through the mesh I lock eyes with Lana. She smiles.

I say, "Erik just wants what's best for me, Mom."

"What's *best* for you is to come with me, *right now*." She grabs both my wrists with a vicelike grip and pulls me toward the door. "I've arranged a meet and greet with some of your biggest fans!"

"What? *Nooooo.*" I look back at Erik for help but he just shrugs.

"Those are actually kind of nice," he says. "Hearing from people who appreciate what you've been putting out there. It's one of the parts I really enjoy. Plus, there's security. It'll be a troll-free zone for you."

"Better than that." Aunt April ushers me toward the castle's canvas exit. "The meet and greet is at your favorite place: *the Fashion Fair Mall!*"

"What?" My whole body goes rigid.

My aunt maniacally grins at me. "Isn't this *wonderful?*"

I envision a sea of young girls clamoring for advice about eye shadow colors and lip tints and about a million other makeup products I know nothing about.

"*Not. Wonderful,*" I say helplessly as Aunt April drags me out of my safe and glittery bouncy castle cocoon.

chapter 20

I grab for Lana and hiss for her to "*Please* come with us" as her mom drags me away from the bouncy castle, but my cousin just gives me a small, helpless shrug and turns her attention back to videotaping the dogs. Zelda, the thing of evil, has clearly taken charge, leading the others on a mission to patrol the drive-in for squirrel intruders.

The next thing I know, Aunt April shoves me into the passenger side of her RAV4 and plops a heavy pink tackle box onto my lap. She gives my face a close look, gives a *humph*, and pats the top of the box invitingly before slamming the door. Based on the rattling sound it makes and the smell wafting from it, the pink tackle box is packed with makeup.

Aunt April pulls away from the concession shack and I see Erik standing alone inside the bouncy castle watching us leave. I have never seen a bouncy castle look so still and sad.

As we drive past Wes and Aunt May, I pleadingly reach out to them and they enthusiastically wave back.

"Nice to see you too, sis," Aunt May sarcastically calls to Aunt April, but my captor just blows a kiss before pulling out of the Starlight.

Passing through the drive-in's exit, we cross paths with Jake arriving in his red Bronco. I practically have my nose pressed against the glass windshield as Aunt April hits the gas and zooms by. We're moving so fast I don't even get a glimpse of Jake.

This is going to end badly. I feel sure of it.

"Go ahead," Aunt April encourages me. "Do your magic. You can't show up for a beauty meet and greet all barefaced and lipstick-less."

She gestures to my clean face like it's disgraceful.

"I really don't think I can put makeup on right now," I say.

"Maybe you should make this into a *challenge video*." She gives me an excited grin before turning her attention back to the road. "Putting on makeup, dot, dot, dot . . . in a speeding vehicle, exclamation point!"

"Maybe you can just stick with the speed limit?" I say.

"Challenge videos are getting all the clicks lately," Aunt April says. "We've *got* to get in on that!"

"Mom." I raise my voice. "How about this for a challenge? *My face is fine, dot, dot, dot . . . the way it is.*"

"Lana Marie! You cannot go to a big event that will be featured in outtakes on social media *without wearing any makeup.* That's *insane.*" My aunt's knuckles turn white as she grips the steering wheel, and she looks at me like *she's* insane.

"Okay, okay," I say. "I'll do my best."

I unhook the latches of the pink plastic tackle box and lift the lid. Both sides unfold like the plastic petals of a giant square flower and the fragrance floats into my face, making me feel carsick. *I'm so overwhelmed.* I think longingly of my backpack filled with horror makeup supplies locked away in the trunk of the Skylark right now. Makeup I'm an expert at applying.

Gingerly, I begin sorting through the bottles and powders and brushes and pencils and pots, lifting lids and sniffing everything. I root around until I find a number of bottles that are skin-colored and select one that looks like a nice neutral shade.

I pick up a midsized brush and then realize I have no idea how to get the foundation onto the brush.

"Do I just dump this . . . or . . ." Aunt April glances over at me like I've got two heads and I say, "Ha. Just joking, of course."

"This isn't the time, Lana!" I detect a slight screech of hysteria in her voice.

Sealing one finger over the opening of the glass bottle, I tip it over and immediately discover my finger seal wasn't airtight.

Liquid makeup runs down my finger and pools in my palm. I quickly place the bottle in the RAV4's drink holder and get to work wiping the foundation on my face, spreading it with both hands.

I have no idea what I look like, but my fingers are too covered in greasy foundation to flip down the car's mirrored visor. I bend my arm and try to nudge the visor down with my elbow, but it keeps snapping back up until my aunt finally reaches over and slams it down for me.

I glance in the vanity mirror at the same time Aunt April sees my face, and we both gasp in harmony.

I picked a color based on my usual skin tone. Which is dark beige. But I'm currently wearing Lana's skin, which, aside from the freckles, is pale as can be.

"*What on earth are you doing?*" Aunt April says.

"Why is this color even in here?" I wail as I try to rub it in, making things even more splotchy.

"That's contour, Lana! Contour!" She gestures wildly to the area underneath her cheekbones. "Are you really going to sabotage yourself right now?"

"It was an honest mistake," I say. "Although we do need to go home now so I can wash my face. It looks like I'm wearing camouflage." I wish I could go invisible.

Aunt April glances over. "No way," she says, opening the center console and pulling out a box of wet wipes. "Get yourself cleaned up and do your face the right way."

Everyone in my family tiptoes around my aunt April when she's upset. Once she goes off there's no bringing her back, and I spot a little vein pulsing in her forehead right now. I'm pretty sure she's close to going nuclear.

Without another word, I get to work, wiping off the *contour* and digging into the other products in the giant pink tackle box. I put aside the things that look completely foreign to me, such as a nubby rubber mitten and a tight silver coil with two pink handles that I have no idea what to do with. I pull out what I *think* is an eyeliner, but it turns out to be a tiny rake complete with a row of sharp metal spikes like teeth that make me shudder.

Once I've pruned out the weaponized makeup items I prop up my phone to watch one of Lana's tutorial videos. Unfortunately, she saves time by fast-forwarding through parts and loses me. I'm left trying to pause my phone while juggling brushes and finally give up on *proper technique*. I start applying all of the products I recognize in the quickest ways possible.

I look over at my aunt, who is still running hot. This observation is based on the way she's screaming at the car in front of us, who is following the speed limit right now. I apply makeup to my face even faster and find that I'm actually doing a fairly decent job.

Perhaps the glamour gene didn't completely skip me after all.

When I'm finished, I proudly slam the tackle box shut and do a final check in the mirror. It's not good by any means, but I don't think I look half bad either.

"We're here," Aunt April announces as she maneuvers through the Fashion Fair Mall parking lot. "Now you need to be quick—we only have about an hour here and then we'll swing by for the convertible and get on the road to LA."

She pulls up to a tall man wearing a reflective vest and leans out her window.

"Hi, I'm here with Lana from *Lookie Lana!*" She turns her head to look at me for the first time.

"*What the*—?!?" Aunt April's rage missiles have been deployed. "Are you *kidding* me right now, Lana?!?"

I duck and cover.

"Do you think you're doing some sort of *Miranda Sings* bit?" My aunt's face gets redder and redder, revealing she's wearing a rather thick coat of foundation herself. Veins pop out of her neck as she shouts, "I. Am. Not. *AMUSED*!!"

The man wearing the orange vest scurries to move a safety cone out of the RAV4's way. "Please, ladies." He looks frightened. "It's all good. You can park over to the left of the entrance. Matt will meet you and escort you to the meeting site."

Aunt April sits staring at my attempted "glamour look" and breathing heavy.

The guard picks up the flag that's on his metal folding chair and tries to use it to wave us forward. But Aunt April's attention stays directed at me.

"You are meeting your fans in less than ten minutes, Lana." My aunt's voice has gone from deep and scary to high-pitched and shaky, which is far more terrifying.

"It's okay," I say, "Watch. I can fix this."

I start pulling out wet wipes and undoing the makeup I've applied.

"I'm just really nervous about what I'll say in front of everyone," I say. "No worries."

"No worries? Ha!" she says. "How about *ALL the worries.*" *I'm beginning to see why Lana is suffering from stress attacks.* A fresh wave of panic flutters in my chest.

Aunt April looks at the parking guard, who has been motioning helplessly with his flag this whole time. He breaks eye contact and looks up into the sky, as if he's watching for a plane he can wave in for a landing here at the mall parking lot.

"This is going to be fine." I look in the mirror and nearly laugh at my makeup-streaked face.

"You look like a wild animal," Aunt April growls as she puts the car in drive and pulls forward, nearly mowing down the parking guard. His little plastic flag slaps the windshield of the RAV4 as he leaps out of our way.

But instead stopping to see if he's okay, or turning the car around and leaving, Aunt April speeds deeper into the lot. She zooms toward the cinder-blocked backside of the mall so fast I wrap both of my thin arms over the top of my head.

She heads directly for a metal door with a very tall security guard standing in front of it. The RAV4 screeches to a stop, landing neatly beside the curb, and I realize the uniformed guard is actually quite average-sized; he's just standing on a Segway.

Aunt April pulls up alongside him and he gives us a stoic nod. "You're the talent?" he says. "Crowd is in position."

"We just need one minute." Aunt April shifts toward me in her seat and clicks her tongue. "You look like someone just did a blindfold challenge on you."

Lifting the tackle box of makeup off my lap, she sets it on the center console between us and gets to work on my face. Roughly, I might add.

• • •

I squeal in pain a few times as Aunt April works with flying hands. When she stops and slams the pink tackle box shut, I dare to look in the mirror and see the on-camera version of my cousin. Big pink lips, huge spidery eyelashes, and not a freckle in sight. Despite all the wet wipes and do-overs, I still have a few dots of glitter on my face and even more of it glints unevenly from my hair.

Aunt April says, "I don't know why you're trying to wreck this opportunity, Lana, but you'd better hurry now because we're already late. You are supposed to be the down-to-earth glamour girl, *not* some diva."

She leaps out of the driver's side and I barely have time to ask the empty RAV4, "*What on earth is a **down-to-earth** glamour girl?*" before she circles around to my door and yanks it open. I hang on to the seat belt and it extends with my grip as Aunt

April pulls me from the car. She slams the car door shut, leaving the belt hanging out the side like a Labrador's tongue.

The security guard maneuvers his Segway back and forth, making a slow six-point turn until he's facing the door. He awkwardly takes out his key, unlocks the door, and carefully backs up on his standing glider, dropping the door handle almost immediately.

The metal door slams shut with a *clink*.

He swears as he glides back in to restart the process.

"Oh, for goodness' sake!" Aunt April grabs the key from him, opens the door, and hands it back. "Thanks for nothing," she says as he gestures for us to enter.

We make our way down an empty hallway that has me wondering what kind of wild illuminati operation needs a secret tunnel system at the mall.

"What is this passageway for?" I ask my aunt. "A Claire's emergency? In case they run out of hair accessories?"

She doesn't laugh.

Thinking of Claire's will always make me picture Lana and me in our preteen years, trying to fulfill the "buy five, get five free" deal. I smile at what a challenge it was for me to come up with five things I even wanted, and how hard it was for Lana to narrow her pile down to five. I'd usually end up letting her pick seven or eight to my three or two.

I genuinely never minded. Making Lana happy has never been easy, which is probably why I always found it so rewarding. I picture her laughing at my Claire's "hair accessory emergency" joke and it makes me smile.

Finally, we come to a set of double doors guarded by two men in mall cop uniforms. Their Segways are parked close by, plugged into the wall. Aunt April tells one of them, "We're *Lookie Lana!* and friend for the four o'clock meet and greet."

"Friend, *ha!*" I say and then freeze. "Four o'clock? The Starlight reopens its ticket booth in less than three hours."

"It's actually four-o-five," Aunt April scolds as the security guard unhooks his walkie-talkie from his belt.

I wail, "Volunteers will be showing up at the drive-in to help out soon." I picture the flow of excited people and Jake and Wes hustling about. *I can't believe I'm not there.*

The guard re-belts his walkie-talkie, apparently satisfied we are who we say we are. *If he only knew.*

Unplugging his Segway and stepping onboard, the guard tells his companion, "Hold the line," as if the mall is under zombie attack.

Standing on his motorized scooter, he pushes the door open and motions for Aunt April and me to follow him.

He glides out across the mall corridor's wide, smooth floor like he's a figure skater on wheels soaring free, forcing my aunt and me to break into a light jog to keep up.

As we draw closer to the open area in the center of the mall where the old fountain used to be, I can hear the din of high-pitched, joyful chattering.

It sounds terrifying.

When we finally chase the gliding security guard through the back of the roped-off area, we find it's filled with over a dozen long rows of girls of various sizes and shades and hair colors sitting in folding chairs. Aside from the wall of moms across the back, and the stray dad here and there, the audience is comprised of a mammoth mob of teens and preteens.

They're buzzing with so much excitement it feels as if the huge, expansive space is vibrating.

The crowd has its back turned to us, facing a large, temporary stage that's currently empty. The raised platform sits before a latticed back wall with a giant flat-screen hanging in the center, surrounded by what appear to be plastic climbing vines. The *Lookie Lana!* logo repeatedly scrolls across the TV screen above a dais table with two short microphones for me and my interviewer.

"I feel dizzy," I tell Aunt April, and I'm not lying.

"Sorry to hear that, honey," she says, "But we're here now. The appearance is no longer optional."

"Wait," I say. "*When* was it *optional?*"

The next thing I know, a blonde girl in the audience turns and sees me. Her face registers utter shock. "*Lookie!*" she calls out, "it's Lana!"

"I see what you did there," I say under my breath. "Clever girl."

But nobody can hear me because their squeals are suddenly bouncing off the marble tiles as the horde of girls moves as one, jumping up from their seats and clapping enthusiastically. Lana's image flashes up on the screen in front and I give a small wave and turn to leave.

I'm stopped by Aunt April, who takes me by my shoulders, aims me toward the front dais, and gives me what I'm sure she thinks is a gentle shove.

I stumble a few steps but catch myself and look back at her. She shrugs dismissively, and I realize that maybe she wasn't trying to be gentle after all.

"We love you, Lana," one of the moms calls out, and I turn

217

to look at her. "Sorry," she says, and then to her daughter she mouths an even bigger, "*Sorry*."

I try to give her a smile, but her fangirling has made me more nervous than ever and my lip starts twitching.

The whole crowd is mostly standing now and every last person in the indoor quad is holding up a phone to record me. *Who on earth is going to watch all of this footage?* I think as I make my way toward the stage in front.

My heart is beating so hard I can hear it.

A man holding a huge video camera has appeared out of nowhere, and he walks backward while filming me. His feed must be projected directly onto the TV in front because I'm walking toward a wide-screen movie of myself walking toward myself in real time. It's a bit trippy.

When I reach the front table, I don't know which chair I should sit in, so I throw a look back to Aunt April. She holds up her hands as if to ask what's wrong with me.

I sit down in the closest spot and fold my hands in my lap, trying to hold the shaking in my right hand still with my shaking left hand. It's not working out all that well. This is decidedly *not fun* for me.

The throng's cheers die down in small increments until the young ladies are all just staring at me adoringly. And expectantly.

Most of them continue filming me with their phones until it gets a little weird. The weirdness factor grows until finally, I give another small wave and Lana's fans go crazy all over again.

Leaning forward, I say into the microphone, "Um, thanks?"

Another high-pitched squeal rises into the air and bounces off the glass ceiling. One voice rings out, "I love you, Lana!" I look to the back and the fangirl mom shrugs as if to say, *That one wasn't me.*

I smile and imagine Lana replying with an insincere, "I love you too." But I'm already being stretched, pretending that I'm Lana. Trying to imitate the fake version of Lana's online persona is just too far beyond my acting capacity.

I smile at my young admirer. "Love yourself first!" The crowd gets quieter.

Either I've completely thrown them by going off script, or they're now expecting me to launch into some sort of talk.

All of a sudden, the full weight on my chest that I woke up with is back. My stomach twists and I feel like all the oxygen has been sucked out of the enormous room.

I catch Aunt April's eye in the back of the crowd and point to my face, indicating I could be about to have a panic attack. My aunt smiles and gives me a thumbs-up. Which isn't at all helpful. *I can't do this.*

All of these phones recording me are just too much. I close my eyes and take a deep breath. I try to imagine how Lana would get through this, but all I can picture is Lana's calm-looking face as her mom dragged me away to this local mall purgatory.

I can't believe my cousin ditched me again the first chance she got. She could've jumped into our path and clung to the hood of the RAV4 and insisted on coming along for support. I again picture Lana's serene expression as she turned away. But her look *wasn't* just calm indifference. I rewind the clip in my brain and watch her turn again. She genuinely felt bad for me, I know it. I zoom into my remembered recording as it replays one more time and there, at her mouth, I see it now.

The tiniest trace of a smile. Like, maybe she also felt something close to . . . *relief?*

Because she knew I'd tank this interview and then she'd be set free.

Gradually, the pressure in my chest loosens.

One kid near the front must hate secondhand awkwardness because she helpfully calls out, "Hi, Lana, how did you get to the mall today?"

I try to smile but my voice is shaky. "My mom drove me. How about you?"

"Same." She sounds disappointed. "My mom drove me."

Another voice comes from the middle of the crowd. "Hey, Lana, who's your favorite makeup artist?"

I actually have an answer to this question. With a wobbly breath I ask, "Have any of you heard of Rick Baker?"

I'm met with a sea of blank stares and I can practically hear crickets superimposed over the recorded video version of this moment.

"*Rick Baker,*" I repeat. "He was nominated for twelve Academy Awards." I pull the microphone closer. "Come on. He won *seven* Oscars for makeup!"

"Was he ever on BubeTube?" a girl asks.

"Gah! He's a special effects artist and he's *amazing*! He's worked on films for over forty years and semiretired recently only because CGI is basically ruining the industry, but . . ."

I stop to take a breath and I'm greeted with more stares. A few girls even lower their phone-holding arms, a sure indicator I've lost them.

I say, "Rick Baker designed the iconic characters in the

Star Wars cantina." I get a few rapid blinks in response to the Star Wars reference, so I go on. "Then he got his first Oscar for makeup on *An American Werewolf in London* in the early eighties." More blank faces. "He did all the looks for Michael Jackson's 'Thriller' video," I say. "And, hey, anyone see the 2001 *Planet of the Apes* reboot? How about Benicio Del Toro in *Wolfman*?"

And I've totally lost them. Murmurs of discontent begin to grow. In the back, Aunt April is now talking to a tall model with a small tiara perched on top of her smooth lavender hair. The model's arms are crossed tightly over her small chest, and with her high heels she stands even taller than the guard on his Segway.

I'm curious why Aunt April is talking to her, but right now this crowd of makeup lovers needs a real education.

I say, "Rick Baker was in high school when the original *Planet of the Apes* was released in 1968. He felt inspired to create his own ape costume, and he used to go out and do this thing where . . ." My grin gets huge. "He'd bring his ape costume to the drive-in and put it on and sneak up to cars and scare people out of their minds. How fun is that?"

I'm surprised the whole room doesn't erupt in applause and laughter at this since it is one of my all-time favorite makeup artist stories.

But nobody seems interested in hearing about Rick Baker. Even Aunt April ignores me as she continues to focus on the towering lavender-haired model in the back.

"Speaking of the drive-in," I say loudly, "that reminds me: starting at eight fifteen tonight, we're having a grand reopening over at the Starlight Drive-in movie theater on Route Eight. It would be amazing if all of you could be there!"

A girl wearing bubble gum-pink lip gloss and about eight million rainbow hair clips calls, "But Lana, you're scheduled to be on the main stage in Los Angeles tonight. I thought you were supposed to sing?"

I cringe. "Oh, right. I forgot."

"*Some sisters are not ready for the main stage*," a loud voice rings out from the back of the room.

It's the lavender-haired model, and without any provocation she strides aggressively up the aisle toward me in her high heels.

"What's happening now?" I say, but nobody can hear me because a fresh wave of excited screams runs through the crowd and up the high walls to the glass ceiling. Every phone is immediately snapped back into filming position as the audience turns to watch the towering beauty's grand entrance.

A glance behind me shows that even the TV screen has switched to her image as she catwalks closer and closer.

I hear someone say, "Ooooh, this is gonna be good," and want to ask them what's going on, because something dramatic is clearly happening right now. And I'd *love* to know what it is.

Especially since I'm somehow smack-dab in the center of it.

chapter 21

With a flip of her lavender hair, Miss Gorgeous Girl arrives at the front of the room and stands close beside my table as if she's waiting for me to do something. Confidently, she reaches up and straightens her tiny tiara. She's even more beautiful and perfect-looking up close.

I stand and sheepishly offer my empty seat to her. "Sorry. I wasn't told there would be someone else."

I slide into the adjacent chair amidst a loud audience harmony of, "Ooooooooh."

"You weren't told there would be *someone else*?" The model uses dramatic finger quotes around *someone* and *else*. "Try royalty!" She flips her hair again and announces, "I am *Her Highness*! Show some respect!"

Why does that name sound familiar? The crowd goes wild and she gives a graceful curtsey before sitting down in the chair I've just left.

"Warmed it up for you." She gives me a look of disgust and I try again. "Hi, I'm Lana."

I reach over to shake her hand and she pulls her manicured fingers out of my reach. "Oh, I know who *you* are." Her voice

223

gets louder as she announces, "You're the girl who thinks she can *take my crown*."

The audience gives another round of "Ooooohs," and I glance at the small tiara perched on Her Highness's head. *Now I remember where I know that name.* Lana and Erik kept mentioning Her Highness as some sort of beauty guru archrival. I had no idea I'd actually have to face her. Aunt April is nervously biting her lip as she watches.

"Is this a prank?" I ask nobody.

"I don't know." Her H leans forward. "Is that *dress* a prank?"

There's a long pause. I don't know how to react, and finally Her Highness waves a hand in front of her face as if she's erasing something.

"Totally kidding," she says. "That dress *slays*." She leans in closer, examining me up and down. "And I don't know how you did it, girl, but that glitter is *wearing me out*. It is *everywhere*."

"Um, sorry?" I honestly do not know what's happening right now.

She laughs, and her teeth are borderline too perfect.

I relax a bit, and Her Highness closes her mouth and stops laughing all at once. Which is terrifying.

Pursing her lips and drawing in her cheeks, she considers me with a side eye and an "Um hum" while she rubs her long fingers together.

I look down at my hands, feeling like I've been using Lana's long pink nails all wrong. They're clearly meant to give dramatic emphasis to my words. I practice making tiny air quotes under the table.

"You should be grateful I'm a queen who grants mercy," Her Highness says into the microphone.

It takes me a moment to realize everyone is waiting for me to respond. "Um, thanks?" I clasp my hands together underneath the table.

"Don't get too excited, this is not a full royal pardon." She dismisses me with a wave and addresses the audience. "Is everyone here aware of the drama?"

Everyone nods and a few more "Oooohs" ring out.

I'm the only one shaking my head no but Her Highness says, "In case any of you just crawled out from under a beauty blender, I'm here to drop the tea with the vile video Lana posted a few short weeks ago."

With a flourish, she gestures to the screen, which flashes with the opening sequence to *Lookie Lana!* featuring her distinct double *L* logo.

"Ugh," Her Highness says and picks up her phone as if she's already too bored to watch. I, on the other hand, turn around in my seat to give it my full attention.

The screen wipes to the image of Lana sitting in her well-lit space that I recognize from her bedroom this morning.

"Hi, everyone, welcome to *Lookie Lana!*" She gives a huge grin and waves. "Today I'm going to be doing another *Versus Video*." In a fancy font, the words *VERSUS* and *VIDEO* flash dramatically.

Onscreen, she holds up an extra-long black plastic compact and says, "As usual, we're going to be trying a drugstore brand on one side . . ." She points to her face with the compact and then shows a long silver compact in her other hand. "And on the other, a luxury version that costs *ten times* as much." She smiles into the camera and says, "Today we're comparing *eye shadows*."

Her tone leads me to think Lana just might make an excellent kindergarten teacher.

She weaves her fingers together, poses them under her chin, and bats her eyelashes at the camera. The crowd chuckles at her cuteness and Her Highness and I both roll our eyes. *This is silly.* Onscreen, Lana goes on to explain that she'll be testing the well-known drugstore brand Norealique against one of the shadow palettes from the "Her Highness Signature Collection."

She leans in and says in a conspiratorial tone, "You may have seen the video Her Highness posted of her sponsor's product blowing other brands away. Well, I'll be verifying her claim, just to keep H honest." Lana gives the tiniest adorable wink.

Expertly holding out the plastic compact, she opens it toward camera, revealing a row of six shadow shades. She tilts it back and forth and begins talking about undertones and texture and something called matteness as she dips a finger into each color and holds up her fingertips for us to see.

When she gets to the luxury brand the screen flashes with the HH logo and a shot of Her Highness, apparently just after eating a lemon, based on the way her cheeks are sucked in.

Beside me, H looks up from her phone and says, "Finally, something worth looking at."

The crowd laughs, and I notice that random mall shoppers have started gathering around the edges of the roped-off area we're sitting in.

Lana reanimates onscreen and opens the large silver compact. "I will say this," Lana says, "the HH packaging is really gorgeous." She opens and closes the compact as if inspecting the hinge. "Just listen to this click." She holds up the compact and quickly snaps it shut. "It sounds like the door closing on a luxury car."

Her Highness says, "Oh yes, she's spilling the tea now."

Onscreen, Lana begins to apply something called an eyelid primer, and although she fast-forwards her application onscreen, Her Highness gives an exaggerated sigh into the microphone. "Sisters, can we please just skip through all this self-indulgent nonsense?"

Obediently, the video speeds up even more, showing Lana applying her makeup at warp speed. Her mouth is moving and her long eye shadow brush is stirring quickly around each of her eyes. Lana even pulls out the spiky rake that made me cringe in the car and runs it through her eyelashes so quickly it looks like a miracle she doesn't gouge out both her eyes. The video finally slows back down as Lana looks at her now-heavy makeup in the mirror, turning her head back and forth, examining her handiwork.

"Here it comes . . ." Her Highness says dramatically, holding up one finger.

Lana purses her lips as if considering. "I have to say . . ." She closes one eye and then the other. "I am *not* loving the Her Highness Signature Collection formula right now."

Her Highness pretends to faint in her chair.

I watch as she comes to and fixes her tiara, then dramatically falls back all over again. Onscreen, Lana is talking about things like the eye shadow's pigment, which she accuses of being "unmanageable." I don't need to know about shadow to know Lana is *not* giving the HH brand a positive review.

The video goes on to show Lana testing the shadow's wear,

going out on a dinner date with Erik and displaying outtakes of her laughing while they play darts.

A few *Awwwws* wend their way through the crowd and Her Highness gives a dismissive wave.

"Clearly fake," she says. "Erik could be my boyfriend in, like, a snap if I wanted him." She snaps her long fingers. "This entire post is packed with Lana lies." She smiles and adds air quotes as she repeats, "*Lana. Lies.*"

"Here we are at the moment of truth," Lana contradicts onscreen. She's sitting back down at her well-lit makeup station, posing in the mirror and winking one eye and then the other.

"To be honest . . ." She pauses and looks at each eye a few more times. "I'm not in love with the way this HH shadow wears either."

Lana leans in close onscreen and points to her eyelid. It looks perfect to me, but she says, "Crease. Crease. Crease." She points to the other eye. "Meanwhile, at a fraction of the price, the Norealique eye is sitting tight."

"Freeze that!" Her Highness calls out. The screen freezes on the close-up of Lana with both of her eyes closed and her mouth twisted unattractively. "You cannot tell me there is any difference between these eyeshadows."

She stands up and traces her long pinky nail along the image onscreen. "In fact, I dare say the Her Highness Signature Collection eye looks brighter and cleaner."

"I bet it can even *see* better," I joke.

Scandalous whispers blow through the crowd while Her Highness leans over me, melting me with her gaze.

Finally, I nod. "Yeah, maybe there isn't much difference

between your shadow and the drugstore brand." I literally see zero difference. "It's still way cheaper though. Are we good now?"

I stand up to go and Her Highness puts a slender-fingered hand on my shoulder and forces me to sit back down. "No, we're not *good now*," she says using air quotes. "But we're about to make this right. Boys?"

She gives two small, commanding claps, and the next thing I know a pair of handsome security guards are moving quickly toward us. They're each carrying shopping bags and their tight sleeves are rolled up to reveal biceps bulging under the strain. They look nothing like the guys riding around on the Segways. As they draw closer I realize they're both wearing tight shorts and also that they're clearly male models just dressed as pseudo mall security.

Everything feels surreal right now. I look for an exit, but the crowd has gathered all around us on both sides.

The next thing I know, the large shopping bags have been placed in front of us and Her Highness is hugging one of the security guards. The other stops to smell her lavender hair, and she poses between them in a way that makes me blush and look away.

The crowd woots and whistles so loud it convinces even more people to wander over from the far reaches of the Fashion Fair Mall to see what's going on. I'm feeling more trapped by the moment and the vise in my chest begins to tighten again. It feels as if the oxygen in this mall is too thick to breathe, and I start to sweat out of nowhere.

Squeezing my eyes shut, I picture Jamie Lee shooting Michael Myers between the eyes in *Halloween II* and begin to relax. I remind myself, *None of this really matters.*

Her Highness has finished nuzzling the guards and pats one on the bum dismissively. "Go wait in the car, boys." Everyone cheers, and Her Highness puckers her lips and adjusts her tiara.

Turning her attention back to me, she doesn't break eye contact while unloading the shopping bags. They're filled with compacts of all different sizes, and she places each of the black plastic ones in front of me, and all of the shiny silver ones in front of herself.

"You like challenges so much, I have one for you." She starts opening each compact and showing them to me one at a time. "These are all eye shadows." She holds one up very close to my face. "Eye shadow. Eye shadow. Eye shadow."

I say, "So, you're saying they're *mostly* eye shadows."

"*All* eye shadows. Go ahead and look at yours." She points to the compacts piled in front of me.

I obediently begin opening each one, confirming they're eye shadows of every shade imaginable. "Yup," I say. "These sure are eye shadows."

"Our challenge is this," she says. "You and I are going to do our entire faces using only eye shadows from our preferred brand. The audience here will judge a winner and the loser must officially apologize."

"I apologize," I say. "Can we go home now?" I look around. "Really. I am *officially* sorry."

"Nice try." Her Highness takes two table mirrors from the bags, sets them in front of us, and hands me a package of wipes. "Get cleaning now—no cheating."

She drags a wipe down one whole side of her face. The smear it creates makes her look insane. So insane, in fact, that when she turns her wild eyes to me, I obediently grab a wipe and start scrubbing at my own face.

The crowd begins clapping in time like a chant and I give a look of desperation to Aunt April, who's still standing behind the last row of chairs. She has her arms crossed, but even from this distance I can read the expression on her face.

She seems pleased.

chapter 22

I try to leave as much of the makeup on my face as possible so I don't utterly disgrace Lana during the challenge. She'll be unfairly branded a fraud if I don't find some way to cheat. Her Highness points to my lips and says, "Nice try."

She grabs a wipe, puts me in a headlock, and begins cleaning my mouth. The cameraman moves in and kneels down so everyone can get a good angle on my humiliated expression up on the big screen.

"This shot's going to be our thumbnail," HH whispers to me under her breath. "We're both going to blow up."

The next thing I know Her Highness releases me, and with a smirk she moves back to her seat. She begins reapplying her own makeup with various brushes and sponges, opening and closing the silver compacts with confident *click, click, clicks.*

She narrates as she goes. "Now *this* palette has a lovely peach that will work nicely for dark undereye color correction." Obviously, she's an expert at this.

I stall for time, opening and closing the various Norealique compacts. They do not give smart *clicks* when they snap shut. They sound more like somebody clipping their toenails.

When I glance back at Aunt April, her face is red as she gestures wildly, *Do something!* I give her a sheepish smile and begin opening and closing compacts faster.

Finally, I find a dark pink that I think could work on my lips. Using the sponge applicator included in the compact, I start applying it to my lips and it looks . . . *terrible*. The color clumps up in the left corner of my mouth and refuses to spread.

And now it looks like I have a sparkly pink cold sore.

As I go back to rooting through the compacts, Her Highness narrates her own perfect makeup application. I'm trying to listen in and learn something, but this isn't like copying someone's math test.

Opening another eye shadow compact, I see a bright green shade that gives me an idea. I give my aunt a big thumbs-up, but she just bares her teeth at me.

I can practically hear her growl the whole way up here.

While I search for the perfect shades and begin applying them, my mind wanders back to the smile on Jake's lips as we did our galloping dance across the blacktop during the Starlight's sound check. *Was that really just yesterday?*

Everything started happening so quickly right after and I wish I'd just kissed him when he was in my arms. I can't believe I was so stupidly stuck on waiting until we were under the stars, and now Lana better not be ruining things with him. Or, taking things a step further. I would really, *really* hate to miss my first kiss!

If Jake is even interested in kissing me anymore.

I drag my applicator through a purple shadow and begin applying it to my face. My insides churn over how much I like him. *What if Jake rejects me after all of this?* I think about my cousin's theory that Zelda hates me because she senses my fear of rejection.

For the first time, I wonder if my obsession with having a magical first kiss is related to my rejection issues. I mean, sure, it's nice to believe in magic and all, and if today hasn't proven that magic exists then nothing ever will.

But when it comes to love, there's never going to be a magic rejection-free guarantee. Not really.

Jake and I could have the most romantic first kiss under the stars and it could be perfect and even magical, and I could still end up dealing with heartbreaking rejection someday. I can't be so afraid of getting hurt that I'm unwilling to take a risk.

My only choice is to take the leap.

I pull out my phone and text Lana:

Please, please, please don't make Jake hate me.

After a moment, I add:

Also, am in a makeup war at the mall with someone named Her Highness. Send help.

I know for a fact that Lana is constantly on her phone, but she doesn't text me back. I picture her in the glitter-filled bouncy castle right now having the time of her life. With Erik. While Jake looks on thinking she's me.

Meanwhile, I'm here, stuck in some spaghetti western-style cosmetics confrontation, about to be forced to take a three-hour car ride to LA so I can sing publicly, *and very badly, I might add.*

And on top of everything else, I will *die* if I miss the Starlight's big night tonight. If Wes decides to sell, this could be the drive-in's final fade-out.

I realize I'm gritting my teeth while applying more and more powder in a way that is making everyone stare at me with their phones held high.

I look around and give a small laugh. "Sorry, I was just . . . trying something."

Her Highness is dramatically putting the final touches of pink shadow on her cheeks with a long-handled brush and gives a snort. Her makeup looks absolutely perfect, and she expertly spins the brush before slapping it on the table.

"Clearly, you've lost it, Lana," she says. "Wait, that should be your new channel name: *Loser* Lana."

The crowd snickers in response and I look in the mirror.

I've used the eye shadows to create giant bruises on my jaw and forehead, plus I've given myself two black eyes. Now I'm currently transforming my sparkle cold sore into the illusion of a fat lip by layering every shade of pink I can find.

"This was supposed to be an eye shadow challenge," Her Highness says. "And you've turned it into a joke. Do you really think makeup is a joke, Lana?"

I look Her Highness directly in her icy-blue eyes, and for the first time I notice a tiny crescent of brown, visible around her iris's edge. She's wearing colored contacts.

I turn and look out at the eager young faces watching us with their phones, hungry to record something juicy.

They're all hoping I lose my cool and cause a scene. Over makeup.

"Sure, makeup can be applied jokingly," I say. "I mean, isn't it *supposed* to be fun?"

"Sorry that I take my business *seriously*," Her Highness says, but her haughty tone seems a bit deflated.

"Just because it's a big industry worth millions of dollars—"

"Try half a trillion," Her Highness interrupts.

"*Really?*" I shake my head, "Okay, so just because it's a half-a-*trillion*-dollar industry, that doesn't mean makeup has to be serious. In fact . . ."

I press a clean finger into a pan of orange eye shadow and reach over to put a line right down the center of Her Highness's nose. "Zoop," I say.

The entire room collectively inhales and holds its breath.

Her Highness calmly runs a fingertip down the length of her nose and stares at the orange powder.

"Did you just smear me with Rusty Savage shadow and say, *Zoop?*" she asks in disbelief.

"Heh," I say, and reach over to wipe the rest of the orange off her face. Except I've been blending my bruises with my other fingertips and so they're carrying every shade of purple and black and yellow eye shadow ever made.

Which I'm transferring directly onto Her Highness's shapely nose.

She keeps her head held high as her eyes swing to the mirror on the table in front of her. Her breath draws in sharply as she takes in the image of her face with rainbowed streaks of color running down both sides of her nose.

"I am *so sorry*, Miss Highness," I say. "Here." I pull out a wipe and begin swiping at her stone-faced expression while the crowd greedily films us.

Finally, she sucks air in through her perfect teeth, and after a beat bows her head. I've clearly crossed a line, and based on the crowd's murmurings I'm about to suffer Her Highness's wrath.

I scan for an exit, but the mob has us surrounded.

Finally, Her Highness raises her pale-blue eyes to look at me and gives an evil smirk. I feel like the fake bruises on my face have gone straight to my stomach and turned real.

Picking up her pointed, long-handled brush, Her Highness slowly dips it into one of my pink eye shadows. She says, "Maybe you should be *Loathsome* Lana." Holding the brush like a pencil, she draws something swirly on my cheek. The crowd goes completely silent as she works.

When she's finished, I hear a few snickers, but when I look into the mirror I see all she's drawn is two capital letter Ls. It's Lana's channel logo. I give a confused look.

Her Highness rolls her eyes and reaches for a wipe. "Revenge is not my style. *These* days." She starts cleaning her nose while simultaneously poking her brush into various colors and swiping them on the back of her hand. "You're right, Lana, makeup *is* supposed to be fun."

She squints at my face. "And I will say, those bruises look *very* authentic."

"Thanks," I say. "Your face looks amazing. I mean, it *did*. I can't believe you did all that with just eye shadow."

"Yes, I'm amazing, I know." She strikes a pose with one hand on her tiara. "But don't allow my display of mercy trick you into thinking we are friends."

"Oh, don't worry. I didn't . . ."

"Hey, sisters," Her Highness calls out to the crowd, "it's time to spill some tea. Let's have your Qs! Lana and I shall give our best As."

She points to a preteen in the second row waving her hand in the air with so much enthusiasm her neighbors are all flinching.

The girl leaps up. "Hi, I'm Ashley, and I have a question for both of you." Her smile barely fits on her face. "What made you get interested in makeup?"

"I was sort of abruptly thrown into it." I laugh at my inside joke that nobody else gets. Clearing my throat, I think about how Lana would likely answer this question.

I look at Her Highness, sitting beside me as she glances at her reflection in the mirror and readjusts her expression. I think about the obvious façade she's wearing. All part of a constructed persona, and she's rewarded for being over-the-top and wildly entertaining.

"I think makeup can be used as a mask sometimes." I look at the diverse crowd and smile. "Dressing up and putting on makeup is a way of pretending to be someone you're not. And who doesn't like to get a break from themselves now and then?"

Her Highness scoffs but I have the herd's attention.

I say, "But makeup shouldn't be used to turn us into homogenized versions of cookie-cutter beauty." I think of Lana. "And it *shouldn't* be layered on to hide our pain. Our unique traits and imperfections aren't shortcomings and our true selves are what the people who matter want to see."

"Wow, that's really deep, Lana." Her Highness laughs. "And here I fell in love with makeup the day I experienced the thrill of shoplifting my first Chanel Rogue Allure lipstick from the cosmetics counter at Bloomies."

"Seriously?" My mouth drops open in shock and Her Highness uses one long fingernail underneath my chin to guide it shut.

"Close your mouth, darling," she says. "It was Coco's cult classic, Pirate Red. And it was just a tester."

"Testers are supposed to be for *everyone*." A voice comes from the back of the room, and I'm so happy to see my cousin striding toward us in her high heels. That is, until she marches right up to Her Highness and flings a handful of glitter directly into her face.

Her Highness lets out a blood-curdling scream that echoes throughout the mall. The muscled security guards immediately spring forward as Her Highness stands up, spitting repeatedly, with glittered drool running down her chin.

"What are you doing?" I ask Lana as I try to help Her Highness brush the glitter off her tongue.

"I saw the livestream and was already on my way here when I got your text," Lana says, gently touching my cheek. "I can't believe Her Highness actually *hit* you! Where was my mom?"

I touch the fake bruise on my eye with my fingertips. "Oh, no," I say. "This was just part of a makeup challenge. Look, it comes off." I rub the shadow with the back of my hand to show her.

"Oh," Lana says sheepishly. We look at each other with wide eyes and slowly turn our attention to an enraged-looking Highness spitting glitter.

"*Lookie, LANA.*" Her Highness's voice is super screechy. "*Who* is your attack goon?"

"Hi there." Lana gives a big smile. "I'm Lana's cousin, Ricki. Sorry H. Just a misunderstanding."

"It's actually a funny story," I say. "See, she thought you'd attacked *me.*"

"*Not* funny, and you honestly thought I would assault another makeup artist?" Her Highness says. "What kind of a monster do you think I am?"

With that, she plants her high heels in a fighting stance and takes a full swing at Lana's jaw.

Thankfully catlike reflexes run in my family, because my cousin quickly ducks out of the way before she can get clobbered.

"Hey!" I say. "You *literally* just said you'd never attack another makeup artist."

"That's right, Lana," Her Highness says, wiping at the glitter on her face while trying to get closer to my cousin. "But this chick *here* is no makeup artist."

Her Highness lunges again and Lana barely manages to leap out of the way. The girls in the audience are going wild and all the phones are positioned at full attention.

"Okay, Erik!" Lana calls between heavy breaths. "Any time now."

A smooth voice says, "Well hello, young ladies," and Erik steps into view from the back of the room. "Any of you pull some cool pranks lately?"

Apparently, this crowd of girls has been holding *back* their enthusiasm this whole time because now they go completely berserk. Erik smiles and waves and is immediately engulfed by a flock of fangirls rushing from their seats.

The security guards leap to Erik's aid since now he's the one in greatest mortal peril.

Lana grabs my hand and starts dragging me toward the break in the crowd behind us. We're fighting against the swarm of teenage girls heading toward her boyfriend, but Lana points to a giant, waist-high planter at the edge of the staging area.

Before I know what's happening, Lana leaps up onto the planter so she's standing inside the enormous six-foot fern growing from the center of it.

All I have time to say is, "*Really?*" before I feel myself being dragged up and inside the fern as well.

While we crouch down in our wild hideout together, Lana says, "I think I may have figured out why we switched places."

A fern frond finds its way inside my mouth and I start coughing. I really thought *I* would be the one to figure things out, not Lana. "Did Aunt May—*cough*—say something?"

"No, she's still glued to Wes," Lana says. "But I found a really big clue. Come on, let's get out of here."

"Way ahead of you." I jump down the other side of the planter and see the outer crowd has mostly left to close in around poor Erik.

"Come on," I say, reaching up to help Lana jump. I know for a fact that the body she's inhabiting is not as spry as the one she's used to.

"Wait." She ducks her head out from the fern. "Hey, Erik," she calls.

A tuft of his blond hair sticks out from the center of the throng, like the eye of the storm that is his teenage fans. Erik's face whips in our direction, and when he sees me he holds a thumbs-up in the air.

He calls out, "I love you, Lana!" like a man who's not sure if he'll make it home alive.

The mob gives a collective swoony *Awwwww*, and Lana leaps down from the fern and elbows me hard.

"Ow." I rub at my ribs. "I'm delicate now. And you're not."

Lana points toward Erik and hisses, "Yell, *I love you too!*"

"You sure?" She nods energetically, so I raise my voice and call, "I've got to say, Erik . . . I love you too!"

The girls all squeal at being a part of this very special and traditionally private moment.

Lana and I immediately join hands and start running away from the scene like a couple of cat burglars. As we make our escape, I have to ask her, "Was that all for the cameras, or did you two just make a mutual declaration of love?"

"Oh, it's real, all right." Lana is grinning from ear to ear as she leads me across the wide expanse of mall. "After all this, it is most definitely real."

She drags me through the food court and we turn down a hallway that leads to the mall's public bathrooms. Lana leads me past the drinking fountains to a door at the end.

I point to a red sign that says "Alarm will sound." "Isn't this an emergency exit?"

"Isn't this an emergency?" she says. "I know this mall. Nothing's going to happen." She shoves open the door, causing a high-pitched alarm to immediately echo down the hallway. She looks at me. "That sound is just a coincidence."

When we step outside, I groan at how much lower the sun is than when we got here.

The mall always makes me feel disoriented, as if time and

space and oxygen are all artificially intertwined. Plus, we've come out a different exit, so I'm completely lost—but Lana grabs my hand, turns me to the right, and runs full-tilt along the outer wall.

"Hurry up," she says. "If my mom catches us, she'll force me to go to LA."

I say, "You mean me."

"Right," Lana says. "We just need to avoid her until it's too late. It takes at least three hours to get to the venue and you're scheduled to be onstage at nine."

Lana's legs are longer, but she's jogging in heels, so I pause to check my phone for the time. I see there's a text message from Jake asking where I am, so I quickly type that I'm on my way back to the Starlight and I'll see him there. I put my phone away and then remember I was supposed to be checking the time. I pull my phone back out and report, "It's already past five o'clock."

"Which means we need to avoid my mom for another hour or else you'll be singing before a huge crowd tonight."

Wordlessly, I pull ahead and continue running faster.

"Wait," Lana says, breathing heavy. "I'm dying. Do you ever exercise at all?"

I laugh and start doing spry leaps in the air. "Nope. Never. But it feels like your Zumba workout obsession is paying off."

"This is so unfair." Lana stops to lean against a parking sign.

"No, what's unfair is the amount of pressure I'm under having to be you," I say. "That whole scene back there was *insane*. I started having an actual panic attack of my own. How do you live like this?"

"Oh, and you think I've been having a stress-free *fun* time avoiding Jake?" she says. "All that boy wants to do is be around you."

"Really?" I smile. "Well, let's fix this switch already. What's the clue you found?"

"Let me show you." She pushes off the sign and starts trotting across the parking lot, and I try to feel hopeful as I fast-walk beside her.

Finally, I spot the pink Skylark way up ahead and I'm filled with the sense that maybe things will work out after all. I speed up even more as I picture kissing Jake under the stars at the drive-in while sitting in the front seat of that magical convertible together.

"I can't believe that after all of this craziness, we honestly might be set free." I cut through the parking lot, making a beeline for the car.

Just then, a familiar voice says, "Going someplace, girls?"

Aunt April steps out from behind a big black van and I actually scream at her disheveled appearance.

Lana and I freeze and lock eyes for a moment. *We're doomed.* The Skylark is still at least two hundred feet away.

Lana glances down at her mother's feet and I see her face spread into a wide smile.

Aunt April is wearing strappy stilettos.

I say a silent thank you to the ruthlessness of fashion as Lana and I sprint toward the pink convertible.

Lana claws at the pom-pom key chain, dropping it once and scooping it back up in one motion.

When we finally reach the car, we run to opposite sides, and my hand is reaching for the passenger door handle when I hear a loud *clomp, clomp, clomp* ring out.

Lana is suddenly tackled so hard, all that's left of her is a cloud of glitter.

chapter 23

When I peer around to the other side of the car, I see Lana is facedown on the ground and Her Highness is on her knees, straddling her. HH narrows her ice-blue eyes at me as she adjusts her tiara and runs a hand down her lavender hair.

Lana gives a muffled, "Hey there, H. Care to help a sister out?"

Aunt April catches up to us, breathing heavy and carrying one heel in each hand. "You have a lot of explaining to do," she tells me.

Her Highness stands, straightens her tight sequined skirt, and looks Lana's mom up and down. "Well, you were right," she says to Aunt April. "That confrontation was a *great* idea. Sure to boost both our channels."

Aunt April and Her Highness share a polite "mind the long nails" handshake.

"I actually expected much more from Lana." My aunt glares at me. "My daughter hasn't been herself today."

"Ha!" I say with zero humor as I lean down to help Lana off the ground.

As soon as she's on her feet she points at her mom. "You

could've at least warned Lana you were planning to have H confront her live that way."

I say, "That guerilla attack was just wrong."

Aunt April shrugs. "You were the one who decided to go off script today with your pranky boyfriend. We needed something big to knock that storyline down."

"Smart," H tells Aunt April. "And I like what you've done with the *Lookie Lana!* brand. I assume you're entertaining an offer from Norealique?"

"Came through during your eyeshadow challenge." Aunt April grins, holding up her phone. "Did you hear that, Lana? Your down-to-earth glamour girl just reeled in our first offer."

Her Highness looks back toward the mall. "Actually, you basically saved my cute butt too, since my stupid manager decided to quit and move to Colorado with her *boyfriend*." H examines her lacquered nails. "And I'm supposed to be in the middle of a comeback."

"Yeah, sorry your channel took a dive, but you know how this business can be," Aunt April says. "You've got the goods. You'll get back on top."

"My manager should've noticed the shift sooner," Her Highness says. "I didn't start changing things up and adding challenges until I'd already lost four hundred thousand followers."

"Ouch," Aunt April says. "Do you sing too?"

"Don't we all?" H runs her hand along the pink convertible's hood. "This is a seriously sweet ride happening here."

"Thanks for bringing it, Ricki," Aunt April says to Lana. "It saves us the trip to the drive-in to pick it up."

"You're welcome, Aunt April," she says. "And hey, could I borrow Lana for a quick sec?"

"Sorry, but Lana needs to get changed and ready to head to LA," Aunt April says. "We need to arrive early to allow for time with fans."

"I've had plenty of time with *fans*," I say. "And I'm already dressed." I brush off my still-glittery pink skirt.

Her Highness and Lana's mom look at me and then at each other a moment before bursting out laughing.

Aunt April points a long fingernail and traces it up and down my pink dress. "That getup has done its work, but everyone will have seen it. You need a serious makeover for tonight."

Her Highness gestures to my face. "And you may want to lose the bruises and fat lip," she says with a shudder. "So *realistic*-looking."

Aunt April says, "And wipe those initials off your face."

I lick my hand, rub it around on my cheek where HH drew the double Ls, and hold back the front of my blonde hair. "Good?"

All three of them shake their heads no, and then Aunt April and Her Highness start laughing again like they're new besties.

"I have the perfect wardrobe change in the car," Aunt April says. "I swear. Without my help, Lana wouldn't have a channel at all, let alone Norealique."

"But have you looked into the ways accepting ad revenue will affect your ranking?" H crosses her arms. "Not to mention folks who will immediately realize that Norealique review was bull."

"Of course I've examined all the factors. And Lana didn't skew her opinion for that review," Aunt April says. "In fact, Her Highness, you may want to evaluate how the brand *you're* aligned with fancies itself higher class when it's just a severely overpriced—"

"Oh no you didn't!" Her Highness points a sparkly nail into the air and raises her voice. "The formulas my sponsor uses are the highest quality."

So much for besties.

A small stream of girls has pursued us in hopes of finding drama, and at the sound of Her Highness's raised voice their phones immediately pop out and start recording.

Lana has moved closer to the car and slyly shakes the pom-pom key chain down low where her mom can't see it. I give a slight nod.

"Even if the two brands are equal in every other way," Aunt April shouts at Her Highness, "Norealique is a fraction of the price and people deserve to know about it."

Her Highness glances around at the crowd then licks her teeth while reaching up to touch her tiara. "You do not know what I've been through . . ." she declares dramatically. "I came from *nothing* and I am now *royalty.*"

The crowd gasps as she yanks the tiara off her lavender head and waves it in the air.

I hold three fingers down low and silently count them down as I move toward the passenger side door of the car. *Three, two . . .*

But before I can get to one, Lana yells out, "Hit it!" and jumps over the side of the open-topped convertible.

I stand frozen while Lana fumbles with the keys for what feels like an eternity. Meanwhile, HH continues to escalate her monologue with, "I swore I would *never* be caught wearing a cheap, chain drugstore generic lipstick again . . ."

Finally, Lana gets the engine to roar to life, and Aunt April notices what we're doing.

She barks an angry, "Hey! Don't you girls dare!"

Lana shifts the car into gear, and I finally unfreeze and dive headfirst into the back seat just as the Skylark jumps forward.

"Sorry, we've got to go," Lana calls as we fly across the parking lot.

When I look back, I see Aunt April is leaning on Her Highness while putting her strappy heels back on and HH is adjusting her tiara. Clearly, they realize chasing us would be futile.

"You can slow down, Lana." I lean forward from the back seat. "I don't think they're coming after us."

Another glance over my shoulder confirms Her Highness has begun posing for pictures with members of the crowd.

But when I look forward again, Lana is recklessly crashing through a taped-off section between two safety cones. We speed away as a mall security officer riding a Segway shakes a fist at us, cartoon-character-style.

Lana gives a *woot* as she launches over a speed bump and the Skylark goes airborne.

"Totally unnecessary," I call out.

Lana cranks up the tunes as she hits another speed bump, and this time I can't help but laugh.

She flings one hand into the air and shouts, "Lana and Lyric ride again!"

The song on the radio drops the bass, and without even thinking I throw my arms open wide and start singing along. Delighting in my unique vocal stylings—off-key and at the top of my lungs.

Lana hits another bump and we are both flying, and for just a second, here in the back seat, I feel like I'm eleven years old again and we're on the greatest road trip of our lives.

* * *

As soon as we reach the highway, Lana slows and turns down the radio.

"Are you ready to have your mind blown?" she asks me.

"Keep rolling steady," I tell her as I start to stand up. "I'll climb up to the front so we can talk."

"No, wait." She raises her arm to block me. "First, I need you to see something back there."

I sit back down and look around but all I see is the journal from Aunt May's yurt sticking out from under the seat in front of me. "You found a clue about our switch in the journal?" I reach down and grab it.

"Not that," Lana says. "On the lower right side of the seat in front of you." I bend sideways and she clarifies, "Other right."

"That's my left," I say, pointing.

"Fine. Just look at the bottom corner."

I lean forward, searching the seat's back cover. I say, "There's nothing—" but then I see it. "Wait, what?"

I run my fingers over the two small initials carved into the leather and sit up, locking eyes with Lana in the rearview mirror. "Is that what I think it is?"

Lana grins and nods her head. "Two *L*s. Lana and Lyric."

"How is this Nona's car?" I say. "I thought our moms sold it. Did Aunt May buy the car back again?" I climb up to the front seat to sit beside Lana, my hair and pink skirt whipping traces of glitter into the wind.

"I have no idea," she says, "but it has to be some sort of clue about our situation, right?"

"Right. Our *situation*," I say, running a hand along the front dashboard with fresh reverence. "This is amazing. What made you even look at the back seat?"

"I was sitting back there, reading Aunt May's journal, and maybe hiding from Jake a tiny bit, when I saw the marks," she says. "I was so surprised I actually squealed, and Jake and Erik came running out of the projection shack to check on me."

"What were the two of them doing in the projection shack together?" I ask.

"Erik was giving a live feed tour of the drive-in and asking Jake questions as he got the place all ready," she says. "It was to promote opening night, and Jake acted like an old-timey ticket taker. You should watch it, it's pretty funny."

I've seen Jake's old-timey ticket taker bit and it's down-right adorable. "Great," I say. "Now he'll probably get BubeTube famous and abandon me too."

"He wouldn't do that," Lana says. "He definitely like-likes you. He kept asking if he could talk to me privately, and well, there's something I need to tell you." She winces.

"Lana! What did you do?" I ask. "You didn't kiss him, did you?"

"Absolutely not, *no*!" she says. "But I did tell him to wait for me inside the bouncy castle and then I grabbed Erik and left to come rescue you at the mall."

"You *what*?"

"I didn't know what to do," she says. "I got tagged on a bunch of posts about your confrontation with H and showed Erik. As soon as he saw that I—well, *you*—needed help, he immediately came up with this plan to sacrifice himself." She looks in the rearview mirror. "The poor thing is probably *still* posing for selfies."

"Poor thing? What about Jake?" I say. "Probably all covered in secondhand bouncy castle glitter and wondering why I'd just ditch him like that." I could cry imagining Jake standing alone inside the bounce house, waiting for me.

"Well, I'm pretty sure he would've left the bouncy castle after I drove off in the convertible with Erik."

I lean close to her face and shout, "*Do ya really think so?*"

"We'll fix it," she says. "I'll say it was an emergency and me and Erik needed to save you. It's not even like that's a lie."

"Speaking of which," I say, "why does Her Highness hate you so much?"

"Her channel's been dropping faster than ever since I posted that video trashing her line," Lana says, "but honestly, her show was due for a redesign anyway."

"I'm sure you would've done better at handling that crazy surprise attack that your *own mother planned*, but I managed to come out on top," I say. "You're welcome."

Lana looks at me and gives a scoff. "Yeah, well, tell your reflection how much you came out on top."

I pull down the visor, and the little mirror reminds me that my face still looks realistically beat-up and bruised, and my cheek is still shiny and pink from the double Ls.

I can't help but laugh.

"Okay, so maybe I didn't come out *completely* on top," I say. "But at least there's no permanent damage."

"I don't know," she says. "That pigment you're wearing is pretty intense. It could have some serious staying power. Here." She opens the glove box and hands me a pack of moist wipes.

"Boy, you have fully moved yourself into the Skylark." I try to keep the annoyance out of my voice, but Lana must hear it.

Defensively, she says, "What? I'm supposed to drive around without wet wipes? Like some sort of animal?"

I pull out one of the thick, quilted wipes. "I guess I'm glad to have them. Thanks."

Leaning in toward the mirror, I start swiping at the pink smear on my cheek. I can still make out the double Ls that Her Highness drew. "What made you use our Ls as your channel's logo anyway?" I ask as I scrub them off my face.

"I didn't know if you'd even remember." She pushes a chunk of swirling brown hair from her eyes.

"Of course I remember," I say. "My feelings were really hurt when you used our cool-looking entwined initials to promote your makeup channel. Like you stole it and distorted its meaning."

"That wasn't my intention at all," she says. "As a matter of fact, I originally pictured the two of us doing our own thing together. Like, you with the horror makeup and me with all the glamour stuff."

"Come on, Lana." I pull out a new wipe and scour my face even harder. "You never invited me to be a part of your show."

"That's because I had that one stupid video go viral and my mom got this wild vision for how to brand me and my channel."

Lana's talking about one of the first videos she posted, where she compared her mother's expensive luxury makeup products to her own drugstore brands. Lana did one side of her face with each and gave a rundown on the places to save money and the items that were important to splurge on. People went nuts for it and Lana's mom took over her channel. And then, apparently, her life.

I grab another fresh wipe. "You have to admit, your mom *has* done an amazing job of promoting your channel. Your fans are . . . enthusiastic."

"Yeah, well, this level of commitment was never really what I wanted for myself," Lana says. "I was goofing around, having fun, and now it's become my whole identity."

"You love the attention and you know it," I say.

Lana grins as she watches the road. "It's definitely addictive," she says. "Like, I'll put up a video and watch the likes immediately start to roll in. It's as if I can hear the viewers applauding."

"So, you just sit there, waiting for people to respond to your posts?" I say.

"It is a quantifiable measure of how well I've done." Her face falls. "Or how *meh*. The comments are the true judge."

"You never should've been reading those toxic comments." I check my face for the last blotches of color. "At least protected yourself that much. If you don't read them, they can't hurt you."

Lana shrugs. "I ignored them a few times, when I really needed a break. But my mom likes me to consider the feedback."

"*Feedback*?" My protective inner wolf is awake and angry. "Telling you to 'go kill yourself' is not feedback, it's abuse. And your mom should've known that those hateful responses would tear you apart. No wonder you've been having panic attacks. Your own mother has been pushing you to drink venom from those anonymous snakes."

With a sigh Lana says, "I think my channel simply got too popular too fast and people started to feel, I don't know, like they could be cruel and forget that I have feelings."

"My mom always tells me that other people's opinions of me are none of my business," I say.

"Yeah, well, mine monitors my ratings and tells me what I need to change about myself to be better."

I say, "How did the two of them grow up in the same house?"

"I have some theories now that I've spent time studying the sisterhood journal—"

"The what?" I interrupt.

"The diary we found at Aunt May's yurt," Lana says. "I'm calling it the sisterhood journal. Anyway, it sounds like Nona was actually pretty controlling."

"What?" I say. "I can't even picture that."

"Yeah, she treated each of the sisters differently," Lana says. "And my mom was the daughter who was never good enough."

"Wow," I say. "Do you think that's why your mom sucks as a mom?"

"She loves me," Lana defends, then after a moment adds, "But she's probably not a great fit for me as a manager."

"Her approach is a *bit* high pressure." I check my clean reflection in the mirror and snap the visor shut.

Lana glances at me. "I always liked the way *Lookie Lana!*'s double *L* logo gave a little wink to our relationship. It helped me stay strong in the face of all that hate. I had no idea you resented me for using it."

"I resented you for cutting me out of your life when your channel took off." I cross my arms over my chest and rest back in the seat.

"That wasn't intentional," Lana says. "In fact, it felt like *you* started acting weird first. I assumed it was jealousy and so I gave you some space. I didn't want to rub my success in your face."

"But you didn't just give me space," I say. "You pushed me away."

I feel a pang of grief at the remembered loss. I'd felt so lonely, spending hours in my darkened room watching horror films alone.

Lana's jaw tightens. "Come on, Ricki. I know we both played a role, but you're the one who gave up on us."

"I didn't . . ." I stop. She is being unfair. I think back to all the text messages I sent that went unanswered and the time she spent cozying up to my mom with all their fashion talk and shopping trips. I remember the stab of envy I would feel anytime anyone talked about my amazing cousin and how much they loved Lana and her channel. Things were really taking off for her. With Aunt April's guidance, she was building something successful.

And I felt so excluded and rejected.

I felt . . . like I was being left behind.

"I'm sorry," I say softly. "Maybe I was a little jealous of all the attention you were getting."

"You think I didn't feel *guilty* for that?" she says. "Everyone wanted to put me up on some pedestal and act like I was special all of a sudden, and meanwhile I knew better."

"Yeah, I knew better too." I laugh. "You're cool and all, but come on, that article called you *the newest Goddess of Glam*."

Lana laughs. "It was all a bit much."

"I assumed you didn't want to deal with being regular old Lana anymore," I say. "Like you wanted to erase that part of you."

"No, I *needed* people like you in my life who know I'm just regular old Lana, and not some sort of glitzy deity," she says. "You were right before about nobody knowing the real me."

"I know the real you," I say. "And I've missed you a lot."

"I've missed you too," she says. "*So much.*"

I slide over in the seat so I'm beside her and give her a sideways hug, and our hair swirls together in the wind above our heads.

"I'm sorry I pushed you away, Ricki," she says.

I say, "And I'm sorry that I let you." I hug her tighter as she drives, and it's as if all the time and hurt between us begins to flitter away.

We are morphing back into close-as-sister cousins again, our brown and blonde hair releasing sparkles into the air as it spins and twirls and twists together.

chapter 24

When the Skylark makes its final turn toward the Starlight marquee, I half expect us to swap places again. But apparently our switch is holding out for something more than Lana and me reconnecting and apologizing to each other in a sincere and heartfelt way.

"I can't believe Aunt May didn't tell us this was Nona's car," I say. "Do you think she even realizes? Or maybe she's had it hidden somewhere on her property this whole time."

Lana says, "It's time for her to spill the tea."

"Oh yes," I say. "She needs to spill a lot of it!" I spot a Jedi talking to a large man in round glasses wearing a wizard cape. "Wow," I say. "Volunteers are already showing up."

Lana checks her phone. "Well, it is nearly five thirty."

We pull up alongside the front ticket booth and three wolf dog faces appear in the booth window, inspecting us as if they're in charge of security. They stand in a row, panting happily as their giant front paws rest on the waist-high window shelf.

A little yap sounds from below and two of them immediately jump back down, disappearing inside the booth. The third continues sniffing at us through the screen a moment before giving a sharp yelp and dropping down out of sight.

Zelda pops up and walks along the sill, like she's the one truly in charge of inspecting our vehicle. She bares her teeth and growls at me, and the next thing I know the three other dogs leap back up so their faces are in the window.

The Chihuahua gives a short, commanding yip, and the wolf dogs start wildly barking at us.

Wes steps up to the window wearing a cowboy hat. His fresh Starlight T-shirt is paired with the glowing *Starlight* Sapphire pendant from Aunt May, and it hangs perfectly between the silhouetted couple on the front of his shirt. The ones about to kiss under the stars. When Wes sees us he says, "Oh, thank God you're here."

"What's going on?" Lana asks.

Aunt May appears from the back of the booth dressed in full Glinda the Good Witch regalia, from cylinder crown to floor-length poufy pink dress. She pulls on two of the wolf dogs' collars, trying to get them to calm down. "I just called your mom, Ricki," she says. "She needs to come and get her little demon dog."

"Zelda's been stressing the poor wolf pups out this whole time," Wes says. "They respond to her command, like they've all accepted her as alpha. It's bizarre."

"She's the worst," Aunt May says. "Poor Wulf keeps rolling onto his back in submission, and now they're *all* out of control!"

"We had a volunteer turn around and leave already," Wes says. "We need to get Zelda out of here."

Aunt May passes Evil Z through the open window to Lana. The Chihuahua immediately starts licking her face hello.

As soon as she's done kissing Lana, Zelda turns around and gives a low growl to the wolf dogs watching from the window.

Their ears drop down as she reams them out with three sharp barks and, one at a time, they drop back down out of sight.

"Such a tiny tyrant," Wes says, shaking his head.

"My sweet babies are traumatized." Aunt May bends down to give the closest wolf dog a hug. Meanwhile, another pup sticks his whole head inside the cylinder top of her crown.

"How're things looking for tonight?" I ask Wes. "Do you think we'll make our quota for the bank loan?"

"I really hope so, Lana." He smiles, "I think we've done all we can do." He looks at Aunt May as she reclaims her crown and stands back up. "The rest is up to fate."

She smiles at him. "It's been a pretty fateful day."

"Yeah," Wes says, rubbing the blue starlight pendant and smiling back at her.

I give them a moment, then say, "Speaking of fate, do you think we can maybe talk to you, Aunt May?"

Lana adds, "It's about the car."

"Is there something wrong with it?" Aunt May asks. "I had my mechanic look it over before I gave you girls the keys."

"Oh, it drives just fine," Lana says.

"We want to talk more about the *origin* of the car," I say. "We have a few specific questions about *where* it came from."

Aunt May widens her eyes, and then glances at Wes. "Do you mind watching the boys?"

Wes responds right away that he'd love to get to know them better.

"Good luck with that," I say under my breath.

Lana must hear me because she chuckles. "This is not the first time Aunt May has fed a guy to her wolves."

Our aunt steps out of the booth and walks around to my side of the Skylark.

I scooch even closer to Lana, and Aunt May squeezes her big, puffy skirt in through the door. "Ricki, you mind driving us someplace with a bit more privacy?" she says.

The convertible kicks up a small cloud of dust and Lana hands the Chihuahua across my lap to Aunt May as she drives toward the huge movie screen in front. Zelda growls under her breath but doesn't snap at our aunt.

I watch the parking lot whiz by from the middle of the front seat. A number of cars have already laid claim to some of the prime-viewing center parking spots, and costumed volunteers are milling about, greeting each other.

But Jake and his red Bronco are nowhere in sight.

I check my phone and realize he's responded to my text, that he had to take care of an emergency errand. He says he'll meet me at the Starlight later.

I type:

Do I get to see a costume preview?

I wait and watch as the three dots indicate he's answering me. I start to panic as it takes longer and longer. Lana parks the Skylark beside the playground and she and Aunt May climb out their opposite sides, leaving me sitting alone, staring at my phone.

Lana takes Zelda from Aunt May and the two of them head

for the swing set. My cousin turns back as if she's about to say
something and realizes I'm not following them.

Tucking the Chihuahua under one arm, she moves back to
the car. "Are you coming?" Evil Z growls at me from her arms.

"Sorry," I say, "just waiting for a response from Jake. I still
can't believe you abandoned him in the bouncy castle."

"I'm sorry, I really didn't have a choice," Lana says. "And
come on. This is important."

I start to climb out of the car just as my phone buzzes with
his response.

> No preview. Surprise. And just so you know want-
> ed to meet you in the bounce house to apologize.
> Promise I'm not a creep. Just misread signs. I'm
> really truly sorry, thought I was being romantic.

I want to cry.

Sorry couldn't bounce with you! I write back. **Lana
needed help. You were never a creep! Wish I could go
back and get a redo.**

He doesn't respond, and Lana is pulling me out of the car by
one arm. In case it isn't clear to Jake that I wish I'd kissed him,
I quickly add:

> I want us to EXPERIENCE THE MAGIC OF THE
> STARLIGHT tonight.

It feels as if my heart goes whooshing off into space along
with my text, and I'm too afraid to check if he's working on

another response. With a small whispered prayer that Jake is reading my words right now and deciding to give me another chance, I put away my phone, climb out of the Skylark, and grab my backpack filled with horror supplies from the trunk.

I tell Lana, "Well, I just laid it on the line with Jake. Now all we need to do is switch back so I can hopefully seal things tonight with a magical kiss."

"You do realize you sound like a desperate Disney princess right now," Lana says.

"Yes, it's humiliating," I say. "I just don't know what I'll do if he ends up rejecting me."

"Hey," Lana says. "There's no shame in being rejected. It means we tried something we weren't sure we could do."

"Yeah, it's hard to put a positive spin on rejection," I say. "But thanks for trying."

When we reach the playground, the slide and merry-go-round are crawling with screaming children, some already sparkling with bouncy castle glitter. We join Aunt May where she's waiting for us in the empty swing set area.

Her bracelets jingle and her poufy skirt sighs as she hikes it up and squishes it onto the swing. "I *love* swinging," she says with delight. As she pumps her feet we can see she's wearing hiking boots underneath her authentic Glinda dress.

"Okay, Aunt May . . . spill it," Lana calls to her between passes. "Lana and I know . . ." She pauses to wait for the swing. "For a fact . . ." Pause. "That you gave us . . . *Nona's car!*"

Aunt May drags her boots in the dirt to slow down her swing. "How on earth did you two figure it out?"

"Ah-ha! So you *admit* it." Lana points at her accusingly. "Wait. You admit it?"

"Do your moms know?" Aunt May asks.

"No," I say, "we just figured it out."

"Please don't tell them," Aunt May says. "It'll just make things complicated."

"Complicated how?" Lana asks.

I say, "Because that car has been making things *extremely* complicated for us today."

"Is it running okay?" Aunt May asks. "Sometimes you just can't tell with these older cars."

"It runs fine," I say. "It's just . . . having a strange effect on Ricki and me."

Lana nods and points at me. "Understatement."

Our aunt laughs. "That's just *nostalgia* taking over. You girls had some amazing times in that Skylark. Driving in it together must be bringing up potent memories."

Lana points to the Skylark with the Chihuahua she's holding. "That car gives new meaning to the term *wild ride*."

Aunt May's eyes are wide. "Do you girls remember that amazing road trip we took after Nona died?"

Lana and I both sit down on the swings on opposite sides of her, and Zelda settles in on Lana's lap.

"That trip was amazing," I say. "A once-in-a-lifetime experience."

"Yeah. One time only," Lana says. "Because *Aunt May* captured the car and held it hostage without telling anyone. I can't believe you've had it all this time."

"It's a whole thing," Aunt May says, which is an explanation that usually means we'll never know the full story. She adjusts her cylinder crown. "But basically, after that road trip I just couldn't give up the car."

"We did have a really great time," Lana says.

"I was in charge of selling it, and so I just claimed that I got less than book value and paid off both your moms."

I slap Aunt May's arm. "I *remember* my mom complaining you weren't savvy with the Skylark sale back at the time."

"That's funny." Aunt May points at Lana. "I thought Ricki's mom was the judgy one. I guess I let down both my sisters."

"Not at all," I say with a grin. "Because you *kept* Nona's car!"

Aunt May tells me, "Your mom called to thank me and said you're riding the Skylark onstage at Digifest tonight." She squints at the sun, getting heavy in the sky. "Wait, aren't you and your mom supposed to be on your way to LA by now?"

Lana puts Zelda down on the ground and the Chihuahua immediately charges across the playground toward an unassuming group of children. My cousin looks at her phone and grins. "It's almost six o'clock. We just need to avoid my mom for a little bit longer and it'll be too late to go to LA."

"Wait, why are you girls avoiding *your* mom, Ricki?" Aunt May asks.

Just then, my parents' silver minivan pulls past the ticket booth and heads in our direction.

"We're not really avoiding her." I gesture. "In fact, here's Aunt June now."

I point to Zelda, who is busy herding the now-screaming children to one corner of the playground by nipping at their kiddie ankles.

"Oh, right," Lana says. "I'd better grab my mom's dog."

Which is when Aunt April's RAV4 comes roaring past the ticket booth and stops with its engine revving at the drive-in entrance.

"Eeep." Lana freezes on her way to collect Evil Z. "And here comes *your mom* too, Lana."

I instinctively duck so she won't see me, but Aunt May stands up and starts waving both arms like she's hoping to be run over.

"*Both* of my sisters," Aunt May says. "This is a rare treat. *Too* rare, in fact."

The RAV4 speeds in our direction while kicking up gravel. As it gets closer I can see through the front windshield that Aunt April looks furious. Her Highness is perched beside her in the passenger seat, one hand gripping the dashboard while the other dramatically holds on to her tiara.

My mom's minivan pulls up next to the pink convertible, and the second she opens her door she calls out in a high-pitched voice, "Zelda Fitzgerald! Who's a good dog?"

The Chihuahua leaps away from Lana's grasp and takes off toward my mom, waggling with so much joy she can't even run in a straight line.

We all scream as the shadow of Aunt April's RAV4 falls over the dog, threatening to hit Evil Z. But luck is better than sense for a dog, and the Chihuahua leaps neatly into my mother's arms just in time.

Aunt April opens her driver's side door and hops down, landing with both strappy heels together and not bothering to shut the door. She rushes toward the swing set.

Lana has jumped back on her swing and the two of us

instinctively start pumping our swings back and forth as fast as we can. As if we can swing high enough to get away from her mom.

Thankfully, my mom manages to head off Aunt April at the edge of the playground before she gets close to reaching us. Shaking the Chihuahua in Aunt April's face, the two of them start yelling at each other.

"What on earth are they fighting about now?" Aunt May asks us as Lana and I relax our swinging. "I mean, I get June's rage over nearly having her dog squished, but why is April coming in so hot?"

"That would be because of me," I say. "She's upset because I don't want to perform tonight."

"Lana's going through some stuff," Lana says. "She needs a break from her whole *Lookie Lana!* world. It's time for her to get honest with her mom and start living offline."

I look over at her as we pendulum back and forth. "Are you *totally* sure about that?" I ask. "This can't be about letting the haters win."

Lana relaunches herself and pumps her swing higher while I wait for her to answer. Finally, I relaunch as well and work to catch up.

I'm already gaining on her when she finally answers.

"The haters only win if I allow the hate to get inside of me and make me hate. I need to break free and start spending more time with the people I love. *That's* how hate gets crushed with love."

"Well said." I point my tiny feet as they go soaring high in the air.

Lana and I look at each other, and in that moment our swinging falls into perfect sync. I feel dizzy as we lock in our gaze and glide back and forth and back and forth together while the rest of the world dips and rises in a blur. We stay connected as we swing, and the knot in my chest loosens. This moment feels . . . *real*. And it is filled with forgiveness, and acceptance, and love.

I don't know what's next.

But I do know Lana and I will have each other's backs. No matter what.

chapter 25

M y cousin and I keep our swings in sync for an unnaturally long time, but I finally break eye contact when we hear a sharp "Lana!" from down below.

It's so disorienting, I nearly fall off my swing.

Everything blurs for a moment and I blink a few times, trying to force my eyes to focus. I see Aunt April storming toward us and I falter, making my swing lurch awkwardly.

Aunt May stands up from her swing and steps too close as she fluffs out her skirt. I avoid kicking her by shifting direction in midair and start twisting and untwisting out of control.

Ignoring the way my swing is halting and jumping through space, Aunt May points at me and says angrily, "If you don't want to sing tonight, Lana, you shouldn't have to."

"I literally *cannot* sing," I call as I start dragging my feet to stop my clumsy spiraling.

With that, Aunt May pivots and storms toward Aunt April. But my mom is chasing after her sister too and beats Aunt May to the punch. Or maybe that should be she beats her to the *pull*, because that's just what she does.

Before Aunt April gets to the edge of the playground, my

mother yells, "April! We're not finished!" and shifts her precious Chihuahua to one hand so she can reach out and yank her sister's hair.

Aunt April's head snaps back so hard, Lana and I both flinch and say, "*Oh!*"

She covers her head and screams, "What the heck, June?"

My mom yells, "Do you have any idea how long I wouldn't have spoken to you if you'd actually *hit* Zelda? She's part of the family."

"Well, it's not like we talk much anyway," Aunt April says. "And *Zelda* has bitten every member of this family, *including* me. Why are you even here, June?"

"I'm here to pick up my dog, who *you* nearly ran over."

"Yeah, well, I'm here to pick up my *daughter* and bring her to one of the most important performances of her life," Aunt April says.

Across from me, Lana launches her swing again and straightens her arms so that on the forward upswing she's practically upside down.

Aunt May cuts into her sisters' argument, "Hey, April? Did you ever bother to ask Lana if she *wants* to sing? Or if she even cares about being famous? Or is that still *your* dream?"

"How about you float off in a bubble and let me handle this, *May*," my mom says. "Since you somehow couldn't even handle a little three-pound Chihuahua." Zelda starts licking my mom's face in the greatest display of phony innocence of all time.

"That little demon creature has been torturing my poor babies all day," Aunt May says.

"*They're not babies*," my mom and Aunt April yell in unison.

Which is my cue to tune out. I've managed to get my swing going strong again, and my arms and legs are tired from pumping but I push myself to swing even higher.

Lana starts humming so loud she's practically screaming with her lips closed. I join in, less in-tune but loud enough to block out the arguing down below.

We swing higher and higher together.

Our moms and Aunt May all love each other, but almost every time the three sisters get together, things get heated. I've come to realize it's not worth getting upset over. They always work things out, but the way they clash will never stop making me uncomfortable.

And the three of them are building up to a big, bitter sister battle right now.

I'm swinging so high it feels as if I just may achieve my life's dream of flipping all the way around when a strong voice interrupts my concentration.

"Is this swing taken?" Her Highness asks as she sits primly between us on Aunt May's swing. Apparently, she got sick of waiting in the RAV4, and has already hung her bedazzled backpack on the swing set's crossbar, above where I dumped mine on the ground.

The veteran beauty guru hikes the skirt of her dress up a bit, walks her swing backward, and launches for a strong start, pointing her high-heeled toes together. "So," she says to me, "you're supposed to be the next big thing on the beauty scene?"

"Actually"—Lana slows a bit to talk to Her Highness—"Lana and I were just discussing the sacrifices involved and deciding whether or not it's all worth it."

"Any advice from Her Highness?" I call as I swing past.

"This life can be all consuming and exhausting," Her Highness says. "And believe it or not, the more well-known you get, the *more* lonely and isolating it gets."

"So why do you do it?" Lana asks her seriously.

"Because I am in *love* with this." Her Highness swings higher as she builds speed. "It's just who I am."

"If you didn't love it, just maybe enjoyed certain parts of it, would it still be worth doing?" Lana asks.

HH swings for a few beats, thinking. "Okay, so the money can be *sick*," she says, "Like, I cannot *believe* how much I'm able to pull in when I hustle. But at some point, the money is meaningless. It all just owns you. The show, the brands, the fans." She swings a few more pumps and adds, "If I *wasn't* in love with it, I probably wouldn't love it. Know what I mean?"

"Kind of." Lana leans back on her swing. "Lately Lana just feels so *buried* by it all."

"Yup, *under six feet of stress*," I affirm as I swing by.

"Just wait," Her Highness tells me. "You only get buried more once you sign with sponsors. I have to be careful with what words I use and where I'm spotted. For instance, it would be death to my brand if someone ever posted a photo of me in the drugstore cosmetics aisle."

"You can't even buy cotton balls?" I ask as I continue swinging.

"I basically use beauty blenders for everything," Her Highness says. "And with my latest deal, I'm required to post at least five videos every week. Even more when a new product launches."

Lana says, "I can't be creative under pressure. I need to

be inspired. I don't even think I *can* churn out decent videos quickly on demand."

"I didn't know you had a station too." HH looks Lana up and down. "Um, glamping style shortcuts maybe?"

Lana looks at her and laughs. "Good one," she says. "But I'm actually a movie buff with sophisticated taste in classic horror films. I've developed a fascinating philosophy that views Jamie Lee Curtis as a sage who holds all life's wisdoms."

The two of us look across at each other and smile. "She's the ultimate scream queen," I say as I glide higher.

"Nice," Her Highness says. "Did you know Curtis was one of the first female celebrities to appear in a women's magazine without an ounce of makeup or retouching?"

"Really." Lana sounds fascinated.

"Yup, she did a whole *before and after* photoshoot with and without makeup and Spanx to show what a dramatic difference it made," HH says. "Very *real* and empowering and fabulous!"

"Zero surprise," I say. "JLC is pure royalty."

"My blue-blooded sister." Her Highness takes a hand off the chain to touch her crown.

"That is, with an emphasis on the *blood*." I laugh, and the others look grossed out. "Because of the horror movies . . . ?" I start to explain and give up.

Her Highness calls out, "Who's ready to jump with me?"

I say, "Jumping at this height takes skill."

HH pumps higher. "I take swing dismounts to a whole 'nother level."

"Oh, but dismounts happen to be *my* specialty," I say.

She warns, "Style counts as much as distance."

It is on!

I even out my pace and feel for the rhythm so I'll be able to time my jump perfectly.

"Wait." Without missing a leg pump, Her Highness turns to Lana. "You, brunette horror girl."

"It's Ricki," Lana says.

"Can you record Lana and me jumping off the swings? It could be a perfect clip for us to share as a follow-up to our scene at the mall."

"Let's just be fully present for this." Lana smiles at me. "Keep it ours instead of sharing it with the world."

"Fine." Her Highness grumbles. "We'll do this dark, but it feels like a waste."

All three of us pump ourselves higher and higher.

I reposition my grip on the chains, pulling my elbows down and around so they're pointing forward. "Ready?" I say.

Her Highness and I count down together, "Three! Two! One!"

Lana straightens her legs and starts dragging her feet. "Yeah, I'm not doing that," she says, which doesn't surprise me since she's never been good at jumping off swings.

What *does* surprise me, however, is the effect my lighter body and smaller size have on my legendary classic dismount.

I'm gleeful when I launch myself into the air at the moment of maximum velocity. It's not until I'm careening through space that I realize my mistake. I'm much more aerodynamic today.

Like, *much* more.

Her Highness has jumped just a half beat before me and so I watch her do an admittedly impressive dismount in what feels like slow motion. My body is still flying higher and higher as she lands softly with her high heels together. She pops her arms proudly in the air, Olympic-gymnast-style.

I careen toward her, watching helplessly as she holds her pose. I can't slow down or shift my trajectory and she is directly in my path.

She gets closer and closer, faster and faster, and I have no choice but to use Her Highness as my landing pad.

I slam into her so hard that despite my lightweight physique and her firm gymnast stance, I completely take her down.

The two of us tumble on the ground and roll over each other a few times before coming to a stop next to the slide. Her Highness is laying on her back and miraculously has both her high heels still on her feet despite the skewed angle of her legs.

"I'm so sorry," I say. "I haven't done a swing jump in so long, it's like I'm a different person."

Lana laughs so hard she can barely catch her breath. "Wow, was I ever wrong about not recording that. It was *epic*."

I'm brushing as much dust as possible off of my pink dress while privately also checking to see if I've fractured any bones. And I'm not talking about just my own. Her Highness hasn't moved since breaking my landing, and although she didn't get hit with "full-sized" me, I flew at her like a blonde bullet. I feel along her arms for any place that bends wrong.

"Are you okay, H?" I say. "Stomp once for no and twice for yes."

Her Highness kicks one high heel into the air and dramatically stomps it down once, but then bursts into such laughter it's clear she'll be fine.

"Why am I even here?" she asks the sky between breaths.

"I figured you came with Aunt April hoping to get a ride to

Digifest," Lana says. "I know your manager left and your channel's been in a slump, but your fans would be really happy to see you."

"Way to kick a gal when she's down. *Literally.*" Her Highness points into the air. "First rule of the slump—never talk about the slump! It angers the wrathful Algorithm Gods."

"You're not cursed," Lana says. "You just need a little reboot."

"Which is why I *was* angling for a ride so I could do a surprise meet 'n' greet at Digi." Her Highness holds out her hands toward me and waggles her fingers until I lean over to help her up. "Except now it seems that none of us are making the trip to LA anytime soon."

We look over at the three still-fighting sisters. Even Zelda is bearing her teeth.

Aunt April waves her arms in frustrated fury as she gestures to Evil Z and shouts loud enough for us to hear, "Would it really be *that* big a deal if I'd hit that vile hairball?"

I tell Lana and H, "Yeah, we're going to be here for a while."

"What time are you scheduled to go onstage?" Her Highness asks me while brushing herself off.

I say, "Nine o'clock, I think?" and Lana nods.

Her Highness straightens her skirt, checks her phone, and gives a low whistle. "It's going to be tight, but wow, what a sweet time slot. Your mom really knows how to *w-e-r-k* werk it, because I've checked out your channel and stats and you're not quite there yet. No offense."

"No offense taken," I say.

"Maybe a *little* offense." Lana wrinkles her nose. "But you're not wrong," she says, "Lana's mom can be a bit of a bulldog, and

Digi bloggers will probably rip Lana apart if she tries to sing onstage. *Especially* tonight."

I point at Lana and nod. "That's a cuppa tea right there."

Lana says, "Not even driving the pink Skylark convertible onstage can save her now."

"Is that why I *had* to get that car for tonight?" I say. "Because I felt insecure?"

"The trolls were going to annihilate you online no matter what," Lana says. "But at least the car would've made for an undeniably iconic image to go with their vile comments."

"So, why do it?" I ask. "If there really is no winning."

"Because you don't just walk away from that type of opportunity?" Lana shrugs. "Whether you want to or not."

"Well, that settles it," Her Highness says. "You *must* make it to Digifest on time. I may be jelly, but I'm still your glamour sister, and that pink convertible will have you collecting clicks like candy on Halloween. This night is your game changer, girl."

Her Highness claps her long-fingered hands together, grabs her bedazzled duffel, and spins on her high heel toward our aunt and mothers.

Lana grabs my arm as soon as H is beyond earshot. "I just had the most *epic* idea for how to get you out of this so you don't have to sing."

"Let Her Highness take the car and the spot at Digi?" I say quickly.

"Yes!" Lana says. "She'll be super entertaining for the crowd. She can drive onstage in the convertible and perform and just be her fabulous self. People will *love* it. Everyone wins."

We look over to where Her Highness has interrupted the

three sisters with her hands held up dramatically. She calls out. "*Sisters!*" as she strides toward them.

My mom crosses her arms and Aunt April looks at her watch and calls out to me, "Let's go, Lana!" She claps her hands. "Move, move, *move!* Or that extra *L* in your logo is going to stand for *Landfill!*"

"Maybe we should record this part after all," Lana says as she takes a deep breath and turns toward the parking lot. "I'm about to provoke the sisterhood."

My heart starts beating with fear. Our moms and their sister are a force unto themselves and I feel like my cousin is charging into the center of a hot-tempered cyclone.

So I charge right in after her.

chapter 26

"This is a once-in-a-lifetime chance," Her Highness is saying when we approach. "You *need* to get this pink convertible and your girl over to that LA Digi-venue now!" H gestures to the pink convertible with two long fingers.

Aunt April waves her arms and tells her sisters, "See? I've been *trying* to tell you two this is huge." She stops when she sees Lana and me approaching. "Thank goodness. Let's go, Lana, you can get ready in the car."

I stop and cross my arms as Lana walks right past the group and continues on to the Skylark. We all watch as she dives face-first into the back seat of the convertible. Her feet kick up in the air while she crawls deeper and deeper into the car, reaching around for something underneath the rear seat.

"I didn't know you were coming too, Ricki," Aunt April says to her. "But whatever it takes to get Lana to LA." She turns to me. "Come on, cousins in the back. Her Highness, you can ride shotgun."

Lana's legs are still kicking in the air and she struggles to stand back up. Her body flails awkwardly as she tries to rock herself up and out of the car. Finally, she just rolls the rest of the way forward and pops up so she's kneeling on the back seat.

"You really have zero core strength, huh?" she says to me, then realizes everyone is watching her. She quickly flings one arm up in the air, showing us she's holding the diary we stole from Aunt May's yurt this morning.

The sisters look at Lana in shock as she points to the silver kissy lips pictured on the cover. "Look familiar?" she asks them.

"Hey," Aunt May says. "That's not yours."

I widen my eyes with fake surprise and say, "*Wow,* where did *that* come from?"

My mom hugs Zelda to her chest and snaps at Lana, "How on earth did you get that, Ricki?" I realize I'm essentially making myself take the fall. Which is totally unfair, since this was all Lana's idea.

I say, "Ricki and I stole the sisterhood journal from Aunt May's yurt! *Together.* In fact, it was mostly *my* decision!"

Ignoring me, Lana opens the leather-bound book and runs her finger down the page. "Sisters of the sisterhood," she reads aloud. "Right here, you all signed your names to this list of promises."

"*Sisters*! Yas!" Her Highness seems thrilled by the overuse of her favorite word.

"We need to get going," Aunt April says.

"No," Lana says sharply to her mom. "For the sake of your daughter, you need to *listen.*"

Aunt April bites her lips, and we all gather around as Lana raises the open book and begins reading dramatically.

"Number one! We the undersigned do promise to never let go of each other, no matter what happens. We promise to always be there for one another and tell our sisters when they have lipstick on their teeth, after we've finished laughing, of course."

We all chuckle and Lana goes on. "Number two! We promise to honor and respect each other's interests, for the world loves to mock the things we girls see as awesome. Let us not fall into that same trap."

We look around at each other and I feel a pang for telling Lana her fans have goldfish brains and for judging the group of girls at the mall earlier. That squealing mob had enough sheer positive energy to light up the world. And they deserve respect.

"Some things do not change," I say.

Lana adds, "It says, *sidenote*: we shall equally share each issue of *Teen Beat Magazine*, with the exception of any pinup posters of heartthrob John Stamos, who shall belong exclusively to June."

I look at my mom. "Seriously?"

She blushes and says under her breath, "He's still foxy."

Lana continues. "We will always follow our dreams and support the dreams of others." She looks up and adds, "But that doesn't mean you should force your dreams on others. Aunt April, Lana doesn't really want to be famous. Can't you see that she's been riddled with anxiety ever since *Lookie Lana!* took off?"

She looks at me and I wring my hands, trying to look as anxious as possible.

"Her mental health should be more important than her channel stats," Lana says. "Do you really want her to become one of those tragic train wreck people who can't handle fame?"

Aunt April looks at me with open surprise. "But Lana is special," she says.

"Of course I am," I tell her. "But special and famous are very different things."

"That's some tea there," Her Highness says. "Plenty of famous people are nothing special."

I say, "And plenty of special people have zero desire to be famous."

Aunt April is looking at me. "You really don't want to be famous anymore?"

I look at Lana as I say, "I'm so sorry, Mom. But I don't think I ever did."

My mom says, "I tried to tell you, April . . ."

And Aunt May says, "Aw, shut up already, June."

"*The sisterhood list goes on,*" Lana loudly interrupts. "We make a pact to call each other on their crap." She points at the sisters one at a time. "Well, *I'm* calling it. The three of you need to start paying attention to what is happening in each of your lives."

The sisters move closer to each other defensively. Zelda gives April a warning growl from my mother's arms. But they don't move apart.

Instead, my mom hands Zelda off to Her Highness, and the Chihuahua immediately shows her approval by climbing onto H's shoulder.

"And the one final rule," Lana says. "Which is actually written in as an *official* addendum."

My mom says, "In April's handwriting, I'm sure."

"Always the official one." May laughs.

"The addendum reads"—Lana looks up from the book—"always, always, *always* say *yes* to a road trip."

The sisters share a look of surprise, and Lana says, "Signed April, May, and June."

She snaps the book closed and the three of them continue

standing close, looking back and forth at one another. Her Highness whispers under her breath, "Sisters."

"So, road trips are always a yes," Lana says. "And right here, in your faces, is an *epic* pink convertible! And here's the thing. This exact car? The very pink convertible right here in front of you—?"

She points to the car and nods at me.

"It's *Nona's* Skylark!" I shout the punchline.

Aunt April and my mom both gasp, while May takes a step backward, breaking up the huddle. All three sisters start talking over each other at once, which is how they communicate when they're amped up. Lana and I smile at each other.

"You actually had the car all along?" Aunt April asks. She sounds angry.

My mom asks, "How could you keep such a big secret?"

"You guys were busy with your families and just moved on from your grief," Aunt May says. "I felt all alone and couldn't let go of Mom."

"I was *devastated* all over again when I thought the car was gone," Aunt April says. "Especially since I thought you'd under-sold the value."

"I can't believe it was with you this whole time." My mom hugs herself and stares at the car.

"I'd been so bonded with Mom, caring for her when she got sick." Aunt May absentmindedly fluffs out the skirt of her costume. "She asked me to keep the car parked on my property and said I'd know when it was time to share it."

"Typical Mom," Aunt April says. "Controlling us, even from beyond the grave. God, I miss her."

My mom says, "I didn't even notice how much the three of us have grown apart since she's left."

"We all handled the loss in different ways," Aunt May says. "Me? I grieved by getting another wolf dog and burying myself in furry love."

Aunt April says, "And I never stopped trying to prove I was good enough for Mom. And now I see how that's affected my own daughter." She turns to me. "I'm really sorry for pushing you so much, Lana," she says. "And we're going to work on getting you help for your anxiety. Reconnecting with your cousin is a great first step."

Lana and I look at each other and smile.

My mom says, "Yeah, well, as always, I've handled everything perfectly since Mom died." The others groan, and she holds up a finger to add, "*Except* for the part where I started to isolate from my two closest friends because I didn't know how to be sad with them."

"You think we couldn't handle you being sad?" Aunt April says. "You were such a gloomy teenager. Before college you were *always* sad."

May says, "Adolescence was not a good look on you."

"Ah yes, I've missed this." My mom laughs, and I try to picture her being anything other than bright and hopeful when she was my age.

"I guess nobody knows us quite like the people who have known us all along," Lana says, and the sisters all nod at the truth of this. But Lana is looking at me when she says it, so I tip my head to her and give a long blink in agreement.

My mom says to Aunt May, "So when you saw Lana and

Ricki were growing apart, you decided it was time to bring Mom's car back?"

"That was really selfless of you," Aunt April says.

"They're the next generation of the sisterhood." Aunt May smiles. "You two bonded while you were pregnant, and it was like you had your own secret pact. You can't know how outside of it I felt." She looks back and forth between her sisters. "But now, I helped them reconnect. So I'm a part of it too."

"Yes, you are!" my mom says. "My goodness. Just look at the two of them, sneaking around and stealing our sacred journal together."

"That's nothing." Aunt April chuckles. "You should've seen them speeding away from the mall together like they were Thelma and Louise. I wanted to murder them both!"

The sisters crack up laughing and hug and start talking over one another again.

I exhale with relief. Surely this is the reason why Lana and I switched places. To get the sisterhood back together.

"Wait a minute." Aunt April turns to me so quickly I swallow a chunk of air. "So, we're really just *not showing up* for your big performance at Digifest right now?"

"I'm sorry," I say weakly.

"*Lana*," she growls, "do you have any *idea* how many phone calls it took for me to secure you that spot? And then the *miracle* of getting the car added in?" Her eyes dart back and forth as if she's searching for what she should do next.

"I'm *really* sorry," I say.

"Oh, well, as long as you're *really* sorry!" Aunt April says sarcastically, and then seems to realize she's getting out of control. She grabs a chunk of her hair and starts twisting it.

Aunt May and my mom move to either side of her. Each of them places a soothing hand on her back.

"April, honey," Aunt May says. "This is okay."

"We're here for you," my mom says. "But it's Lana's decision. Just let it go."

Aunt April takes a deep breath, and immediately breaks down crying.

Lana and I look at each other with wide eyes at seeing her like this. Her sobs get louder and louder, until, finally, she starts trying to talk. "Meyyyyy fiiiir gt shuuuu dounnnn," she says between sobs.

May and my mom share a puzzled look, trying to decipher what their sister just said. They both shrug, shake their heads, and pat her back even more vigorously.

Her Highness shifts Zelda to the other shoulder and moves so she's facing the three of them. "Okay, April, that's enough." H snaps and Aunt April turns her tear-streaked face toward her.

Her Highness asks her, "Have you even considered managing someone you didn't breed yourself?"

"April has been working in entertainment law," my mom says protectively. "She just celebrated ten years at her firm, right before shifting her focus to managing Lana full-time."

Her Highness says, "Did you not just hear her say her *firm got shut down*?"

"What?" Aunt May looks back and forth between them. "How did you understand what she just said?"

"It's true," I say. "Mom didn't want anyone to know."

My mom lunges to hug her older sister. "April, why on earth didn't you tell us?"

Aunt May joins in the hug. "That stinks, sis. What are you going to do?"

Aunt April clears her throat. "I don't honestly know," she says. "At first, I was applying for interviews at other entertainment law firms, but there are only a handful of them here in Fresno, and no way are we moving to LA." She looks at her sisters. "But then I saw that Lana's channel had a few popular videos, plus that one that went totally viral, so I started studying up on the BubeTube business. It turns out it's a market that has been *exploding*, and meanwhile my law firm turned its nose up on the whole sector. It was only interested in traditional showbiz and in representing *real* stars."

"Probably why they had to close," Lana says as she climbs back out of the Skylark.

Her Highness nods. "BubeTube-famous doesn't mean famous-famous to most folks over thirty. Meanwhile, many of us have a much larger audience reach than most celebrities do."

Lana adds, "Walk-of-fame stars only go to people in music, movies, or broadcast television."

I say, "Remember when I asked what the funny boxes with Vs were the first time I saw the stars in the sidewalk in LA?"

Aunt April wipes her eyes and points at Lana. "I thought Ricki asked what the televisions were."

"Lana thinks everything's about her," Lana says and winks at me.

"Say, Ricki," I ask her dramatically, "didn't you have a good solution for Digifest?"

"Actually, I thought *you* had that great idea, Lana," she says.

"Listen up!" I raise my voice above the still-chattering sisters. "Ricki and I have a great idea!"

Lana cuts in. "Since Lana has no desire to pursue fame, and Aunt April has managed to secure this awesome spot at Digifest . . ."

She grins at me and I nod. "Mom, how about if we give my performance spot to Her Highness?"

Aunt April looks over to Her Highness, who's been elegantly petting Zelda. "What do you think, H? Ready to hit that stage tonight?"

"That would be ah-mazing!" Her Highness sings. "But I'll do you one better. April, baby, I see your talent and I want you to be my new manager. What do you say?"

"I don't know," Aunt April says, "I really need to focus on finding a job . . ."

"Oh, honey," Her Highness says, "managers get twenty percent. And since this afternoon's *stunning* display at the mall, I already have two new sponsors knocking down my door. Or should I call that *our* door?"

Her Highness leans in to whisper numbers into my aunt's ear. As she listens, Aunt April's lips move with the quick math she's doing in her head.

Her lips stop a beat before spreading into a smile. With her eyes wide, she says, "Um, yes, Her Highness. I do believe we can work with those numbers in helping you achieve your long-term goals. I'm happy to act as your official manager."

She offers H a handshake, but Her Highness ignores her outstretched palm. Instead, she passes my mom her Chihuahua and tackle hugs Aunt April.

"And now a hug with all my new *sisters!*" Her Highness opens her arms wide and gathers us into a giant group hug right there at the playground's edge. "Come on now," she scolds. "Everyone, get yourselves in here. You too, Miss May, with that *fabulous* look of yours."

I'm not entirely sure H knows the Glinda outfit is a costume.

Lana and I end up squished together in the center of the six-way hug and whisper together, "Sisters."

After a beat of sentimentality, Aunt April peels off from the group and looks at her phone. "We need to leave right now if we're going to get Her Highness to LA on time. Time to move, move, *MOVE!*"

Her Highness laughs. "I like your moxie. We're going to have fun working—"

"Now!" Aunt April shouts, and we all disperse.

Lana whispers to me, "Better H than me. I am *not* going to miss all that shouting."

"Even though I'm not singing, if you need me to ride along with your mom, I understand," I say. "Your relationship with her is more important than the Starlight's reopening."

"Are you kidding?" Lana says. "You're so close to everything you've worked really hard for. No way are either of us missing this!"

Aunt April is investigating the convertible. "Is there anything we need to know about the car?"

"Just that *I'll* be driving you to LA," Aunt May says, gathering up her skirt and twisting it into a knot. "This is too close to a spontaneous road trip for me to *not* come along."

Aunt April looks at my mom. "June, what do you think?"

"My book group will hate me." My mom looks at her sisters. "But far be it from me to break a pact I signed almost thirty years ago."

Aunt May punches one fist in the air and calls out, "*Road Trip!!*"

"Let's get Elvis cued up in case May gets us pulled over again," Aunt April says.

"*You're* the one who was speeding," Aunt May says. "I didn't even drive the last road trip since I'd lost my license for . . ." She looks at Lana and me.—"Reasons."

Lana and I look at each other and my mom leans down to whisper to Lana, "She was a *scofflaw.*"

"A scofflaw?" Lana sounds scandalized.

"Unpaid parking tickets," I explain, and Lana nods.

"I'm so excited," Aunt May says as she climbs behind the wheel.

My mom says, "I didn't even realize how much I've missed you guys." Her eyes are shining. "April, I'm so sorry I had no idea you were struggling to find work. We need to *share* each other's burdens."

Aunt April snaps. "I am going to share my burdens right on your heinie if we don't get moving now, now, *now*! Let's go! I have a client and I need to get her to a very important venue!"

Aunt May says, "And she's back, folks—our sister April."

My mom slides into middle front seat of the Skylark and Her Highness jumps in the back. The Chihuahua climbs along the front headrest so she can investigate H's tiara. Her Highness immediately picks up Z and begins to snap delighted selfies of the two of them together in the back of the pink convertible.

Aunt April looks at me and Lana. "That's a big back seat. You girls coming?"

"We'll catch the next wild road trip," Lana says. "We have a drive-in celebration to help with tonight." She looks at me. "And it's really important, *to both of us.*"

I grin at her.

Aunt April jumps into the car and we move out of the way and start waving goodbye.

"*Road trip!*" Her Highness shouts gleefully.

"Bye, Miss Highness," I say. "Good luck!"

"Wait one second," HH says as she rifles in her bedazzled duffel. "Ah yes, here." She leans out of the convertible to hand me a folded-up silk robe with a smooth ribbon around it. "A parting gift. Your sacrifice shall be remembered."

"Um, thanks?" I say.

Lana snatches it from my hands and hugs it to herself. "One of your signature robes!" She points to the double *H* logo. One of the *H*s is wearing a tiny tiara.

Lana looks delighted and so I try to match her enthusiasm.

"It was a promo gift at a Sephoxie opening, no biggie," Her Highness says with a wave of her long fingers. "We're truly sisters now. Thanks for sharing all your moms."

"Good luck with the drive-in, honey," my mom says to Lana. "You can drive my car home."

"Bye, Mom. Have fun!" Lana calls, and my mom throws her the keys to the minivan.

"*Great.*" Lana shakes the keys at me. "Trade you rides?"

"What, and give up the chance to drive a ten-year-old tan RAV4?" We laugh at how utterly downgraded our wheels just got and watch with longing as the cotton-candy pink Skylark convertible pulls away from us.

"Stay out of trouble now," I call, and everyone laughs.

Lana adds, "And *be beautiful—to each other.*" I give her a shove at her phony channel sign-off and she defends, "What? I'm keeping the tagline. It's a great sentiment, when you mean it."

I watch my mom put an arm around each of her sisters from the middle seat and tell Lana, "I guess it's not the worst."

Her Highness screams out, "Onward, pink chariot—these fabulous four sisters are ready to take on the open road." Zelda gives a yap and H picks her up to face the wind. "Sorry, I mean five—*five* sassy sisters off to conquer LA!"

Aunt May peels out, kicking up drive-in dust, but when they reach the front ticket booth, the Skylark screeches to a halt.

Lana and I look at each other and start running toward the booth, afraid something's wrong.

We watch as Wes leans out toward the car. Aunt May pulls off her crown, jumps up, grabs the front of his T-shirt, and drags him toward her for a long kiss.

Her sisters whistle and *woo!* loudly.

Aunt May slaps at them as she sits back down in the car. Then she turns and gives high fives all around. I check the sky and see some early stars showing through the pre-twilight.

Zelda gives an approving yap, and with an engine rev and a cloud of sparkly dust, they're off.

Lana and I stand side by side, waving until long after the Skylark is out of sight.

We turn toward each other and I give a huge smile. "That went great," I say.

"Yup," Lana says. "Except that we probably just waved good-bye to any possibility of us switching back tonight."

"Oh." My smile drops. "The Skylark. You're probably right," I say. "Guess we should've helped our moms reconnect over the pink convertible some other time."

"No, this was good," Lana says. "Her Highness deserves the break and my mom is going to do an *epic* job as her manager."

"I guess today wasn't really about us after all," I say.

"Today has been *awful*," Lana says, "but I can't say I haven't had fun. Because of you."

We bump shoulders and smile at each other. "I'm glad we're back to us," I say.

"But wait," Lana says. "We didn't even figure out *costumes* for tonight. Dressing up was supposed to be one of the best parts of this grand reopening."

Looking at the HH Bathrobe™ Lana is hugging, I look toward my backpack still sitting by the swing set and feel an impish expression cross my face. "Actually, I think I have a really good idea."

chapter 27

The Starlight is starting to buzz with costumed volunteers and early customers, and the bouncy castle has come alive, rocking and twitching from little ones jumping inside.

"Hey, Wes," I call as Lana and I approach the front ticket booth. Wes gives us a big wave, which one of the wolf dogs takes as a command to jump up and give a full-body hug. Wes disappears from sight for a moment.

He pops back up with a grunt. "Welcome to the Starlight drive-in grand reopening!"

We laugh. "I may not be a fan of Zelda," I say, "but at least she forced the wolf dogs to keep four paws on the floor at all times."

"Your aunt asked me to watch the boys until she gets back." Wes grins.

"Um, congratulations?" Lana says.

"Nice wolf-wrangler costume," I say, pointing to the cowboy hat he's wearing.

"Thanks." He tips his hat at me. "Butch Cassidy, pleased to meet you. What are you girls dressing up as?"

"It's a surprise," Lana says.

"We don't want to take over the bathroom to get our costumes on," I say. "So do you mind if we use your office to get ready?" I gesture to the backpack I'm wearing on my shoulder.

"That's fine, Lana," he says to me. "Just please keep Ricki from dressing too scary."

"You got it," I say, and then mash all my words together as I start striding away. "We'll also need to borrow some of the first aid backup supplies you keep in your office okay great thanks."

Lana runs to catch up to me. I don't break my stride as I point to one of my bedazzled flip-flops and ask, "What size shoe do you wear?"

"Eight, eight and a half, why?"

"That can work," I say. "Let's go grab your makeup kit from your mom's car."

"Hopefully she didn't slip it into the trunk of the Skylark when we weren't looking," Lana says.

When we peek through the windows of the RAV4 and spot the pink tackle box sitting neatly in the back seat, the two of us celebrate with one of our complicated hand slap routines, ending in a high five.

Lana opens the door to grab it and I hear a smooth, "Hey, good looking," come from behind me. "Wanna go to the movies?"

I turn quickly and see Erik leaning out the passenger window of Jake's red Bronco.

Jake sits beside him, dressed as a very authentic-looking classic Wolf Man.

"Great costume, Jake," I say with a grin, and Erik waves a hand in front of my face, making me realize I'm staring at Jake's Wolf Man with open adoration in front of my supposed boyfriend, who recently risked his life for me before publicly declaring his love.

"Oh, sorry, Erik," I say. "So glad you got out of the mall in one piece."

He laughs. "It was a little touch and go there for a while—those meet and greets can get *intense*."

"Tell me about it," I say.

"This guy here came and rescued me." Erik gives Jake a pat on the back. "I owe Chewbacca big time."

"Wolf Man," Jake and I correct in unison.

I'm openly crushing on Jake again and call to Lana, "Hey, cuz. Check out the guys' costumes."

Lana steps up beside me and I hold out an arm like a spokesmodel and gush, "May I present the Wolf Man and, er, Erik, *sweetie*? Who are you dressed as?"

Erik runs a hand through his slicked-back hair and smooths down his black T-shirt. "I'm Danny Zuko from *Grease*." Erik grins. "This was totally last-minute." He points to Jake, who looks super uncomfortable in his full fur regalia. "Not like *this* guy."

"Wow, Jake," Lana says. "You really went *all out*."

Jake gives a small nod. "Yeah, heh. Feel a little silly now."

"No, it's perfect!" I practically shout, and everyone looks at me. "I mean, doesn't he look just perfect, Ricki?"

Lana looks at him. "Your costume is totally . . . *elaborate*." She whispers to me, "That is *so much* hair."

"Just wait until you see *our* costumes," I say. "Erik, honey, you're going to wish you'd put in a bit more effort."

"Yeah, well, I had to post a video explaining why I'm not going to be at Digi," he says. "So I ran out of time."

"Plus, of course you were a prince rescuing Lana from the mall," Lana says, meeting Erik's gaze. "You sure you don't mind missing Digi?"

"Happy to ditch," he says. "I'd do anything for your cousin."

I move between them. "Well, I'm thrilled that we're *all* here, but Ricki and I better start getting ready."

"Right!" Lana shuts down the flirty exchange with her boyfriend, holds up her tackle box of makeup, and the two of us turn to go.

"Wait, Lana." Erik jumps out of the Bronco and catches me by the arm. "How did your mom take the news about you missing Digifest?"

I look at Lana and she grins. "It all worked out," I say. "I ended up giving my performance slot to Her Highness."

"*Plus* our cool car," Lana says, "and our moms too, I guess, huh, Lana?"

"What?" Erik says, "I thought you and H were sworn enemies."

Lana says, "Never underestimate girls' power to bond over a common obsession."

Erik looks at me and I shrug.

"We both like makeup," I say. "Plus, I was feeling generous because I finally told my mom I'm quitting my channel."

Erik gives a whoop and grabs me and spins me around. "I'm so proud of you," he says.

I laugh and go with it. "I'm proud of me too!"

As Erik spins me, a Princess Leia lookalike catches my eye and I take in the fun costumes on display all around us. We have everything from Beetlejuice to Zoolander, to *Pretty in Pink*'s

Andie and Duckie. There's even an actual DeLorean parked near the front, made up to look like a time machine.

I marvel at the number of volunteers who have come, some with children. People who believe in this place. Families that are here to build memories together.

When Erik finally puts me down I call to Jake inside the Bronco, "I was thinking maybe Ricki and I can do a little face painting for the kids."

"That's an amazing idea," Jake calls back. "The children are going to have so much fun tonight."

"Oh yes we are," Erik says, and we all laugh.

A guy in a trench coat crosses between us with a boom box held high over his head and Jake asks, "What movie characters are you two dressing up as?"

I grin. "It's a surprise."

"That's right," Lana says. "Just wait until you two see how we're dressing up."

Everything shifts to perfection as Lana and I turn and confidently walk together down the long center aisle of the Starlight's parking lot. Each carrying our precious makeup supplies with us. Hers *glamour*. Mine *gore*.

Lana whispers to me, "So, how *are* we dressing up, anyway?"

I laugh. "I promise you. It's going to be *epic*."

Lana gives a happy gasp. "You used my word."

"Yes, Lana," I say, "*epic-ness* is guaranteed."

• • •

Despite rushing as fast as I can, it takes us over a half hour to get ready, and it's getting close to twilight by the time we come strutting out of the back room to reveal our costumes.

Jake and Erik are standing behind the snack counter together, getting the hot dogs cooking on the rollers when we step up behind them. Jake is wearing a hairnet over the head of his Wolf Man costume. It's so adorable I feel myself falling the rest of the way in love with him.

Lana clears her throat and the boys both spin around at the same time.

"*Aargh!*" Erik clutches his chest. "You two scared me," he chastises.

Jake says, "Great costumes, guys, but sorry, employees only behind the counter."

"Employees?" Erik looks at him. "Really? So, I'm getting *paid*?"

"Oh. No, sorry, I meant . . ."

"Kidding!" Erik says. "Man, are you an easy mark. So gullible."

"Guys!" I say. "It's us!"

The two of them turn back around, and this time they take a moment to look us up and down.

Finally, Jake says, "No way! Those costumes are amazing."

"Wait." Erik looks confused. "Who's who?"

My grin presses against the bandages around my mouth. My plan is working perfectly.

I wave my hand. "Ricki here," I say, stumbling forward in the heels Lana has been wearing all day. But it's fine that I seem stiff since I'm dressed as the Mummy. Stiffness is expected.

Also, it's perfectly natural that I'm wrapped in grungy gauze from head to toe and wearing white contacts over my brown eyes.

Lana stands beside me, completely covered in Ace bandages,

except instead of distressing her dressings with coffee grains and fake blood like mine, we've left hers clean and smooth.

She's also wearing dark sunglasses, a pair of Wes's old slippers from his office, and the signature robe Her Highness gave to us.

Erik runs a hand through his hair, trying to slick it back. It's clear his costume is the worst one here. "Who are you supposed to be, Lana?"

"She's *the Invisible Man*," Jake and I say in unison, and then laugh.

I say, "From the 1933 classic film."

"I usually prefer super cute costumes," she says. "But I thought 'going invisible' would be nice and symbolic to celebrate me stepping away from BubeTube."

In actuality, the whole time we were getting ready she kept stopping to wail, "I can't believe we're not dressing up *cu-u-ute*."

"I'm so happy you're taking care of yourself, Lana. You are so precious." Erik moves in close to her and pauses. "Boy, that costume makes you seem taller."

Lana points a toe of her retro men's slippers and says, "Lifts," while simultaneously pretending to stumble into Erik by accident. It's the perfect distraction. Heroically, he reaches out to catch her and she falls into his arms so neatly it seems choreographed.

"Wow," Erik says as he struggles to adjust to catching my weight instead of Lana's, "that robe must be made of lead."

"Hey," I say. "*Rude*," but Lana just gives a flirty laugh.

"Silk is so *heavy*," she says. "Plus, I have bricks in my pockets."

"What?" Erik raises an eyebrow.

"Bricks of *color*," she says. "Look."

Lana pulls out stacks of makeup palettes from each deep pocket of her robe.

I say, "For face painting the kids."

"You guys are the best," Jake says. "And thank you." He gestures to our costumes. "I was starting to feel like the only freak who loves any excuse to dress up like a classic horror film character."

"This is so much fun!" I say, "I think we may need to find a Classic Monster Cosplay Con."

"Or start one." Jake's eyes smile at me through his wolf makeup, and it feels really good to have him look at me like I'm *me* again.

"Half man. Half wolf. Compelled by a hideous curse!" I say with a flirty tone. "How's that dual personality working out for you?"

"Hey, I'm not the only one here having an identity crisis." Jake laughs as he gestures to me. "Are you dead? Are you alive? You need to decide."

The two of us stand, our faces obscured, but our eyes locked for a long moment. And despite the white contacts and the layers of gauze I'm wrapped in, my heart feels ready to be exposed too.

Finally, Lana says, "It's getting late. Ricki will make a face painting sign and I'll set up the paint station on the picnic table over by the bouncy castle."

"Thanks, Lana," Jake says. "Glad to have you helping out. The turnout is already looking *really* amazing."

I'm so excited. "We did a *fantastic* job," I say. "And Jake, I've had the time of my life working with you to make tonight happen." I wish I could unfurl the bandages from my face and kiss his furry lips right now.

"Yeah, it's been . . . great." Jake glances at Lana, and my mind rolls through all the times I flirted with him by accident today while he thought I was her. I wince.

"We'd better finish setting up the snack counter," Erik says. "Inspect the place for any stray motorized mice before the hungry mob hits." He smiles at Lana and she dips her chin in a way that would probably look fetching if her head wasn't completely wrapped in Ace bandages.

I'm impressed that she's managed to act flirty with such an unconventional costume. I can only imagine what she could accomplish dressed up in something somewhat cute.

She and I turn to start walking away and Lana slows her stride to match my uneven, wobbly steps.

"Nice and authentic, Ricki," Jake calls after us.

I turn with my arms out and give a deep, creepy, "*Mmmmoohh!*" while taking a few stiff mummy steps.

Jake responds by aiming his furry face toward the ceiling and sounding a loud, "*Arrrroooooo!*"

"Well, it's clear you two are made for each other," Lana says while guiding me toward the glass doors. Leaning close to my ear she hisses, "It looks like the boys are buying it."

We shuffle through the puddle of glitter that's worked its way from the threshold of the concession stand throughout the entire drive-in. I say, "Now we just need to hope we switch back before the night ends."

Lana says, "You mean you don't love this so much you want to keep it up for the rest of the summer? Heck, Halloween is only five and a half months away."

"If we don't switch back, Halloween will be the next time we can hang out with our boyfriends as ourselves," I say. "That is, if Jake ever becomes my boyfriend."

My ankle gives an awkward twist and I grab on to Lana, and the two of us stumble toward the picnic tables beside the bounce house. A man recoils in horror at the sight of us and holds a protective arm in front of his girlfriend as we pass by.

Lana mumbles, "I really wish we could've dressed cute."

● ● ●

Daylight is barely hanging on as we work our way through the never-ending line of kids thrilled to be getting their faces painted.

A little boy I've just finished painting says, "Thank you," in his cute little boy voice as he picks up the hand mirror from the table. With a smile, he holds it up to get a look at his reflection.

And immediately begins screaming at the sight of his own face.

Lana looks up from the fresh unicorn she's drawn on the cheek of the princess beside her and joins the small boy's screams. "What are you doing, Ricki?"

"You know." I gesture to the kid who's now crying inconsolably. "Painting faces."

"Why would you paint anything that scary on a child?"

I look at the little boy with oozing wounds across his adorable cheeks and say, "He said he wanted to be a Ninja Turtle and, well, I don't know how to do one of those. So I made him another movie character who lives in the sewer."

"You made him into . . . Who is he even supposed to be?"

I smile and pull up the hood on the kid's yellow sweatshirt.

"See?" I say. "Now he just needs to go get a red balloon from the volunteers handing them out and he's Georgie from *It*."

"Seriously?" Even with her face bandaged, Lana puts a hand up to hide her smile. "Ricki, you're the worst."

"It feels good to be called Ricki again," I say.

"Are you okay?" she asks the boy as she wipes his tears.

"I *told* Mommy I didn't want her to do my Ninja Turtle," he says, pointing to me. "And I was right!"

"But isn't getting to be right kind of wonderful too?" Lana asks.

The kid blinks at her a few times. "I want a balloon."

"Go ahead," Lana says, pointing to where a volunteer is handing them out. She adds with a giggle, "Make sure you get a *red* one."

"Tell your mommy, 'I told you so,'" I say as he stands to leave. "Also, see if she can fold you an origami boat."

He runs away, and Lana reaches across the table to slap my arm. I tell her, "This is fun."

She says, "The goal is not to send all these kids into therapy."

Our line is steady, and Lana and I have a great time painting faces for almost an hour straight. A few cool youngsters are even into the blood and gore I'm serving.

Two brown-haired *pre*-preteen girls keep whispering to each other as they wait in line. When they finally sit down to have their faces painted at the same time Lana asks, "Are you two sisters?"

The girls launch into a fit of giggles at this, and the one in Lana's seat says, "I love it when people ask that!"

"Our parents are best friends," my girl says. "So, we're basically like *cousins*."

Lana turns her sunglasses my direction. "This is my *actual* cousin, Ricki, and we used to tell people we were *sisters* when we were your age."

"Wow," one of the girls says. "Did people believe you?"

"Nope," Lana says. "Underneath all of these bandages we look nothing alike."

I say, "Boy, do I ever wish we had two blue baby doll dresses for you girls to wear right now. You'd be perfect as the Grady twins from *The Shining*."

They look at each other and look back at me with furrowed brows.

"Don't tell me you two haven't seen *The Shining*?" I turn and say to Lana, "What are they teaching these kids today?"

"They're like, seven, Ricki," Lana says, and turns to them. "Never mind her. What movie characters would you two like to be made up as?"

"That's the problem," my girl says. "We can't agree."

"I want us to both be Disney princesses," Lana's girl says. "But *she'd* rather be something gross, like a monster or Harley Quinn."

"Harley Quinn isn't gross," I say. "And I can use pink and blue shadow to color your hair." I scoop my girl's hair up into two pigtails. "Just need to do your eyes and lips all crazy and write *rotten* across your right cheek."

"That's not going to look cute," Lana's girl says.

Lana laughs. "I hear you." She leans down and asks her girl, "Which princess would you like to be?"

"Well, I really wanted us to be Anna and Elsa from *Frozen*, but now I don't know who to be." She crosses her arms and slumps her shoulders.

"I understand," Lana says. "Sometimes we don't know who we are when we feel abandoned by the people we love. It can be *really* hard to feel so alone."

The girl looks at Lana for a beat and says, "Yeah, I'll just be Elsa."

I hold a long, rubber scar up to my girl's face and ask, "Would you like your Harley a little extra-scary?"

She grins up at me. "Yes, please."

Lana and I clean our brushes and get to work on their faces. The two of us work smoothly in sync, sharing colors and trading brushes without needing to say a word.

After a while I say, "You know, girls, staying close as you get older isn't always easy."

"True," Lana says. "Communication is really important."

"Crucial, really," I say. "Like, don't hide how you're feeling from each other, because how can you help each other if you don't share what's going on?"

Lana has stopped making up her princess and is looking at me. "And don't ignore problems. Clearing the air can be a good thing."

I say, "Fighting can be ugly and painful sometimes, but it means at least you're trying. And arguing with each other is so much better than totally cutting each other out of your lives."

I look down and realize the two girls are watching us with horrified expressions.

"We just wanted our faces painted," Lana's Elsa says. "We could never ever, *ever* stop being friends."

"I love you, bestie," the girl in my chair says, and she leans over to hug her little friend.

Elsa hugs her friend back and says, "I love you too. This is going to be such a fun night!"

"Is my Harley Quinn almost done?" my girl asks with a grin, and I realize I've made her a little over-the-top creepy with the cuts on her face and undead-looking eyes.

"Er, sure, I think we're finished here," I say.

"Can I see?" She points to the hand mirror sitting face down on the table.

I say, "That mirror's broken."

The girls look at each other and smile. Harley tells Elsa, "You look beautiful!"

"Oh wow. You look so *scary*," Elsa says, then smiles. "You're going to *love* it!"

The two of them actually hold hands as they run off to find their parents, and when I turn back I feel Lana's hand in mine.

"Do they remind you of anyone?" she asks.

I laugh. "Just a little." I look at my cousin. "You know I'll always have your back, right?"

"Ha," she says. "*Literally*! Get it? Because you have my back and I have yours."

"Too soon," I say and give her a playful shove.

Lana laughs and then stops and looks at me a moment before lunging in for a hug.

I catch her with a grunt and wrap my arms around her. We rock back and forth a few times.

Lana says, "Besties?"

And I whisper back, "Always."

Lana lets out a shaking sigh and I half expect us to change back. But when we separate I stumble a bit on my high heels and know that nothing has changed. Even though truly, *it has*.

I feel a tap on my shoulder and turn around to see Wes standing behind me in his cowboy hat.

"Hey, Ricki?" he says and then looks back and forth between Lana and me. "You are Ricki, right?"

"Yup, I'm the Mummy," I say, pantomiming a straight-armed grope as I give a few half-hearted *Mmmmooh*s. "Lana's the Invisible Man."

Wes says, "First of all, I really want to thank you both for doing this face painting today. Really. So great. But see . . ." Wes doesn't seem to know how to finish what he's trying to say.

Lana cuts in, "Ricki's been doing all the gory-looking ones."

"I *knew* it," he says. "Seriously, Ricki, you need to *stop*."

"What? I think everyone looks great." I look around and see that there are several ghoulish children crying hysterically with mothers swiping at scars and oozing sores. "They were already crying like that before I did their makeup."

Wes points and says, "That kid you turned into little Georgie from *It* is pretty upset."

"*That* kid? He's barely even made up," I say. "What I really wanted to do was tuck in one arm and make his loose sleeve all bloody. Now *that* would've been a good Georgie."

Lana and Wes just look at me for a few beats.

Finally, Lana says, "Sorry, Wes. I tried to make her stop."

He sighs. "Anyway, I really need to talk to you, Ricki." He gestures toward the snack stand. "Privately?"

I stay sitting. "If this about the face painting, I've just run out of fake blood, so I think we're good here."

"No, there was one other thing." Wes sounds uncomfortable,

which is not at all like him. "I have Jake managing the ticket booth. Can we maybe go talk in my office?"

"I've got this," Lana tells me, gesturing to the small line of children still waiting. "And don't worry, Wes. I only do cheery face paintings." She points to a boy with a Captain America shield on one cheek and adds, "Superheroes are my specialty."

I stand and take a few shaky strides in my heels. "All set," I say, "Aaand if you don't mind, I'll just stay completely in character, cool?"

"You're acting so strange today, Ricki. Even for you," Wes says as he slows his pace down to match my wobbly one. "And that's saying something."

"Oh, I am aware," I say as I focus on not falling.

The outdoor lights switch on, signaling it's getting close to movie time, and I'm grateful for the extra light, but feel like time is moving so much faster than I can shamble along.

chapter 28

I manage to teeter the whole way to the concession shack with Wes. Once there, I use the countertop to help me stay upright as I drag myself along, hand over hand, making my way to the back. Finally, I find myself clutching the door handle to Wes's office.

"Wait!" Wes shouts too late. "*It's booby-trapped!*" I hear him just as the door pops open, and I wince in anticipation of more glitter. Instead, I'm immersed in furry full-body slams from my aunt's three wolf dogs.

They knock me to the ground, thanking me for releasing them by licking my face until they're dangerously close to exposing my identity.

Instinctively, I reach up and begin massaging the closest wolf's ears. The giant dog gradually rolls onto his back and gives a happy grunt.

Moving quickly, I manage to subdue the other two dogs before my Lana face is uncovered. With three dogs and only two hands, it's a bit like playing a game of whack-a-mole.

"That's amazing," Wes says, "it totally blisses them out." He drops to his knees to help me massage pointy ears.

"Was this what you needed help with?" I ask as we continue to sit on the ground with the docile wolves.

"Not exactly. You see . . ." Wes opens his mouth as if he's about to say something, then closes it, reconsiders, and tries again.

Mutely, I watch him struggle to find words, and a fear begins to grow in my chest. "Are you accepting the MegaMart offer from that real estate guy?" I ask through the lump in my throat.

"What?" He sounds surprised. "No, that's silly. Folks have been after me to list this property for *years*. People who only care about money, and that guy is the worst one yet. Can you believe he had the nerve to go ahead and find a buyer without my okay? And then to come in here badgering me right when we're in the middle of an *outstanding* reopening. I mean, obviously MegaMart is offering a *lot* of money . . ."

"So then what *did* you want to talk about, Wes?" I cut him off before he realizes "a *lot* of money" may be too much to pass up.

"It's about your aunt," Wes says and then looks at me. "Those white eyes are freaking me out, Ricki. Can you maybe lose the contacts while we talk?"

I think about Lana's blue irises underneath these contacts. "Sorry, I forgot contact solution. What do you need to ask me about my aunt?"

Wes blushes. "I was kind of wondering if May is, er . . . free? I mean, not *free*, but available?" He sighs. "I don't normally do relationships, but Ricki, I really like your aunt May."

"Well, based on that drive-by kiss I saw her give you earlier, I'd say you're in."

"Oh, you saw that, huh?" Wes gives a bright smile. "Yeah, I mean I know we like each other and all, I'm just thinking I might be ready for, you know . . . like, if she might be open to a just her and me for good sort of thing."

"I have never seen you so uncomfortable, Wes," I say. "It's nice. And hey, look, you're already bonding with her wolf babies and that's a really big step."

"Yes!" He grins and leans down to give a belly rub to one of the dogs. He's immediately whacked in the head with a giant paw that knocks off his hat. Wes laughs as he places his hat on the desk. One of the pups instantly accepts it as a gift and sniffs the inside thoroughly before moving on to chew the brim.

I ease the hat out of the dog's mouth before he can do too much damage.

"Well, if you're asking for my blessing to date my aunt, you've got it," I say. "In fact, I wish you luck because you both happen to be two of my favorite people."

Wes rubs some of the slobber off the brim and puts his hat back on his head.

"I may need every bit of that luck," he says. "Remember how you and I were discussing whether or not she was avoiding me earlier today?"

"She wasn't, I told you," I say. "And look at the amazing pendant she was busy making you."

Wes wraps his hand around the twinkling blue stone at his chest and takes a deep breath. "But that's the thing," he says. "Tonight's movie was supposed to be our first date and a really big deal. And now here I am, with *The Wizard of Oz* all cued up as a special after-the-movie movie surprise, and here she is, well, *not* here." He lets the pendant drop to his shirt. "I'm really worried about her deciding to take off for LA just now—does she know I'm serious?"

I think a minute and then shake my head. "If you under-stood the bond that my aunts and my mom have, you'd know that she *had* to go with them. No matter what. My aunt April is going through some stuff and needed the support."

"So, you think I might have a shot with May? For, like, some-thing real?" Wes pulls at the hem of his shirt.

"Here's the thing about my aunt," I say. "First of all, May is amazing. She's the most unique and creative and *generous* per-son I know. She will make you see nature though a new lens of beauty, and I can promise she'll make you belly laugh at least once every single day. She is absolutely worth loving."

Wes says, "I can see all that in her. It sounds like you were about to say 'but.'"

"I was just going to add that there are no guarantees. There are reasons the both of you have gotten to this point in your lives single, and you're each a bit set in your ways."

His face falls.

"But that doesn't mean you shouldn't pursue this!" I say. "If I *guaranteed* she would say yes to a real relationship with you, that would be cheating. Fear of rejection is part of the journey."

Wes says, "Rejection is the worst."

"I totally agree," I say. "But someone special recently told me that getting rejected means you tried something that you weren't sure you could do. And that's a pretty cool way to look at it."

Wes's eyes light up. "So, you really think I should go for it?"

"Yes, I do." I give the brim of his hat a playful tug. "But you'll have to ask her all this yourself because, Wes, this is not high school."

"Don't kid yourself, Ricki." Wes straightens his hat. "The whole world is high school."

I laugh. Wes puts a hand on my shoulder and I steady myself by putting one back on his.

He says, "I want you to know I'm really grateful for all the work you and Jake have put into saving the Starlight. You two jumped in right when I was starting to run a little low on hope for this place and it truly means a lot."

"We've loved every minute," I say. "This drive-in is incredible."

"Yes, it is," he says. "And so are the two of you." He pauses a moment. "Can I ask why you've been avoiding Jake today?"

"Wow, *Uncle* Wes, feel free to barge right into my business."

"Sorry," he says. "It's just that you don't run a drive-in for as many years as I have without developing a knack for spotting couples in love. I've been watching you two for a while now, and today was kind of hard to witness."

"It's complicated," I say. "But I haven't been avoiding Jake."

"You told him to meet you in the bouncy castle and then drove off in that crazy pink convertible with your cousin's boyfriend," Wes says. "Poor kid looked crushed."

"You don't understand," I say. "That wasn't really me."

"Well, it sure looked like you," Wes says. "And anyway, that wasn't the first time I saw that crushed look on Jake's face. Am I wrong about you liking him?"

"That's not . . ." I start, and then try again. "I was waiting for . . ."

"Waiting for what?" Wes raises one eyebrow.

"Fine!" I growl. "I was waiting for a Magical Starlight First Kiss Under the Stars. There, I said it. To my boss."

Wes laughs so hard the dogs all rush to his face to check on him. He pushes them away and says, "Holding out for one of those magic Starlight kisses, huh? You know who came up with that legend?"

I keep my white mummy eyes turned on him, but he just grins and nods. "Seriously?" I say. "It was *you*?"

Wes tips his hat to me. "Turns out, it's easier to start an urban legend than you'd think. Just tell a few folks a success story or two using specific examples. Make up a catchy slogan to put in your ads, and voilà: A Kiss Under the Stars at the Starlight turns magic. Next thing you know, we're all wearing the T-shirts."

"But wait," I say, "what about all the people who were still together after sharing their first magical kiss here? I talked to some of them. Still totally in love after *years*. The magic works!"

"There are actually two explanations for that," Wes says. "First, I believe that going to the drive-in together is a pretty kick-butt way of getting to know someone and starting off a relationship. The Starlight does get folks going on the right foot."

"Okay, so that's definitely true," I say. "What's the other reason?"

"Well, did you really interview *everyone* who ever shared their first kiss here?" Wes laughs. "Or were you only talking to the long-term couples *because* they were still together?"

"Oh," I say. "I guess you're right."

"I told you about all the people who came to the drive-in while dating, then eventually got married and brought their children here," Wes says. "But trust me, I could give plenty of examples of folks who came with different dates for years and never made a lasting connection with any of them."

"That's sad," I say.

"I've seen plenty of couples fighting and leaving early over the years too," he says. "The magic of the drive-in is really all about who you share the experience with."

"It's still magic though, right?" I try to sound positive, but my voice cracks and gives me away. "With the right person?"

"Absolutely, Ricki," Wes says. "I didn't mean to make you lose faith."

"But I really may have ruined things with Jake already," I whine pitifully.

Wes says, "You *just* told me that fear of rejection is part of the journey."

"But that was when I was talking about *you* and *your* love life."

Wes laughs, and I gradually join in. He puts a hand on my shoulder and says, "Well, it's my turn to take over the front booth. Jake will be freed up if you want to spend some time with him."

"I do," I say. "I just wish I was feeling more myself tonight."

"It's up to you, but the movie starts soon," Wes says. "Whether you're ready for it or not."

"Let's go," I say and begin hobbling along in my heels.

I put my arms out and give a few groans to really sell it, and Wes shakes his head and laughs as he ushers me out the door. The three wolf dogs fall into formation as Wes and I make our way out of the building and across the drive-in lot.

Lana has finished painting faces and I spot her leading Erik into the bouncy castle. I marvel that she is willing to risk her heart with someone so reckless. But then Erik seems worth it. He really does love her, and whatever happens with their relationship, I'll be here for her. She and I make each other brave. And I'm glad she's back in my life for good.

We pass a couple dressed as Mia Wallace and Vincent Vega, dancing together beside their car, and my cousin's giggles ring out across the sparkling lot.

I look up at the stars poking through the darkening sky. "Here they come," I say quietly.

"What's that?" Wes asks.

"The magical stars," I say. "I'm choosing to believe."

"Yes. It's a pretty great night." Wes rubs the ear of the wolf dog closest to him and snickers. "And don't the five of us make quite the pack."

To all of the people in their cars getting ready to watch the movie, we probably look pretty awesome. Butch Cassidy and the Mummy just passing through, surrounded by three giant wolves.

Who would ever guess that Wes and I are both cowards when it comes to love, and that the three dogs at our sides are obsessively scanning the landscape for the one thing they're truly frightened of: a three-pound Chihuahua no bigger than a teacup.

I rub the head of the closest dog and whisper to him, "You've got this." Looking up I see Jake's silhouette in the ticket booth window and think, *We've got this.*

● ● ●

Wes and I arrive at the front booth just as two guys dressed like zombies pull up in a Mercedes and stop outside the window to buy tickets.

"Whoa, classic," the driver says when he sees Jake and me. "The Wolf Man and the Mummy!"

His friend in the passenger seat adds, "Noice."

"You guys look great too," I tell them as Jake takes the credit card the driver hands him.

"I'm a zombie from *Z*," he tells me.

His passenger says, "And I'm a *Night of the Living Dead* zombie."

Jake laughs. "Well, I think we've already got zombies from *Zombieland* and *Warm Bodies*, so it sounds like you two are just in time." He hands back the card with their tickets.

I say, "And here's a free popcorn coupon for coming dressed as your favorite movie characters tonight."

"Keep the coupon, we're here to *spend*," the driver zombie says.

"Tonight is all about saving this adorably timeless drive-in!" The passenger zombie gives the driver a sharp high five.

"We're huge fans of Erik's channel and cannot *wait* to see what prank he has planned for tonight."

"A *prank*?" I look at Jake.

"It's a surprise," Jake says as we watch the cross-film zombie duo pull away.

"Wait, so you *know* about Erik's plan?" I say. "Is he pranking me or Lana? Holy cow, is he pranking *all* these people? What on earth is he up to?"

"Wes?" Jake says. "I think it's time."

"Already made the call," Wes says. "Should be here any moment."

"Come on, Ricki, you can help me," Jake says.

"What is happening?" I'm starting to get nervous.

Jake takes my hand. "You want to know what the prank is? You can help me do it."

The way Wes looks at me as he rubs one of the wolf dog's ears makes it clear; *this is it*. Time for me to let down my guard and take a risk.

I nod to Wes as I turn to do my mummy-walk after Jake.

He looks back from a few strides ahead and stops to let me catch up. "Nice commitment, Ricki," he says. "But we *actually* need to hurry."

I shuffle a little faster, and Jake slows so we're moving side by side.

A small child isn't looking where he's walking and bumps into Jake's leg. The little boy stops and looks up, leaning back so far it looks like he's going to topple backward.

Jake waves at the little boy and we both hold our breath.

Finally, the boy's face expands into a huge smile. "Hi, dog-gie," he says, and we both sigh in relief.

"Enjoy the movie," I say, and the boy looks over at me and gives the highest-pitched scream of all time. We hurry past as his mother rushes to his side.

"Sorry," Jake tells her.

The two of us start laughing as soon as we're out of earshot. I can't help but think Rick Baker would be proud.

As we continue on, Jake explains to me that Erik posted a cryptic promise on BubeTube at the end of their livestreamed Starlight theater tour.

"He said he's going to be performing a prank here at the drive-in after dark tonight and everyone is welcome to come and witness it firsthand."

He looks around at the lot. Nearly every single space is already filled with cars.

"It definitely didn't hurt our turnout," Jake says.

"I guess we owe him a thank you," I say.

"Well, we *are* thanking him by helping him with the prank," Jake says. "Everyone's watching, so he's staying visible with Lana and we'll execute the prank in private.

We're almost at the projection shack. "So what is this big caper we're pulling?" I ask.

"You're about to see." Jake grins, baring his wolf fangs at me. "I'm so glad we're doing this together, because you're going to love it."

chapter 29

W ow," I say. "Just. Wow."

Jake and I are standing next to each other inside the dimly lit projection booth.

The new equipment Gwen and Brad set up is occupying most of the space, and it is impressive-looking, but I'm staring at something on the ground in front of our feet.

It's a fully inflated, oversized kiddie pool, filled to the top with red Jell-O.

Jake gives the giant pool a kick and the Jell-O jiggles in response. He says, "Perfectly congealed. This stuff is awesome."

"This is *amazing*," I say. "How many gallons of Jell-O are here?"

"It's actually something called Fun Jell," Jake says. "It's this powdered stuff Erik works with for pranks because it makes huge quantities of Jell-O without being boiled."

I bend down to poke it and the Fun Jell gently wiggles back and forth. "I can't believe you guys made so much."

"We used the whole hundred-gallon bag," Jake says. "It's what people use for Jell-O wrestling."

"You want to Jell-O wrestle me?" I ask. "Wait, is this supposed to be for me and Lana?"

"No." Jake laughs. "It's for the *prank*."

"So where is all this Jell-O going?" I ask.

"This whole pool of Fun Jell is going directly into the Property Prince of Doom's trunk."

I cover my mouth bandage with both hands. "You were right. I do love it!" I say. "Wes was just telling me what a lowlife that guy is."

"Here, get an end," Jake says, gesturing to one side of the kiddie pool. "We need to dump this into his trunk so I can get back here in time to start the movie."

I toddle over. I'm getting better at walking in the heels, but I'm concerned I won't be able to keep my balance while helping to carry such a massive load. When I test the weight I find that either Fun Jell is lighter than it looks or Lana is stronger than she looks, because I have very little trouble lifting the pool waist high. Still, it's awkward to carry while walking in these shoes.

"When did you and Erik mix this up?" I ask. "And I mean the plan as well as the Fun Jell."

With a grunt, Jake walks backward, and I follow him out the double-wide door of the projection room. "When Erik brought the bounce house, he originally planned to try filling it with Fun Jell as a new stunt to film."

"Erik has some fun ideas," I say. "But I don't think Wes would've approved."

"Agreed," Jake says as we continue moving out the door with the jiggling pool. "That's the sort of thing that I'd love to *watch* but have no desire to *experience*."

I laugh. "This stuff looks super messy."

"It doesn't even smell or taste good," Jake confirms. "But

when Erik told me about his plan, it clicked in my mind how we could teach our nasty real estate villain a lesson."

"I like how your mind works," I say in admiration.

It's dark enough that Jake and I feel confident leaving the projection booth with our jiggling secret delivery. I'm glad we're dressed up because a) nobody can tell our identity and b) people will just assume we're working for the Starlight, which, technically, we are.

As we slowly make our way around the concession shack with our massive pool, Jake explains how he pretended to need the real estate guy's keys in order to move his car earlier, and then jimmied the trunk so we'll be able to pull a string and release it without the key.

"Erik and I used the hose to fill the pool hours ago, so it's had plenty of time to congeal," Jake says. "And Wes should be distracting Mr. Property Prince of Doom right about now."

We turn the corner and Jake suddenly reverses position so that he's lunging back toward me.

The only problem is, my brain gets the memo that we're changing direction long before my body has time to react and shift my heels into reverse.

The resulting *squish* is the sound of Mummy meeting Fun Jell as we both drop the pool and I fall headfirst into it.

"Aaaaaah." I slip and flail about inside the kiddie pool as I unsuccessfully try to stand up.

The next thing I know, Jake is lifting me by the arm while shushing me and trying not to laugh.

"I am *so* sorry," he says. "Our target must have been getting a jacket or something out of his car. I didn't want him to catch us."

I'm upright, but still kneeling in the pool of red Fun Jell. "I can't even believe that just happened."

I look up at Jake and he flashes his wolf fangs down at me. "You want to pull me into that pool of Fun Jell with you right now, don't you?"

I nod. "I'm calculating what sort of an effect it will have on your Wolf Man fur," I say. "Because you deserve to be jellied, but that costume is perfection."

"It's supposedly washable," Jake says, and with that, he hops right into the kiddie pool beside me. The next thing I know the two of us are half wrestling, half tickling, and mostly just goofing around as we toss handfuls of Fun Jell at each other inside the pool.

A car shines its headlights on us and someone calls out, "Wolf Man versus Mummy!" while a small group of people holding buckets of popcorn stop to watch.

"So much for staying low key," I say to Jake.

"This is actually a pretty great preshow."

We both stop and turn toward each other, out of breath and covered in bandages, fur, and Fun Jell. It's a really great moment, and I rest inside it for a beat before responding to the urge to fake left and spin around so I can jump on Jake's back.

I pump my fist in the air and try to get a chant started: "Mummy! Mummy! Mummy!"

Jake just stands there, completely impervious to my presence on his shoulders. "Um, Ricki? We should really get this Fun Jell where it needs to go."

"Oh, right." I hop down, using Jake's shoulder to steady myself.

We look around at the people watching us, some recording us with their cellphones. Two guys dressed as Bill and Ted give each other a high-five and call out, "Excellent!"

Jake says, "And now this is going to be a little tougher to pull off privately."

The two of us wave awkwardly and a woman dressed as Holly Golightly offers elegant applause. Jake takes my hand and leads me in a theatrical bow. We stand waiting and waving until the crowd realizes we're definitely finished and begins to disperse. I don't mind since we're still holding hands.

Eventually, Jake gives my hand a squeeze and steps out of the pool to check back around the corner.

Moving quickly, he rejoins me and we each grab a pool end. "Let's go," he says. "This is it."

The two of us shuffle our way around the parked cars with our enormous kiddie pool now dripping with Fun Jell. We take speedy little steps down the aisle and stop when Jake hisses, "Here!"

Carefully, we put the jiggling load down on the asphalt behind a black sedan. Jake starts fidgeting with the car's trunk and I pretend I'm not with him as I casually lean on the SUV beside it.

"Hey, you, with the bloody bandages," comes a voice from inside the vehicle I'm resting against. "Do you mind? You're scaring my kids."

"Oh, sorry." I stand up straight. "I'm not actually supposed to be quite this gory," I start to explain. "You see, there was this Jell-O incident . . ."

I gesture to the kiddie pool in front of me, but see that Jake has gotten the trunk open and is leaning down to pick up one end of it.

"How are we going to dump this whole thing in there?" I ask.

"We put a liner inside the pool," Jake says. "It will make it easier, plus, we don't actually want to ruin this guy's trunk and get sued."

"Good idea," I say, and the clear plastic liner definitely makes it easier to lift the Fun Jell up out of the pool, but once it's released from the inflated pool, its jiggly nature is set free and it's much more difficult to control.

"Whoa!" Jake says as a big wave of red Fun Jell runs down my front.

"Seriously?" I hiss.

He looks at me and stifles a laugh. "I guess you didn't look gruesome enough."

I look down to find the Fun Jell is clinging to my front and making it look like my guts are spilling out of my chest. I give Jake a proud shimmy.

Once we've managed to get most of the Fun Jell into our target's trunk, we slam it shut and give each other squishy high fives.

"Excellent," we say jokingly at the same time.

Jake pauses a moment, and the way he is looking at me in the light from one car's headlights makes me check to make sure my bandages are still covering my face. They are.

"Mission accomplished," Jake says, his voice deep.

"I *loved* that." I want to add *I love you*, but instead I simply put a hand on his hairy bicep.

We lean toward each other and Jake looks into my white,

cloudy eyes a moment before shaking his head as if he's just woken up. "I need to go fire up that projector and get the previews started!"

"Yeah, I should probably go get cleaned up." I feel like I'm made of Fun Jell as I look into his Wolf Man face. I want nothing more than to kiss him right now. "Well, good luck . . ."

A voice comes from behind me. "Hey! What are you monsters doing by my car?"

It's the real estate villain, and Jake and I take off in opposite directions, leaving the big, empty kiddie pool behind.

• • •

I head for the bathroom to clean up, and hear a familiar giggle ringing from the bouncy castle as I pass by. Lana and Erik may be missing Digifest, but they're clearly not *missing* Digifest. I wonder if Erik even remembers about the prank. I glance back and see a number of phones recording the Property Prince of Doom opening his trunk and shining a light on the mound of red Fun Jell inside.

"*My trunk is filled with Jell-O!*" he rages, and laughter rings out. "Wait, no, yuck! This isn't even real Jell-O!"

"You got pranked!" someone yells.

"Eww," someone else says. "Why would you taste that?"

Another voice rings out, "Hashtag *Erik Pranks!*"

I hear Erik give a *woot!* from the bouncy castle, and his laughter marries Lana's giggles as the two of them bounce around like little kids.

I'm happy Lana and I managed to get some time to be

ourselves with Jake and Erik. But I wonder what will happen if we don't switch back tonight. Our sacrifice in giving up the Skylark tonight may have been a really, *really* dumb idea after all.

● ● ●

The movie is starting soon, so the ladies' room is packed when I arrive to wash up.

A basic Disney princess girl takes one look at me and bursts into tears. Her mother hustles her to the exit and gives me a loud *humph* as she moves past.

The speaker in the bathroom comes to life and Jake's voice fills the room.

"Hello, ladies and gents, and welcome to the grand reopening of the magical and legendary Starlight Drive-in!" He sounds like an over-the-top gameshow host, and I smile as I listen. "Our main feature will be starting in just a few moments, so now is a good time to find your way back to your vehicle and settle in to *enjoy the show*."

I make my way against the flow of people leaving the bathroom and finally find myself clinging to the edge of the sink closest to the back wall.

Jake continues talking overhead, suggesting a quick trip to the snack bar and reminding people to turn their key to the auxiliary position to avoid draining their car battery. "I forgot to do that once, and ouch." He imitates a car engine unsuccessfully trying to turn over. "Although I will say, my adventure ended with an *adorable* meet-cute."

He's talking about us. I grin so big at that I can feel my cheeks press against my bandages. I look up at my reflection in the mirror and shudder. No wonder I've been making children cry.

The original distressing of my bandages is barely even visible underneath the grime and Fun Jell of the past few hours. My white eyes look absolutely haunting, and it's easy to tell right where I face-planted into the kiddie pool because it looks like a gaping head wound.

The contacts are bothering my eyes, so I unwrap enough of my head to put water on my face. As I slowly unwind the filthy rags, I half hope I've switched back to myself.

Of course, I'm not shocked when I see Lana's face emerge in the mirror instead of my own, but I do let out a sigh. The older woman next to me gives a consoling look to my reflection.

"Long day?" she asks as she washes her hands.

I give her a weak smile. "From beginning to end, it's been just . . . freaky."

She smiles back at me, and something about her reminds me of Nona. "Well, you know what they say." She winks. "A wise man adapts himself to circumstances, as water shapes itself to the vessel that contains it."

She cups her hands and allows the water to fill to overflowing.

"Let me guess, fortune cookie?"

She closes the faucet and turns to dry her hands. "Ancient proverb."

I say, "My Nona used to save those little paper fortunes and give them out to my cousin and me at just the perfect time . . ." but when I turn to look, the woman is gone.

With another sigh, I turn on the cold water and cup my hands under the faucet.

I think back to the adorable meet-cute Jake just shared with the whole Starlight drive-in. Me rescuing him. The way our eyes met as he placed the charging clips on the battery of his Bronco.

I remember feeling glad for the excuse to talk to him and the way he seemed to take his time, letting the engines run as they stayed joined together. Feeding off of each other.

I would hate to lose my relationship with him. Taking things to the next level is such a risk. And knowing that the Magical Kiss Under the Stars™ safety net isn't foolproof makes this even scarier. I could seriously get hurt, and so could he.

My mind rolls through the possibilities of how our relationship could end. Us growing apart. Wanting different things. The potential for rejection is infinite.

But then I picture it going well. Jake and I sharing new experiences and adventures together. Trips to mini golf and Fat Jacks, maybe saving other drive-ins down the line. And I would not rule out a bit of classic horror cosplay.

And then there are all the movies we will watch together—*oh my goodness*, the movies. Starting with this one here tonight.

I stare at the water overflowing from my cupped hands and think of the old woman's words. We all must change and adapt to our circumstances. Even impossible ones like Lana and I did today.

With a sigh, I release the water, watching it all go down the drain together as one. Readapting and moving on.

All of a sudden, the lights in the bathroom begin to flicker and I feel as if I'm being pulled backward and into the air.

screech

    whoock

       zzzap

Incredibly, I rise up and burst through the roof of the ladies' room. For a split second I'm above all the rows of cars, facing the giant white movie screen that flashes with strobe lights. My stomach dips as I hover there for just a moment before being roughly thrust into the glittery bouncy castle.

The inflated canvas floor rebounds a few times from the force of my landing and everything goes completely dim.

"Am I dead?" I say out loud.

A smooth voice answers, "Yes, and this is heaven, babe."

"Babe?" I raise my head, and in the reflection from the concession shack lights I see Erik leaning over me with a grin. I put a hand up to rub my eyes and realize I'm wearing sunglasses.

I pull them off my face and turn them over in my hand incredulously. They're Lana's sunglasses.

"I'm the Invisible Man," I say, and laugh as I feel the silk robe I'm wearing. Despite my shock, my brain is able to register the fact that, "Wow, this is some *quality* silk."

"Are you feeling okay?" Erik stares at me strangely and adds, "You look different, Lana."

He's trying to look into my eyes, and I immediately thrust the sunglasses back over them.

"Actually," I say, "I really need to go to the bathroom. Like, right away."

Erik laughs in a flirty way and leans in as if he's about to kiss me.

But I am not having that.

Shoving him back away from me I say frantically, "I said *right away*. I have stomach *issues!*"

"Oh!" Erik makes a face. "Sorry."

I swim my way toward the exit and awkwardly scramble out though the canvas opening.

"Do you need help?" Erik calls.

"Oh *god* no," I say.

"Sorry, Lana," he says. "I hope you feel better."

I take off running full tilt toward the bathroom. My feet feel amazing in Wes's old slippers, but one keeps falling off and I need to stop and slide it back onto my foot twice.

I pull off my sunglasses and begin to unwind my head bandage as I burst into the bathroom's entryway. I make my way along the pink-tiled hallway and hear someone screaming like they're being murdered in a cult-classic slasher movie.

When I round the corner to the bank of sinks, Lana is standing near the back wall. She's covered in dirty bandages stained with Fun Jell, and her face is half unwrapped, and it is *her* face. Lana looks like Lana. And that must mean . . . I run to the mirror and lift my sunglasses and look into beautiful brown eyes.

I let out a huge cry-laugh of relief.

Lifting the remaining bandages off my head, I reveal my full face. *My full face.* "Hello, me," I say.

Lana is still frozen with her mouth open. Her face is white as she looks at me. "I thought we were dead," she says. "Why am I covered in blood?"

I give a small laugh. "Heh. It's Fun Jell."

Lana reaches up and takes out one of the white contacts. She leans in close to the warped bathroom mirror, blinking quickly. Finally, she rests her forehead and palm on the mirror.

"Wow, cuz," I say. "Am I ever glad to see you in your own skin."

She turns from the mirror and runs to fling her arms around

me. I feel like a hulking giant as she attempts to pick me up. "Nice try," I tell her and easily spin her around.

"Ricki, Ricki, Ricki," she repeats over and over, and I echo, "Lana, Lana, Lana."

Taking a step back, she holds my face in her hands. "This was horrible, but I couldn't have gotten through one minute of it without you."

I say, "And there's nobody else I'd ever want to embody."

After a few more minutes of celebrating, Lana stops. "What do we do now?" she asks.

"I think we exchange costumes and go back out there as ourselves." I take off the silk robe and begin to unwrap the rest of my Invisible Man bandages. "Wow, your costume stayed so much cleaner than mine."

"No lie," Lana says as she peels off layer after layer of Mummy filth and Fun Jell. "Did you really think this get-up needed to be grosser?"

I laugh and tell her about the Jell-O prank gone wrong. As the two of us start helping each other exchange bandages, she describes the farewell video Erik helped her post on BubeTube. He filmed her painting a few kids' faces as the Invisible Man and joked that this was her new makeup artist gig. And then she gave her fans a heartfelt goodbye.

"I got honest about my anxiety and my need to take care of myself," she says, handing me the white contacts.

"Walking away for the sake of your mental health sets a great example to your fans." I toss the white contacts into the trash. "You should be proud."

"I'll admit I did find it empowering to admit I've only been showing the pretty parts of my life," she says. "I warned viewers, 'the shiny things we see in our feed do not tell the full story.'"

"I love it! Helping to crush the lies of perfection and comparison."

"Well, I guess I was inspired by that thing Her Highness told us JLC did with her realistic photo shoot." Lana stops reapplying her bandages to point a finger at me. "She's more than just the Ultimate Scream Queen you know."

"Yes!" I punch the air. "You getting real about your struggles and imperfections will help set others free from the insecurity trap, cuz! I do believe you're a dang hero."

Lana stretches a wide bandage across her forehead and begins rewrapping her face. "I'm ignoring the video's comments, but I've already been getting alerts about a conspiracy theory circulating that it wasn't really me making the announcement," she says. "Erik thinks the rumor is the perfect subversive end to *Lookie Lana!* But little does he know, if people examine that video closely, they might put together I really *am* you in disguise."

"Nice mystery twist for your fans," I say.

"I thought you'd like that," she says. "Oh, and I heard Jake's meet-cute story! He better have been talking about when you two met."

I nod. "I'll tell you all about it sometime."

"I want every detail," Lana says. "It looks like you're going to get your magical kiss under the stars tonight after all."

I draw in a deep, nervous breath. "If it was truly magic, I'd know exactly how my whole future will work out. What's the fun in that?"

"Wait," Lana says. "So you are actually jumping in and risking rejection without some imaginary magical safety net?"

"Yup," I say. "Not allowing the fear of getting hurt stop me."

"Well then, I'm proud of you too, cuz," Lana says.

The two of us smile at each other and I put an arm around her.

"It's not easy for me," I say. "But it helps having *you* as a safety net."

"That's right," Lana says. "No matter what!"

I say, "Like I could show up with a dead body and I know that you will help me bury it."

"Why does everything end up being about dead bodies with you?" Lana laughs and shoves me away as she tucks a bandage under the collar of her robe.

I say, "How about we just promise each other a road trip on demand whenever either of us needs it?"

"You got it." Lana grins. "And I know the perfect vehicle."

"Yeah, if we ever get it back from our moms!" We've both finished reapplying our costumes and I turn to face her. "Okay, how do I look?"

Lana reaches up as if to fix something and then stops and makes a face. "Gross as can be," she says. "And me?"

I straighten the lapels of her silk robe. "You look lovely, and I'm going to need joint custody of this robe."

"We can definitely arrange a mutually agreeable schedule for sharing our Her Highness signature robe." We laugh.

"Yes," I say. "I do believe we've *finally* learned to share."

Jake's voice breaks in overhead and announces the previews are about to start. I point to the speaker and say, "I'm heading for the projection room. Wish me luck."

"Luck," Lana says. "And I'm off to watch the movie with my boyfriend in the bouncy castle."

I wince. "About that," I say.

"Ricki? What's wrong?"

"I may or may not have implied to Erik that I had diarrhea when he thought I was you."

"You *what*?" Lana screeches, and I rush for the door.

"I'm so sorry it was unavoidable and hey how about you get extra time with that robe." My words mash together, and I take a steadying breath. "Don't worry. Erik really, *really* likes you. I can tell."

"Yeah, he probably wouldn't have hung in there today if things weren't pretty solid," Lana says as we walk out the bathroom exit.

"Jake too," I say. "It was *quite* a day."

The two of us hug. "I'll see you after the movie," she says as we continue holding on to each other.

I whisper in her ear, "I promise to never let go again."

We squeeze our hug tighter a moment and then release one another.

Lana teases, "Who are you? Rose from *Titanic*? You *literally* just said you'd never let go!" We laugh, and she turns toward the bouncy castle.

"Oh, so you want me to come with you now?" I offer. "Maybe I can explain about the stomach issues?"

"No, *please*," she says. "No more helping."

I take two strides toward the projection booth and am engulfed by a walloping silky tackle hug from behind.

"I love you, cuz," Lana whispers.

I barely have time to respond, "I love you too," before she is off, skipping toward the bounce house in her Invisible Man outfit. I admire how strong her steps are despite the heels she's now wearing and make a mental note to work on learning to walk in them.

Because I have to admit, tall girls walking around in heels is kind of epic.

On my way to the projection booth I pass our evil real estate villain, still standing at the open trunk of his car. He hasn't noticed the liner so he's still scooping the Fun Jell back into the kiddie pool with both arms. People are filming him and laughing as he calls out, "Come on! Are you kidding me?"

I think, *That will teach you to try to bury the Starlight's magic under some big box store.*

Because now I truly believe the Starlight is magic. But the magic doesn't come from some enchanted ability to protect hearts against heartache. It doesn't make a no-risk love guarantee. The magic of the Starlight comes from the time spent here and the memories built.

We are connected to it by the moment we're sharing right now.

I look around at the people sitting in chairs or inside their cars, some eating popcorn, as the preshow ads roll. Amused smiles spread across their lit-up faces while they watch cartoon hot dogs jump through hoops in the vintage snack commercial that's playing onscreen. Wes insisted we keep the old-timey reel, so we should see a huge jump in quality once we switch to digital for the main feature.

I open the door of the projector booth and find Jake standing behind the machine, watching the grainy-looking snack ads play.

He's taken off his Wolf Man makeup, and I watch his profile as the light from the projector plays across his features. His hair is messy and his flannel shirt is rumpled, and I can't help but notice how far down it's unbuttoned.

"The wolf has turned back into a man," I say.

He turns to look at me and gives me a half smile that makes my stomach dip.

After a beat he takes a step in my direction, and I'm glad I have all these bloody bandages holding me together, because otherwise I'd probably explode from the way he's looking at me right now.

"Well, we did it," he says in a deep voice as he moves in front of me. "The Starlight is saved."

I say, "For as long as we can possibly hold on."

He wraps his arms around my waist. "I guess you're right. There's no guarantee that the drive-in will still be going strong five years from now. Or ten. There will always be new real estate bad guys to thwart."

"All we have for sure is this moment right here," I say. "But then, isn't that what makes this special?"

Jake leans closer. "It makes this *magic*."

There's a click behind us.

"Speaking of magical moments, the vintage reel is almost finished." Jake moves back to the projector and I follow him. "Are you ready?" he asks.

He reaches for my hand and places it on a plastic switch under his.

Jake says, "Here we go."

I say, "Here's hoping Gwen and Brad got this thing online and running right."

Jake gives me a nervous look and we keep steady eye contact as we count down together, "Three. Two . . . One!"

Applying gentle pressure, we flip the switch and I feel a surge of happiness. The picture clicks ON and the film company logo whirrs to life on the giant screen outside.

We both exhale together.

I love the sense of starting something new, and it's only right that Jake and I hit the control together.

Looking out the small window at the movie, I say, "This is going to be good, I can tell."

"Yes, it is," Jake agrees, but when I turn I realize he's looking directly at me. "You took the white contacts out."

I bat my eyes at him and he laughs.

Reaching up, he touches the bandage on my cheek and asks, "May I?"

"You've had enough of the gore?" I tease, but help him unfurl the edge of my bandage.

He continues unwrapping my head and I stop helping. Standing perfectly still, I hold my breath.

Out of nowhere, I'm hit with the sudden fear that when he finishes I'll be wearing Lana's face again and everything will be even weirder than before.

I feel the air on my cheeks and look up at him nervously, trying to read his expression in the flickering light reflected from the projector.

A smile spreads over Jake's face and he whispers, "There you are."

He dips his head forward as if he's about to kiss me and I close my eyes and lift my lips expectantly. And I feel . . . *nothing*.

I lick my lips and dip my head back even more obviously,

pantomiming kissing the empty air. Still nada. Finally, I straighten my head and open my eyes.

Jake is just watching me.

"What are you waiting for? An invitation?"

"Actually, yes," he says, and adds dramatically, "Ricki, may I kiss you?"

Before he gets the chance, I lunge to kiss him first.

And he ducks.

"Gotcha back," he laughs, and I grab his face with both hands and pull his lips toward mine.

My mouth is firm and lands on his in a direct hit. Jake straightens in surprise, but then he slowly melts into our kiss.

And it's perfect.

I mean, sure, nothing could ever *really* measure up to the fantasy kiss I've been holding out for and imagining underneath the stars in the front seat of the Skylark convertible.

Plus, in my eagerness, I did zoom in a little harder than necessary, so my first kiss with Jake is less "tender" and more "mashy." And okay, since I'm listing things, I haven't had a mint in a while and so my breath smells a bit like the popcorn I ate for dinner, and there's a chance I may even have a kernel or two stuck between my teeth. So, actually, I guess my first kiss *isn't* perfect.

And yet, somehow, it is.

I can't wait to compare notes with Lana later, because my second kiss comes right on the heels of that first one, and I have to say so far *that* kiss is the best one yet.

Acknowledgments

his book, at its core, is about the importance of family, and I could not have written it without the support of mine! I can never thank *all* of my families enough, but here I shall try. *clears throat*

To my Blink family: Hannah VanVels, Jacque Alberta, Jennifer Hoff, Annette Bourland, Londa Alderink, Ron Huizinga, Gwyneth Findlay, Denise Froehlich, Jillian Manning, and the Blink squad of rock star authors. I have adored every single Blink family member I've met. Thank you for making this publishing journey an absolute dream!

To my EMLA family: Ammi-Joan Paquette, Erin Murphy, Tricia Lawrence, Kevin Lewis, Tara Gonzalez, Dennis Stephens, and the über-gifted tribe of Gangos and Emus. Thank you for the magic with which you usher each EMLA book into the world! I am humbled to be surrounded by such immense talent.

To my extended family: Pops, Momma, Gerry, Zach, Christina, Jackson, Alessia, Adalina, Jenna, Kaylon, Dorene, Eddie, Nicolette, Dylan, Arianna, Kylie, Tori, TJ, Danny, and all the others. Thank you all for keeping life fun and exciting and filled with love!

To my church family: I am blessed beyond measure to be a part of what the Lord is doing at Intercessor! Thank you for the privilege of worshiping together. May you always have a praise song in your heart and Church Candy in your pocket. See you all on Sunday!

Turn the page for an excerpt from

LAURIE BOYLE CROMPTON'S

Pretty in Punxsutawney,

where after a *Pretty in Pink* viewing gone wrong, Andi must relive
her first day of school over and over again until she can get her
first kiss and break the curse … at least, that's what she hopes.

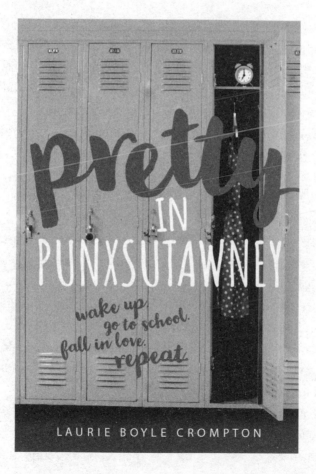

chapter 1

The ground races toward me so fast that my muscles tense instinctively. With a nauseating dip downward, everything goes dark for a beat before an explosion rattles the walls.

Good old Dolby digital cinema surround sound.

The hero striding toward us onscreen is so cool, he doesn't even give a backward glance toward the burning ball of fire growing behind him.

"Yes!" Colton punches the air in triumph and aims his 3D glasses in my direction.

I grin at him just as the theater door swings open and light spills over his handsome smile. "Shoot." He grabs the glasses off his face and shoves a final handful of Raisinets into his mouth.

The theater manager, Tom—aka, the bane of our existence—makes his way toward us. "Break's over, Colt."

Colton's grin bounces back as he quickly chews. "No problem, boss-man." He brushes his hand along my arm as he stands. "You want to stay, Andie?"

I glance at the screen. One of the best scenes is coming up, but I've already watched this movie with him twice, and I find that CGI explosions lose their appeal around the third viewing. Besides, action movies are only my sixth-favorite type of movie. They come after romantic dramas, rom coms, regular coms, suspense, and parodies, but just before horror and foreign films—unless, of course, the foreign film is an epic romance, in which case, *swoon*. Speaking of swooning, I can still feel the trail of warmth Colton's fingers left on my arm.

Following him out of the theater, I squint at the brightness of the lobby and stagger slightly as if I've just woken up. Post-movie disorientation: one of my favorite feelings.

It's amazing to think that when we moved to Punxsutawney just two months ago, I was sure my life was over. Summer break had barely begun, but I was already anxious about starting at a new school. Now the first day of senior year is tomorrow, and I can't wait. Colton is giving me a ride, and he's promised to show me around and act as my student guide. I'm fairly confident he'll be acting as my first boyfriend very soon as well. If my wishes have any power to come true, the two of us are *definitely* happening.

He gives me a micro-wink as we both move behind the lobby's glass snack counter. I twist my auburn hair into a knot and secure it with a cheap plastic pen from the pile beside the register before I start handing out 3D glasses to a family of five.

"Whoops, let's try that again," I say to a sticky-looking little girl who grabs hers by the lenses. I give her a clean pair and hold the smeared ones up to the light. Somehow, she managed to deposit about one hundred teeny-tiny fingerprints during the split second she held them.

Tom is standing at the far end of the counter, spraying cleaner into a rag. He aims the bottle my way as if to ask if I need it, but I just shake my head and use the edge of my T-shirt to wipe the glasses. Tom shrugs as he starts wiping the counter. He's a bit older than us, but takes his job so seriously that I'll always think of him as "boss-man."

"Hey, Colt," Tom calls, "make sure your *girlfriend's* clear she's fine helping out, but you're responsible for the register."

Even though Tom already knows Colton and I are not together, we tell him in stereo that I'm *not his girlfriend*. Of course, saying it out loud makes my insides go all slasher-flick angry. I've had a thing for Colton ever since our adorable meet-cute.

In case you don't know, a meet-cute is the point in a romantic movie where the two lead characters meet each other for the very first time. I'm not sure where the name comes from, but I assume it has something to do with how quirky and adorable these meet-cutes always are. Colton and I had ours the first week my parents and I moved here, when I came to the theater alone so I could drown my sorrows in a nice light romantic comedy called *Sundae Sunday*.

I was looking forward to the movie, whose trailer promised the comforting formula of girl-meets-boy, girl-loses-boy, girl-and-boy-realize-they-are-each-other's-everythings-and-finally-get-to-the-point-of-the-whole-film: *true love's kiss*.

When I walked into the cinema, Tom greeted me from behind the snack counter with a genuine smile. "What would you like to see today?" he asked with such enthusiasm that his love for his job was immediately clear.

He struck me as borderline cute, so I tried not to look like a friendless freak as I told him, "One for *Sundae Sunday*."

"You must be new around here," he said as he rang up my ticket.

"We just moved into town." I reached into my shoulder bag to get my wallet, and the plastic bag I was holding slipped from my hand. The bag dropped to the red carpet and the carton of malted milk balls inside rattled loudly. *Very* loudly.

Tom peered over the counter to see what was happening down by my feet. "Care to explain that rattling sound?" His friendly voice had turned crisp.

"Oh, that's just my Whoppers." I picked up the bag, pulled out the large tan carton, and grinned at him as I gave it a hearty shake.

"No outside food." He looked offended, as if he was some aspiring Willy Wonka who'd made the theater candy by hand and I'd insulted him by bringing my own personal stash.

"Sorry, I didn't know if you sold them or not, and I can't watch a movie without my malted milk balls." I scanned the snack menu. "Either way, it's cool because I'm buying popcorn."

"Why would buying popcorn make it cool for you to sneak food into the movie theater?"

"I wasn't *sneaking* it." I raised the flimsy bag and waved it in his face. The milk balls rattled noisily. "This bag is totally see-through."

He put his hands on his hips. "I'm going to need to confiscate those chocolates."

"Listen"—I squinted at his nametag—"*Tom*. This is my favorite movie treat . . ."

"Do you have any idea how much a theater like this depends on refreshment profits? Do you even care if we keep our doors open? There is *no outside food* allowed. I'm sorry. No exceptions."

I gestured to the row of candy under glass. "You don't even

carry Whoppers, so it's not like you're missing out on a sale. My old theater didn't carry them either, so they just let me bring my own."

"You are welcome to leave your malted milk balls with me. And may I interest you in one of *our* tasty chocolate confections to enjoy with your popcorn?"

Tom and I stared each other down for a few beats. He steepled his fingers like a Bond villain, and I noticed he was trying to hide a grin. Like he'd been hoping to have a Whopper standoff against someone all morning.

Finally, I snapped, "Fine." I pulled out my carton and peeled open the spout on one side. Shaking out a large handful of the chocolaty balls, I defiantly shoved them into my mouth and started chewing in his face with a loud *crunch, crunch, crunch.*

I found his wide-eyed reaction satisfying enough to push a *second* handful into my already bulging cheeks.

Which was exactly when the best-looking boy I'd ever seen in real life swooped in behind him. It was Colton.

Everything in the theater lobby shifted to slow motion when I saw him for the first time. I could practically feel my pupils dilate. My hearing sharpened. I began to salivate. Literally. As in, the milk balls in my mouth were dissolving into thick chocolate drool.

Colton—who I immediately dubbed "Drop-dead handsome-face" before I knew his name—gave an easy grin and asked us what was happening. Tom threw a hand over his mouth, covering his shocked laugh, and all I could do was stand there, breathing through my nose and trying not to choke on my chocolaty spit.

Tom filled him in on the contraband candy situation, emphasizing how much outside snacks were hurting the theater. "She's new to town." Tom gestured to my face. "I had no idea she'd take it this hard."

Colton leaned over and handed me a napkin, presumably to wipe the trail of brown drool off my chin. I tried to smile at him, but my cheeks were already stretched as wide as they could go.

"What did you do, frisk her?" Colton asked, looking at me curiously.

"No, the carton of Mighty Malts dropped and made a huge racket," Tom said. "I couldn't just ignore them."

I tried to correct him with a muffled, "Whoppers," which only served to send a fresh stream of chocolate drool down my chin.

Colton handed me a new napkin and winked at me. "Perhaps you're willing to buy an extra-large tub of popcorn for your snacking pleasure? You can keep your candy and we'll call things even."

I nodded and tried again. "They're Whoppers." More drool. I swiped the napkin Colton had given me across my chin.

"Missed a spot there," Colton said, and then—get this—he took the napkin from my hand and gently guided it along my chin. Meanwhile, his other hand swiped two Whoppers and popped them right into his beautiful mouth. "Mmmmm, chocolaty." His voice was so deep and his eye contact so intense, I had to take the napkin from his hand before I impulsively tried to lick his fingers.

Even if my mouth hadn't been packed with dissolved malt and chocolate, I would've been speechless.

About the Author

aurie **Boyle Crompton** is the author of several YA books, including *Pretty in Punxsutawney*, *Adrenaline Crush*, and *Love and Vandalism*. Laurie graduated first in her class from St. John's University with a BA in English and Journalism. She has written for national magazines like *Allure*, survived a teaching stint at an all-boy's high school, and appeared on *Good Day New York* several times as a toy expert. And yes, "toy expert" is an actual profession. She grew up in a small town in western PA and now lives near NYC with her family and three fuzzy "dog toy experts."